W9-BCQ-784

It was our destiny to [illegible], too late, the truth. The fair, bearded one was not our eagerly awaited Lord of Dawn, but Cortés of Spain, come not to free the people of the land from the brutal yoke of the Azteca, not to lead us back to the peaceful ways we long ago knew. No, he came to conquer us, to grind us under the mighty boot of his Spanish king and his Catholic God.

Still, and after all these years, it is an astonishment to me that my sister had willfully—as I had unwittingly—brought so much of this about. "Queen of Death," she was called, and then, simply and with disgust, "La Malinche," the traitress-whore of Mexico.

DAUGHTERS OF THE SUN

"Praised by some, damned by others, she is one of history's most controversial women—Malinche, who surrendered herself, her homeland and her entire people to an alien conqueror. Impeccably researched and grippingly told, this new chronicle of her life may be the truest account yet written."

—Gary Jennings, author of *Raptor*

"Sally Hayton-Keeva is a writer with an exquisite prose style and a flair for turning an amorphous impression into a beguiling anecdote." —*The Press Democrat*

"I was caught up in the extremity of events—the Aztec rituals of human sacrifice, the terrorism of the invading Spaniards. The two narrators, the sisters Malinalli and Xochitl, are especially fascinating. To read about the conquest of Mexico through their eyes, twice removed from the standard viewpoint of the European historians, is a fresh and provocative experience. And all the more so since Malinalli's contribution to the events is grounded in historical but long overshadowed fact."

—Ella Leffland, author of *Rumors of Peace*

ONYX (0451)

FLAMING PASSION

☐ **NO GREATER LOVE by Katherine Kingsley.** Beautiful young Georgia Wells is plunged into a vortex of desire when the handsome Nicholas Daventry returns to Ravenwalk to reclaim his legacy. (403029—$4.99)

☐ **HEARTS OF FIRE by Anita Mills.** Their flaming passion lit their perilous path of love. Fiery-haired Gilliane de Lacey's love for Richard of Rivaux ignited in her a burning need, but Richard was honor-bound to wed another. Yet nothing—not royal wrath or dangerous conflict—could stop Gilliane and Richard from risking all for love, giving all to desire. (401352—$4.99)

☐ **THE EDGE OF LIGHT by Joan Wolf.** Two headstrong lovers vow to fight to change the world rather than forfeit their passion—in the magnificent tale of Alfred the Great and the woman he could not help but love. (402863—$5.99)

☐ **NEW ORLEANS by Sara Orwig.** Chantal was the daughter of the most powerful family in Louisiana and lived like a princess on a vast plantation. Now in a city of pride and passion, she must choose between a man who offered her everything she had ever wanted and a man who led her to ecstacy beyond her wildest dreams. (403738—$4.99)

Prices slightly higher in Canada.

Buy them at your local bookstore or use this convenient coupon for ordering.

PENGUIN USA
P.O. Box 999 – Dept. #17109
Bergenfield, New Jersey 07621

Please send me the books I have checked above.
I am enclosing $__________ (please add $2.00 to cover postage and handling). Send check or money order (no cash or C.O.D.'s) or charge by Mastercard or VISA (with a $15.00 minimum). Prices and numbers are subject to change without notice.

Card #__________ Exp. Date __________
Signature__________
Name__________
Address__________
City __________ State __________ Zip Code __________

For faster service when ordering by credit card call **1-800-253-6476**

Allow a minimum of 4-6 weeks for delivery. This offer is subject to change without notice.

DAUGHTERS OF THE SUN

SALLY HAYTON-KEEVA

AN ONYX BOOK

ONYX
Published by the Penguin Group
Penguin Books USA Inc., 375 Hudson Street,
New York, New York 10014, U.S.A.
Penguin Books Ltd, 27 Wrights Lane,
London W8 5TZ, England
Penguin Books Australia Ltd, Ringwood,
Victoria, Australia
Penguin Books Canada Ltd, 10 Alcorn Avenue,
Toronto, Ontario, Canada M4V 3B2
Penguin Books (N.Z.) Ltd, 182-190 Wairau Road,
Auckland 10, New Zealand

Penguin Books Ltd, Registered Offices:
Harmondsworth, Middlesex, England

Published by Onyx, an imprint of Dutton Signet,
a division of Penguin Books USA Inc. Previously published
as *Unholy Sacrifice* by Sagn Books.

First Onyx Printing, March, 1994
10 9 8 7 6 5 4 3 2 1

Copyright © Sally Hayton-Keeva, 1992
All rights reserved

REGISTERED TRADEMARK—MARCA REGISTRADA

Printed in the United States of America

Without limiting the rights under copyright reserved above, no part of this publication may be reproduced, stored in or introduced into a retrieval system, or transmitted, in any form, or by any means (electronic, mechanical, photocopying, recording, or otherwise), without the prior written permission of both the copyright owner and the above publisher of this book.

BOOKS ARE AVAILABLE AT QUANTITY DISCOUNTS WHEN USED TO PROMOTE PRODUCTS OR SERVICES. FOR INFORMATION PLEASE WRITE TO PREMIUM MARKETING DIVISION, PENGUIN BOOKS USA INC., 375 HUDSON STREET, NEW YORK, NEW YORK 10014.

If you purchased this book without a cover you should be aware that this book is stolen property. It was reported as "unsold and destroyed" to the publisher and neither the author nor the publisher has received any payment for this "stripped book."

"My interpreter was an Indian woman who was given to me as a present with twenty other women at the beginning of our conquests. Humble and obedient, at our insistence she renounced her false beliefs and came to the true knowledge of God and our Holy Faith. Though but a woman and born a barbarian, she rendered no small service to us and often, in the latter days, would tell one and all how I had conquered Mexico and all the other lands which I held subject and placed beneath Your Majesty's command."

—Hernán Cortés,
from a letter to
King Don Carlos V

1

Xochitl

It was on the day the conquerors came in triumph when I once again beheld the face of my sister, my twin, Malinalli, the most-reviled. Events had not dimmed her beauty, I saw even at a distance, as they had mine. Suddenly she smiled upon the stranger she stood beside, the man we thought a God. The great Quetzalcoatl we thought him, Lord of Dawn, come again to his people from the eastern reaches of the sea and the heavens beyond the sea and the nine underworlds of death. This was our fate and unavoidable. Between us, my sister and I had brought this ruin to pass.

I drew nearer. Leaving the other women behind, I made my way past the warriors, splendid in their masks of eagles and jaguars, ferocious before the opposing men who seemed fiercer yet, astride their giant deer. All wore shining helmets of gold but for one of them, the one upon whom my sister did smile so sweetly. He stood bareheaded, his beard as fine and skin as pale as those of Quetzalcoatl, seeming indeed to be the God foretold.

My Lord Moteczoma stepped forth, jeweled and shod with golden sandals. To my astonishment, my sister calmly addressed him, then, apparently knowing the God's strange tongue, turned with the Ueytlatoani's words and spoke them to the Lord of Dawn. I could not hear the words she spoke nor see into her eyes, but I knew who she was and that her demure manner was but a shield over the face of a jungle cat.

My Lord spoke again, and my sister once more gave his words to the God, then turned to smile into my Lord's eyes. This was an act punishable by death for all but a few of my Lord's intimates. I awaited breathlessly my Lord's dark anger. The moment passed and, as if all of us had awaited answer to the same question, it was with a universal gasping breath that we saw Moteczoma touch that pale, outstretched hand.

Swiftly, at my Lord's command, treasure was laid at the stranger's feet: a jade necklace of wondrous design, gold worked in many marvelous ways, golden birds and the heads of serpents inlaid with rare and beautiful stones, necklaces of golden bells and bundles of the capes our artisans sew, covering the cloth with many thousands of hummingbird feathers. The fair-skinned one in return gave to my Lord a necklace of blue stones, clear as the sky. With a gracious gesture my Lord Moteczoma, ruler of all the One World, Anáhuac, welcomed the strangers inside the very walls of Tenochtitlan. All was lost in that moment. Unlikely indeed would it have been for us to welcome them so graciously had we known our lives were in deadliest peril.

The strangers were led to the late Lord Axayácatl's palace, where the last Great Speaker had lived in most sumptuous ease, even as did his successor, Lord Moteczoma, in a palace nearby. Women and food and drink were brought them, and many more gifts of gold and chalchuite stones, and the strangers, according to the word of our servants, spoke loudly over them and divided them among themselves. I suppose my sister took part in this, since she never seemed to leave her Lord's side.

It was our destiny to discover, too late, the truth. The fair bearded one was not our eagerly-awaited Quetzalcoatl, Lord of Dawn, but Cortés of Spain, come not to free the people of the land from the brutal yoke of the Azteca, not to lead us back to the peaceful ways we long ago knew, out from under the crushing weight of

Huitzilopochtli and Tezcatlipoca and their thirst for blood. No, he came to conquer us, to grind us under the mighty feet of his Spanish king and his Catholic God.

Still, and after all these years, it is an astonishment to me that my sister had willfully—as I had unwittingly—brought so much of this about. It once was said that if Cortés had not had my sister by his side he could never so easily have entered the fortress of Tenochtitlan, the greatest city of the land of the Mexica. My sister's words hurled thousands of our people, Azteca, Acolhuas, Huexotzincans, down into Mictlan. "Queen of Death," she was called and then, simply and with disgust, "La Malinche," the traitress-whore of Mexico.

We were born in Coatzocoalcos, near where the river pours its waters into the sea. Our mother had been the most beautiful woman in all that part of the land, but it was said my sister and I were more beautiful still. All of us as women were slender and large-breasted, with narrow hips and golden skin. All of us had the long dark eyes of the jaguar and lips full and, unfortunately, tempting. It was good for us that rape was considered a punishable offence, for my sister and I even as young girls could see the effect we had on that part of a man he cannot well control. On the days we did honor the young Goddess of the Tender Maize, Xilónen, dancing in the young corn with our long black hair flowing and breasts bare, men both old and young sought to be near us. My sister would laugh at the more obvious desire of some of them, dancing away, and I would blush at the burning hunger in their eyes.

I have often wondered why we were cursed with such a gift. Almost every bitter thing that happened to us happened because we were beautiful women, when but to be a woman is hardship enough. Our mother knew that. Her mother and her mother's mother, back in time to our fabled homeland of Tollan, all knew what the world was for women and sorrowed for it. Through time the women in our family, and other families as well, taught us to remember we had not always been the slaves of men and their Gods.

To know these things reassured our hearts, but did not make our lives easier to bear. Still it was our duty—and yes, sometimes our pleasure—to live among men and to lie with them in the darkness and to bear their children. (My sister swore to me she would never belong to a man and never bear a child. I, more surely under our mother's influence, bowed to the inevitable.) As our mother said, our world was not the world Malinallxochitl walked upon. She who was the greatest Goddess of them all, who ruled all beings by sorcery and tamed the wild beasts with song; she, who let all people live in the peace of women's arts until her brother, Huitzilopochtli, maddened by envy of her power, advised his priest in a dream to kill her so he might rule in her stead. Thus was Malinallxochitl destroyed, even as was her younger sister, Coyolxauhqui, and thus in time did the Azteca come to our land from the cold north and conquer us, ruling through the warlike strength of heart and arm instead of the inner knowing dark of female power.

It pleased our mother that we were born in the year Malinalli, year of Penance Grass, so named long ago in the Goddess' honor. My sister was born first and therefore into the first part of that magic name while I, brought forth but moments after, became Xochitl. Malinalli and Xochitl, Penance Grass and Flower, we were two living reminders of one lost Goddess, however ill did we represent her on this earth.

Father was a warrior and held in respect. I think my mother did truly love him, and perhaps he cared for her as well. He was not a man given to speaking his heart, being for most of the time only a very large shadow in our house. We heard him and my mother in the night, and it was not always in silence or in pain that she received him into herself. I like to think they were close in this way, if in no other.

Most of the time Father only spoke to us when he needed to be brought something from beyond his reach, and we obeyed him in silence, as children were expected to do. He was neither kind nor unkind to us, which was the way with most fathers and daughters. It was their sons fathers took notice of, teaching them of men and war. That was in the order of things then, my mother told us, but it had not always been so.

"Had I only been born a man!" my sister often said when she grew rebellious at her female tasks. "I would far rather die in battle than bear some man's babes!" She would toss her head and run off somewhere, returning late enough to merit a beating at our father's hands, a beating she always bore in stoic silence.

With a sigh Mother would watch Malinalli run off toward her beloved river. "Do you wish for me to run after her?" I would ask. Eyes sad and busy hands idle for the moment, Mother would answer, "No. Let her lose her restlessness in the jungle. She will return when her fire cools."

As the shadows lengthened and Father was due to return for the meal he, as a male, always ate first and alone, Mother would go often to the doorway and scan the riverbank for a sign of my discontented sister.

"She will be beaten again today if she does not come."

"She says she does not care," I told her, both in truth and to ease her worry.

A small sad smile touched my mother's lips. "Perhaps it is the only combat she can seek." At this she turned to me and took my uncomprehending face in her palm and gazed at me a long moment. "It is harder for her than it is for you, my Xochitl, to look down the road of the years and see no reason for singing." It was not long before I understood what my mother meant, that in the beatings my sister did feel herself a warrior. Not only a warrior but, in a curious way, a warrior whose foe was her own warrior-father. This is not to say she hated him. She held him above all beings, submitting to his punishment with an odd satisfaction. It was in being beaten that she became the warrior she wished she were by birth. The pain his hands inflicted gave her, at least for the duration of the beatings, what she sought more eagerly than anything else on earth: escape from the curse of womanhood.

Punishment aside—and it was fair, if harsh—our early years were pleasant ones. The Gods brought us our seasons of rain and maize and, if we did them honor, they watched benevolently over us. Tonatiuh, the sun, shone down upon us and kept us warm. We loved to run and play in the sand beside the ocean, and we would narrow our eyes and try to see Tonatiuh's face, but we never could. His capes were all made of fire.

We were given tasks suited to our age. Until we were four years old we did little but play and sleep in the shade of our home, which was built of wood and earth and stood a sensible distance from the waves that were made angry in the season of storms. Then we were given the daily task of finding wood and grinding maize, the one suited to my sister's restless nature and the other to mine. I did not mind grinding the maize, though it had to be done while the world was yet dark and Tonatiuh still on his journey through the underworld. I would sit on my heels and press the lime-softened kernels between the stone pestle and the metatle, rolling and crushing, rolling and crushing, the resulting fine powder of the maize whitening my hands until they looked like those of one dead.

Sometimes my mother sat near me, sewing in the firelight, repairing my father's elaborate feather headdress, and she would tell me stories of long ago. Often she would tell me the story that we were once the children of the jaguar, born to be proud and strong, but never cruel. And she would tell me of a time still older when our ancestors in the fabled Tollan, birthplace of my people, carved statues most wondrous and painted scenes more lifelike than life itself. These grandfathers of grandfathers and grandmothers of grandmothers did not sacrifice people as we now did, but crushed the brilliant bodies of butterflies and the petals of the most beautiful flowers upon the holy altar of the king-turned-God, Quetzalcoatl. Our own special God he was, Malinalli's and mine, for he was God of twins. The Feathered Serpent, Lord of Dawn, he was a lover of the wondrous arts, of learning and light.

Great tragedy it was indeed when he was lost to us, tricked, my mother said, by rivals to his power. These rivals did by stealth and cunning trick Lord Quetzalcoatl into becoming drunk and, therefore, lecherous. In night's darkness made yet darker by his drunkenness did he desire the beautiful body of his sister and he did overpower and possess her. After this crime, Mother said, he fled sorrowing near to the very place in which we lived, on the yellow fringe of the eastern sea. There he boarded a raft with dwarves and other sorcerous beings, promising to return in the Year One-Reed, bringing peace and plenty. Then would he send the Gods of warfare and human sacrifice, Tezcatlipoca and Huitzilopochtli, to the underworld. The Goddess Malinallxochitl would return, and the ways of woman, the birth and bearing of children and the springs of most fruitful desire, would once again be praise unto the earth. This my mother told me and my sister—when my sister was present to hear—in the words of her mother and her mother's mother. Games we played about the return of the Lord of Dawn, my sister and I. Powerfully did the prophecy take root in our minds, and in our hearts as well. Quetzalcoatl's return was our hope that the world could be again the way it once was.

"And then I will be a sorceress," my sister said, her eyes flashing, "and do anything that pleases me!"

I laughed at her and we danced and then my sister

said, "And you, my sister? What will you be when our Lord comes?"

"Probably a woman with more babes than I can count," I said, half in teasing. Then in all seriousness I added, "That would be a better fate than some."

"Than what?" Malinalli cried scornfully.

Something dark took hold of my heart and I could not reply. As if in a dream I heard stones falling and cries of agony. My sister took my arm and her grip tightened at, I imagine, the horror in my eyes. "What is it?" she whispered. "Why do you look at me so oddly?"

"Nothing," I answered and made myself seem light-hearted as before. I did not tell her the truth; I could not. Suddenly before my gaze my sister's eyes had filled with flame and in those eyes, black against red fire, were skulls staring hollow-eyed. And they had stared at me.

"Let us go bathe in the river," I said, turning away from her and, shrugging, she followed me in silence.

While I ground the maize and patted out the tlaxcallis for our main midday meal, my sister gathered wood. That task took her, gratefully, away from the house and its daily female tasks, into the jungle. There she prowled like the jaguar's great-great-granddaughter she was, finding curiosities and ruins in the underbrush and singing beside the wordless chant of the river.

Sometimes we went together, and though she would refuse to show me the most sorcerous places she had found, she showed me enough for me to see she must have spent very little time gathering wood! Indeed, I believe she must have snatched up a hasty armful just as Tonatiuh began his descent from the sky into the first of the underworlds, leaving our world dark and cold and longing for him. She would come home, dancing a little and humming under her breath, only falling silent at our doorway. Then she would solemnly place the wood near our cooking fire and tend the tlaxcallis browning on the hot stone of the cumal or stir whatever was simmering in the pot over the fire; squash and beans and tomatoes, dense and hot with chiles, fragrant stew or, sometimes, roast dog or turkey or maguey worms. Usually we ate well, for maize was abundant in those days, along with the potent grain amaranth, upon which it was said the power of the Azteca depended. Father was a fine hunter, also, and we were thus fortunate to have whatever he could kill.

There were some things my sister and I could not escape, and those were the sacred festivals of the Azteca, so much more fearsome than our own used to be. Prostrating ourselves before the Gods, we must thrust maguey thorns into our tongues and earlobes and scatter our blood upon the earth. There would be sacrifices in which pretty women or children, whose tonalli at birth had shown their fates, were drowned or slain to please the Gods. Men taken in the many forced battles were given the honor of the Flowery Death, from which they would rise and live forever in a paradise of flowers and food and, I imagined, fields of beautiful, silent women.

It had worried our mother that my sister and I, for our beauty, might be sacrificed. Early in our childhood she asked our father to speak to the priests to see if our tonallis foretold this fate. He returned home with the priests' confusing words that we would grow fully into womanhood and, while we would not be slain in sacrifice, one of us would live a life of sacrifice and the other would be sacrificed in death. Our mother told us this, and, being young, we pondered for a moment and then lost interest in the odd prophecy.

"Do you not feel, Mother, that our sacrifice would be pleasing to the Gods?" I asked her once. "For they say the seed of the Gods falls most plentifully when beauty's blood is shed."

"Yes," she answered carefully, "but I trust there are women beautiful enough, as there are men brave enough, for the Gods not to hunger for you, too." Which was as near to irreverent speech as ever I heard her say.

My sister, heedless and wild as always, said to me when we were alone, "Never will I sacrifice myself to a man or at a man's bidding. No, not here on earth or anywhere else!" I gasped at her blasphemous words, for one never knew which words might descend into the underworlds where the Gods moved with such power and stealth.

I myself could never have wished to die in such a way, with my breast torn open and my heart ripped out, spurting blood to feed the hungry Gods that nourished us in repayment. But I did understand why such sacrifice had to be. Maize could not grow if blood did not wet the thirsty fields of Xipe Totec, and Tlaloc would never send rain or Tonatiuh the warming rays of the sun. It was an honor to die that way. Still it was not something sought by those with other destinies. I believe it was different for those children who knew, from their first word and breath, that it would be their destiny to die for the Gods and their people, and that it was a pleasing fate for those warriors who knew they were but bloody seconds from eternal life. The rest of us just die. After enduring the knives and winds of Mictlan, we unhonored ones rest in cold and silent blackness until the end of all time.

There were many chances for warriors to die gloriously, for there were many wars in those days. The Azteca, feared and hated, claimed tribute from us in the form of food, gold and treasures worked by our artisans, and not those things only, but also our men, forced to fight both for and against the Azteca, depending on the enemy and Tenochtitlan's need for men to sacrifice. Many fathers, brothers and sons entered the gates of that great city, never to return.

In one such Flowery War, when my sister and I were twelve years old, our father was wounded and made captive on the battlefield and taken to Tenochtitlan where he was slain.

My mother tore her hair and cut herself with knives and pierced herself with thorns in her black sorrow.

And so also did my sister and I, all of us staying in the darkness of our house, my mother weeping. Malinalli and I wept too, more because our mother wept than from grief at the loss of the great dark shadow that had been our father, and little knowing that we had full reason to weep. Our lives changed with our father gone, and all the rest of our lives, in that bleak unknowing time, was laid out before the two of us as one road, and one road only, stretching forth from where we stood.

For the first few months life did not change utterly. Mother finally stopped her weeping and my sister and I did as we had always done. But in the month of Ueytecuilhuitl my mother remarried. He was a warrior her age, still youthful. He came to live with us in our house where he made lusty and frequent love to our mother in the darkness. During the day he was dignified and concerned only with the concerns of men. At night he was insatiable. My sister and I sometimes crept out to sleep by the ocean, half-burrowed in the sand like turtles when they lay their eggs. The rhythmic hushing of the small night waves buried the sounds of pain and pleasure as we curled close with our arms tight around each other, willing sleep. I must add that my sister and I were not squeamish, for children early heard the night sounds of men and women. Yet it did bewilder us that he was not our father; it did not seem to us that Mother had needed to bring him into our house and to her sleeping mat.

Especially did this enrage Malinalli. "Our mother did not have to take another husband!" she said through her teeth. "The three of us could have lived alone and well. With all her weeping," she added in a voice sharp as obsidian, "she seems to have comforted herself for the loss of our father with shameful speed."

"But, Malinalli," I told her patiently, having heard from my mother what she refused to lend ear to, "she felt it would not be seemly for a woman of childbearing years to live without a man. What might the people think? There would be suspicion, and that would be unsuitable for a woman like our mother, widow of a great warrior." Saying these words, still did I sigh over them.

My sister looked for a moment at me with silent contempt, turned on her heel and left me.

Singing rather less along the riverbanks, and then not at all, Malinalli did everything she was asked in a cold silence disturbing to me and painful for my mother whose attempts at comforting her were mutely rebuffed. My heart flew to her in her pain, but she would not be consoled.

Shortly after our second father came to live with us, my mother was with child. When she grew heavy and slow with the babe, our second father turned to us in the night, and it was only due to the Goddess' blessing that our bellies did not also swell with his seed. At first our mother pleaded with him, and we fought, but his hand was powerful from years of training in the arts of war and we were no match for even the slightest of the blows he spared none of us. Bruised and silent, my sister and I, one by one or both together, lay beneath the heavy hot body of our second father, while our mother sat, weeping, in a corner of the room.

It mattered not at all to him that we were maidens. With rough fingers did he spread our thighs and seek the opening of our tipilis. If we flinched from him he would strike us openhanded on face or breast until we lay passive and open to him. Then, hard and swollen, his tepuli would thrust inside. Flooded with pain, we would wait, teeth clenched, for him to take his pleasure. Then, without a word, he would return to his sleeping mat and command my mother to join him there. She did not dare refuse him. More and more did he enjoy his power over us, becoming tyrannous. As the hour of his coming approached, our days would darken, and while he ate his solitary meal we would await his desires with foreboding. As man, he was our master, and his bidding, our law.

If this behavior of our second father's had become

public knowledge he might have been severely punished, but he warned us that if we made the least outcry he would sell us into slavery. For a beautiful woman slavery was no better than prostitution, in itself a terrible transgression. We endured.

Oh, the shamed silence in which we lived! My mother, sick at heart and weary, tried to smile and make light speech when her husband was from home, but it was difficult for her. I understood her shame for us and her unwilling passivity in the face of such a crime against the Gods. My sister hated her for it. Her face grew hard and without emotion, like a mask; her long, jaguar eyes turned to cold stone, her soft full lips folded tight. She began to pull her long black hair not into the fashion of a mature woman, but back into a hard knot, and she bathed many times a day in the waters of the river, as if they had the power to wash the memories of the night from her slender, bruised body. I bathed with her often and tried to comfort her, but she railed against me for my loyalty to our mother and walled her heart away from mine.

One night Mother began to groan, and since it was the custom to bear children in a warrior-like silence, we knew she was in great pain and that the time of birth was near. Our second father left to alert the midwives and then remained at a comfortable distance from the result of his actions. My sister and I lighted the fire and I sat beside our mother, washing her sweating body with warm water infused with cooling herbs. When the midwives came we shrank back into the shadows to watch them at their work, burning their sacred grasses and chanting the songs of childbirth, giving my mother strength to endure her pain and bring a brave warrior or courageous woman into the world.

It was horrible to watch. Shining in the firelight, her body arched and twisted, her great naked belly convulsed like a serpent with a live dog in its bowels. The midwives gave her potions to drink and rubbed her muscles with unguents and burned incense that made the air fragrant and indistinct with smoke.

At last, my sister and I clinging to each other as we used to do as children, we watched as Mother was helped to squat, legs spread wide, while a midwife reached between her legs and pulled forth a child. He was covered with blood from his own hard journey, and the midwives sucked at his mouth and nose and covered him with a cloth and put him into my mother's arms.

"This is a warrior," the midwives chanted, "As a warrior he will grow to be strong and dutiful to his Gods, Huitzilopochtli and Tezcatlipoca. He will live his years in modesty and courage and do the Gods all honor."

"Honoring most Quetzalcoatl, Lord of Dawn," Mother added softly in words Aztecas would have frowned upon—and even her own husband, had he heard.

With that was blessed our brother's entry into this world. They put a small shield into his tiny hand and then took it to be buried with the cord they severed at his belly. Solemnly they put the shield and the bloody cord into a hole they dug by the fire. This was done so he would grow to be a courageous warrior, if that was his tonalli.

Our second father was pleased with our mother's gift to him of a son and he praised her and the child with honeyed words. Yet next night he lay with my sister and me in the presence of his wife, and continued to lie with us for two months, until custom allowed him to lie with Mother again. One cannot imagine the relief we felt, Malinalli and I, to be rid of the weight of his body and the pain of his shameful desire.

Our relief was to be short-lived. He told us one day to come with him to the marketplace. It was a request never made of us before and one with which we, most unwillingly, had to comply.

Near our small pyramid and its teocalli, wherein the

priests conducted their rituals in honor of the Gods of war and rain, was a square, flat, barren place where the market was held. Twice a month many people came to sell or buy what was grown or crafted. People sat on the ground and spread their wares before them: tomatoes or chiles, maize and tidy heaps of beans, necklaces and clothing, turkeys strung by their feet, and the skinned bodies of scrawny little dogs which dangled fur-less in the sunshine.

"Wait here," our second father said, and we waited while he walked off a little way and stood in speech with an ugly man who stared appraisingly at us, head to foot, and nodded. He handed something to our second father, who then beckoned to us to join them. My sister stiffened and, at first, would not move.

"I do not trust what he is doing," she whispered to me. Though I agreed with her with all of my heart, there was no purpose to be gained in either remaining motionless or attempting flight. The man looked pleased as we drew near, looking at us just as if we were not wearing our huipillis and as if our full young breasts were naked and our tipilis open to his gaze. Our second father turned to us. Quietly he spoke so no one but us could hear.

"Your mother and I have decided our son is the rightful heir to that which we possess, and therefore you will now go with this man and obey him in all things."

With these words he turned from us and strode away. Even my outspoken and rebellious sister could do nothing but stare speechless at his back, her hands hanging limp at her sides.

I looked up at the man, whose face was coarse and lined with cruelty, and I asked him with a most uncharacteristic bluntness, "Who are you? What do you want?"

He looked from one to the other of us, a smile brutish and carnal on his mouth. Lips trembling, I managed to cry out, "If he has sold us to you, he has done great wrong! Our mother will surely come and take us home!"

The man's smile widened so that it was impossible to see the few teeth that remained to him. "Your mother? Your mother agrees to the sale." Then he reached out a hand, and, before I could avoid it, he took painful grip of my arm. Still smiling, he added, "As for doing wrong, they have full right to do as they will. Your lives are as nothing."

"You lie!" I spat at him, oblivious to the stares my noise had attracted. I think it was this attention that made the trader in flesh decide it would be easier if we departed, and he took my sister's arm also.

"You lie about my mother!" I cried in anguish, and he dropped my sister's arm and struck me across the head so that I fell at his feet. When he bent to pull me up, I looked desperately at my sister, standing so strangely without protest. Her face was set like the face of one dead.

"It is a lie about Mother," I whispered to Malinalli as the man began to pull us along, one on either side.

"It is the truth," she answered in a voice of stone.

We left our home and our land, then, sold as slaves into a world we did not know existed, destined for a future not the wildest of dreams could have foretold.

Naturally the trader in flesh used us both that night. It was probable that never before had he lain with women so identically young and beautiful. It was a disappointment to learn our second father had lied to him and we were no longer maidens, but he taught us how to pretend we were so that we would command a higher price. My sister asked, with a quiet scorn such a brutish man could never perceive, "And why should we be concerned with the price we bring, since it is only you who will benefit from it?" He did answer, "Since you will command a higher price, you will be more valuable. Hence you will possibly be beaten less and perhaps not so readily sacrificed on one of our holy days."

As young and ignorant as we were, still we could see the truth in that. So we learned the crude tricks he taught us, the tricks of low women who straddle the road, and submitted to whatever he asked of us, and endured.

Two days later my sister was sold. Our one road, for a time, was divided. We embraced as we had not done since childhood, looking long into each other's eyes as if to find the maidens we once were mirrored in their dark depths. Then she walked away in harness like a proud lithe beast. It would not be for some five tumultuous years that I would see her face again.

2

MALINALLI

Oh, my Lord, my God, my Tonatiuh! You who warmed my body and made me dance for joy! What a friend you were for a lonely child who stood upon a riverbank and wondered if all the waters of the world passed by her there.

Tlaloc! Your waters were tears upon my body. I was clothed with the sky. Ehecatl, God of Wind, your breath the very flowers, and Xipe Totec, who filled the barren field. To you have I always given honor. But none have I honored as I have honored you, Quetzalcoatl! Lord of the Morning Star, you who stood beside me in the darkness of the jungle, who led me safely home from all my wanderings, who loved me; your name was always first on my tongue, in my heart. I knew that whatever befell me in this my life, you would stand beside me, above me and around me, and I would take shelter. No matter how dark the night or how haunted by spirits made restless in their pain and grief and anger, I would be protected by you and comforted by the golden light of your being. I would prostrate myself at your holy places, before the great stone faces of the ancient Gods who remained to me nameless, for I worshipped only you in their shadows. Surely you would stay by me and I would be forever your child, kneeling at the hem of your golden robe. So many ages ago you left us, and we lost our way. Yet never did I see in my dreams that you would lie and return to us no more. Never did I glimpse in my dreams your betrayal.

I knew the Goddesses for what they were. I knew. They held no surprise for me, no treachery. Cihuacoatl! Goddess of sacrificial death and the pain of childbirth. Joy for you there is in the suffering of women. And Acuecueyotl! You of the waves that drive all before them, consort of storms and drowning. Rejoice!

And Mictlancihuatl! Can I forget the consort of death itself? No, my Lady Death. We all await your glad feasting upon our flesh!

Only Malinallxochitl, cunning sorceress, rests blameless in the heavens, disemboweled by your brother for your courage. Did you truly think yourself to be the ruler of the All? Foolish woman! Did you truly forget Huitzilopochtli, God of War, your most dangerous brother? Did he slay you while you slept, unarmed? Do you still peer down at us from your flowery abode to watch with horror blood pool in the fields of combat and stream down the steps of the teocalli? I tell you, there is great joy to be had in war. I have feasted upon the sight!

We know it is Ipalnemohuani who gives to us our life, and Huehueteotl who gave us fire. And, yes, another God more kind than any Goddess uneasy in the heavens or restless for death in the realms below; Xipe Totec, who dies and is reborn to give us maize! Hail! And Tepeyollotl, Jaguar God, he who puts the cunning of the jungle in our hearts and the hunger of the jungle in our eyes! I prostrate myself to you also, ferocious Lord.

I knew from the first day of this, my life on earth, that it would be to the Gods alone I would owe my allegiance, never to the Goddesses interested in nothing but the agonies of birth and the flaying knives of death. It would be to Quetzalcoatl I first would turn—and then to the Gods of war and revenge. To that I swore in my own blood, tasting my oath in the thorn through my tongue and in the flames I passed beneath my feet.

And yet none of you could save me from the vengeful hands of the Goddesses! Not even you could stop them from giving me up to the uses of men. Not even you could forbid their violations, the violations of the night I tried to wash from my body as I stood naked in the river at dawn and prayed most desperately to you, Quetzalcoatl, but not even you could comfort me or change the path the Goddesses lay before me. I prayed and prayed for you to shield me again, Quetzalcoatl, as once I knew you did, and I sacrificed and cried for the strength of your strong and shining arms! But you deserted me and so I was forced to succumb to the ways of the Azteca, to war and dark cunning, to the mighty Tezcatlipoca and Huitzilopochtli, until even they fell before yet a mightier God who conquered us all.

Tonatiuh, with your bright eye fixed upon this earth, did you not see? Did you not hear me calling you, as you swept in splendor across the sky? Where were you when I fell crushed to earth, screaming for pity? All I had left then was the hope that your brother, Quetzalcoatl, would come to us again, that he would sail across the seas as he once promised, to make righteous once again our land and free us all from slavery. I kept my eyes on the east, watching. My heart stood still, waiting for him to come. Quetzalcoatl! Light of my eyes! Did you betray me for my sister, softer than I, kinder than I, Xochitl? In the cold stones in my heart, she, like a serpent, coils. . . .

3

XOCHITL

I was sold into slavery at fourteen years of age, and before I was fifteen I knew everything about the shameful acts of men and women. For the first two months of my captivity I was sold by the hour, and though the price my owner asked was high, it was willingly paid. Youth ensured the smallness of my tipili and the firmness of my breasts. Only on the days of my bleeding was I free of men and, given hunger for certain tastes, not always then.

My owner had use of me as well, whenever another of his slaves did not please him, and I grew accustomed, however unwillingly, to the way he would have me straddle him so he could fondle my breasts as I was made to ride him like a beast. It was a blessing from the Goddess that he could not wait long for his pleasure, but was soon grimacing and writhing beneath me. I hated him with a hatred so round and full and deep I thought it must loom up around me like a foul shade.

For most of his female slaves, my owner would find buyers as quickly as they appeared, barter goods in hand. Of course he did not ask, nor did he care to know, for what purpose his slaves were being purchased. He did not care what was to befall me, either, for he had not the capacity for affection, keeping me longer than usual only because he waited for the higher price I would command. It mattered not at all if I were to be bought as a whore, as an object of brutality or unremitting labor, or if I were to have my heart torn from my body and my body itself thrown to the beasts.

After those first two months I, too, became careless of my fate. What was it to me, life? I had seen too many faces grown slack with desire, felt too many thighs part mine, too many tepuli push too soon into my tipili, and had seen nothing behind the faces twisted with pleasure so near to my own. I lay beneath them wondering if they had daughters, and what they would feel if—given the unlikely possibility they cared about them—their own kindred were being treated so. Fathers there were who took me, and their sons and brothers. The traveling pochteca, also, (sometimes a caravan of them, waiting patiently for their time with me, speaking of business and smoking their little pipes) and warriors there were, laying down their shields and macquauitls beside my sleeping mat. And men of the land, if their season had been fruitful, and men who hunted the wild pig and turkey, paying for my body with dried corn or beans or the bloody bodies of animals. I lay beneath them as limply as one of their hunted things, and they took me as passionlessly as they would make water in the jungle, their faces stone carved with cruel fingers.

Then came the night my owner forced me to straddle him and then fell into a sleep deepened both by pleasure and cups of octli, forgetting to first tie me by my hands and feet. I crawled serpentlike from his hut, staying close to the ground, like the shadow of a cloud passing the moon.

When it seemed I was far enough from the camp I began to run, only to find myself pursued by someone swifter.

"Malinallxochitl!" I cried beneath my breath. "Goddess Mother!" But my pursuer came swifter yet, with long strides closing in as if to a kill. He grabbed me as I ran, throwing me to the earth, pressing a knife to my throat so I knew I was but one stroke from my death.

"Will you struggle or lie still?" he demanded in a rough voice. All I could do was move my head. He drew back then and pulled me to my feet, looking closely at me in the whiteness of the full moon's face. He was startled by me, as men always were, and I knew the smallest price he would exact would be that which all men exacted.

"You are the slave of Icpitl?" I nodded and he looked long at me. "You are beautiful," he said in a voice less rough, "like a flower."

Never had a man spoken so to me since the first day of my captivity. I could only stare at him, waiting for what was always next to come.

"Are you frightened of me?" he asked; a foolish question I did not answer. "Do not be so, maiden," he whispered, and I came almost to laughter that he should call me so. Maiden! Not the whore I had become, but maiden once again! I could not guess by his face what he wanted of me, but I recognized him.

"Your task is to catch the slaves as they run from their master," I said coldly.

"That is my task," he agreed. "I am a slave as well."

"Let me go," I urged him in sudden hope. "Take me here on the earth and then let me go!"

Could there have been a sadness in his face? Almost I think there was.

"If you should run away, Icpitl would find you. Your beauty would be remarked upon, and there is a heavy price to pay for sheltering slaves who have escaped their masters. Do you know what our master would do to you? I have seen what he does, and to you he would do the same, taking care, of course, not to mar you and thereby lose some of what he hopes to gain." He was quiet a moment and I was silent, shivering in the warm night air that gathered around us as if it listened with the ears of Icpitl.

"He would beat you, very painfully, but so it would not show upon your skin, and he would use you as no woman should be used, even with his animals, so to break your spirit. He would see to it that your beauty was unchanged, but you yourself would only long for death. That, too, would he know, and thus he would keep you bound hand and foot every moment you were not being used."

He spoke harshly, and I did not doubt he spoke the truth. As his words lay spoken but still present on the air, there was a cry from the direction of the camp, a cry echoed by others, and then the flare of torches.

"He has discovered that you have gone," this slave said to me. "You must do exactly what I say. Come with me, then." He took my hand and held it until we were almost within sight of the camp, then dropped it and told me to follow him. Other slaves gave cry at our presence and Icpitl came running and made as if to snatch me by the arm, but the man stepped between us.

"Master," he said in a pleading voice, "do not be angry with me, I beg!" Icpitl, in his surprise, looked away from me and at his slave, who bent slightly beneath the weight of his plea and cowered before him. It was a performance of cunning, I knew, and sensing in him the price he paid with his dignity, I was moved to gratitude.

"Well, what is it?" Icpitl demanded in a hard and impatient voice, his hands aching to give me pain.

"This woman, here, stepped forth from your hut for a breath of the night's air, and I saw her, and . . ." he paused and wiped his forehead as if the sweat of fear had gathered there, "and . . . please do not beat me, Master! I could not help myself!"

The slave cowered further, and his voice grew high with a fearfulness I hoped was feigned. "Master, I have not had a woman in many months. When I saw this beautiful one, I had to have her. I put my hand over her mouth, for she tried to scream, and I carried her into the darkness to make use of her."

"And did you use her?" Icpitl demanded in a fury.

"I did not," the man replied in a voice low with shame. "It has been so long I could not get my tepuli to rise to her." And with that he dropped his eyes to the earth in expectation of the ridicule that indeed followed.

"A slave has no use for a tepuli," Icpitl said through his coarse laughter, "no more than he has a right to so beautiful a whore. I will have my men bind and beat you, but I will let you return to your task in the morning. If you can yet crawl!" he added, in another burst of laughter.

Icpitl motioned for me to step into his hut. The night's high humor had renewed his lust. Perhaps there was the seed of suspicion in his mind, for he used me roughly, spreading my legs and climbing over me, for once, pushing his tepuli into me most cruelly, pulling me up to him by my long hair, then pressing down upon me with the full force of his strength.

I heard in the distance the sound of a whip and a beaten man's brave silence, and so I also was brave and uttered not a sound. In the morning I was not bruised, just as the slave had told me, but my tipili was bloody from that night's work.

I saw my rescuer several times from a distance, but could never approach him. I longed to tell him of my gratitude, but that was not possible. Within the week a buyer was found for me and I was led from camp without speaking the words.

At last I lost count of the days. I knew the tenth month of Xocotl Uetzi must be coming to an end. In the teocallis it was time for worship of Xiuhtecuhtli, God of Fire. Many prisoners taken captive in the Wars of Flowers would be sacrificed, even as my father years before. In the Azteca city of Tenochtitlan hundreds of men would be sacrificed, their chests torn open to procure hearts for the thirsty Gods who watched the sacred ceremonies from their dark and smoky temples and from the sky above and the nine underworlds below. Within smaller teocallis would be enacted smaller ceremonies with fewer warriors going to meet the Flowery Death.

After the people watched these sacred rites, then young men would compete to climb a pole greased with human fat to try and possess parts of a huahtli-paste effigy erected at the top. It was amusing to watch and there was much laughter and slapping of hands. The people did not attend all the sacred rites, as there were too many for any but priests to attend them all, but it had always pleased me to go to them when the month was one for rejoicing and we could laugh and feast and so reassure the Gods we were grateful for the abundance of their blessings.

It was midday when the slave traders arrived. They had come many miles in search of women fit to be sacrificed in the eleventh month of Ochpantzli, when Gods in the earth sweep a path for the Gods in the heavens. It is in this ritual, come to us from the Azteca of Anáhuac, that a woman, untouched and most beautiful, was dressed in fine clothing and led with dancing and music to the teocalli to be beheaded in honor of our Earth Mother, fertile giver of life to all. It was honor as well for the woman so beheaded, for she thereby ascended to the joy accorded a warrior killed in battle or sacrificed. I had seen this ritual one time before, holding tightly to my mother's hand as she breathed with a shaken breath beside me.

"Mother?" I had asked her, staring with curiosity into her face, "would you be glad if you were chosen for such a sacrifice?" And she smiled a very small smile and sighed.

"It would ill become me if I did not," she answered in that way which does not answer and I continued to stare into her face. She looked away from me, though, and the swollen pupils of her eyes were pools of night.

Icpitl chose ten of his seventeen female slaves and harnessed us, naked, by collars to a pole and paraded us before the men who had come to buy. They looked long at us, from the front and back both, measuring us carefully with their eyes as they would measure the plumpness of a fowl or the length of a quetzal feather. Then they pointed at me, and at two others, and so began to argue with Icpitl over our price, taken singly or purchased as a group.

It became apparent they wanted me most eagerly, for though they kept their voices low and faces expressionless, their eyes were drawn to me again and again. My breasts grew hot under their gaze and my hands joined in forbidden modesty to cover the lips of my tipili. One trader came close to me and his eyes were like fire and another came up behind and lifted my long black hair to inspect my back and buttocks for any blemish.

"I have looked over these women and in every place both private and not private," Icpitl told them, with the smile men reserve for other men when they discuss the bodies of women, "and they are all three of them perfect. Each one will be chosen for sacrifice, I promise!"

"And you have not touched them?" one of the men asked.

Icpitl looked offended. "They should each be whipped to death if they have been violated." This truly should have made the traders smile, for they all knew about their lewdness with the female—and often male—slaves in their possession. It was common knowledge among them, carefully hidden from others.

They paid a high price for me, so high that they had to return immediately to Cholulan, from which sacred city they had come. They harnessed me to a pole with some twenty other females, paid for me in the form of quills filled with gold powder fine as dust, and Icpitl was pleased. From the time I was harnessed to the trader's pole, he never looked again at me.

It was a long journey to Cholulan, and one made arduous by the ruggedness of some of the trails, though the main road from Huatusco to Acatzinco was firm and level enough. We created little interest in the towns we passed through, although some male eyebrows raised at the number of beautiful women collared to the same pole. The traders moved us like valuable livestock, but as livestock, nonetheless, sometimes forcing us to walk twenty miles in a single day. We were fed three times a day in sufficient quantity so that our flesh would not press upon our bones, and they allowed us to bathe and wash our hair in the few rivers we passed.

We were a passive and silent row of yoked animals. Now and then one would hear a muffled cry or a plea to some God or Goddess, but we did not speak to the traders nor to one another. That did not seem strange at the time, for we were all of us intent upon survival and the coming sacrifice and our future if we were not to be that sacrifice. I could guess from the many sidelong glances cast at me that I was considered the slave most likely to symbolize the Mother of Earth, and such a fate seemed acceptable. I did feel that it was a fate any one of us would have embraced, both for the honor of it and because any other future we might envision could not inspire hope.

Strange, indeed, did it seem to be so far from the sea beside which I had spent my short girlhood. The nights seemed empty without the sound of Acuecueyotl's hands moving the waves onto the shore and back again, ceaseless and soothing as a mother's soft singing to her weary child. That sweet soothing had been mine every night of my life until I became a slave, and I was restless in its absence and lay for hours in an exhaustion sleep would not heal.

In the mornings we all rose before Tonatiuh and the bonds were taken off our hands and feet and the collars fastened around our necks once more. All of this in silence, and still in silence were we used by the three slave traders, one after another; quiet as death as they sampled us all. I never knew which of the traders had me, nor how many times each, because such activity took place in the darkness and without words and, for me, without thought. I never heard one woman make a sound of any kind, except those one would make when asleep and dreams ruled her speech.

It was as if we dreamed in the daylight also. The

hours would pass as we moved along, bare feet stirring the dust, the sun rising above us, then slowly lowering us all into the dark underworld we endured until Tonatiuh rose again. Day after day, around the southernmost edge of the mountains we trudged, and at last to the banks of the Atoyac River, resting beside and bathing within its coolness, readying ourselves for the next day's entrance into the sacred city of Cholulan. The traders sat watching us as we disrobed and waded into the shallows of the water, and I was reminded of the many times I had stood in a river, thus, with my sister. Where is she now? I thought. What has her life become?

4

MALINALLI

Oh, my mother, you who bore me, you who abandoned me to the violations of your husband, who allowed him to sell me like an unwanted dog, hear me! I send you no greeting but a curse, you who surrounded yourself with pleasure and lived your days in your own house and with no master but the husbands you took to your sleeping mat. All men are my masters, Mother, and all sleeping mats those I must share.

Upon that day I first was sold, I was sold again. This man sold me to another, after he had made use of me, to work for a Tabascan cacique in a village larger than the one in which I was born, some unknown long-runs south in the city of Cintla. I walked there, harnessed to a pole by a collar around my neck, in the company of some seven other slaves.

It was unbearably hot in the middle of the day when Tonatiuh's pitiless eye was upon me, and the insects rose in stinging clouds from the surrounding marshlands. One of the slaves was bitten by a snake, and though he screamed out and then could only stumble, our master whipped us on until the man fell in his pain and weakness, and the trader cursed and took the collar from him. In the jaws of death he begged to be released from pain. He had value no more, and so the trader cut his throat there in the middle of the trail. Since it was yet six hours to go before we could expect to lie down for the night, the trader directed myself and another woman to cut the corpse into manageable pieces, which we did with difficulty given the blunt knives he handed us, wary, perhaps, that we might use them on ourselves and so be also out of his reach.

It was an awkward butchery, but we cut from him his head and then his limbs, slicing whatever meat still clung to his bones and skinning the flesh. This we wrapped in cloth and bore away in our arms, bloody bundles that began to stink with a sticky sweetness before that long, hot day was over.

After we made camp, the trader directed us to make a stew of the slave meat, and to season it with chiles and other spices he had in his possession. Then he ate it, sharing bits with those of us who pleased him. It had been some weeks since I tasted meat and I was hungry for it, finding the flavor not unlike dog and as sinewy. That it was human flesh did not bother me more than the whine of one member of that cloud of stinging insects. Had it been the flesh of a woman, perhaps I would not have been so unmindful.

Well-satisfied with his benevolence, the trader then had me lie down by the fire and, with the other slaves watching or not as they chose, he forced himself upon me and then bound my hands and feet and allowed me rest. He took another woman sometime in the night, and then he slept. The moon, Huitzilopochtli's slain sister, Coyolxauhqui, watched impassively from the sky. I was learning, Mother, to feel nothing.

And are you pleased also, Mother, that we rose on that day and came to Cintla, where I entered servitude? I was led to the door of a fine stone house, accepted by another slave and shown where I was to sleep and what work I would be expected to do. I, who never before had rested indoors if I could be out, was given tasks in the kitchen, crushing maize into flour, stirring pots of beans, sweeping clean the floors. It was there, in the kitchen and during my duties in other parts of that noble house, that I learned the language of my master, that ancient speech of the Maya. I learned rapidly and well. I was suddenly aware, my mother, that to understand in secret what you are not expected to comprehend can bring one much interesting knowledge.

I show but one example. Knowing I was a Nahuatl-speaking slave, but not knowing my desire to listen and learn and to turn knowledge into a weapon for my survival, my master paid little heed to me if I were near. One day I overheard my master tell his son that to travel anywhere in the One World, all one need do is learn the paths of the stars and follow them. This I had not known, believing the stars to move at their own whim. I hid in the garden as the old man pointed the stars out to his son who, to my benefit, learned with exceeding slowness. Though there was much that was beyond my comprehension, I learned one or two things I kept in my mind.

It was a life of the daily round and nothing more. I was not bothered by men in the house, neither slaves nor the family of the cacique, because of my master's orders. No slave could be beaten unless a serious transgression was proved against him, and it was forbidden for freemen to lie with slaves or for slaves to lie with slaves. Still, some nights the gardens outside the windows moaned and sighed with more than the hot breath of Ehecatl on his night's journey. Never did I add my breath to those nights, but kept my body to myself and my mouth closed and my ears always open.

Thus did I hear my master tell his son that a travelling group of pochteca had brought into Cintla from the far great city of the Azteca, Tenochtitlan, news that great houses had been seen upon the waters of the eastern sea. It was, so he said, a matter of discussion among the wise men and sorcerers and priests whether these houses were abodes of men or of Gods, or even, as it had been foretold, Quetzalcoatl returning to us in the coming year of One-Reed.

That was a moment when the heart in me felt like the heart of a child, and I sang beneath my breath and waited with a trembling and a hunger.

"You! Slave!" I heard over and over in those waiting

days. "Do you dream to be whipped, or will you work?" And I would find myself rudely returned to slavery from the riverbanks of the Coatzalcoalcos a lifetime away. My hands grinding corn were the hands of that girl, and the air I breathed smelled of salt; I slept sweetly in the imagined sound of waves rushing across sand.

Quetzalcoatl! Oh, Mother, what a dream that one name painted in my mind. Many nights as I lay in that narrow land between waking and sleep, I could almost see him. He would be pale of skin and his hair not black or even dark brown, but fair, and he would be dressed in shining gold and come among us like the God he was, and set us free! Flowers I would throw in his path and so would I hunt in the jungle for the rarest of blossoms to place upon his altar. Jaguars I would snare to make a cape for him, and butterflies would I trap and give to him for his pleasure.

All of this I kept in my heart, and went about my work in a silent way. Though slaves in this house were treated well and were kind to each other according to the nature of each, I stood back and watched and listened and called no one friend. Day by day I built hope upon hope, waiting for him to come for me.

Four years I spent in that house. Four years I ground corn for other mouths and swept the floors of a house not my own. I could have suffered worse, my mother, but greater suffering was yet to be.

5

Xochitl

From a great distance one could see the pyramids and teocallis of Cholulan. There were hundreds of them, whitewashed and painted with bold colors, fearsome serpents coiling from the walls, their jaws gaping full of sharp stone teeth. In the center of this sacred city was a pyramid so enormous one could only gasp at its size. At the peak had stood a statue of pure green chalchuite that was Quetzalcoatl, Lord of the Breath of Life, and though the teocalli still rose in our Lord's honor, the statue was no more.

The streets of Cholulan were paved with stone, and of stone were made the fine houses and teocallis also. Priests bore incense and incense burned in all the hundreds of teocallis, so that the very air was white with the fragrant smoke of copal. Everywhere people came and went and the marketplace was a wonder. Never had I seen such a grand one before. So many people and so many things to buy: wondrous jewels of gold, pottery of red and black and white, exotic fruits the like of which I had never seen, foods of other kinds, known and unknown, which lay in piles like small bright pyramids.

There was little curiosity as we passed, perhaps because in Cholulan slaves were a frequent sight. Sacrifice was a daily task; our many Gods required the bodies of many, many slaves. As I walked toward the great teocalli, that wondrous place, like the work of a sorcerer so amazing and beautiful it was, I found myself resigned to the sacrifice. Nay, even with a feeling of honor did I begin to hope for such a thing. Surely in that holiest of cities my blood would be spilled for good reason, and my spirit soar from earth to the heavens in the moment my heart was torn from me.

On we went even to the great teocalli itself, to a doorway on its eastern side. The traders ordered us to stop. One of them entered the doorway and soon returned with a priest whose black garments and long hair were crusted with the blood of many sacrifices. So might my blood, I thought, stiffen his robe and clot in his hair. I trembled then, and felt cold. The priest looked long at us and then, without uttering a word, pointed at me and at another woman. The traders took off our collars and bid us follow the priest into the heart of the pyramid.

Corridors stretched in all directions, one leading to another and that to another in a way most bewildering to me. Silently we followed the priest past walls upon which butterflies and insects of yellow and black had been painted. There was an air of utmost holiness in the pyramid. Almost could I imagine the presence of my dear loved Lord, the softness of his breath upon my cheek.

At last we arrived in a large room lighted by holes in the stone above. In the room were two kneeling priests chanting beside bowls of burning incense set before two idols with eyes of glittering jewels. This was a sacred place, and I felt in my heart that surely we were to be sacrificed if we were allowed to see it.

The other woman and I stood, hands clasped before us, still as two slaves of stone, while the priest who had guided us knelt between the others and chanted with them. The incense seemed to thicken the air and the stone images wavered before my eyes and suddenly I felt I would be ill. Horrified at the prospect of such sacrilege, of defiling this holy place with my body, I knew I would deserve for it a speedy and ignominious death. I hardened my belly against itself and held my breath, lest I disturb in any way the holy rites of the three priests. I found myself praying desperately to my Lord Quetzalcoatl, pleading for him to spare me from committing such outrage, asking him to let me be a worthy sacrifice for him.

"My God, my Lord of Breath and Lord of Dawn, giver of life and joy, let me die in your service! Let me be of use to you, my Lord!"

The walls then seemed to shudder and the stones loosen from the white tetzontli that held them in place. Copal filled the room so that the priests and the glittering idols appeared at great distance. And then darkness overcame me, and I was given up to the God . . .

My spirit wandered far from me. It passed up through the temple, through the holes in the stones, between the very stones themselves, curling like smoke through the very heart of the pyramid, up to where the great glory of the temple had once stood, and now stood again. For there the great green image of my Lord Quetzalcoatl rose before torches of flame. And my spirit knelt before him, and all was still. Then down the shining length of him blood flowed, and it flowed over the dais he stood upon and over me as I knelt before him so that my hands and limbs were dark with his blood. The air grew full of the sound of wings and the cries of animals and birds and the whine and whisper of insects so that it seemed I was in the jungle once again and the very trees themselves did whisper.

The flames flickered in a sudden wind and went out, and in the temple there was blackness and all voices were stilled. From the green image of my Lord there came a light, and it filled the God until it glowed clearer and more green than the edge of the sea when it lies shallow and warm in the hollows of the sand.

I knew the image spoke to me, yet it was as if the words did not enter my mind but passed from between my own lips, and though it now seems strange, I felt no fear. There came the smell of many flowers, and such a joy arose with their perfume that the heart in me was made glad. I was a child again by the sea, and my mother stood behind me with her warmth at my back.

Then all was darkness. I heard voices again, this time the voices of men speaking low, and I opened my eyes most cautiously, remembering where I was and knowing that I would surely die for my impious conduct. The three priests were standing above me with their eyes staring and wonder upon their faces. I did not dare speak before them, but lay where I had awakened upon the floor. The woman who had been with me was gone. Surely now I would die.

"Do you know what you have done?" one priest asked in a harsh voice, and I barely had courage to shake my head.

"Did you dream?" another asked, more gently. Encouraged by his softer tone, I nodded. "Would you then tell us what you saw?"

I told them all that I had seen and heard. I spoke of the words which had passed from my lips but which were not mine. I did not say they seemed to come from the image of my Lord, for such words seemed sure sacrilege. And then the first priest asked, "Have you told us all?" and I nodded, and the third, who hadn't spoken, said, "Why did you not tell us you were with child?" I could only gape at him, feeling my body grow suddenly strange, as if it were no longer mine.

I shook my head and whispered, "But, Master, I did not know."

They stood and looked at me a long moment. Then the soft-voiced priest reached down and helped me to rise. I lowered my eyes, for I could not look at them.

"Come, child," the priest said to me, and took my hand as if I were indeed a child still and led me from the room.

"Master?" I asked him, and he stopped and turned to look at me.

"Yes, child?"

"Master, am I not then to be sacrificed?"

Almost a smile touched the furthest edge of his solemn mouth and he shook his head. "That would be most unseemly."

We stood wordless for a moment and then I gathered my courage to my breast and asked, "Because I am with child, Master?"

He did not come near to smiling then. "No woman with child can give her heart in Ochpantzli, but you will give your child in your stead when the time has come. And there is also something more than this."

I looked swiftly into his face and then away, unable to form the words to ask him what "something more" could be. He turned from me and led me on, down the corridors and out into the blinding sun, then on to the biggest house I had ever seen, like a palace of the fearsome Moteczoma himself! A white-robed woman with her hair flowing down her back glided toward us from another chamber. The priest spoke low words to her, then turned to go.

"Master . . ." I made bold to stop him at the threshold, reaching out a hand I did not yet dare to place upon his arm. "Master, what is the second reason I am unfit to be sacrificed to my Lord?"

He looked at me most gravely, so gravely that my heart travelled into my throat and stuck there, rendering me speechless even if courage had given me words. And he said, "Our God has spoken through you in your dreaming, and therefore you now belong to him forever in all of your acts and thoughts. You were saved from the one great honor for another, greater one, and your life must be lived in his service."

With that, the priest did indeed turn upon his heel and leave. The woman in white came forward and took my hand, leading me into the vast whiteness of that most holy house of women.

Entered I so into a world made fresh; thus appeared the road which led my steps a little way before it was lost once more in the mist of the unknowing. It was destiny for me to be the happiest I was ever to be, since early girlhood, in that house of women, and for the next months until Atahualco, the first month in the great and holy round, so would I remain.

On that first day I was taken to the temazcalli to purify my flesh. Pouring water on the hot stones, the young woman who was my guide bid me undress, and so I left my huipilli and cueitl, both torn and filthy, on the floor outside. Alone I entered the steamy chamber of the temazcalli, then rubbed myself with herbs and beat my skin with grasses to cleanse it. It had been many days since I had washed myself with more than the waters of a river and I sweated with a glad heart until my skin was red as fire.

My guide returned and bid me dress. She had brought soft cotton cloth which I wrapped around my waist and a new huipilli to cover my breasts. All this was in silence for she did not speak and I had not courage to raise my voice in her wordlessness. She brushed my hair and bound it smoothly into the shape of a shell. Lastly, she made a mark with a white paste upon my forehead, and very solemn was she as she did this and with grave eyes.

Leading me then through three corridors and to a door into another chamber, she motioned me to enter. It was a goodly-sized room and all of it white. Before me, seated in a low chair, was a woman dressed in white, with a headdress of white feathers and white sandals on her feet. She beckoned me to approach and I did so, kneeling as I drew near, keeping my eyes down in all respect.

"Look at me, child," she said in a voice not unkind, and I looked up. Her countenance, while solemn, was not cruel, and I took hope. Surely it would not be bad fortune to spend my life in slavery to such a woman and in such a place!

"I am on earth the spirit made flesh of Ixtacciuatl, the White Goddess. Other priestesses there are in this calmecac, all purifying themselves and learning to become cinatlamacazqui so that our sanctuaries will be kept forever in readiness to honor our Gods with their fires ever burning. This you may not do for you are with child and thus would dishonor those who must be honored."

My skin stung with shame and I cast my eyes down again. What would I be if stained with dishonor? Not to be sacrificed and not to be servant either? I was bewildered before this noble woman who looked to be the very Goddess Ixtacciuatl herself.

"Do you know why you are here?"

I shook my head and was miserable.

"Look into my face," she demanded, and I made haste to obey and did not take my eyes from hers again. "I have been told you were given visions in the teocalli of Quetzalcoatl. That you lay as one dead and spoke words wondrous and strange. For that you are to stay with us until you bring forth your child. It would not be fit for you to be trained in the spirit while your body is filling with life, but here you will stay and do as you are bid, and then when your child comes into this world, you will begin your training to become cinatlamacazqui." She stared at me severely for a moment and then added, "I need not instruct you, child, I am sure, that you are to keep yourself pure for your service and though you have obviously known man," and at that I had trouble not lowering my eyes again, "you may know man no more. Will you obey?"

I nodded. Pleasure I had never had from lying with man, and to give up all such acts in future was a promise I could happily—nay, joyfully—make to my Lady Ixtacciuatl. She was a wise woman, this priestess of Cholulan, and she saw the relief in my eyes and smiled, the smile blossoming upon her grave face like a flower upon snow.

"I believe this promise is not made with too divided a heart, child?" and she laughed as she spoke with a small bright laugh, like tiny silver bells, and motioned with her hand for me to go. "A woman awaits you outside. Her name is Oxomoco, and she will instruct you in your duties." I turned to leave and as I reached the door she spoke to me again. "What is your name?"

"Xochitl," I answered shyly, "and I have a sister, my twin, whom my mother named Malinalli."

At this my lady's gaze grew keen. "Ah, Malinall-xochitl," she breathed with the sound of wind through dry reeds. "Ah," she breathed again, lost in thought. Quietly I backed from the room to find the woman Oxomoco waiting for me. Hair grey with her years, face homely from birth, she was slightly deformed and walked with a limp, and yet on that unhandsome face there was the look of great peace. She took my hand and led me, as a mother does a child, to a room where there were sleeping mats upon the floor and she indicated the one where I was to sleep.

"You may leave anything you possess here beside your mat where it will be quite safe," she said, but since I owned nothing but the clothes given to me, I stood with hands clasped and motionless, awaiting direction.

"What is your name?" Oxomoco asked with a gentle curiosity in her voice, "and where have you come from to this city of Cholulan?"

I told her what she asked, though my village was too distant for her knowing of it more fully than it was east of Cholulan and beside the sea, which she had never seen.

"I am from Cholulan," she offered with pride, "and I was born with this penance," she said cheerfully, indicating her bent back and her legs, one being shorter than the other. "Since it did seem to me most unlikely that I would ever wed someone who would not beat me, I offered myself to this calmecac and herein have I lived my life these forty years."

I did not know what to say to this, but I smiled to show I heard her words and they had pleased me. She reached out and took my arm and pressed it kindly, saying, "It is hard work to become cinatlamacazqui, but it is a great honor to so serve the Gods. Tasks there are in plenty, and it is proper that we live in all modesty and with only simple pleasures and possessions, but it is a life with purpose and thus a life of value. Serve well, Xochitl, and you will be as happy as your tonalli and the Gods allow."

This I took for the fair speech it was, and kindly meant, and I placed my hand upon her arm and she smiled. "Xochitl, you are a woman with fewer words than an old crone has teeth!"

I laughed, the first such laughter in three years; rusty with disuse but a pleasure to feel bubbling up inside me like a fountain of light. "It has been long since I could speak without fear," I faltered, "and perhaps there are many words waiting to be spoken, too many to break free and pour forth."

"There are many days for them to flow," Oxomoco said smiling, "and many years to hear them, and no need for you to fear."

Thus it was I became part of that world of women, a world as full of joy and grief, sacrifice and shrewd cunning as ever the world outside, but safer and, because men were small part of it, more sweet. My belly grew and my child moved within me and, dismissing the words of the priest in my joy, I looked forward to motherhood and to this one possession that would be mine. All else had been taken from me, but this little being enclosed in my body, like a seed within a pod, could be held, caressed, looked upon and watched fondly as it grew from the shadow I cast and out into the sun.

I swept floors, cooked meals and busied myself while the other women took instruction and had their sacred duties to fulfill, and I was happy. Time passed as if enchanted. I grew heavy and was slow in completing my tasks, but there were no harsh words for me. Many women glanced at me with pity and curiosity but they asked nothing. We spoke of many things but never the child. Though in all truth I did long for such speech, it was unseemly in that house of maidens.

Still, I thought of my child in almost every waking moment and dreamed of it at night, feeling the little body beneath my swollen breasts.

At last my hour came and I awoke in the early dawn, breathless and with the hands of birth tightening around my belly. I waited until the conch shell had been blown and the others awakened and went to Oxomoco, by then my very dear friend, and whispered to her shyly that my baby was soon to be born.

"Oh!" she gasped, her eyes wide and mouth startled open and round, "so this is the day!"

"I think so," I said. "I feel as if the breath is being crushed from me."

"Do nothing until the midwives come," she ordered, hurrying with her clothing and leaving her hair half-fallen around her face like a crazy woman.

"Do you think my child waits for my convenience?" I said to her, laughing. She did not join in the laughter but hobbled from the room with her face paled by worry.

At the command of Lady Ixtacciuatl, Oxomoco led me to a small room some distance from the main rooms of the calmecac so that the sounds of birth would not penetrate to where the words of the holy mysteries were spoken. Midwives from the city were brought, and they burned herbs and gave me potions to drink. Oxomoco, given permission to stay with me, rubbed my body with lotions and tried bravely to smile. My naked belly humped and convulsed as if it were no longer part of me, and as time passed there were fewer moments of peace between the pains.

I had learned something of birth from my mother and so I knew not to cry out or make any sound. I prayed without ceasing to the Goddess Cihuacoatl to ease my suffering and aid me in my silence. Sweat gathered and fell and gathered once more while I rocked back and forth in the throes of birth. Xocomoco rubbed my back and whispered small words of courage to me, and though I was grateful to her, I could not speak for fear that from my lips would issue screams. Or worse, curses, for I grew astonishingly angry and would have said unspeakable things to the midwives who sought only to bring my child safely into the world and preserve me from the honor of dying the warrior's death in childbirth.

Time passed so slowly it seemed I must have lain for months in that dark and narrow chamber. Oxomoco never left my side, even when in utter weariness I closed my eyes and slept. Whenever I was thrust back into wakefulness it was to find that good woman kneeling beside me still. She knew nothing of birth and I do believe she must have worried more in those hours than I, and felt a goodly measure of the pain! I saw the dark concern in her eyes though she sought to hide it from me with her smiles and hopeful words.

At last the end drew near. I could not stop from pushing with all the force left in me, Oxomoco holding me half-sitting in her arms, her body bracing mine from where she knelt behind me. So it was I saw, through a gushing of blood and water, a small head make its way into this world, and the rest of its body—so small I wondered at the size of my belly—follow behind. The midwives held her—my daughter!—and cleaned her before passing her into my hungry arms. Then they spoke the words over her;

"Oh, precious stone, oh rich feather! Thou wert made in the place where are the great God and Goddess which are above the heavens. Thy mother and thy father, celestial woman and celestial man, made and reared thee. Thou hast come to this world from afar, poor and weary. Our Lord Quetzalcoatl, who is the creator, has put into this dust a precious stone and a rich feather."

They did not bury the severed cord with miniature symbols of my daughter's domestic future as servant or wife, an omission I chose to believe was made necessary by the fact that she had been brought forth not beside her mother's hearth but in a sacred calmecac. It was an omission, however, that made me uneasy. I turned the uneasiness from my mind as I reached for my daughter, and forgot all but my joy as I held her in my arms.

6

MALINALLI

Oh, Mother, it is I, Malinalli, the daughter you bore only to betray. Listen!

Long were my days of servitude; long my nights of lying awake in a great and hollow emptiness only my God, Quetzalcoatl, could fill. Only he, and only when all things were made plain and peace was returned to this earth the Azteca—and you, Mother, and the man you took to your sleeping matt—had made intolerable.

You would be glad to hear, Mother, that I spent my time quite well. Does that surprise you, you who thought me capable of nothing? Not only did I learn from that old man, my master, as he taught his stone-skulled son, but I learned the ways of the ancients, of the women and men who have long known the craft of magic and the mixing of herbs and grasses and the blood of trees for their strange and potent effects. There was in the old man's house, unknown to him of course, a woman who had been taught the ways of sorcery by her mother, as her mother had before been taught by her mother's mother. She was powerful in the knowledge and devious in her use of it. Thus when a cruel overseer died, writhing in agony, no one thought to ask why it was that this woman had brought him a delicious soup but moments before the agonies began. She moved like a shadow in the night, choosing her herbs with the aid of the moon and uttering words guttural and foreign beneath her breath.

This woman had no daughter to whom she could bequeath her craft, but when I sensed in her the power I forever and in all ways did seek, I made myself useful and pleasant to her. In time she grew to trust me and she would show to me the plants she gathered, the words to say over them to distill their power and how to make drinks and potions from them. She taught me many charms, to heal and to kill. There was not time enough to learn them all but, in that final year of my servitude and her teaching, I learned that which would be most useful to me.

I cared nothing for her. She smelled sour with age and her fingers were twisted and ugly. In the foolishness of her many years she thought me fond of her, and so that she would continue to teach me I pretended to such fondness. It was not necessary to tell her the truth, because by the time that year had passed I left my master's house, never to return to slavery.

My Lord had placed his feet upon our shores, Oh Mother, and by that act freed me to go to him, as was my destiny.

7

Xochitl

How can words express the inexpressible? They elude me and I am speechless. My being flooded with joy when I held my daughter in my arms, feeling her small mouth on my breast. Her long dark eyes were my own and her honey skin and delicate fingers. It was simple for me to pretend she had no father, for she resembled only me. I threw whatever man he might have been into the mist of my forgetting and kept my daughter to myself, in and of myself, the heart of me that had left my body and now lay in my arms.

So began the teaching of the Mysteries, now that spirit had become flesh. In the first light of dawn we rose with prayers in honor of Tonatiuh for returning to us from his perilous journey through Mictlan and the shades of death, ascending to the heavens once more, his glory upon the waters and upon the earth he warmed with his touch. I fed my daughter, whom the Lady Ixtacciuatl permitted me to name Xochitl Xocomoco in honor of my friend and also so my child would bear my name on this earth after I had left it. Xocomoco was pleased and brought my child many small gifts: flowers and gourd rattles and even a necklace made with a chalchuite stone carved in the likeness of a flower. I did not know what she must have bartered for it, for though it was not a necklace of great value, no priestess possessed much with which to trade!

Through the day I carried my daughter with me, feeding her when she wished. She was a very good child and never cried or grew restless, but lay in my arms with her solemn eyes fixed upon mine or closed in quiet sleep. The other girls and women smiled upon her but were not seized with longing. I found such lack of longing to be strange for, indeed, I longed for my daughter even as I held her in my arms.

The months passed with their ceremonies and rituals and I learned the ways of the priestesses and life for me was full of peace. The Mysteries I also learned, but with half a mind for my thoughts often lay elsewhere, in the person of my child. The Lady Ixtacciuatl learned of this and called me to my tasks, and though I would do all I could in her service, my mind slipped from my grasp like an oiled snake.

Thus did the days pass and thus the weeks, and the last month of the eighteen, Izcalli, came round and we honored the God of Fire and I pierced the ears of my child and drew her blood and stood with her before the flames in the teocalli to show her, in the honored way, to the God. Even at that she did not cry, though I felt tears spring to my eyes as I pressed the thorn into her sweet flesh. I would have kept all pain from her if I had been able, but our Gods were thirsty Gods and our blood needed to be shed in their honor for life to continue upon the earth. It was the way in which we lived, the way in which we all believed.

It was in this month that Xocomoco began to be strange. She was not her familiar self, talkative and humorous and kind. She kept herself away from me and did not often hold my child, and when I looked into her eyes they were sad.

"Why is it that you stay away from me?" I asked her in a joking manner. "Is it that I need to bathe?"

She kept her eyes turned from me and the smile she put upon her face was like a mask. I grew afraid for her and worried she was ill, but when I pressed her further she shook her head and told me she was only weary and getting old.

"You will never be old, Xocomoco!" I protested,

laughing to cover my alarm. "Say not so! Indeed will I someday be a toothless crone, but never you." I put my arms around her and so did she also embrace me, but I could feel the sadness like a chill inside her flesh. It seemed so unlike her to be suddenly taken captive by the fears of Mictlancihuatl, consort of the Lord of Death, but she denied all else and so I believed her.

Through these many months I did not know another fainting dream. The Lady Ixtacciuatl asked me if I had and seemed unhappy at my reply. But I was greatly relieved such fainting was in the past, that I was not to become one of those rare prophetesses who rave and speak in strange tongues and writhe in the coils of unseen serpents. I had heard of such women but to become one of them was horrible to contemplate! Content was I to remain a student in the calmecac and mother to my child.

And so the month of Izcalli passed and then it was the first month once more. Altacahualco, it was, the month of the stopping of the waters. It was a time to honor the God Tlaloc so that he would bring the rain back to us so plants would grow and we could eat. When the rains slowed and then ceased and the earth lay broken with thirst, one was most forcibly reminded of our great need for Tlaloc's blessing.

I was summoned to the Lady Ixtacciuatl, and in her white chamber I was surprised to find the priest who had conducted me to the calmecac months before. I bowed my head in respect and he said in his low voice, "And do you, Xochitl, remember my words to you in the teocalli of Quetzalcoatl when you bore your child within your body and you did speak the words of our God?"

I nodded, but all speech died in cold foreboding. What had his words been? Had I, in my bewilderment and terror, forgotten what he had said to me?

"Do you therefore remember that you are to give your child to Tlaloc as sacrifice in your stead?"

I could only stare at him in horror and clutch my child tighter in my arms.

"It is now the time," he said, stepping toward me. I also stepped, but backward and away from him, the thought of running away suddenly in my mind. I could escape, I thought, and go to live somewhere in the jungle or as servant to someone who need never know who I was. I could work to keep my child alive and watch her grow into her beauty and fill my eyes full of her when I died. I think the priest caught my thoughts as they flew about like butterflies, for he stretched out a hand as if to hold me in my place and the Lady Ixtacciuatl spoke a warning into that room. "Xochitl, it is your duty to honor the Gods. It is your life of service that we speak of here. Do not dishonor the Gods your tonalli it is to serve."

I looked down at my daughter. Her eyes were grave as always and fixed upon mine. I could not keep her from her destiny, I had not the power. The Gods needed to be served her warm and living flesh and taste her blood and thus close forever her eyes which were so like my own. I saw the little skull beneath the silken covering of her honey skin and knew that long before the time came to cease my journey on earth that skull would be white and eyeless.

The priest stepped to me and this time I did not step back. But before he took my daughter from my arms I bent to rest my cheek a moment against hers and willed her eyes to hold only the image of my face until the moment she died and could see no more. Her image was carved forever in my sight and upon my heart and there would never be time enough, in this world or the next, for forgetting.

The priest walked quickly from the room, the Lady Ixtacciuatl and I following. She said nothing and I did not look at her for fear I would dishonor the sacrifice by falling to my knees, weeping. We went up the steep narrow stairway of the teocalli of Tlaloc where a deep pool of water ran just outside the God's sacred chamber. There were many priests and all were carrying children, some no more than freshly born and some two or three years old. Some of the babes wept, and all stared with frightened eyes at the priests who held them.

I searched that holy crowd for the face of the priest who carried my child and soon I found him, for he was first to lower his burden—my daughter's body—into the pool. He pressed her down into the water and though I could not see her struggles from where I stood, I felt my body fight not to breathe in the water and then did my lungs fill and my body, too, grow numb with the dread of death. And it was indeed my death I witnessed, for never again would I feel alive with that aliveness of motherhood. The priest lifted her still and dripping body from the pool and the people raised their voices in praise and supplication to the God Tlaloc, and the drums were beaten and the conch shells sounded and her body was dropped without ceremony over the side of the pyramid.

That night I faced great danger, but it mattered not. I left the calmecac without permission, and in defiance both of the Lady Ixtacciuatl and ancient ceremony I went to the teocalli of Tlaloc. There I searched by small torchlight among the little bodies for that one of my own flesh. Dawn was near before I found her and held her in my arms once more, her beautiful eyes glazed and sightless. I carried her outside the city and buried her in the earth so that her flesh would not be eaten by beggars scavenging in the streets or by the roaming beasts, and I spoke some poor words over her grave and left her alone there. Xocomoco was awake when I returned at first light to the calmecac, and she pulled me down beside her and held me in her arms for what was left of that night.

Tonatiuh soon rose and for once I did not praise his coming, for my daughter needed him to light her way to the underworld where it would be dark, and she would be afraid.

Thus ended my first life and so began my next. I rose from Xocomoco's sleeping mat a different woman from the one I had been before, seeing nothing but endless days before me, and years of ceaseless grieving.

8

MALINALLI

There were rumors, Mother, of war. It was said the great houses of the Gods were once more to be seen upon the breast of the eastern sea, and I waited in an agony as rumors changed to certainties and I learned that warriors from all the surrounding villages and cities were to be sent to attack the strangers on the shore. Thus, it was said, they would discover if they were truly Gods, or mere men, for Gods would not die. I was in a fury at such stupidity, but to whom does a female slave address her agony of spirit? And who would care, except for that doting old fool who taught me enchantments and who mattered not at all?

We were ordered, all women and children, to leave the city and seek shelter in the sparse jungle while the men made war. But I determined not to leave, even if I were to perish. I stayed in my master's house and, as he was old and a noble cacique and his mind full of the war to come, he paid me no attention. I made myself useful to him so that I could hear from his lips what was done and what was to be.

There were rumors of war and then the day dawned for war itself, Mother! I could hear the screaming of our warriors as they pitched headlong into battle and the cold and ghostly drone of the conch shells and the beating of the drums. And then also there came a sound I had not heard before, thunder that came without a storm, again and again, sometimes small crackling thunder and sometimes a great roar that rumbled from the shore and along the plain.

All day did the battle continue. All day was I tense as a jaguar, prowling my master's house for any word, any sign. In the slaves' empty chamber I burned copal and prayed to Quetzalcoatl, bidding him hear my words of praise and welcome through the drums and thunder, and then I prowled on, listening at doors but always near that of my master, as if I stayed thus only to more swiftly serve his needs for food or drink or to fan him in the heat. Thus it was as I stood fanning him the caciques of our town and the others came to him, as he was eldest and poor of health, and made solemn talk among themselves. And so they came also the next morning, a day in which I awoke to a silence deeper than that of early dawn. It was the silence of death, Mother.

I made haste to go to my master to help him dress and support him into the large chamber to which the other caciques came hurrying early that day and with grave news. Word had passed from mouth to mouth that he who had landed must be our Lord Quetzalcoatl! Eight hundred of our warriors lay dead, but not one of the strangers had been killed. The Lord of Dawn had vanquished our warriors in a battle made terrifying by his attendant Lords, who were half man and half giant hornless deer, and by the great beasts that could rend a man from breast to knee with one snap of their jaws. These warriors wore shining garments and carried sticks that belched flame and made holes in the bodies of our warriors so that they died. All of this was said in horror, and in all the land only I was glad!

There arrived at my master's house two of our warriors who had been taken captive. Quetzalcoatl had given them necklaces of blue and green stones and had spoken to them of peace. The caciques there assembled spoke among themselves and with heat, a few crying for peace and others among them speaking still of war.

"We must have time," my master cautioned them, "to decide what to do, for we dare not offend these strangers. Certainly is this true if they are Gods. And if they are enemy we must not let them advance further than where they now stand."

The other caciques agreed with this wisdom while hot words blistered unsaid upon my tongue. Among them they decided with cunning to do the strangers honor, but not great honor, and so walk the middle of the road, without giving offence or encouragement. Thus it was that they sent fifteen male slaves with their faces painted with a magic paint so as to make them more fearsome, carrying in their arms food, maize cakes and fowl and fish, to present this offering to the strangers. Wise they were, these strangers, my Mother! Offended they must surely have been by the rude appearance of slaves and the humble gifts they brought, and they spoke angrily to them, nevertheless giving them necklaces of green and blue stones, and sent them back to us with the message that they wished to see our caciques and so seek peace.

There was excited talk, some speaking one way and some another, but it was decided they should do what the strangers bid and so present themselves. Oh, how I longed to go with them, but when I suggested such a thing to my master, he silenced me with a wave of his hand. At the next dawn our caciques dressed themselves in all of their warrior finery and marched to the edge of the plain with many slaves behind them bearing a greater gift of food than they had sent the day before. Their procession led them past the hundreds of our warriors fallen dead—already their bodies were rotting in the sun, their wounds full of worms that spawned quickly in the heat.

Our caciques were wary and would not speak of making peace, even to the very face of the Gods, Mother! But only that they wished to speak among themselves and return the next day, and that they wished to bring with them more slaves so that the dead could be buried before vultures and jaguars came to feast on their flesh. The Gods permitted this to be and the caciques returned to our city and caciques from even farther away in the land of the Azteca gathered there also in my master's house. Thus I heard everything that was said.

There were those who still thought the strangers were men from strange lands across the sea, but more believed them to be Gods, and so argued forcefully for peace. "For what will the Gods do to us if we persist in this sacrilege?" they demanded.

It was decided, after hours of heated talk, that they would go at midday on the morrow and that they would bring more food, but as yet no great gifts of honor. Our caciques dressed even more finely than the day before and took with them more slaves and a greater abundance of food, and these slaves also were to burn and to bury our warriors' bodies. Such a task took days and the air was full of the smell of roasting meat, but with a smell different from the roasting of flesh that has not lain for days in the sun and grown sweet with worms and rot.

These caciques came back with words of fear and excitement. They exclaimed among themselves that the Gods—for they finally had agreed the strangers must indeed be Gods—had metal sticks like serpents that were angered by us and that they spit death in their fury. And although they rode great ferocious beasts, they were not part of them, but the beasts were angry at us, also, and would only be soothed by the God Quetzalcoatl, who most kindly had his Lords lead them away where they could not do the caciques harm.

It was then I learned that they were to do the Gods true honor next day. They were to gather treasure from their storehouses, and twenty of our most beautiful women were to be presented to the Gods for their use, if they should be fitted as men and given to such hunger. So it was that when my master went into his garden to rest in the last hours of that day, I went to him and knelt at his feet and did not raise my eyes to him as I made my modest supplication that I be one of the women given to the Gods.

"But why?" he asked, as surprised at my daring as by my request. "They are mighty and of great power and you are not. Do you not fear that in coupling with them they will destroy you?"

It was then that I raised my face to his with magic willed into my eyes and he relented, as I knew he would.

"Indeed, you have great beauty," he said. "Be it so." And my heart beat as with a fever, so did I long to be in the company of my God.

Thus went I forth next day, a slave no more, and joined the twenty other women who wept and bewailed their fate as we walked from our city to the edge of the sea in a procession of honor and ceremony.

There were hundreds of our warriors yet lying dead, but I felt nothing to see them. The putrid flesh, the swarms of flies, the high stink of death, hardly did I notice, Mother! All I had graven in my eyes and in the thoughts of my mind was the image of my Lord Quetzalcoatl, and when I saw the attendant Lords with their golden breasts and helmets bright in the sun, I came to them singing, just as in the days of joy when I was a child. I could see their houses on the water and their restive deer and dangerous beasts and my heart was dancing.

So was I the only woman who walked to her fate without weeping, my eyes bright with magic and longing for sight of my God!

9

Xochitl

Steadily did I grow more beautiful as my heart grew cold. Even the priests, whose blood had been thinned of desire, would look up from their sacred rituals to stare upon my face and down the length of my body. My blood did not heat. It was as if the female in me was no more. Yet I was still woman and at the same time greater than mere woman; filled with power, though I knew not from whence that power came.

As I had done before in the teocalli of Quetzalcoatl, I began to swoon and prophesy. In those dreams I was witness to beauty and terror and my lips formed words that were not mine and rose from my mouth like flame. I saw teocallis fall to dust and the crumbling of cities and streets running blood. There was fire in the sky and the sounds of thunder and of the hooves of great beasts and the screams of children and the smell of rotting flesh. I would awake from these dreams and the priests and priestesses around me would be frozen, their eyes dark with horror. Of them I would ask the words I had spoken and they would tell me, and it would be much like what I had indeed seen most vividly.

Such dreams wearied me greatly, so much so that there were times I could not rise from where I had fallen. Priestesses would fetch a pillow for me to rest upon and I would lay motionless upon the stones for hours, the pictures still painted inside my head and the sounds echoing in the bones of my skull. Xocomoco would always come to sit by my side and stroke the hair from my face and soothe me. As I grew in power so was she allowed at all times to be with me, though priestesses were not supposed to feel friendships for one another but to keep the love in their hearts only for their Gods. I must confess the only true love I felt, pale indeed beside what I yet felt for my child, was in those days felt solely for the person of Xocomoco, and that in great part, perhaps, because I knew she had also loved my child. I knew I felt peace only in her company and in the few gentle dreams the Gods gave me, for it was not peace I felt in the enactment of the Mysteries, but power.

As I stood by the braziers of copal and breathed in the sweet fragrance of the burning resin, there would come a slow and unsettling heat to uncoil up my legs and arms until I was more serpent than woman, feeling the depth of the heavens and the carnal and incarnate will of the Gods. I was smoke, also, and even to my own mind indistinct and without form. My flesh and bones and blood melted into air and the air in the teocalli embraced me and swallowed me so that we were One and divided no longer. Thus I learned to feel the great sacred secret of the Mysteries: that man, purified of small thoughts and all desire, was but part of the wholeness and that wholeness not Gods and beasts and earth and men, but the great power behind and within the All, and that All was both God and Goddess, Ometeotl, the One Who Created All, and is All, and contains All that is or was or shall be, in a world that has no end. This I knew, and yet felt nothing. For even with the power of this knowledge I was not at peace. My spirit was restless within me, and I knew I was being made ready for a life not yet shown to me. I knew such a life awaited me in the road of my days as the destiny I could not escape even if I wished, and so I counseled myself to wait with patience and learn whatever I needed to be taught before that life met me on the road and took me captive.

The days passed until the month of Atahualco came

once more, then that of Tlacaxipehualtzi, and there was fire in the heavens and a quaking in the earth and talk of the great Ueytlatoani, Moteczoma, who was said to be calling upon all the wise men and priests in the One World to tell him if in their dreams and prophecies the God Quetzalcoatl was indeed returning to wrest from him his empire. Just so had I seen his ruin in my dreams and, swooning, spoke words of dire prophecy. This knowledge passed from mouths in Cholulan to ears in Tenochtitlan. Thus the great and powerful ruler of the Mexica, Moteczoma, summoned me to be brought to him to tell him what I had dreamed and to speak the words of our God.

One day was I bid to the chamber of my Lady Ixtacciuatl. She looked gravely at me. "The Ueytlatoani, Moteczoma, honors you greatly, Xochitl. He has summoned you to the Heart of the One World to hear you prophesy. You must go at once."

A trembling seized me and a dread of something I could not put name to. My life was meeting me in the road and though I could not but obey my destiny, the winds of fate were cold.

"I think you should know," the Lady Ixtacciuatl told me, "that the Lord Moteczoma has put to death all those who have prophesied for him. He seeks to learn his fate and the fate of the One World, but when he does not approve of what he hears, he sends the prophet to the teocalli of Tezcatlipoca and the Flowery Death."

She paused and I nodded. "I thank you, my Lady, for this knowledge. I will be prepared to face what I must."

She sighed and then inclined her head so that the feathers in her headdress quivered, "You have been brave, Oh Xochitl. I cannot but wish you a kinder fate."

"I thank you," I said again and bowed my head to her and so took my leave, feeling nothing in my heart but sorrow for having to part with Xocomoco.

"And will I never see you more?" she asked me through her tears, and I embraced her.

"If the Gods allow, dear friend," I answered, and thus I left her and made myself ready for the journey to Tenochtitlan.

Lord Moteczoma had sent slaves with a litter so that I need not walk, and thus it was a trip of great luxury for me through the mountainous passage between Cholulan and the heart of Anáhuac. Between two volcanoes the road led, the snow-drowned and most lofty peaks of Popocatepetl and Ixtacciuatl, and we rested that night close to the stars in a small dwelling in the city of Cuauhtehcac. We were on our way again at dawn, Tonatiuh painting the snowy peaks the colors of flowers and jewels. All day the slaves walked on while I rode in the litter, uneasy that my weight bore too heavily upon their shoulders. I had been too long a slave myself not to feel a fellow slave's burden and glad was I when we stopped midday to eat the food that had been brought for us to share.

I took my portion and ate as I walked a little way into the forest, stretching limbs grown stiff with sitting. Birds were in the trees, singing most beautifully, and the air was sweet. I lost myself a moment and was filled with peace. How I wished it were possible for me to stay forever in such a place, I thought, and played with the foolish notion of how it would be to run away and build myself a little house of branches and live on seeds, like a squirrel. But a slave came to fetch me and I returned into myself and followed him to the litter and was borne away.

It was dark when we reached Ayotzinco on that day and the slaves were weak with weariness. They had been given orders to proceed to Tenochtitlan with all speed and thus could not take their ease along the way. There was nothing to see of Ayotzinco in the darkness but the inside of the chamber given me. I slept badly that night in expectation of entering the presence of the Lord Moteczoma, the fearsome and merciless, and thus was dressed and out upon the road with the first light of the sun.

Immediately was I struck dumb with wonder at the sight before my eyes. Below me, at the end of a long stone causeway, lay cities upon a great lake, with teocallis massive and beautiful and so tall they seemed to graze the sun. Pennants and banners of feathers drifted from rooftops in the soft morning wind, and everywhere there were gardens of vegetables and flowers floating upon the waters. I knew this magnificence was due to the fearful tithes the Azteca rulers had levied upon the people of the land, but at that moment all I could feel was awe: it was a mighty Lord, indeed, who would decide my fate!

My wonder mounted as we proceeded. The lake stretched far on either side and cities of white stone rose as if by magic from the water. I had never seen such splendid teocallis, even in that most sacred city of Cholulan. They were vivid with dyes in every imaginable hue, and as we drew yet closer I could see the sculptured heads of the Gods peering by the hundreds from the walls of the pyramids. The causeway led to gates set in the high wall and we passed swiftly into the Heart of the One World, Tenochtitlan.

I had small time to stare about me as we made our way through the streets, all paved with stone, and past the marketplace full of wondrous goods and noise and smells and bustling with people. Soon did we come to the serpent wall which surrounded the sacred Heart of the Heart of Tenochtitlan and just outside of which the Lord Moteczoma dwelled with his wives and concubines and priests and, on occasion, the other two Lords of the Triple Alliance, all living in a splendor to stop one's breath.

The slaves bore me to a large and elegant building where they bid me step down, one slave assisting me and leading me inside. Another servant came to me then and guided me to a room where she bid me take my ease until the Ueytlatoani should summon me into his presence. I could scare enjoy to the fullest the elegance of the chamber in which I waited in fear and trembling. I washed my face in a basin of perfumed water I found upon a low table and smoothed my hair and counseled myself to have patience. One could not guess the whims of a lord as powerful as Moteczoma, and it was possible, indeed, that I might have to wait long and perhaps not even be summoned in the end after all. Even so, the fear and trembling did not abate and I had to walk back and forth across the chamber, back and forth, and try to slow the beating of my heart.

I did not wait long. A servant came to me and bid me follow him and thus did we walk together down corridors and up stairs, through a magnificence I could not then appreciate, to the doors of my Lord's audience chamber. The servant then gave me rags to wear to show my humble station and instructed me to approach my Lord with body bowed and never to look into my Lord's face and not to speak until he bid me and then, when told to leave, to walk backwards and bowing all the way until I was once more outside the door. Then the servant opened wide the door and I was bid to enter and to approach the throne of the Ueytlatoani.

Keeping my eyes upon my feet and my body bowed double, so did I draw near my Lord. When I reached the dais upon which stood the royal icpalli, I did touch my finger to the stone and then to my lips in obeisance.

"What is it you prophesy?" came a soft voice, not the harsh one that had bid me enter. "What of Tenochtitlan and our God Quetzalcoatl? Speak."

My body froze as if I stood in the snows on the peaks of the two volcanoes and I could not reply. There was nothing in my mind but emptiness and nothing for me to say, and thus did I stand in silence and most unwilling disobedience.

"I wish for you to speak," came that soft voice again, but this time with a silken hint of menace.

I tried desperately to find words for him and could

not. In desperation did I pray to my God Quetzalcoatl to let me not fail. "Fill me, Lord." I prayed to him, "and use me to speak your truth." But all was emptiness and silence.

"Speak or die!" the harsh voice shouted, and then, with the rush of many wings and brightness as of fire and the sound of voices murmuring, my God possessed me and I fell to the ground at the feet of Moteczoma.

10

MALINALLI

We left that plain of death, Oh Mother, and the shore before us swarmed with life. Our caciques walked in all ceremony and with copal did they give the Gods due honor and present them with treasure. Into their hands did they place gold in the wondrous shapes of lizards and ducks and other creatures, and earrings were there, and golden soles for royal sandals, also two masks of the God Quetzalcoatl, marvelously wrought with chalchuite stones and the precious blue jewels of fire. Also were there many other things of lesser value and baskets of fruit and cakes of maize and other good food. If that was not treasure enough it was because we possessed nothing finer after so many years of paying tribute to the hated Azteca and their master, Moteczoma.

Then the caciques told the Gods that they had also brought them women, and the looks turned upon us were those even the most chaste could recognize. The others blushed and looked away, but I turned the full of my face to them and so looked upon the breast of my God, not daring to look higher, and willed his eyes to meet me. This he did not do, but returned to his speech with the caciques.

These Gods spoke a sacred tongue and thus could only speak their words to one Lord Interpreter who then spoke them in the tongue of the Chantal Maya. So trained was I in the female art of listening that I could hear most of what was said and could understand some of it. They spoke thus: that the God Quetzalcoatl, whom the Lord Interpreter called the "Great Captain," wished all women and children of our towns to return to their dwellings and so prove their desire for peace, and this within the space of two days. Also he wished us to worship his God and so forsake our own, and then did he show to us a statue of a Goddess with a young God in her arms, lying as if dead. We understood it to be the sacred mother of Quetzalcoatl and as pretty was she to look upon as Lady Precious Green, our caciques told him most politely, bowing their heads.

Then they departed and the Lord Interpreter came to us women and bid us make camp, so we built a fire and rested in the shade of the scrawny trees at the edge of the shore. There was much talk among the women about what was to happen to us. Some of the braver ones spoke in whispers about their curiosity to know how much like *men* the Gods were to prove to be. It was a restless night and while the other women cried out in their dreams, I waited impatiently for dawn.

Soon after first light our caciques returned, and again I drew as close as I dared and listened with the whole of my body and sought the attention of my God. He stood in all his shining armor and spoke quietly but with strength. He asked why our warriors had attacked him when he came in peace and our caciques answered him that they had wished him no dishonor and had already, indeed, begged forgiveness. Though this seemed fair speech to me, I could see the God Quetzalcoatl shake his head sadly as if our caciques had answered him not. Then his words turned to the gold we had given to him and where it and the jewels had been found. The attendant Lords gathered close and listened even as did I, and it was possible to see in their faces hunger for gold even as they did thirst for blood. Our caciques were cunning men, though, and did pretend the gold came from some magic place, and the Lord Interpreter shook his head and on the faces of the Lords was grave displeasure.

There were more words I did not understand and then all were dismissed. Of course the other women could talk of little else but their fate and, needing something to do, busied themselves and cooked and brushed each other's hair, while I took myself off some little way alone and kept my own counsel.

In the hour when Tonatiuh enters again the jaws of the serpent of Mictlan, the Lord Interpreter came to us from the Lords' camp and made speech. Said he that his Great Captain would give us to his most powerful Lords the next day, but first we would have to do worship and thus be purified for such honorable service. We did not know if that service was to be our sacrifice or the service of woman to man, and again we rested uneasily until the first light.

Then the Lord Interpreter bid us follow him to Cintla, where an altar had been built upon which was set a sign of this worship in the shape of two sticks crossed. Upon this altar stood also the idol of his Goddess Mother and he bid us bow down to her and this we did. Then did a great priest of Quetzalcoatl give us speech the Lord Interpreter passed on to our ears in Maya and thus did we hear about the Great and Most High Majesty across the oceans and the sky. We were to pay him homage, said the priest, and render him all obedience, and if we did so he would give us protection from our enemies and all the blessings of life would flow to us from the heavens and the earth. This we took to be the God of All, Ometeotl, and the caciques, of course, pledged submission to him. Turning to us then, the Great Priest spoke to the women fair words and bid us submit ourselves to the service of the Lords and then he sprinkled us with water as if in honor to Tlaloc, God of Rain.

It was then the God Quetzalcoatl stood forth and spoke words we could not understand and which the Lord Interpreter did not repeat, and one by one the Lords stepped forth and took a woman's arm and led her away. I willed much magic into my eyes and turned them full upon the very mouth of my God but at last when I, most beautiful of all, stood alone, it was not he who took my arm but another Lord. Thus was I led away from Cintla and some small distance into the trees, out of sight of my beloved God.

Oh Mother, I give you leave to laugh! He was not God at all, but man! He pulled the clothing from his legs and his tepuli made to stand as straight as ever man's did, but no larger than most I had before seen, and he took from me my clothing and so stood I naked and before the eyes of any who might pass. Without speech he pushed me to the earth and most roughly did he spread my legs apart and push into me his tepuli, and I lay awash in the pain of it. Almost more painful yet, Mother, was the smell of the man! He must have journeyed far in the service of his God for his body was rank with rotten odors and the breath of his mouth was most foul. It was hard not to retch at his stink. Glad I was he had been so long without a woman so that his seed was swiftly planted.

He got to his feet with a grunt and pulled on his clothing and waved his hand for me to follow him. Thus it was I walked with him to his camp and was made to cook for him and to follow him into the jungle when his male heat again arose. This I did and silently, my heart despairing. My God Quetzalcoatl took not a woman to himself, keeping his heart on more lordly concerns, and though I followed him with my eyes, he observed me not at all. The warrior who was now my master was called "Alonzo," and he alone possessed me although I could see the heat I aroused in other men. They watched with their eyes on my body, but made no move to possess me. Perhaps this was because they feared their God, and Alonzo, though mere man, seemed to be my God's favorite, for they were often together, scratching with sticks upon the earth and walking together solemnly along the sand.

So passed that day and the days following. Several times in the day and night, and without speech, would my master use my body for his pleasure. My thighs and breasts ached from the weight of his body, my skin rubbed raw from the hair on his face. The last day on shore I cooked him maize for his morning meal, as always, and then walked behind him in a procession of all the warriors and their women back to the village of Cintla where we again worshipped at the wooden altar now covered by branches in a ceremony most sacred but beyond our understanding. Two of my God's warriors then made to carve the symbol of the two crossed sticks in a great tree, and we were then bid to worship this tree also while our God did kiss this symbol and then bid the caciques, there with their women and children, farewell.

Slaves came bearing fowl and fruit and other foods and Quetzalcoatl bid at last for the caciques to care well for the altar and to render all obedience to his God and to his King from across the oceans, promising them maize would grow in plenty if they did this in true reverence. Our caciques gave their promise and returned to their villages while we returned to the shore.

Late in that day, strange canoes were brought to the water's edge and the hundreds of us were taken out to the great houses resting on the sea. The greater warriors went first and so I was also among the first to go. Never had I been out upon the sea, and though my heart was heavy with my lot, there was excitement also at such a rare and dangerous journey. We drew near the houses and then could I see they were only much larger canoes they called "ships," with great reaches of cloth that caught the wind and held it captive in their white bellies.

Alonzo showed me a large chamber in which it seemed we were to sleep on wooden benches. Though he motioned for me to wait upon his bench, I heard much shouting and the sound of whistles and then the ship grew restless on the water. Curiosity drove me at last to leave the chamber and stand at the side of the ship, and so it was I stood and watched with wonder as we drew further and further away from the shore. I still stood in wonderment when my master, Alonzo, found me and struck me with a heavy hand so that I nearly fell. Speaking to me in harsh and foreign words, he pushed me back toward the sleeping chamber where all the women were to remain caged in the ship as if we were beasts.

Small comfort was it to have the other women with me. They made childish talk, some of it in sorrow and some in ridicule. It was better, a few said, that the strangers had turned out to be but men because surely lying beneath the weight of a God would have killed them. Some said it would be better if we were all dead. All made faces of disgust at the stink of the warriors and laughed softly at their filthy ways. We all of us were silent when a warrior came into the chamber, however, and modestly turned our heads when he possessed his woman there before us as if they were but beasts rutting in a field. Late in that day we made food and then lay beside our masters, and the air in that close chamber was fetid with stinks and noisy with groans and cries. My master possessed me once and then, perhaps because of weariness from all the tasks of that day, fell into a deep sleep by my side.

The great ship was rocking upon the waters, but it was not soothing to me. I longed to be out in the sweet air with the ocean spread around me and the stars above my head. I could not bear to be caged on my first journey with my God. However humble my place in that army of warriors, I determined then in my heart not to remain a beast. With great caution I drew myself away from my master and crept past the other sleeping benches to the door. It was difficult at first to know how the door opened, but at last it moved under my hands and I slipped out into the night.

The moon was full and bright were the stars in the heavens. The air, after the stink of the chamber, was fragrant as with a thousand flowers. The ship was moving swiftly and within sight of the land as it passed hills and hollows, dark where a river spent its water in the sea and pale where the moon touched the sand. The breath of Ehecatl filled the belly of the white cloth above and bore us northward toward the Home of the Dead and land of the unresurrected God of Maize, yet it was not fear which filled me at this thought but the sweet breath of Ehecatl speeding us on our journey. Knowing not where I was to be taken nor what would happen to me along the way, still the restlessness I had always felt was soothed for the first time as I watched the land pass before me.

Suddenly and without warning I was seized from behind and pulled roughly around. I thought to see the face of my master, but it was a warrior as yet unseen. He covered my mouth with one hand and with the other pulled at my clothes. I could feel his tepuli naked and thrusting against me and knew I had to let him take me quietly and without struggle in the darkness, lest my master discover I had left his side. As I felt his hand hot upon my tipili, he was seized in turn and pushed so that he lurched and staggered away from me. As he disappeared into the darkness I grasped hard the side of the ship so as not to fall—and then I looked up into the face of the warrior who had rescued me.

It was my God Quetzalcoatl! He had struck his own warrior away from me, a mere slave. He reached out a hand and put it gently on my shoulder and spoke to me soft words I could not understand but knew were fair and kind. I fell to my knees before him and he put his hand on my head a moment and then lifted me to my feet. My heart swelled within me at this sign of his graciousness, and when he led me to the door of the sleeping chamber and opened it and again put his warm hand at my back, I returned to my master's side in joy and reverence. Great were my God's blessings, Mother, and kind was his lordly heart. I knew then I would serve him all my days.

11

Xochitl

So it was that I saw before me and around me all the land of this earth, and it reached the oceans that surrounded the land and held it cupped as did the waters of the Lake of the Moon cup Tenochtitlan. Cloudlike I was, swooning, and prone upon the sky. As I rested the land grew smaller beneath me until it seemed but a green seed in a drop of water, and that drop held suspended in heavens without end. It drew farther from me still and was no more than the smallest mote of dust before I plunged toward it at mighty speed so that it swiftly grew to seed again and then to the vast reaches of the land, and then I saw below me the banners and pyramids of Tenochtitlan, and all afire. Idols toppled from their teocallis and broke before me into ten thousand fragments upon the stones, and the streets were rivers of blood. Houses burned and fell into the reddened waters of the lake. Over all was silence.

Where were the people? the thought came to my mind. Burning to death inside their dwellings, buried beneath the fallen teocallis and the broken idols and uttering not the smallest sound? I could hear nothing. Not screaming, not the thunder of stone falling upon stone, nor the serpent's hiss of burning wood as it tumbled into water. Nothing. And then I sank down still further, but more slowly, and then stood upon the threshold of the one teocalli left standing. Filled with dread, I entered, and before me loomed two Gods. One was of black obsidian and his eyes were flame. The other was green and with milky eyes, as were the eyes of the blind. Upon the breast of the black God shapes like shadows moved, and as I gazed raptly upon them they took form and to my horror there lay clearly pictured bodies mutilated and skeletal, mouths slack with death and eyes round with horror. This is where the people were, then, I thought, and it was with a cold shuddering that I saw what had become of them.

The air in the teocalli grew dense with smoke. It was not the sacred copal but the smell of burning flesh. With the smoke came also the sound of thunder and the cries of beasts and the screams of men and beyond all those sounds came there also to the ears of my mind the steady drumming of the ocean upon the shore. The forms on the surface of the black God then grew shadowlike once more and then also did the blind God and the black one lose shape and substance and become but two more shadows in the growing dark which swallowed me with the jaws of Mictlan, and all was no more.

Slowly I returned to myself and felt the stone beneath me. I did not open my eyes but lay yet awhile, afraid. To what would I open my eyes? To whom? Well did I know I had dreamed prophecy again, but had I given it speech? Within me there was dire foreboding of disaster. If that had indeed been my prophecy, then soon would I die. So be it, I thought, unmoved. Better it was to face what must be faced than to remain in that shadowland between the worlds. I opened my eyes.

The Great Moteczoma no longer sat upon his icpalli but stood upon the dais with his hands over his eyes. A priest in his holy black robes stood also nearby, but his eyes were burning down upon me and with a fierceness that made me rise trembling to my knees, where I remained.

"She has been schooled to say this," the priest did say, and the Ueytlatoani slowly shook his head but made no reply.

There was stillness in the chamber and then said the priest, "Shall I take the woman now to feed

Tezcatlipoca, Lord?" and he stepped eagerly toward me as if impatient and expecting assent.

My Lord Moteczoma then did take his hands from his eyes and look full upon me kneeling at his feet and say, "She is a prophetess of great power and shall not be sacrificed."

"But my Lord!" the priest protested with ill-concealed heat, "she is just another one who speaks falsely of our doom, and but a woman!"

"Raise your eyes to me, prophetess," said Moteczoma, and so I did this thing which was most impious without consent, and I took care to have some but not all of my power shine through my eyes. The Ueytlatoani looked long at me and though I felt his strength also, so was I certain that I wrapped skeins of my power around him. "She shall live," he said at last, "and live here in my palace with the women."

I lowered my gaze but not before I had made a clear image of him in my mind. Truly a Lord did he seem, slender yet well-formed, with a narrow face and solemn eyes. His mantle was oversewn with many thousands of hummingbird feathers so that it shimmered with all the colors of the green earth and the sky. He wore a crown of gold with jewels encrusting it and also the royal plumes of the quetzal bird. The maxtlatl around his loins was bright with thousands of feathers, green from hummingbird bodies and scarlet from their throats.

"Go you now, Chimalpopoca," he commanded, and the priest, with one last look I felt cold upon me, walked backward and with hurried obeisances to the door.

"I would see your face again," the Ueytlatoani said, and willing power to shine forth again from my eyes I raised them to his breast. He studied me closely from all sides, as if I were but a lifeless object that gave to him an obscure pleasure.

"From where have you come?"

"Coatzocoalcos, my Lord," I answered him.

"And when was it you left your home?"

"I was sold as a slave by my mother's second husband, Lord, when I was fourteen years of age, and was taken then to Cholulan to be sold as sacrifice in the teocalli of Quetzalcoatl."

I could see the slightest small quivering of a muscle in his cheek, but he was a man of firm control and could conceal what he did not wish to make known. "Why then were you spared that great honor?" he asked. Almost could I hear a flicker of sarcasm in his smooth, soft voice and I wondered what he meant when all knew without question the honor of such a death.

"Two reasons were there, my Lord, the first being that when I entered the teocalli I fell into a swoon and prophesied even as I did, my Lord, at your own feet. The priests of Quetzalcoatl chose for me to serve our God with my life rather than my death."

He nodded. "And the second?"

It was with sudden pain that I looked swiftly down and so my Lord commanded, "Lift back your eyes to me," and I did so, and thus he saw the sorrowing in them and the grief that had no end.

"I was with child," I said abruptly, "and therefore unfit."

He gazed upon me for a moment, his eyes searching the shadows of mine as if he tasted my sorrow on the tip of his tongue and savored it as a rare delicacy. "And what of this child?"

"She was given to Lord Tlaloc in the month of Altacahualco when she was yet not one year of age."

"And her death was not glory for you?" he asked in his silken voice. "Was it not a fine and fitting death for the daughter of a priestess of Quetzalcoatl?"

Here then I knew I was standing upon broken ground, and dangerous indeed could be the words I gave voice to.

"I loved her well, Lord," said I, "and though honor it was for me to have borne her and honor for her to die so, her death was great sorrow to me and I grieve for her still."

A thin smile flickered at the edge of his mouth, but there was no warmth in it. "Surely it is sacrilege to feel grief when you should, in all honor, feel but joy?"

It was difficult not to turn away my eyes, for though I had learned to wear a mask of my own face, still there was this one weakness which could bring feeling from the depths in which I kept all passions caged.

"That is so, my Lord."

"Surely if this is so, then it is improper for a woman who has become a prophetess known even to me in the Heart of the Heart of the One World?"

Then I knew the Lord Moteczoma toyed with me. Even though he was so great a Lord, anger rose within me that he would make mockery of me and the mask of my face hardened once more. "Agreed, my Lord," I said calmly, "but I was woman before I was prophetess, and mother before priestess. It requires time to learn not to be one and to become the other."

"Perhaps so," my Lord said, and I saw something move in the shadows of his eyes and though I could not have been sure, it seemed that the Ueytlatoani then looked down upon me with no increase in pity but with a growing respect. I had no need of the former, indeed, but the latter was of great value.

He then sat down upon his golden icpalli and bid me rise. "You will have enemies in Tenochtitlan. Even before you came to this city this was so, and more will you have now." He paused, probing my eyes for a fear my face would not show. Then, as if disappointed, he said indifferently, "At least in my palace, among my women, you might be safe. But perhaps not even there."

I lowered my eyes so that my words would not seem to challenge his. "Surely no one would dare lay a hand on a priestess of our God Quetzalcoatl?"

"There are those," he answered, "who believe our God Tezcatlipoca is far greater than his ancient adversary, Quetzalcoatl, even though it is I, most powerful ruler in this world, who rules through descent from that great ruler-turned-God. Some now say it was through the divine blessing of Tezcatlipoca that we Azteca remain supreme in all the land and not through the Lord of the Morning Star. That he is, indeed, but a lesser God and with small power and it is a falsehood that he will return and reign over us once more. Chimalpopoca is most firm in this."

These words were sacrilege to me, so terrible and so like thunder in that great room that I waited for the Lord of Dawn to appear in anger and, like the great feathered serpent for which he was named, devour us both for our impiety.

"That is not what I myself have seen," I said with a bravery I did not feel.

Quetzalcoatl's mortal successor gazed watchfully upon me and from the edge of my eyes I saw his hands tighten upon the arms of his icpalli.

"And do you then believe, prophetess, that he will come again, as has been foretold?"

"I do, Lord," I answered in a low voice. "This I have not yet myself seen, but still do I believe it."

All was stillness in that chamber and so it remained for long moments. I could feel his gaze upon me, searching with that strange hunger I had earlier seen, a hunger restless and insatiable.

"I will direct a slave to take you to your chamber," he said at last in a voice grown indifferent once more, "I will send for you when I have need of your services."

"I thank you, Lord, for the honor you give me. I will serve you with my life," I promised, "and as long as you have need of me." I bowed low and backed across the room to the door, opened it somewhat awkwardly behind me, and bowed again. Once outside I drew breath and leaned a hand against the wall in a weariness I had not known I felt. I heard a golden bell and as I dressed once more in my white robes, a slave approached me, bowing humbly, and led me down corridors to a large and sunny chamber painted with pleasant scenes and flowers.

"If you have need for anything, Lady," the slave whispered, "there is always someone outside this door to fetch it for you." I nodded and the slave bowed, then left me alone in the chamber.

I sank down upon a bench soft with pillows and let myself feel to the full my weariness. I would have to have all of my wits about me, I thought, and even then I might not survive the intrigues in that palace. That there were intrigues I did not now doubt and that I had formidable enemies I could not question. It was only by my power that I could hope to live out my days, and then only by the grace of the God I served, Quetzalcoatl. Even in that lovely chamber, fragrant with perfume and bright with flowers, could I feel within my own body that there was great menace in Tenochtitlan, and blackest evil.

12

MALINALLI

Oh Mother, I could not sleep! My God had saved me and laid his hand upon me in blessing and not even my master's noisy slumber could deaden my joy. In first light we arose and went out into the good air and every one of us drew it deep into her body to cleanse from us the stink of the night. We were given cold maize cakes which most of the women ate meekly inside the chamber, but I alone stood by the side of the boat and ate as the land flew past my eyes as in a dream.

The sun had not risen full before I saw that the land we passed held memory for me: the shore and its marshes, the low hills, and then the mouth of a river and in the distance high mountains with snow upon their peaks. I could not see the dwelling from which you banished me, Mother, but I did see the jungle I could no longer walk within—happy in some way and singing of my God Quetzalcoatl—and the sacred ruins that were no longer mine to explore and the shore with the treasures it takes from the sea. All had been lost, Mother, lost. And yet as I stood there I knew that everything was well lost if I had gained this knowledge of my God and the chance to serve him. So, Mother, do not pity me for what I had become, for you yourself could never know such joy.

At my side there appeared the Lord Interpreter, Aguilar.

"You do not look sad to be here and far from your home, among strangers."

I turned upon him with a smile, a smile I knew served me well but came rarely to my face and more rarely yet to my heart. "Even as you speak, my Lord, I was looking at the river I bathed in often as a child. Strange it is that at this moment you should ask me."

He tried also to smile, but his face was too full of my smile to smile easily in return. "Your home?" he asked, and turned his eyes toward the river. When I did also turn my face to the shore I could see his eyes travel back to my face and there remain.

"Coatzocoalcos," I whispered with magic in my voice to touch his heart and bind him to me.

"Coatzocoalcos," he repeated as if I had bid him do so.

There we stood a long moment with the sun warm in the sky and the air soft and scented with salt and sweat and the green smell of the land.

"Do you miss your home?" he asked at last.

It was then I decided to begin to take honor and power into myself, and thus I said to him that I had been daughter to a powerful cacique with many slaves and that my mother had married after my father had been killed and then had she born a son. This son, said I, had been greatly prized and thus it was I was sold into slavery so that he might inherit my father's lands and slaves. Made I no mention of my sister, Xochitl, still no doubt at your breast, Mother, in her dreams!

"Then do you speak the tongue of the Mexica, Nahuatl?" he asked of me in the Mayan, many words of which I now knew well.

I nodded, "Yes, Lord. That was my mother tongue. In slavery did I learn much of the Chontal speech of the Maya."

"In Cintla, that would be, where first you joined us?"

I smiled within myself. In truth I had quite willingly joined them, but he knew this not. He saw me only as a bartered slave, and this suited my purpose well. The less truth he knew of me the more complete my mastery would be.

"How did your father die?" the man Aguilar asked and as if any question would suit his purpose if it kept me by his side. The words were thorns thrust into my heart, but this I showed him not.

"He was taken captive in one of the Flowery Wars the Azteca continually force upon us and was sacrificed in Tenochtitlan."

"Què barbaridad!" he muttered low and though I knew not what he said, a thought, wondrous and strange, flooded my body at the words and my life took shape and my purpose grew clear before me.

"Do you not speak Nahuatl?"

"It would suit my Captain if I did," he answered, shaking his head, "for being now in Nahuatl lands I would be much handier so."

"I do speak both Nahuatl and Chontal Maya," I said quietly, letting the power of my thought breathe gently through my words so he would not wonder at my purpose but be most subtly moved by it.

For a long moment stood he with a mind as empty as a summer sky. Impatient with him but speaking not, I allowed the idea to come to him as if it were his own.

"But then you could interpret Nahuatl from the natives into Mayan, and then I take those words and give them to my Captain in his Spanish tongue."

I let my face cloud over with bewilderment and suspicion. "But will your Great Captain, as you do call him, will he allow a woman to take a place so near to him?"

Aguilar, as I had wanted, straightened his shoulders in that way men have and spoke in a strong voice. "My Captain listens well to me and trusts my word. I will take you to him now. Come!" he said, and went before me the length of the ship and down wooden steps to a door. He made noise upon it with his hand and then the voice of my Lord God spoke words and Aguilar opened the door and waved his hand for me to walk inside.

Quetzalcoatl was sitting at a wooden bench with drawings on thin white bark in front of him and a look of weary impatience upon his pale, lordly face. He spoke words soft but with an edge to them and Aguilar then answered in a voice less brave than the one he had used to me outside and spoke at length. Though I did not dare raise my eyes to my God, I knew he was watching me and with no little interest. He spoke again and again spoke Aguilar, who turned to me and said, "Captain finds this idea of mine acceptable. It will be as I told you." Then Aguilar told me that his Captain desired to look full upon my face. I raised my eyes to his eyes and I filled them with all the magic my spirit held. The blackness in the center of his pale eyes swelled and took my magic in, and then when I saw them waver with my power—and even he, a God!—I looked down in all maidenly modesty.

My God spoke in a low voice and Aguilar replied in a voice rough with feeling, and my God spoke words again in his sacred tongue so that Aguilar turned to me. I looked with hidden curiosity into his face.

"My Captain wishes me to leave you here and he will see you back to your chamber." His voice was full of longing and there was anger in his eyes and my heart plunged and raced with both fear and exaltation. He then did go to the door and close it behind him and at that the air in the chamber of my God simmered as water set over flame. He rose and came slowly toward me with a limp in his gait as if his long journey had done him injury. I felt the heat of his sacred body as if it were heat in my own, and when he drew quite near I fell, overcome, to my knees at his feet.

"My God!" I whispered, "Oh, my Quetzalcoatl!" and he reached down for my arms and pulled me to my feet. His radiance flowed around me as the river of my childhood, but it was not coolness that engulfed me but a most divine fire. Gently did he place a hand beneath my chin and lift it and, whispering in his sacred voice, he put his lips to mine and had he not placed his arms about me then would I have fallen. Even so did I sway against him, the length of my body pressed against his, and then did he put his tongue upon my lips and, so gently, so tenderly! bid them open. I could not breathe for joy. Slowly did my God let me go, leading me over to his sleeping bench and laying me down upon it and then bringing to me liquid fire in a wondrous cup. I drank this and I felt it warm me down to my womb, and though it scorched me, it also eased my breathing.

Taking the cup from my hands, he returned to where I sat full of such a strangeness that I seemed not to be myself but possessed by another being entirely. Sat my God then down beside me and tenderly put his lips to my neck and gently as a woman did he then unwind my long hair. He took from me my huipilli and placed warm hands upon my breasts and bent to them and took each in turn into his lordly mouth and so my nipples swelled and thrust against his tongue.

With an arm behind me he lowered me back upon the bench and placed his lips once more upon mine and upon my neck and breasts and then down to my belly, and though no man had ever touched me thus, nor had I ever felt the smallest desire for the work of woman and man, still did I lie back in languor and without protest. He spread open my cueitl and stroked my legs with the touch of hummingbird wings and then did they grow slack and my tipili was open to him.

Never had I known such exquisite hunger possess me. His lips moved soft as sunlight over me and his tongue sought the lips of my tipili and then deeper. I moved my hips against him and moaned in a voice I had never heard before. Between my legs did he finally remove his clothes. Revealed at last was his white and sacred body and his tepuli, like that of a man, long and stiffened straight from his body. Lifting me full upon the bench, he climbed over me and my tipili tilted toward him, hungry as a babe at breast, and he entered me. Shuddering in his arms I felt the movement of him and the strength of his thighs, and then was I truly possessed! Wild and new this feeling was, like that of flaming serpents swarming into my tipili and thus into my belly and breasts, and I did hear myself cry out as I felt my spirit leave my body and the winds of Ehecatl carry the empty husk of me into the sky.

Then it was I felt, and from a distance, my God grow rigid with pleasure and swift did his tepuli move in me and then did he lay still with his body wet and hot upon me, yet I was not crushed beneath his weight nor did my flesh blacken with his fire. It was as he lay there that I did dare at last to open my eyes and look long at him, wondering that such a God should have the form of man and yet be with woman so much more than man. In sleep he did move from me and I slipped away. Trembling and with rapid breath I dressed myself and left his chamber, wishing to hold his hands and lips and breath upon my body some little time more and in rapt stillness and alone.

That was not to be. Outside his door, Aguilar stepped from the shadows, took me hard by the arm and pushed me against the wall. "So he has had you too, has he?" he said roughly, but in a voice too low to arouse his master.

I was bewildered by the anger within him and was then in turn angered by his daring to touch and speak to me so, and my body still afire with the passion of our God!

"How dare you treat me thus when I have lain beside our God and by his desire?"

Aguilar then, to my great wonder, threw back his head and laughed a short bark of laughter that anger made sharp as obsidian.

"You think Cortés is a God?" he said to me. "Cortés?" and while pain was still in his eyes, his voice was bitter with ridicule. "Foolish woman! He is a man like the rest of us, as I should think you would know by now!"

With black fury did I struggle to free myself from Aguilar and with all my power against him, muttering oaths and curling my fingers like talons to claw his flesh. But I was weak from spent desire and all struggle was in vain. Aguilar then pressed me to the wall and at last I grew still. His eyes were dark with passion and he held me in their grip.

"Malinalli, he is but a man," and into his voice I heard creep a pity more hateful and grievous to me, for in that pity there was truth.

Truly then would I have fallen if Aguilar had held me not. Swarms of insects, black and fire, filled the corridor where we stood, the humming of their wings too loud for me to hear what Aguilar at first did say. Weak enough almost to swoon, I held on to the world with my teeth.

"Then he is not our God Quetzalcoatl, returning to us as has been prophesied?" I whispered, bringing the words up from the center of my spirit and feeling the pain of them as they rose to my lips.

"He is only a man," Aguilar repeated, "but he is a great captain, Hernán Cortés, and we are proud to serve him and our King. But he does not come from the heavens, Malinalli, but from a country that is called Spain."

I swayed against Aguilar as I had only long moments before swayed against the man I had thought a God, but this time my body grew languid not from passion but despair. Gently he took me in his arms and I put my head upon his shoulder like a child, and he held me thus awhile until life returned to me.

"Would you like to return to your Coatzocoalcos?" Aguilar asked. "I can arrange it so, Malinalli."

I looked long into my mind, at the house where I was not wanted and at the men who would see me only as a woman who had straddled the road and as a slave, and I shook my head.

"There is nowhere for me to go."

Aguilar pushed me slightly from him and looked

into my eyes with what I knew was love and pity, and though I felt nothing for him in return, I was grateful that at least from him I could learn truth. Even so bare and hard a truth.

"Come with us, then," he said eagerly. "We are on a great adventure for our King and God, and you can be of much use. You need have nothing more to do with Cortés if you do not wish to. He will not want to cause bad feeling between you and Alonzo. As for myself, I will stand always halfway, protecting you with my life, Doña."

I pulled myself from his hands and lifted my head. "But I do not wish for you to stand between my Lord Cortés and me," I told him proudly. "I wish never to leave his side."

"But, Malinalli, he is . . ."

I stopped his words with the flat of my hand against his mouth. "If we have been abandoned by our God Quetzalcoatl, then it is good for us Cortés has come in his place to save us from the hated Azteca. No one need know in this land what you have revealed to me."

Though it was with black grief and empty loss that I felt to be thus forsaken, still at that moment I knew, even through the smoke of pain and sorrow, that Cortés could indeed appear to others, if no longer to myself, as the God foretold. Perhaps, I decided at that moment, it was my destiny to have them so believe.

Also it was strange, but also true, that I did still love Cortés even though he was but man. I had given my body to him in worship as I had given the words of my mouth and the thoughts of my mind and my heart's devotion. Even then in my shock and sorrow was I aware, even with gladness, that a God could only be possessed by many—but a mere man could become wholly mine. Indeed, he *would* be mine.

"I wish to speak to the Captain Cortés," I said to Aguilar. "There is something I must say." And though he protested most vigorously, he at last consented and sought my Captain's permission to enter his chamber and again we went inside.

"A great treasure of gold and jewels lies in the Aztec city of Tenochtitlan," I told them, "far to the west where the sun enters the underworld. It is ruled by the hated Ueytlatoani, Moteczoma, who will fear you and pay to you great tribute."

After Aguilar told Cortés these words in their tongue, my Captain turned to me with fresh eyes, saying, "Will you tell us where this city lies?"

"I will lead you there."

So thus it began, Oh Mother, what they did later call the Conquest of Mexico. And it began because of me.

13

Xochitl

Many beautiful women there were for the Ueytlatoani's delectation, as he was a man given to the enjoyment of sensual abundance. A first wife had he, Green River Flowing, and gracefully was she aging; in her time she had borne her Lord healthy sons and now was held in high respect. Concubines had the Ueytlatoani in plenty and, to relieve his tedium, in every imaginable shape and hue. Some were dark and thin as reeds and others honey-skinned, as was I, and full of breast and round of thigh. Many nights he had no taste for women, or was chaste in obedience to sacred ritual, and there were nights one would be bidden to present herself to him, and sometimes indeed more than just one.

Whispers I overheard about Moteczoma's strange ways, and glad was I to be priestess and so above the reach of all men. It was said his hungers demanded more than his numberless concubines could satisfy, but to voice such knowing would be to bid for death. These concubines not only warmed the Ueytlatoani's bed, but also served his meals so that he need not look upon any ill-favored slave as he dined. And *well* did he dine, indeed, as his musicians entertained him and dwarves sought to make his heart light with their antics. There would be thirty dishes and more at each of his solitary meals, and all of a variety scarce to be believed. Dainty in all his ways, Lord Moteczoma took from each golden dish small morsels of roasted fowl or succulent fish brought to him from the sea by running slaves, and waterflies, also, with their little and bitter eggs but hours from the swamps, tasting what seized his fancy and leaving the rest for the hunger of his noble Lords. Sometimes he sipped but a cup of cacao and all the many dishes he left untouched, which would alarm the cooks. If the food gave heat to his blood, then would the Ueytlatoani bid stay the concubine most to his savoring, and he would take her body like a sweet there in the chamber where he had dined.

This I did learn and more, not in the first day I lived with Moteczoma's women, but slowly in the months that passed. Naturally of a chattering nature, these women knew it to be unwise to talk too freely. A concubine jealous of another's greater favor might well seek to advance herself in the eyes of her Lord by a word of scandal or guileful gossip. Rare indeed was this, and yet had it occurred. More than this, the palace itself seemed to have ears and foolish was anyone who spoke thoughtlessly. As priestess, I was for some while regarded with suspicion and not a little awe, for priests and priestesses often did discover the most hidden of secrets and it ill-served one to have one's name ever on the lips of priests, however innocent one might be of fault.

With this and in spite of this, however, life in Moteczoma's palace was of a bewildering luxury. His women did indeed live there as Goddesses, with but the finest cotton to wear and with jewels and necklaces of gold and dining in all sumptuous delight.

At festivals we would gather to hear musicians play their flutes and shells, sounding as if Ehecatl himself made music of the very wind. Drums would be beaten so the dancers could keep time to perfection. Not only would slaves dance, but all the women as well, as even our Lord would, too, at rare and sacred ceremonies. One such festival was in the time of the Tocontin, when he would rise from his golden icpalli and step forth through the flowers strewn upon the dais and dance with three children as other dancers fell prostrate at his feet and there rattle ayachachtlis and sing in reverence. All dancers at such festivals would dress even in such finery as Moteczoma, in the feathered mantles and sacred jewels of Tenochtitlan's dead rulers. Yet even in this dancing was the Ueytlatoani grave in his manner and most solemn in movement, for it was not proper that the Ueytlatoani should behave before the people ever unlike an aged and wise old man, though he was in years still young.

Then there were the other festivals in which noblemen entertained each other, to give due reverence but also to be amused, and also were we so entertained in the palace. Slaves were chosen from the marketplace who did dance and sing the most beautifully and were brought back to the palace to be caged in the night like birds. For the evening meal next day they were brought forth and bid to dance and sing before those at the feast, and great was Moteczoma's special pleasure if they were unusually skillful.

Then were the slaves gently washed and strangled, then cooked slowly in hot oil and served in golden dishes with maize—their tongues and toes the greatest delicacy—and savored hungrily by all but me. For I, who heeded Quetzalcoatl's teachings, did not feast on human flesh nor sacrifice life lightly as indeed did the Azteca followers of the fierce and merciless God of War, Tezcatlipoca. This feasting was customary in the fifteenth month of Panquetzaliztli, which did honor to Huitzilopochtli, and was a festival with other more sacred entertainments in the palace as well. Male slaves would be chosen for their skill at singing or dancing or for their beauty, and they were washed and their hair cut from their heads and they were then bid to dance before the Ueytlatoani. Later were they bid to do battle with true warriors, dressed in their masks and finery, but while the warriors carried shields and wooden swords, the slaves did battle with nought but small arrows fit to kill birds. If a slave did indeed wound a warrior and bring him down, then was that warrior flung on his back over the still-echoing drum and his heart cut from him, so the blood that gushed from his body might bring new life to the palace. After these mock battles the hearts were cut from the slaves to become the precious-eagle-cactus-fruit that nourished the hunger of Huitzilopochtli, second God of War and dark companion of the yet darker God, Tezcatlipoca.

Many festivals there were and much honor given to these two Gods in Tenochtitlan. Amazed was I to learn, indeed, how little ceremony was done in honor of Quetzalcoatl, whom I served with utmost devotion. Common people and even the sons of the Azteca noblemen knew little of him and this did so amaze and displease me that I dared to question the Ueytlatoani soon after I had entered his palace and he had thought to call me into his presence once again.

"May I speak, Lord?" I asked with my eyes respectfully upon the ground.

"It is permitted," he did make answer in his soft voice.

"Then, Lord," said I, "may I make bold to wonder at the little honor done our God, Quetzalcoatl? I hear his name on no lips but your own."

There was deep silence in the chamber. Perhaps I had crossed the boundary of my station and the Ueytlatoani was angered by my daring. I trembled not in the face of this thought, however, for it was my first duty in life to serve my God and not even his mortal successor on earth, Moteczoma, should be allowed by priestly silence to let the God be thus forgot. At last he spoke and his voice was still smooth and silken to my ears.

"Does it seem thus to you, indeed?"

"Yes, my Lord."

Again was there silence, but more swiftly broken. "I serve Quetzalcoatl with my every living breath, priestess, but for my priests it is their duty to worship and give honor to our other Gods. I am satisfied to have a priestess of our gentle God in my palace, and also to have priests serve and do just honor to Huitzilopochtli and Tezcatlipoca in the teocallis of this the One World. If this so satisfies me, your Ueytlatoani, do you dare to question what you see?"

"No, my Lord," I answered, but my heart was rebellious, for it did seem to me that my Lord would be well content to have our savior, Quetzalcoatl, come to Tenochtitlan unhonored and unheralded, as if he were the merest slave. And all the while great honor was done the Gods the Azteca treasured more, for they were the Gods of death and war and devastation who had led them from their humble origins in Aztlán to a place of glory and power over all the Mexica, whom Quetzalcoatl did call their "brethren." Thus they were forgetting in the passage of time that Quetzalcoatl's coming was foretold for the year One-Reed, and that year was fast approaching.

"Indeed you will join the sacred ceremonies with the other priestesses and also do honor to our God, Quetzalcoatl, even as I bid you. And now may you leave me."

Thus was I dismissed with my heart uneasy in my breast. It did seem to me, as I thought long upon his words, that the Ueytlatoani did most subtly bid me keep silence while permitting his priests to profess their favored Gods' greatness with all noise and ceremony. Thus did the idea enter into me that Moteczoma would be content to forget Quetzalcoatl's coming and so perhaps remain upon his golden icpalli for the years left in his destiny. That this was greatest sacrilege—and founded upon most ill-advised thought—I had no doubt. And yet it seemed to be the truth, this plot of evil devising.

Thus, as I was bid, I joined less in the luxurious ease and small entertainments in the women's chamber but made my way gladly out of the palace and into the teocallis where priestesses did honor in the round of rituals for the Goddesses the Azteca still did worship. I was reminded of my mother's words, that once there were Goddesses in plenty and with most divine power, now enjoyed by the Gods, but that in the passage of years the Goddesses had been slowly lowered and shrouded in darkness as were the Gods raised and made shining. Thus was the truth made visible to me in those sacred rites wherein priests did honor in place of the priestesses, even as the next in power to the Ueytlatoani, Snake Woman, was a man and never again woman at all but in name only. This is not to say the Goddesses were without power, but it was a lesser power, as if at the permission and whim of the Gods, even as if they permitted the Great Mother to sprout maize in her season and at their command.

I was a most rebellious priestess as I went forth from Moteczoma's palace, and one watched most banefully by her brother priests. Black-robed in the smoky darkness of their teocallis, I knew they spoke of me and that their eyes glittered at my name. This did I suspect, and soon I was to learn my suspicion was well founded, indeed!

It was soon before the eighth month and the ceremony in honor of Xilónen, Goddess of the Tender Maize, for which a maiden was always chosen to be sacrificed, and I heard my name spoken as deserving of that honor. It was said that though I was no maiden, still I was chaste enough in my sacred service to merit a maiden's reward. And this was said by the priests to my Lord, and my Lord listened well to them. Bid to my Lord Moteczoma's chamber I was therein told what was to be, and honeyed words were said about this honor, but I knew it was the priests' way of making certain that I would be given no chance to lead my Lord's heart from their dark keeping. I would be beheaded and my heart cut from me and thus be silenced forever of Quetzalcoatl's name.

14

MALINALLI

Much was it to my satisfaction that I was renamed by my Captain, Marina. And due to the belief that I was of noble birth, they gave me the title of respect, Doña. Thus I was Doña Marina to the Spaniards, and though soon I would be given another name, Malintzin, by the Mexica, Doña Marina was mine for ever more. Not only I, but all of the women were renamed, for we had all of us been sprinkled with their God's holy water and such was their custom. Most were not pleased—only the two or three who had been given to men of gentle manner—and used only their old names among themselves.

With my new name came new respect. Justly was I turned to as the one among all who knew the ways and customs of the people the Spaniards sought to bring to the feet of their God and King. Never more was I seen as mere slave, Mother! No, I was treated well and as befitting a woman of cunning knowledge and noble birth. I was back in Alonzo's bed, alas, but he no longer used me as if I were wooden and mindless. There was no delicacy to his lusts, but he would not force himself upon me if I loudly resisted.

Aguilar was often by my side when Alonzo was not, and soon he became my confederate in all ways and spoke the words I gave to him without protest. Well did he serve my interests, as even did I serve my Captain, Cortés. Oh, my Mother, what a truly Godlike man he was! Kinder to me than any God had been, kinder to me than all except my father, the man you did betray, Mother, in your weakness. In my Captain I placed whatever remained of my earthly trust and pledged to him all my power to lay the One World and all its riches at his feet. Even as the tyrant Moteczoma spilled my father's blood needlessly down his teocalli steps, so would I bring the Ueytlatoani to his knees and see him slain. This I did swear with the whole force of my being.

Sailed we on. The land passed us by with the hours and the voyage of the sun. Aguilar spent much time with me, explaining strange words, and so I began swiftly to learn the language of my Captain, beloved tongue that lay upon his lips and now also upon mine! Learned I also much about our ship and what the sides of it were named and that the clouds of white cotton which caught the wind and sent the ship over the water were called sails, and each one with a special name also. My Captain often stopped near us on his rounds and though I knew fire was in my eyes when I gazed upon him, his were cool and mild with curiosity at the land we passed, as if that time of our passion had never been.

At last we were in sight of the island of sacrifices and Aguilar did tell me of the time he had landed on the island to find altars and the many bones of the sacrificed, and I could see from his words that the Spanish held this sacred and terrible rite in disgust and Aguilar swore that it was their purpose to put their God over all and thus end such pagan ways, as he called them. It seemed to me their God had much in common with Quetzalcoatl, the God of our abandonment, and so this coming of Captain Cortés was in a strange way the coming of that God, also. This pleased me for it gave strength to me in the plot of my devising.

On a sacred day they called Holy Thursday, we entered the port which had been renamed San Juan de Ulua and dropped anchor in the quiet water. It was the year of their Lord, 1519, although in the reckoning of the Mexica it was in a farther and darker time that priests had begun to count the sheaves of the years. It mattered not to me what year we placed ourselves on the earth, nor what the months were called, nor the days. I had a new life and it suited me to put an end to everything I had known in my past and change all.

My Captain's ship was soon brave with bright pennants and flags of their Spanish King, and swiftly did word pass and two large Azteca canoes come across the water, their passengers bidding permission to climb aboard. This I spoke to Aguilar, and he to our Captain, who then did say they were to come. They were not people of low respect but warrior caciques dressed, not in all the finery reserved for war, but as did befit their rank and in respect for my Captain.

Much it was to their surprise that they must address their words to a woman and she honored to carry those words to my Captain, but I kept my eyes upon them without modesty. When they learned they were speechless without me, they did address me with greater attention, if not greater respect.

"And who is this, your Tlatoan?" they asked.

I raised my chin proudly and half-lowered my eyes. "And who seeks word with him, and he the greatest of Lords?"

Long they looked at me and well could I see their hands burn to punish me for my insolence.

"We come from the Heart of the One World, from the Ueytlatoani Moteczoma, who seeks to know what manner of men are these."

"Men?" I replied. "Do you think it is but mortal man before you?" and I inclined my head in the direction of my Captain, who was silent while Aguilar told him that I sought to discover from where and for what purpose the caciques had come and that he should not, until it was time, make speech.

The Azteca were uncertain now. I could see in their eyes that they were full of doubt and uneasy in their minds whether they stood in the company of men or within the sacred presence of a God.

"He has come, even as was foretold, and with him these much lesser Lords to serve him. I bid you treat them with all reverence, for their power is great, and though they come in peace, yet will they seek revenge for sacrilege."

Then did they bend their knees to my Captain, and say they had been sent by their Ueytlatoani to supply us with whatever we needed. All this I spoke in fair words to Aguilar who spoke them to my Captain.

Well was he pleased, Captain Cortés, to find these messengers from Moteczoma so eager to give him honor, and thus did he give them food and wine and necklaces of blue stones, and after they had dined he bid us say to them that he had come to trade with them and to have no uneasiness for that was all he had come to do. This did not suit my purpose, so I altered his words and told them that my God and his attendant Lords had come as foretold, and that it would be to their good fortune if they remembered who and what he was and why he had come. The caciques bowed their way to the ladder and left our ship, and only I knew that the eyes they did not raise were eyes lowered in reverence. Yet even then I knew there was doubt in their hearts and I would need to be vigilant that those seeds of doubt were not watered with reason so to sprout and flourish.

My Captain returned to his cabin and Aguilar stood with me at the rail. "Sooner or later, Doña Marina," he said quietly, "they will discover Cortés is but a man. Then what will you do? What vengeance will they seek?"

I looked from him to where fires lighted upon the shore marked the encampment of the messengers of Moteczoma. "There is no reason why they should discover it. Long have the people expected our God Quetzalcoatl to return to us. This year One-Reed is the year foretold. Why should we not make use of this knowledge and the ignorance of the people?" Aguilar stared at me through the gathering darkness, and I knew he struggled with the vision I had at last shared in full with him.

"This you will do, Doña Marina, even to your own people?"

I turned to him in a fury and swiftly did he draw back from the dangerous magic in my eyes. I knew his body felt the chill in mine so that his flesh did shiver. "Never will you know what the Azteca have done to me, Aguilar," I told him in a voice of ice, "and why this is revenge most just against my enemy and the enemy of all who hate Anáhuac."

"Marina," he answered, and there was pleading in his voice, "I do not seek to insult you. It seems, however, strange to me that you could have such allegiance to us, to whom you owe nothing."

Unwarmed was my voice in answer. "It is not to you I give my allegiance, Aguilar, nor to your God nor to your Spanish King. It is to my Captain, and only to my Captain that it is given, and with the whole of my heart!"

I felt my words turn to thorns in his breast, but I cared not. He must be forced to see what I sought to do and to cast his lot with mine, giving to me *his* allegiance as I, in turn, gave mine to my Captain. In the days past I had skillfully wound skeins of enchantment around him and bound him to me, and I waited—with a heart like the fluttering of wings, Mother—to know if he were captive, indeed.

"Do you know that Cortés would consider this blasphemy, if he learned that you are calling him a pagan god? He could very easily have you flogged and put onto another ship, and you would be nothing but a slave and a woman forever defiled in his eyes."

A last struggle was this, and though it needed skillful fingers it was easily won. "We will not tell him of this you call 'blasphemy' then, my friend. There is no need for him to know he conquers not as a man but as a God. And I promise you," I added in a voice now hard as jade, "that only as a God will he conquer the

Azteca, and if they find he is but man, his life and yours and mine will be forfeit! It is too late an hour," I added, "to return to where we first stood."

Aguilar turned from me and gripped the rail with his two hands, staring a long moment at the shore and the brightening fires, then sighed. "Very well, it will be as you wish. I will not give the lie to your words. But may God have mercy on us."

I put a gentle hand on his arm and sought to make my voice warm with gratitude and womanly softness. "I am thankful to you, Aguilar. You will look back upon this day and know the righteousness of what we do."

"I hope you are right," he said with a second, less mournful sigh, "for to my mind it is indeed blasphemy, and so may God forgive us indeed, though I am sure Cortés would not."

I moved close to him so that my breath was sweet upon his cheek and the warmth of my breasts was upon his arm. "Worry not, my friend," I said to him with a small laugh, triumph and relief flooding my body, "we will not give your God offense. And if we do, then let his revenge fall only upon *my* head, and only my head be ever bowed in penitence."

Said I so, Mother, laughing.

Alonzo came in search of me and then must I follow him to the sleeping chamber in the manner of a humble woman, the fool not having the smallest knowledge of my triumph or my power as I lay unresisting in his arms. I had indeed learned, Mother, a woman fulfills her purpose best if she shows her power only when it is most urgently required and that at all other times she must wait in patience and observe all things with passive composure. Thus did I seek to do always, to restrain the passions of my heart and flesh in service to my Captain and so to prove to him my devotion.

We set foot on shore next day and the iron cannons were set upon the hills of sand. An altar was built at my Captain's command and all of us did worship there while their Spanish priest spoke in a strange tongue so that I knew not one word of what was said. Our five hundred soldiers were bid to build shelters for themselves and also for the horses, lest they stray. Curious, I went to see those fierce beasts and when one drew near I put my hand lightly upon its back but it harmed me not. While I stood there patting the great beast and stroking its smooth fur, the honored soldier, Alvarado, came close to me and spoke to me fair in words now grown familiar. I replied in his tongue and saw he met my words with surprise.

This man was wondrous to behold and of a strangeness seen but once in the land of the Mexica. His hair was golden, even as was that of our God Quetzalcoatl, and his skin was fair. Large were his eyes and as smooth as polished stones, yet when he turned them to mine I could see the cruelty in them and the cold fire, and I felt a trembling in my limbs and looked away. He said words I could not understand and took my arm and forced me to face him, and I then raised my eyes to his lips and they were full and red and the lips of a passionate and brutal man. His grip upon my arm was fierce and fiercely did he pull my body to his and seek to put his mouth upon mine, but I struggled against him until I weakened at the pain in my arm and so stood still. Words harsh and low came from his mouth and, fearful, I looked into his eyes and then he smiled as if I were but slave once more and let go my arm, and then turned from me and walked away. In arrogance did he walk and in arrogance did he speak to me some hours later, and as if he would give me pain another time and at his pleasure and as if I would be powerless to make him let me go. Even as my body trembled with a heat most loathsome to me, so did I also tremble in hatred for him.

Slaves were sent from the villages next day to cut down trees and build sturdy dwellings they then covered with cotton cloth to lessen the great heat of the sun. Also did they bring food and fruit and some golden jewels which they presented to my Captain, telling him the news that their caciques would come next day to pay him honor. My Captain gave them fair speech and gifts of little worth and they departed, bowing.

It was a sacred day that dawned, one they called Easter Sunday. As had been promised, two caciques from the palace of Moteczoma presented themselves, and their names were Cuitlalpitoc and Teuhtlilli. Following them were many slaves and peasants bringing baskets of food, all of them standing first upon a hill to make obeisances to my Captain as if they were approaching a God. Such sign of their humility pleased me, and yet as these were powerful Azteca warriors I knew well the need for utmost wariness.

My Captain bid us make the caciques welcome, and so we did. Then did he approach them to grasp them in friendly manner by the arm, and by such familiarity I feared he might give them cause to doubt what manner of God he was. Thus did I swiftly say to them, "Lord Quetzalcoatl wishes to touch you and in so doing know of what kind of flesh you are made."

They looked at me with expressions most strange and then cast down their eyes in reverence. My Captain asked of Aguilar why this was so and what it was I had told them, and then Aguilar said only that I had spoken words of greeting in the tongue of the Azteca. Lightly I told Aguilar to say to my Captain that it was not customary in my country for men to embrace, and so from that time on my Captain's dignity was not again offended by his familiar manner.

My Captain then bid us say that it was the hour for worship and that the caciques and even their slaves were most heartily welcome to worship with us. This was put in words suited to my purpose, more like a God's command than a man's polite request, and everyone knelt upon the sand and the priest sang his sacred words and though so many of us knew not the meaning of one word, much of this ceremony yet did seem customary to us, for singing and music always did honor in our sacred rituals.

After our worship we dined together at wooden tables the soldiers had built, and when all was eaten my Captain, the two caciques, Aguilar and I went a little way from camp to make speech among ourselves.

My Captain told Aguilar to say that they had come from the greatest King on earth and that they served the Christian God, which was the greatest God, and that they came at their King's bidding to make trade with the Mexica in friendship. In turn did I say to them that my God Quetzalcoatl, who honored them with his presence, had come from across the oceans as had been prophesied and that he sought the ears of the Ueytlatoani to tell him that what had been foretold was now at hand.

The cacique Teuhtlilli, with swift, shrewd scrutiny of my face, then cast his eyes down humbly and replied that they were deeply honored and that they did beg him to receive their ruler's gifts, though poor they were and unbefitting a God.

"Tell my Captain," I said to Aguilar, "that these caciques are not certain Moteczoma will wish to see him, as he is busy with important royal matters." This I spoke in the Mayan tongue strange to both my Captain and the Azteca, saying words of such irreverence so that my Captain would not then seem to be unduly eager for common friendship nor greatly pleased by their gifts. It was as I had wished and my Captain, offended by what he believed them so to say, grew cool and his face impassive and proud.

The cacique Teuhtlilli then bid a servant to carry forth a chest which he opened upon the sand. In it were many pieces of gold in wondrous shapes, set with jewels and crafted with a skill unequalled. But my Captain, displeased by what he thought was Moteczoma's message, received this treasure with cool smiles, and even when the cacique bid slaves to bring forth many loads of feathered mantles and other fine clothes, his manner did not warm. Graciously, however, he accepted these gifts for his King, though I told the caciques he accepted them without mention of the King but only that they pleased our God. Then did my Captain give the caciques the necklaces of blue and green stones which were strange to the Azteca and, though neither of value nor sanctity, I told them the stones came from the sacred land where Quetzalcoatl had dwelled in his years of exile and were therefore sacred things and did great honor to their Ueytlatoani Moteczoma.

My Captain said then he wished to trade with all of the people in the land and barter more of the green and blue stones for their gold, and thus I said, "The God Quetzalcoatl does bid all gold to be given him in due honor, and when this has been done he will give to all these sacred stones which are of greater worth."

My Captain then commanded that a chair be brought forth. Carved skillfully, but not so skillfully as would our artisans do the work, it was inlaid with bright stones that had been carved also. This he presented to them as well as a necklace of stones wrapped in cotton with a strong scent. I told the caciques that it was the scent of the God's copal and powerful as only such holy resin can be when it is brought forth from the sacred trees of Quetzalcoatl's vast and magic jungle. They made haste to put the necklace and the cotton in a small box so the scent would not fade before it reached the nostrils of Moteczoma.

At last my Captain presented to them a strange gift, a headcovering, soft of fabric and blood-red in color, with a disk of gold upon the front of it in the likeness of a warrior spearing a most enormous lizard. Swift of thought, I told the caciques it was symbol of the God in all his power and of the awesome serpents he had slain upon his long journey. The caciques tried to seem indifferent to this news, but were filled with wonder and no little fear.

After this ceremony had passed, my Captain bid them take these things to their ruler, Moteczoma, as signs of his friendship. Severely then did he bid them declare a day for meeting their great ruler, and so did I say in turn to them that my God wished to hear when Moteczoma would do him just reverence, and that when he did so my God wished for him to be seated in the carven chair and wearing on his head the red headcovering as a sign he did his God true honor.

My Captain listened to the caciques with patience and all unknowing while I made the words clear to the mind of Aguilar, and as I turned to him I saw some men a little way from us, looking carefully about and painting marks upon the thin bark they held in their hands. Coolly I added at the end of my speech to Aguilar, "It seems Moteczoma needs further proof of who we are and the force we bring with us." He noticed also that these men were gazing long at us and at our beasts and men and cannon, and I said, "Even yet they are not sure of what manner of man or God our Captain is. Perhaps they do not yet believe the strength of our arms and therefore look upon us as but a few and, in the face of their many thousands, easily defeated."

Aguilar then spoke to my Captain, and though I did not understand his words well, I knew to what purpose they were spoken since Captain Cortés first looked at the painters with narrowed eyes, then turned to Alvarado who stood at his side and spoke some words to him.

Bidding the caciques to wait there upon the hill, he went with Alvarado to where their horses were. Attaching small bells to the armor of the horses, they then rode swiftly along the shore where the sand was wet and their horses' hooves would not sink and make them stumble. This was wise of him and well did he ride, my Captain. But even in the hatred of my heart I could still see how more skillfully Alvarado rode, and with bravery did he make his horse stand back upon two legs and plunge and kick and utter cries that rang fiercely to the low hill where the caciques stood in amazement. Then did they leap gracefully from their horses and give them to soldiers to hold while my Captain said quiet words we could not hear to some other of his men.

After all of this was done, Captain Cortés approached even as I made my quiet way around the caciques, coming up behind the painters to see the fair likenesses they had made of us, even of our great dogs and the ships and horses and cannon. Strange it was to see myself made small upon the folded bark. Indeed, to myself I looked a different woman than the one drawn with face uplifted to Captain Cortés, and it was with wonder and no little disappointment that I saw I seemed to others so womanly mild. After learning what was to be learned, I slipped away unseen, and as I drew near my Captain there was the sudden awful thunder of the cannons and stones from them flew with a loud whistling into the jungle.

When the caciques could find breath to speak, so surprised and overawed had they been, they hurried to make fair words, calmer in speech than I knew their true words would be! Teuhtlilli then startled at the sight of the helmet one of our soldiers wore—for in that heat the soldiers had worn them not—and with a shaking voice asked humbly if he might hold it in his hand. Gazing upon it with startled eyes, he told Cuitlalpitoc that it was very like the helmet left them by the hands of their ancestors, the helmet of the ruler, Quetzalcoatl, before he became a God. This was new knowledge to me and most welcome.

With heads bowed, Teuhtlilli asked if they could take the helmet also to Tenochtitlan. Nothing did they say about it being like the helmet of Quetzalcoatl, nor did I. My Captain nodded graciously that they could do so, but that he wished for it to be returned filled with gold dust so he could send it as a gift to his King. To the caciques I did not say this. I said only that

Quetzalcoatl required the helmet to be returned to him full of gold in order to do him honor. This, they said humbly, they would do.

Thus the first cacique, Teuhtlilli, turned from us, bowing, and made haste toward Tenochtitlan with the gifts and paintings and helmet while Cuitlalpitoc encamped nearby and waited.

Seven days passed. Slaves came from the villages laden with their small golden jewels, having little of grandeur left from the greed of Moteczoma whose hand took from everywhere and all at once. In payment, Captain Cortés gave them the necklaces of stones he believed the people loved overmuch as they were of little value. Indeed, he did begin to look down upon the people in their ignorance, not knowing that I had told them they were sacred stones and full of power, or that the people took them to their teocallis and there used them in their worship. This I knew but was silent in the knowledge, and I also waited, and most watchfully.

15

XOCHITL

The month of my death drew near. Perhaps it was this which made my Lord, Moteczoma, uneasy, for he knew that what his priests sought to do was grave dishonor to Quetzalcoatl in this, the year One-Reed. My Lord, at the urging of Chimalpopoca, decided that the great sacrificial stone of the Aztecas was not grand enough for the grandeur of his empire and its dark Gods. Thus did he order his finest stonemasons to search the land for a stone of enormous size and bring it to Tenochtitlan to carve. This they did, finding a stone so ponderous that it required a hundred men to drag it from its mountain dwelling to the Heart of the One World.

That stone was still living rock and the spirit within it groaned upon the journey, and then as it neared the city the slaves heard it mutter curses. Messengers were sent to bring this news to my Lord and he was then afraid. In the first light when the stonemasons touched it, their hands grew red with a bloody dew, and as they moved it so did it shriek of disaster, and though the masons were sore afraid, still did they journey toward Tenochtitlan.

Now in the days of the Ueytlatoani Ahuitzotl, that ruler had commanded a conduit be made to bring water from Coyoacan to Tenochtitlan, and the priests and sorcerers had seen signs in the heavens of grave disaster if did he so. But the Ueytlatoani, blinded by his glorious enterprise, did command this task be done, and his slaves hastened to obey. Thus when the conduit was built and fresh water flowed into the Lake of the Moon, a priestess dressed as Goddess of the Waters did throw herself, singing and playing the music of death on her omichicahuatstli, into the water and so did drown. However, a disaster did indeed befall Tenochtitlan; in a great flood many were swept away and the palace of Ahuitzotl was ravaged by the angry waters even as the priests and sorcerers had foretold.

Moteczoma's stone rolled slowly, cursing and weeping blood, until the frightened slaves at last reached the conduit where the priestess dressed as Goddess of the Waters had thrown herself in to drown. There did the great stone roll upon the causeway and slip from the slaves' hands and fall into the water, taking many men with it to their deaths. From its watery grave it could not be moved, as the stonemasons made haste to tell Moteczoma when they returned with empty hands to Tenochtitlan. In his fear, Moteczoma had all of these stonemasons sacrificed in the teocalli of Tezcatlipoca and that of Tlaloc, God of the Waters, and took solemn counsel with his sorcerers and sages, all of whom shook their heads and spoke of doom. When he called upon his priests of Huitzilopochtli and Tezcatlipoca, they advised him in comforting words that the stone's drowning did not foretell his doom in the future coming of Quetzalcoatl—Chimalpopoca among others did not believe the God was upon our shores—but was a sacred sign for the Ueytlatoani to carve not a stone of sacrifice but his own image where all in his empire could worship him during his reign and for all time.

Moteczoma chose to heed these pleasing words and bid stonemasons from Cholulan to carve a most enormous statue of himself upon his icpalli from the living rock in Chapultepec where stood a great cliff that rose high above the trees. The work progressed apace and people stood all amazed at the grandeur of the statue and its excellent likeness to our Lord.

During the whole of this time I completed my duties as priestess and made myself ready for death. It was, indeed, a simple task, for I was unafraid to die. Sometimes I yearned for the day when I might see again my little daughter in Mictlan—if her spirit yet rested there and had not traveled on to the heavens of the drowned where she would find solace in the company of Lady Precious Green and her Lord Tlaloc. Since my death would not be by drowning, I could not join my daughter in her watery world in the heavens above the earth, but would travel on to the fields where went those who died the Flowery Death. There I might at least see my father, though I doubted I would find his face nor he mine among the thousands of phantoms.

No longer had I need to fear the priests, for they but waited for the eighth month to do their work. I knew they smiled with pleasure at the prospect, especially since I had not ceased from counseling my Lord Moteczoma. Whenever he bid me to his chamber I warned him to ready himself for Quetzalcoatl's coming and to prepare a teocalli and fill it with fruits and flowers and butterflies in his honor. The dark priests stared narrowly at me as I told my Lord these words and they muttered to themselves and cast dire looks one to another. This troubled me not for I sought to do what I still could as priestess before death claimed me for other duties.

The month of the sprouting maize came at last. That morning Tonatiuh rose in splendor from the underworld to which I would that day descend. The night before I had fasted and prayed in the teocalli, surrounded by priestesses who bore me solemn company on my last night. It was a sweet night, for I spent it remembering my lost sister, Malinalli, and how she and I had once passed the following day dancing barebreasted in the tender new maize with the other maidens, our long hair sweeping below our knees to wave behind us as we danced like the pliant young plants under Ehécatl's eager breath. They were golden days I remembered, with the rays of Tonatiuh upon our bare bodies and the soft caress of the wind through our hair and over the small mounds of our breasts. Well did I remember our mother standing near the field smiling, perhaps reminded of the days of her maidenhood when she also danced. We had but rarely gone to the teocalli after the dance to watch the sacrifice in honor of Xilónen, Goddess of the Tender Maize, for Mother wished for the ceremony to be as it was in the field, and with the young girls and the music and dancing and happy laughter, and not darkened by the rituals of the priests.

"This is a time of birth, not of death," she told us in a careful whisper, for such talk was sacrilege and she bid her own death with those words. Later I learned what she meant as I grew to womanhood and looked into the smoking mirror the priests held to the face of the sun to darken our days.

At dawn I put memory to sleep. I dressed in the robes of a priestess of Xilónen and slaves then placed a wreath of tender maize upon my head and left my long hair flowing. Then were the conch shells sounded in the teocallis and the teponaztlis were struck so that the very sky seemed to thunder. Down the steps of the teocalli of Quetzalcoatl I walked in solemn procession with dancing priestesses shaking their rattles with the sound of angry serpents, and across the Heart of the One World more priestesses were gathered on either side of the path my steps would take. Beyond them were crowded many hundreds of the city's people come to do Xilónen honor so she would bless them in this year with maize. Dancers wearing flowers and garlands danced delicately and with joy; young girls bare-breasted in the sun as my sister and I had been years before. Marching past the Tzompantli rack, where my skull would soon join the wall of skulls placed there in honor, and past the great teocalli of Tlaloc and of Huitzilopochtli and Tezcatlipoca, at last we came to the stone of Tixoc where I was to die.

The music of rattle and drum and conch shell rose to a frenzy. There was the low thunder of many voices chanting and Tonatiuh shone brightly upon the vivid paintings and with blinding light upon the white stone of Tixoc. So dazzled were my eyes I could see through the light as if it were but bright water that shimmered before me. Then all was silence. The harsh grating of the omichicahuatsli began and the low thumping of the priestesses' drums. I looked up to see Chimalpopoca emerge from the teocalli of Tezcatlipoca. Like a shadow torn from other shadows, slowly he descended the many steep steps cut into the pyramid's side until at last he stood before me and with triumph in his eyes. In proper silence did he bid his fellow priests approach, and they did so, pressing me backwards upon the stone, untying the robe at my throat and lowering it so that my breasts were naked to the sun. Then did I see more than holiness in those hard eyes, and I was well-amused that for all their menace and their sacred ways they were still but men and with mortal heat!

Chimalpopoca saw me smile and he trembled then with anger so that the sacred dagger he held quivered in his hand. He would first plunge it into my breast, I knew, and then with his sacred axe cut from me my head, and then upon my body would Moteczoma and his caciques dine—the priests, no doubt, upon the tender morsels of my breasts. This I knew and cared not, but as I saw Chimalpopoca lift high his dagger I did pray to my God Quetzalcoatl to pluck the spirit quickly from my body and I closed my eyes so as to see more clearly the Lord of Death.

Swiftly indeed did my God fall upon me and with great force, so that the breath was crushed from me and my body filled with light brighter than Tonatiuh's rays upon white stone. A rushing of wings swept down from heaven and a far thunder rumbled across the land and shuddered beneath me. Many voices then began screaming and beasts bellowed in fury in their stalls and the roar of the earth cracked beneath the stone of Tixoc and the teocallis around me splintered into dust. I heard a closer cry and it seemed to call me back from the sky. Unwilling to return, I opened my eyes slowly. Chimalpopoca still stood over me and his eyes were wide with horror. As he looked down upon me I heard a voice issuing forth from me, not only from my mouth and nostrils, but from my breasts and between my thighs, and it did roar and the priests stared upon me, motionless with terror.

Then did I see the sky and it was all aflame; winds from heaven made the flames leap and coil like serpents and then the fire fell like blazing stars and the people cowered beneath this radiant storm and many fell senseless to the ground.

As the thundering in the earth grew fainter, my eyes did close without my will and I felt the flames like water upon me and cool as night rain. Then did I feel hands upon me, lifting my body from the stone, and though patiently did I await the axe to sever my neck, it fell not. Gently was I carried to the teocalli of Quetzalcoatl and tenderly cared for. I could not walk without aid for many days and found the act of taking breath almost beyond my power. In my weakness I listened to the awed words of the priestesses as they related what had taken place during my swooning dream, not only in the Heart of the One World, but beyond. At the moment when I had closed my eyes, they said, there was a flash of lightning in the sky and the distant roar of thunder. The earth did then begin to quake and there was the noise of giant beasts pounding with their hooves swiftly across the land toward Tenochtitlan. The people were thrown to their knees from the force of the earth's shuddering, as if it were a beast itself which did shake them in its mighty jaws.

Most wondrous and fearful of all, said the priestesses, was that when I did open my eyes they were all of a green and sightless glow, and all did stare down upon me in horror. A mighty voice issued from me, they said, filling the sky with prophecy that the end was near and Tenochtitlan was doomed. Fire then streamed across the sky and quivered in a strange cold wind while the earth trembled—and then all was still and silent, with a silence more still than silence is, and not a breath nor a whisper disturbed the air while the sky flamed on and fell down upon them. Then it was I closed my eyes and blood fell as rain from the sky and the people were sore afraid and wept and lamented the evil of their ways and then did beg salvation.

"Quetzalcoatl comes," I said when first I could speak, and the priestesses looked solemnly upon me, saying that even the priests of Tezcatlipoca did fear this might be so.

"The Ueytlatoani Moteczoma has ordered a teocalli prepared in his honor, and a palace for his comfort he has commanded to be made ready."

This was sweet to my ears, indeed, but truly Moteczoma still did not do this only because of the many signs and portents all could read in the earth and sky that day, but also for a reason closer to his heart: stonemasons had returned to Chapultepec late in that day to find the statue of Moteczoma had been broken from the living stone, and that in its hand where had been the staff of power, the quaking earth had carved in its stead the bone instrument played at the funeral of Azteca Ueytlatoanis. Moteczoma was carried upon his litter to Chapultepec to see for himself if what he had been told was truth and, bewailing his doom, returned to his palace promising to exile himself from all pleasures and so await the end.

16

MALINALLI

We waited there by the ocean most impatiently to hear what Moteczoma would say in answer to my Captain. Upon the seventh day came the message that the caciques, Tleuhtlilli and Cuitlalpitoc, would come to our camp that day, bringing many slaves heavily laden. Such a sign pleased me and I sought out Aguilar.

"It seems Moteczoma honors our Captain," I said, "to send slaves heavily laden with gifts and not with weapons." With this he did agree, but nothing was said to our Captain for it suited me that he should not seem overeager for gold or reverence but that he as a God should expect such honor.

Moteczoma's envoys duly arrived and with one hundred slaves. Also, in some strange cunning, they brought a man who bore uncanny likeness to our Captain whom the soldiers called "the other Cortés," which pleased me not for it lacked respect. This man gazed at me most fixedly, not with the look of hunger, but of curiosity and awe. Suddenly I was addressed by all as "Malintzin," adding the "tzin" of nobility to my name most courteously.

First the caciques brought forth copal and waved braziers of the fragrant smoke in the direction of my Captain and his men. I suspected this was due more to the Spaniards' foul odor than to reverence, but I told my Captain this was Azteca ceremony which, indeed, it turned out to be. We seated ourselves and Tleuhtlilli bade us most heartily welcome and said other idle words of pleasantry and then bid the slaves to bring forth their burdens.

My Mother, such treasure was surely never before seen gathered into one small place! My Captain and his soldiers were struck all amazed. First Tleuhtlilli uncovered a great calendar, round as is our way and carved with the days and months and years of our time. All of gold, it shone like a brother to the sun. And, wonder upon wonders, they then uncovered a *second* calendar, sister to the moon and all of silver and most skillfully carved. The man whom they said looked like Cortés brought forth the helmet Tleuhtlilli had taken from us to Moteczoma and he put it into my hands with a searching look and I then placed it into the hands of my Captain, though it was so heavy with gold I almost could not carry it. Then were brought forth twenty ducks of gold and other beasts and golden bracelets of artful design and royal staffs of gold, which pleased me greatly for I guessed they were gifts of great honor, as also were the royal headdresses of gold and silver and quetzal plumes. Lastly they placed at our feet thirty loads of cotton mantles all worked with feathers and many more things of costliest devising.

Tleuhtlilli asked my Captain to accept these gifts with the willingness with which they had been given him by Moteczoma and this I repeated in my own way. Then he said that Moteczoma desired nothing on earth more than to see such a great and powerful Lord, but that he would send treasure instead. Bidding us to remain in the port and not to venture forth, Tleuhtlilli told us Moteczoma felt truly that it would not be in all honor for such a Lord as was my Captain to make the wearisome journey to small and poor Tenochtitlan.

Repeating this most cleverly, I told Aguilar to say that Moteczoma was now commanding us to stay where we were because our presence was not desired in Tenochtitlan, and though the riches of the Azteca were great, he would send no more of it to Cortés. My

Captain was most displeased by this, but he wore his displeasure well-disguised. In regal calm he announced to the caciques his thanks, but I embroidered them thus: that he wished to send Moteczoma sacred objects in return for the honor paid him, but as he was the God Quetzalcoatl, come as foretold, he would not be delayed in the journey to Tenochtitlan. My Captain presented the caciques with the necklaces of stones and some cotton clothing, none of it of any value, and a drinking cup most wondrously crafted but which Aguilar did later tell me was also poor trade indeed for such treasure. This the caciques of course did not know, but accepted our gifts with the reverence due holy things. All then departed but for Tleuhtlilli and some twenty of the slaves, and the man who looked like my Captain departed also.

Moteczoma had charged Tleuhtlilli, so were we told, to supply us well with food and so he sent his slaves to nearby villages to seek what we needed. This, I suspected, was to ensure we were not made so restless with hunger as to leave the port where the Ueytlatoani wished us to remain. For several days we were indeed well supplied, and then the supply lessened until only my Captain and his highest soldiers had food to eat and the common soldiers had to use the small golden objects given them as their share of the treasure as barter for food and also did they have to hunt and fish along the shore. Our bread grew stale with age and then at last even my Captain had little to eat.

Finally, Cuitlalpitoc returned and burned copal and made obeisances and spoke many fine and flattering words. He presented my Captain with ten loads of feathered mantles and four precious chalchuites which my Captain thought had little value, but when I told him they were worth far more than gold in this land, he was content with them. Then Cuitlalpitoc told us that Moteczoma was pleased with the gifts my Captain had sent to him but still did most heartily wish that my Captain would venture not to Tenochtitlan nor send any more messengers nor gifts, for that would be to do him too much honor. I said all this to my Captain, but did not speak of the honor, only of Moteczoma's great unwillingness to receive strangers in his court.

This did indeed lessen my Captain's pleasure in the gift, and at the same moment my words whetted his hunger to see for himself what was so carefully protected in Tenochtitlan that strangers were not permitted to even enter the gates. He turned to his soldiers and said to them, "Surely this must be a great and rich prince! Some day, please God, we will disobey his ungracious words and see for ourselves."

At this Alvarado replied, "I wish, indeed, we were already there." Fierce hunger stirred in all the men at sight of the treasure that had been given them and restless were they with the knowledge that there was more to be had.

All this I understood in their tongue, and indeed much more, for Aguilar taught me every day and I listened to him and also kept silence when the soldiers spoke among themselves, although much of what they said would be unseemly on the lips of a woman. In this way I knew Aguilar would soon not be needed more by my Captain, who would then need only me at his side. My Captain would be forced to lean upon me and, like a vine upon a tree, cling tightly and forever.

Aguilar did not suspect me. He had not the cunning to learn Nahuatl and so put distance between my Captain and me. At rare times he would ask me the meanings of certain words; often I told him senseless things. For my amusement, indeed, I once told him the word for "bread" was the Nahuatl word for "shit," and so at every meal I would smile to hear him ask for a chunk of shit to put into his broth. Fortunately he had not my memory and thus when he would ask me another time the Nahuatl word for something I had already taught to him, I would tell him something else completely and he would not guess my cunning. So it was "bird" became for him "stone" and then "kneebone," and with all of this was he satisfied.

Suddenly I saw the narrow eyes of the caciques on *me*. When they saw I was aware of their dark scrutiny, they smiled with their teeth like daggers. "Ask Lord Quetzalcoatl," they said, "to send you with us to Tenochtitlan, for the Ueytlatoani Moteczoma would like to do you honor and speak with you."

I lifted my chin. "I will go to Tenochtitlan when my Lord is made welcome."

Tleuhtlilli turned his palm upward in pleading. "But you will then be able to bring back from the Heart of the One World food for your God and his many Lords, as well as treasure. For the Ueytlatoani will indeed be pleased with you if you obey him, Malintzin, and will cover you in jade."

"What is this you are saying?" my Captain asked.

"Nothing, my Captain," I answered, "I but asked why they have not supplied us well with food these few days past."

"And what do they say?"

"They are sorry, Captain, but food is scarce indeed in these poor parts." I then turned to the caciques as if in reply and I smiled with a gentle mouth and spoke softly. "My Lord bids me say to you that he would as soon be parted with me as with his legs," and at that the caciques' eyes narrowed once more. I was glad it was so simple a thing to defy them, for well I knew that if I should ever go alone to Tenochtitlan, I would never be allowed to return to my Captain's side.

That day, after all words were spoken, the sacred bell rang and all that were Christian fell to our knees in the ritual demanded by my Captain's God, facing the wooden cross my Captain had placed against a tree near the shore. Then the Spaniards sang a holy song in praise to the Great Mother and her son, and many sang badly, and I not at all, for the words were in the holy tongue of the priest and were as senseless as gnats whining in my ears. Tleuhtlilli and Cuitlalpitoc looked from one to the other in bewilderment.

"Why does this great Lord and his warriors so humble themselves before a *tree*?" they said to me when the singing had ceased, and this I told to my Captain who was amused but said to the priest, de la Merced, "This is a good opportunity, Father, to explain through our interpreters matters concerning our most Holy Faith."

The priest then spoke to me and I to the caciques, though I spoke words better suited for their ears. I told them of the God's great God—whom they knew to be Ometeotl, though the priest had spoken of their King Don Carlos—and how he had bid them cross the sea and bring to this land their crossed sticks and images of the Great Mother and her sacred son. They also wished to end all bloody sacrifices and teach the people to sacrifice but fruit and flowers and butterflies in honor of Quetzalcoatl and the images he bore with him.

They listened with curiosity and with an awe that grew as I explained that these were ferocious warriors and that with them and with Quetzalcoatl's sacred power, blessings instead of blood would flow upon this land and its people and ensure to them peace and bountiful harvests. All they would need to do in return was to put images of my God and his Goddess Mother in their teocallis and do them honor and reverence.

The caciques then looked at the earth most gravely but said nothing in reply.

Still there was not enough food for our soldiers and so they bartered their share of the golden treasure for fruit and meat. My Captain did not stop them for he knew not how to obtain food in the nearby villages and not stir unrest at having to feed our great number. Yet in so doing, my Captain made enemies among his men. The soldiers paid no heed to me as I walked silently among them listening to their words to be able to report them to my Captain. Thus he was not taken by surprise when some soldiers asked him to forbid the bartering of gold for food and so lessen the treasure to take back to Spain.

"The pagans in these villages must either give us their food or we will take it from them!" one named Velasquez said with heat.

Though my Captain did indeed forbid the bartering, he did not allow any soldiers to take food from the villages without permission, and so the unrest, as the hunger, did continue.

Fish there was in plenty, but while it filled their bellies it was not the roasting meat they hungered for in their minds. I heard mutterings of discontent. Many said they wished to leave with the treasure they had gotten for themselves and their King, and that they did not wish to further risk their lives in a hostile and barbarous country. I did not speak of these words to my Captain, but kept them locked in a fearful heart. Not only did I yearn to lay Tenochtitlan at my Captain's feet—and Moteczoma beneath them!—but also I feared that if his heart changed and he departed these shores, he would not wish for me to go with him. Aguilar had told me that he had a lady wife on an island named Cuba, and it was not so far away and they were much in love. So I heartily wished him never to return to her, or that she should soon die.

One dawn we awoke to find the camp of Tleuhtlilli had been abandoned in the night. This boded ill indeed. It seemed to me that Moteczoma must be restless in his mind and undecided what to do with this unwelcome God and his warriors, whether to bid them stay or urge them to go. This we later found out to be true.

Then Ehecatl blew ill upon us. An uprising began among the soldiers and those who had spoken ill of my Captain spoke ill again, saying they feared Moteczoma would come with his warriors and take us captive and all would be sacrificed in pagan fashion and eaten as common meat. This talk was stirred by the unaccustomed heat and by the many xexenes that whined around us, biting us unmercifully, as they always did in this season and place of many marshes where they bred. I truly then feared for my Captain, who began to listen well to what I said and bade me to listen to all I could and to report each evening what I had heard. This pleased me well, but Alonzo grew jealous and so he commanded me to stay away from all other men but the Captain and Aguilar.

"Do you think you can command me when Captain Cortés has given me tasks to do? It is not you I will obey, but him." I did not speak these words in anger, but in a voice low and smooth with meaning and in perfect Spanish, and he turned a brighter red in his red face and turned muttering away.

Then did he go to my Captain, asking that I be commanded to do what he wished in bed and in all other ways, and to take my steps from where the soldiers camped because I was but a pagan woman, after all, and not to be trusted as a true Christian woman would be. My Captain answered him that I had been made Christian and that he had no distrust of me. He said that I heard things of great importance and he had need for me to learn these things. Thus he took Alonzo into his confidence. After this talk my Captain said to me that I must obey the will of my master for he was a valuable and trusted soldier and so I was, for that reason, to submit to him at his desire, for women were by God's design made to do so. More than this, I was also to continue to do my work, seeking out unrest to tell him where it lay.

Rage mounted like flames in my heart. I held my tongue and lowered my head and feigned compliance, while I planned vengeance against Alonzo. I amused myself thinking of ways to rid myself of him. Poisons there were, indeed, and evil magic, but his death would not answer. Always there would be another soldier to take Alonzo's place and much as I hated him, still was he not so bad as some who took pleasure in unnatural ways or beat their women when they had nought else to do.

In wisdom I swallowed my anger and did as I was told. Alonzo once again made frequent use of me and I submitted to him as a grass blade submits to the foot that steps upon it, upright again when the foot is gone. Aguilar pitied me, and his jealousy of my Captain lessened for he now believed that Cortés did not want me and that my heart would soon turn from its devotion to my Captain and fasten upon himself. This hope I saw in his eyes and read in his heart, and I used this knowledge to my advantage. Seeing but a sorrowing woman, her spirit weak within her, Aguilar looked upon me with love and spoke kind words to me and to my Captain regarding the good work I did for their holy cause.

Hunger for food grew fierce. The soldiers were day by day more unruly, fighting and cursing and speaking ill of my Captain for forcing them to continue on such a reckless adventure. I showed them how to look for waterflies and their eggs and to cook worms over the fires, but most of them would not eat, speaking longingly of "Christian food." Aguilar ate them to please me and found that he liked them, so we two did not hunger as did the rest.

In search of food, therefore, we often walked the shore a long way and also into the jungle. One day Aguilar and some soldiers and I came upon a group of warriors who fell to their knees at sight of us and babbled in a tongue I could not recognize. In Nahuatl I answered them, and two among them had knowledge of that tongue. They had kept us in their eyes for many days, they told us, and knew my Captain and his warriors were great Lords, but did not come near for they had seen their gravest enemies, the Azteca, come among us. They knew the Azteca had fled in the night so now they wished to seek converse with us and our Lord.

Quetzalcoatl was come to them as foretold, I said with solemn import, and they were overcome with awe and muttered that they did not dare approach so great a God.

"But he has come to rescue you from the yoke of your oppressors," I told them, adding that he had come to rule the empire justly and in peace, asking for none to give up their riches or fight in Flowery Wars and so lose the ablest men to sacrifice in Tenochtitlan. At this the warriors were most joyful and asked us to lead them to our God so they might offer him their praises and obedience. In my Captain's presence the warriors did indeed kneel down before him and touch a finger to the earth, then to their lips in reverence.

"What is it they wish?"

"They are sworn enemies of Moteczoma," I told my Captain, "and they wish to throw off the ropes stretching from Tenochtitlan to bind them captive here in their own lands. They are weary of filling the Ueytlatoani's treasure houses and dying in his teocallis to the Azteca Gods. They seek your protection, Captain, and swear to you their loyalty and many armed warriors when you go to barter with Moteczoma."

Never had I seen my Captain more pleased by anything but gold. "Indeed," he said, smiling, "nothing would delight me more. But ask of these men if there are many in these parts who also hate Moteczoma."

So we learned that many thousands of men in like mind were ready for combat. Moreover, they knew the Azteca were fearful of us and of our great beasts and iron cannon and guns that spit death.

"These men look most fearsome," my Captain remarked, staring at the golden disks in ears and lower lips. "Tell them we most eagerly and happily accept their aid."

This I said to the warriors: that they were most fortunate our God agreed to protect them if they swore loyalty and obedience to him. Eagerly they promised and then asked that we follow them to their city of Cempoalla to hold converse with their caciques. Cortés agreed, saying that soon we would march toward their city, and if talk went ill with Moteczoma's emissaries, then we would plan for war together. He gave to them necklaces which I, as ever, explained were made with sacred stones and full of magic. Pleased, they departed to their land to make ready for our coming.

Fortunate it was for us that those warriors had come, for the unrest in our camp had grown angrier still. The soldier, Velasquez, came boldly and with angry words to say to Cortés that they should return to Cuba and render obedience to the greater captain, Narvaez, who had sent Cortés on this journey. Other words of low respect said he: that it was by cunning that Cortés kept them there, that many of the men were weary of fish and some had wounds that would not heal. My Captain answered in honeyed words that they had come not to trade like mere merchants but to make settlement, and that it would not be possible to land a second time for the Azteca would surely meet them in hostility and in greater numbers. He also spoke cunningly of treasure and thus gained again the ears of the soldiers so that, though many were ranged against him, still most cast their lot with us. We stayed long enough to found a village they called Villa Rica de la Vera Cruz, though rich land it was not and the name did not make it so. Alonzo begged Cortés to stay always captain of their adventures, and perhaps because of his words, Cortés appointed him "alcalde" of the village. Velasquez and some other of the soldiers were still angry, so to render them obedient, my Captain had them confined to his ships in chains.

Alvarado was sent forth at the head of a group of soldiers to seek food, so that the hunger in the camp would at last be lessened and also the unrest. In two days he returned with food and much to tell. The villages they had found upon their way were newly abandoned and in the teocallis there were signs of much sacrifice, he said with disgust, many bodies with their hearts torn out and other parts gone and probably eaten.

I knew the people in the lands around us made sacrifice to their Gods of War to protect them from the Azteca, and all the while hid from us in fear. There were no slaves to carry the food they had found, so the men had carried what they could in their arms and on the backs of their horses. There were various kinds of fowl and maize and other things and though they hungered most of all for meat, they did not dare bring back flesh of what might once have been man.

Squatting near the nightly campfire, I heard Alvarado tell my Captain he had damaged nothing in the villages, even as he had been commanded, but that when he saw the cruel number of the sacrifices, he was so sickened that he longed to spit all such pagans like chickens on his sword.

"You may have opportunity for that, Alvarado," my Captain replied. Then, praising him first for his restraint, he added in laughing words that soon he would have pagan blood in plenty upon his sword and to be patient.

Now that foothold on the land had come with the founding of Villa Rica de la Vera Cruz, my Captain decided it was time to march north to Cempoalla. Wanting loyalty and now direly in need of it, my Captain gave more gold to all those who had stood against him, cheering them with tales of their fierce allies and their King's holy cause, and unlocking their chains and making them again free men. In justice did he also give gold to all the men who had stood by him, as well as honeyed words of thanks for their loyalty and courage. Seldom after this did I hear words of unrest, for treasure and the prospect of war and adventure seemed to appease their hearts as surely as did the food Alvarado brought appease their bellies.

Many towns did we pass on our journey north but they were abandoned and silent with fear. While the women and some soldiers searched for food in the storehouses, many of the soldiers amused themselves by going into the teocallis where they would make crosses upon their breasts with their hands and speak with disgust of the barbarity of the people. After this they would sometimes topple a stone God or scratch the letters of their names in the black soot upon the walls. Hearing them speak as they did, I was ashamed and glad I was no longer pagan but a Christian, even if only a Christian woman and still more pagan than was a Christian man.

We marched along the sand and into the jungle and across stretches of jungle and flat plain, all unsure of the way. We were most heartily glad one day to see a group of men marching toward us, making obeisances to us when still at a distance before coming slowly closer, and then bowing once more. They had come from their cacique, they told us, to lead us to Cempoalla. They had brought deer and pig and turkey, which were most welcome to the men who were by now as weary of maize as they had been of fish. The city of Cempoalla was but one sun's march distant, they explained to us, and we greeted this news with pleasure.

That night we slept in a village where quarters had been readied for the Captain and his important soldiers, and so I slept with Alonzo in blankets most luxurious. The next dawn found us refreshed and the Cempoallan emissaries fed us all we wished to eat and more. My Captain sent six of them ahead to their city with news of our arrival while the rest guided us on our way. Even with such signs of welcome my Captain still bid his men to remain on guard and to march prepared for attack.

When we neared the city, many caciques came forth with sweet copal to honor us. With myself by one side and Aguilar on the other, my Captain listened gravely as they told us that their noblest cacique was too fat in body to come and receive us himself, but longed for our meeting in Cempoalla. This my Captain took in good part and in gracious humor.

We marched on then, and when we had come in

sight of the city, its white walls shining as silver, many of our soldiers cried out that the stones *were* silver in this land and perhaps gold, too, in other cities. Swiftly did they learn their foolishness, but I was pleased that greed did so blind their sight, for greed would keep them tame and as loyal to my Captain as dogs to the master who feeds them.

Soon we entered the streets of that city, and though but of common stone it was a fine place and green with gardens and proud with many teocallis. My Captain and his soldiers were amazed that in such a barbarous and savage country they should find a city as wondrous as this!

17

Xochitl

One day did I return to the women's chamber in the palace, there to find great weeping and lamentation. Moteczoma's concubines as well as his Lady wife, Green River Flowing, were drawing blood from the lobes of their ears and from their tongues with thorns and so it did drip like necklaces of precious jewels. To me they would not speak, but merely stared in awe. A servant came to bid me to my Lord's chamber, the first summons since the day of my swooning upon the stone of Tixoc. There was ferment in the land; I could feel it in my flesh. A time of great change was at hand.

Lord Moteczoma was not sitting upon his icpalli when I entered his chamber, but walking in a fever up and down the room. Priests were there also and they looked narrowly at me, their eyes black with malice and suspicion. Moteczoma ceased his pacing. "Strangers have landed on the shore of the eastern sea," he said, and could scarce control the trembling of his voice. "They have brought with them monsters and hollow tubes that spit death."

"Quetzalcoatl?" I breathed, and my heart took wing.

My Lord clasped tight his hands and looked to his priests. "These say he is not so, being merely man. And yet . . . and yet my sorcerers say he is the God foretold and even now does he march in triumph to Tenochtitlan."

Once more he began to pace and his breathing was ragged as if he had run a great way. Then he stopped again to look hard upon me. "What say you, priestess? God or man?"

"My Lord, you know what I have seen when the God has possessed me. Truly do I feel that the time of prophecy draws near."

"Step forth, priest of Huitzilopochtli," then said my Lord, and one of the priests took two steps forward. "Look well upon him, priestess."

He was a man of waning youth and of features regular though somewhat smaller than is usual with our people and his hair was a shade lighter.

"The . . . the being who has touched upon our shore bears great likeness to this priest. First I did send messengers bearing gifts so to make in secrecy paintings of the strangers and their beasts. When they did return, the features of this God or man did so resemble those of this priest that I sent him to the Tabascan lands with a second group of messengers all bearing treasure so to do reverence to the strangers if they were Gods and to satisfy their greed if they were, as my priests did say, mere men. And all remarked upon this strange likeness. But there was a likeness far more wondrous than this."

They all stood staring upon me a moment, and then said my Lord, "Can it be you do not know?"

"I cannot say, my Lord. All I know is what my God has shown me in my dreams."

"Tell her, priest."

This priest drew close to me and held my eyes within the darkness of his own. "The first messengers did not bother to paint a clear likeness of the woman who accompanies this being, speaking for him so all will understand his words. She was but a woman and therefore of little interest. Yet when I did arrive there I saw that this woman bore uncanny likeness to a woman we priests have seen closely and know well." Then he fell silent and held my eyes while I struggled to find meaning in this strange new knowledge.

"And who does this woman resemble?"

As if the words strangled in his throat, he cried, "You, priestess! In every way does she bear your likeness. Even her voice is low as is yours and her eyes are your eyes and her lips yours, also. I looked long at her and as closely as I now do look upon *you.*"

"Why," my Lord Moteczoma said, "do you send your shadow self to lead these beings to Tenochtitlan?"

Then did I see why they looked at me with fear and malice. Great power would it take to send my shadow self from me, and the deepest sorcery. Yet I had not done this in my willful mind. Perhaps, I thought, it had been in my swooning that my shadow self had slipped from me to that place where my God did stand. And then came to my thoughts the name of my sister, my twin, Malinalli, who had been parted from me in the Tabascan lands. Even yet more wondrous strange would it be if she, and not my shadow self, did stand beside our beloved God. But what could have made her more than common slave, and how had she learned to speak the language of the Gods?

Swiftly did I plan what, under the watchful gaze of the priests and my Lord Moteczoma, it would suit me best for them to believe. Our Gods did indeed have shadow selves—twins, we thought, were but earthly mirrors of the opposites contained within the divine. Especially was this true when the twins were male, or bore a mirror-likeness, as did my sister and I. More than this, Quetzalcoatl was the special God of twins, which had always made him seem even closer to my sister's heart and mine. Was it I who stood upon the shore . . . or she? To the priests, I knew sorcery would have more consequence, and so would it also to my Lord. Thus it was did I say to them, "It appears my God Quetzalcoatl has need of me even as you do, my Lord."

The priests drew back with a hiss at my words and like the eyes of serpents did their eyes glitter beneath their hooded lids. My Lord looked uneasily upon them. "I bid you priests go," said he. "I would have private speech with this priestess." And they went at his word most reluctantly. Despite the sacred power they knew I possessed, I knew I lived now in mortal danger. Since they believed I was leading my God to Tenochtitlan, perhaps they would decide that if they were well rid of me, Quetzalcoatl would not be able to find his way, nor speak his words of comfort to the people.

Moteczoma was silent a long moment. Then he asked me to raise my eyes to his face. There did I read the words he did not speak. Dislike and fear were dark there, and an uncertainty I had not known he felt. "You have heard about the statue made of me in Chapultepec?" he whispered.

"Indeed, my Lord."

"Was it *your* work to destroy it? Or the work of your God Quetzalcoatl, whom you bring to the Heart of the One World to lay it to waste?"

"I know not, Lord," said I in answer. My Lord looked deep into my eyes and knew I spoke truth. "Perhaps, my Lord," said I, lowering my eyes for my words were bold, "if you did honor my God he would spare Tenochtitlan. It may be that my vision will come true only if you resist him. Therefore it would be the greater wisdom to make his journey one of triumph and his arrival reason for rejoicing."

"My priests did tell me this is what you would say," he said bitterly.

"I but speak what I feel to be true, my Lord. Even as I serve my God, so do I also serve you."

"But a *more* loyal servant you are not to me."

And I said softly, "That is but just, my Lord, that I should serve first my God before his earthly emissary."

My Lord did sigh and turn away from me. "I have posted runners in the jungle and they have come to tell me that this stranger has left the shore and marches inland with his warriors. He has met with my enemies, the Totonaca, who have sworn to him their allegiance. In their company does he now march west. Does this seem to you the act of a peaceful God, priestess? Or is he a man who seeks to bring war and ruin upon us?"

I raised my eyes to him unbidden. "Dare you say our God comes to make war upon you? He but comes as foretold to rule this land in godly wisdom."

"Dare you say 'dare' to me?"

In the face of my Lord's fury, I lowered my eyes. "Forgive me, Lord, I spoke in haste," said I, and bowed my head.

"Go. But I may have need of you soon, priestess," he said coldly. Thus did I, bowing, take my leave.

I walked far from the palace then in a restless fever. Thoughts veiled my sight and I walked without knowing where my steps led me. My sister or my shadow self? Even now one of those stood in company with my God, marching west beside him. My mind turned from one to the other in equal wonder and confusion. Suddenly I found myself at the Great Temple of Huitzilopochtli where, in a frenzy, the priests were making sacrifice of captive warriors so that the steps ran red with blood and bodies lay in mounds at its base. Black smoke rose in stinking clouds from the teocalli high above. In the smoke I felt the baneful presence of the priests and knew that in their sacred rituals they wished evil upon me and served well their Gods so that I might be struck down. Sickened by the sight of so much blood and the smells of the many hearts burning in the teocalli's holy fire, I walked on, without knowing where.

For many months I had been in Tenochtitlan, and though I had often heard of it, never had I seen Lord Moteczoma's great aviary of captive birds. I lifted my eyes then to the great building in which lived birds of every color and kind, from the tiny jewel of the hummingbird to the great eagle, symbol of the Azteca's might. I entered, here where these birds were kept in luxurious gardens, flying around their great cages as if they were still free.

"Forgive my boldness, priestess," came a man's

deep voice close by my side, so startling me that I gasped and rounded swiftly on him.

"You?" I whispered when I could draw breath to speak.

"Indeed, it is I," he replied, and I looked wonderingly upon the face of the slave who had rescued me from the wrath of the slaveowner, Icpitl, on that distant night when, like a frantic bird intent upon its freedom, I had sought release from captivity. In silence did we gaze into each other's eyes, and strange magic held us in a world no larger than that of our two selves. At last he smiled upon me, satisfied, and though I did manage to smile also, my heart trembled at the kindness in his face.

"You are no longer slave, priestess."

I shook my head but could not look full upon him, for my face was flushed with shy heat as if I were but a maiden and still innocent of men.

"And you?"

"I am slave still, sold by Icpitl into my Lord Moteczoma's service." He then shrugged his great shoulders and smiled again. "It appears to be my tonalli, and I do not struggle against it. At least," he added in a softer voice, "I have not until now."

I could not look up, or force myself to speak. I saw his hand reach toward me, and slowly, as if it moved outside of time, and softly did he place it upon my cheek. His flesh was no cooler than my own. He raised my chin and forced my eyes to meet his. "I know it overbold of me to speak thus, priestess, and sacrilege as well, but I have dreamed of no one but you since that night you sought escape. Many times have I cursed myself, wondering whether it would have been safe to let you go and to face Icpitl's wrath by myself in the morning, rather than lead you back into captivity."

"You did what you thought best for me," I answered, feeling myself grow faint at the fathomless depths I saw in his eyes, as if I were in danger of falling.

"I did, indeed. But after that night I have never been certain." He put his hands upon my arms and then slid them to my waist and then around it. This was, indeed, sacrilege, but I cared not. Standing thus for a moment, in the circle of his arms, I lay my head upon his chest and breathed in the male fragrance of his body.

"I know not even your name," I whispered.

"And yet do I know yours, priestess. Xochitl, you are called, and a most great priestess have you become." I could not restrain a sigh, for in his arms he did remind me I was no mere woman possessed of my own heart.

"I am Atahualpa," he said, "Would I could serve you all my days."

I looked up into his face and saw truth upon it. He smiled sadly. "It is not my destiny to do more."

I knew the truth of his words, yet they gave me pain. I yearned to deny them. "But we may at times speak with each other, Atahualpa? Surely there is no sacrilege in that."

"And if in truth it *is* wrong for us thus to meet, what then?"

I drew a shaking breath. "Then we shall do wrong. But I cannot think it so!" I cried, but softly, passing my hands around him and pressing his body to mine so that I felt the quivering in us both, and our desire.

With difficulty did he draw away from me and, lingeringly, we ceased to touch. "This could be of gravest danger for you," he said. "You are not without enemies, Xochitl."

"At this moment, Atahualpa, I do not care." A radiance transformed the sorrow in his face and he took me in his arms once more, holding me so tightly that it almost gave me pain. We were swept in that moment back into the universe of our small world, and did not see the eyes that glittered through the leaves of that lush chambered garden nor hear the stealthy footfalls then recede.

* * *

Many times in the days to follow our meeting did I seek Atahualpa—whose name in my mouth was honey—in the aviary gardens. We would sit upon the benches and converse, the small fingers of our hands scarce touching. My body trembled in the nearness of his and grew weak with desire. Eyes held eyes captive and with but a look did we each plumb to the very soul of the other. Rarely was it safe to do more than look, and then could we exchange but the briefest, and yet most searing, of kisses. At other times, when someone came also to walk or work in the gardens, we would stand apart and as strangers, the priestess and the slave and their enchanted garden. Yet even then would we dare glances at each other that would quicken breathing and draw fire into the loins.

There were times when we were quite alone and then would Atahualpa whisper to me the poetry he kept in memory for me during the hours we were apart. All lay hold upon my heart, but none so dearly as the one he told me often, at my request, so that I would remember it always.

> "One by one I proclaim your songs:
> I bind them on gold crabs as if they were anklets:
> like emeralds I gather them.
> Clothe yourself in them: they are your riches.
> Bathe in feathers of the quetzal,
> your treasury of birds' plumes black and yellow,
> the red feathers of the macaw
> beat your drums about the world:
> deck yourself out in them: they are your riches."

He would bring to me precious feathers he found in the cages and lay them softly upon my hands and breast and hair, and then would I seem not impoverished priestess, but Goddess. It was well we had this enchanted time, for soon it ended as the forces of darkness did their work.

One morning when I came to the aviary, Atahualpa was not there to meet me. Thus it was also the next day and the next, while another slave was there to tend the birds and collect their feathers. Again and again did I return for the next long week, but never did I find him waiting. Even when I asked the new slave where Atahualpa had gone, he said he knew not. There was no one else I could ask. With a heart as heavy as it had been light, I performed my tasks at the teocalli of Quetzalcoatl and obeyed my Lord's commands and yearned for Atahualpa.

The priests of Huitzilopochtli and Tezcatlipoca approached me not, but in my flesh I felt their sorcery and I appealed to my God, Quetzalcoatl, to forsake me not and to hurry upon his way to Tenochtitlan. Often was I bid in these days to the presence of my Lord Moteczoma. What dreams had I dreamed, he did ask, and what prophecies had been given? But no dreams had been given me since the last upon the stone of Tixoc, and no prophecies. Thus in silence would I stand watching him as he paced up and down his chamber speaking of Quetzalcoatl's coming and then, in his next breath, the triumph of Tezcatlipoca.

Most eagerly did he wish my God would leave our shores with the treasure already given to him. But the Ueytlatoani's emissaries despatched to spy on Quetzalcoatl always returned bearing messages that the journey continued and with an increase of armies hostile to Tenochtitlan. Great warriors, priests and sorcerers came also to Moteczoma's chamber, and made enchantments and plotted battle. But Moteczoma, like a blade of grass in a contrary wind, did bend this way and that, believing one thing and then the other. There were times I listened to this talk and saw my Lord grow forceful and speak of war. Then would he look to me and in a pleading voice ask did I truly think the beings who marched with Quetzalcoatl were men or Gods? I did tell him at these times that whether they were men or more than men, still were they Quetzalcoatl's warriors and deserving of honor and not war. My Lord would often order us all from his chamber in angry confusion. Sometimes it would be his whim to order great numbers of captives sacrificed in the Flowery Death in all the teocallis, and at these times he would do reverence and abstain from women and from all pleasure. Also did he, to the fury and consternation of Chimalpopoca, command that the palace of the dead Ueytlatoani, Axayácatl, be prepared in all sumptuous splendor for Quetzalcoatl's coming. One hour would Moteczoma curse his tonalli and plead for the aid of his dark Gods, and in the next hour send gifts to Quetzalcoatl.

The priests, of course, were not content with sorcery against Quetzalcoatl. They sought too to take my tongue captive, to render me helpless to speak for my God. In my sleeping blankets I found objects of great magic—once a beetle with golden wings and once a small figure of clay with its female breast cut wide. There were times as I ascended the pyramid to conduct sacred rituals I felt the force of ghostly hands pushing down upon me, seeking for me to fall. Yet my prayers to Quetzalcoatl were unceasing, and thus I felt protected.

Days and days did pass, and it was again the sacred month of Ochpantztli, in which priestesses had still much to do to help ensure fertility in beast and man. As the most powerful priestess in Tenochtitlan, I was chosen to enact the sacred role of the Goddess Tonantzin, honor indeed though not of my desiring since my God desired that no blood be shed, while the priests were adamant for that sacrifice. Thus it was that day I proceeded in solemn procession to the stone of Tixoc, accompanied by dancing and singing and the hollow drumming of the teponaztlis and the priestesses' rattles. A huehuetl I carried beneath my arm and another priestess took it from me as I reached the stone.

Four beautiful women waited there, naked to the waist and with their long hair flowing. Priests stood there also in reverence and Chimalpopoca took his place by my side. Then did I take the obsidian dagger from where it hung at my waist and looked upon the women. Young they were and frightened, but their eyes were glazed with potent drink so that they did not scream nor run but stared down upon their bodies in a kind of stunned amazement that they did stand thus naked before the multitude. With compassionate swiftness I slit open the first woman's breast. Blood flowed gushing from it into a golden bowl one of the priests held while another stood behind her as she leaned half-swooning upon him. Quickly did I slit her other breast, and then the breasts of the other three, and many were the golden bowls filled with their rich female blood. Priests lay the women down upon the stone and did behead them one by one.

With these heads we then proceeded in solemn ceremony to the tzompantli where, after they had been scraped and scoured clean, the skulls would be placed on top of the skulls of those thousands of others gone before to Mictlan. Then did I in my sacred guise as Tonantzin, take back my huehuetl and throw it down and step my foot upon it. Shells were sounded and the teponaztlis struck, and a golden bowl was put into my hands and I drank blood yet warm from a woman's body so to nourish the Goddess within me so that she would bless us with fruit in the wombs of the beasts and swell the bellies of our women.

In reverence and joy, then, the people danced. A bowl of blood was taken in ceremony to Lord Moteczoma in his palace, and did he also drink. There would be feasting later in the day and much honor given Goddess Tonantzin and praise for her work in this world—but this I would not see. I had tasted human blood before and knew it for the salty drink it was, but this woman's blood had been embittered with her fear, I thought, and thus had tasted strange to me. After I had drunk, it seemed a swarm of xexenes flew into my skull and I staggered as a man drunk upon octli. Priestesses rushed close to support me, but

Chimalpopoca bid them in a voice unnaturally kind to permit him to lead me to a sleeping chamber nearby so I might rest the sooner. This was improper, but Chimalpopoca was the most powerful of all the priests and priestesses in Anáhuac, and the priestesses did obey him. I could not compel my tongue to make the words needed to resist.

So was I led from the sacred revels; the priests had all but to carry me to the teocalli of Tezcatlipoca in which an opening like a serpent's monstrous jaws stood agape. Through this did we walk into the pyramid and past flaming braziers full of hearts black and smoldering. Upon that rank vapor did I choke and feel my belly sicken. Away from that foul place we went and down many steps and through a long dark corridor lighted with but a few torches fastened to the walls, then through another opening, this one carved like a grinning skull with open, toothless jaws. We were inside a large chamber, indeed, and I tried to force my eyes to see what was contained in the many large cages against the walls. The two priests stopped before one cage, within it a jaguar that regarded us with baleful eyes before it returned to dine upon the torn and headless body of one of the women I had sacrificed that day. Growling deep in his black throat he fed, while the priests carried me on to the next cage and the next, and inside of each were wolves or foxes or jaguars or other beasts. This was, I now saw, Moteczoma's famed and fearsome menagerie. It seemed to me that this was Chimalpopoca's design, that I should end thus humbly and food for a beast. Yet even he must have been too fearful to commit such dire sacrilege.

At the far end of the chamber were cages no larger than the rest but placed somewhat apart. Stopping before the first of these, Chimalpopoca directed my gaze at what it did contain. A man so twisted he scarce could lift his head from between his knees was inside, and in the cage next to him was another with a great lump of flesh upon his back. A girl with dead eyes sat behind the next cage's wooden bars, the small shriveled body of a child protruding from her side in a terrible mockery of birth. These pitiable monsters were naked and gazed sorrowfully upon us as we passed to the last cage where I did look upon another man. It was Atahualpa. My body began to swoon and Chimalpopoca swiftly held a foul odor beneath my nose so that I coughed and my eyes watered fiercely from its sting. Thus he prevented the swoon that might have led me into the arms of my God and beyond the priests' possession.

Atahualpa was naked, but for a ragged maxtlatl, and his flesh was red and broken from beatings. He looked up at me from where he lay upon the cage floor, then struggled to rise to his feet and could not: his legs had been broken and could no longer bear the burden of his once-perfect body.

"My love!" I whispered, and tears I had once thought scorched dry long before came to my eyes and fell as rain.

Atahualpa's face, which had in his humiliation been dark with shame, lightened with this evidence of my devotion.

"Do not worry for me, Xochitl," he said quietly and in the strong voice I loved well and well remembered. "No one on this earth will take from us what we have even so briefly known."

Chimalpopoca raised his voice to put an end to further words between us. "The Ueytlatoani Moteczoma, in his merciful kindness, did not choose to put this slave to death after he had learned the sacrilege of his daring to hunger for the body of a priestess. Here will we not speak of *your* shame, Xochitl," he said to me, smiling coldly. "The Ueytlatoani, in his wisdom, will not allow foul passion unbefitting the chastity of a priestess to defile the teocalli of Quetzalcoatl, and thus will save your honor and that of your God by taking you to himself as his Second Wife."

"This is but greater sacrilege," I cried even in my

weakness, "to marry a priestess against her will and so sunder her vows!"

"But I know," Chimalpopoca said in a silken voice, "as even did your Lord Moteczoma, that only time would it need for you to sunder those vows yourself, and in the ignoble arms of a slave. Lord Moteczoma wishes to gain possession of your body before your shadow self returns to you. And, perhaps, with this marriage your shadow self will no longer have the power to guide your God to Tenochtitlan."

"You cannot forestall his coming, priest."

"And you," hissed Chimalpopoca, leaning toward me so that I could smell death upon his skin and breath, "you cannot forestall the slow and agonizing torture of this slave . . . but by doing as you arc bid."

I looked into the cage and into the face of Atahualpa. Well did he make stern his features and so mask his sorrow. "Do nothing for my sake, Xochitl, but for your own."

In silence then did I bid him farewell, with the light of love in my eyes turned full upon him as he did also look full upon me. For a moment we were again in that small universe which contained our love and nothing more, and he smiled upon me to give my heart courage. I turned upon the priest and masked my face with coldest fury. "You will do as you have promised. And I promise *you,* priest, that if this man dies so will you die, and more horribly. I swear to that!"

Chimalpopoca's fury almost equalled my own, but he masked it also. "A woman no longer priestess would do well to guard her words. But as it is promised to you, so will it be done and this man's petty life spared. At the hour you are married and again but a woman in the Ueytlatoani's arms, then will he be released into freedom, and exile."

"So be it." With one last look at my love, I allowed the priests to support me from that chamber of horrors and out another door and through dark passages that ran like deep rivers beneath the streets above our heads, thus to the very palace of my Lord Moteczoma. At Chimalpopoca's command, slaves took my arms and led me to the women's chamber where one and all now called me Xochitlzin, in honor of what I was soon to become.

Slaves and concubines did that day bathe and dress me in finery equal to that of Green River Flowing, and take down my hair to wash and oil it and wind it in elaborate coils and then place upon it a feather head-dress. Priests returned to lead me to a chamber where with a dagger they cut through my nostrils. Upon stanching the blood, they fit into my nose a golden jewel with the figure of Xolotl carved upon it. By this I knew them to be working rare enchantments, for Xolotl was the dark twin of Quetzalcoatl and the monstrous overlord of Quetzalcoatl's passage through the underworld of night. Thus did they seek to bring back my shadow self from its sacred journey.

In a procession of dancing women I was led to the chamber of my Lord, wherein he and I were bathed together in a golden vessel and prayed over by the priests of Tezcatlipoca and Huitzilopochtli. Not one priest or priestess of Quetzalcoatl attended, save me—and was I still a priestess or but woman once more? The Gods were called to look down upon us as we were led to my Lord's sleeping chamber, and we were left there alone.

I looked into my Lord's eyes and saw he gazed at me uneasily. "Why did you this, my Lord?"

"Did the priests not tell you?" he said in a voice not without disquiet.

"It is sacrilege for a priestess to be compelled into marriage, no matter how noble the man."

"But you are priestess no longer," he said, and with sudden restlessness did he begin to pace the chamber. "They told me you allowed the fond embraces of a slave, and did permit him to speak of love to you. Thus did you defile your chaste calling and sunder your vows. Was that not so?"

"No sacrilege was done and no defilement." This I said with my eyes steadfastly fixed upon his, bidding him in silence to hear me and to argue not. Thus as if I had spoken did he step forth and stand near me.

"Did you feel a fondness for this slave?" I yearned with all my being to speak that most dangerous truth. I thought of Atahualpa encaged and how I needed first to free him.

"He was a most well-formed man and pleasing to my eyes. Nothing more."

Moteczoma then took my arms in his hands, looking long at me and in the half-longing, half-hurt way of a child, asked, "This is the truth, Xochitlzin?"

"Indeed, my Lord," said I, willing the sorrowful visage of my love to leave the eyes of my mind.

Moteczoma then bade me undress. He did pass covetous hands over my body, saying that my form and flesh were all perfection. Then he bade me lie down upon his sleeping mat and I did so in sorrow while he untied his maxtlatl, murmuring all the while that though I was no longer priestess of a God, I was now priestess of fleshly desire. Long had he yearned to possess me, he said, and now I was of his belonging and could be possessed by no other. In truth, however, it was only my flesh he did possess and only as a man, for I felt nothing in my body or spirit to equal possession by a God. I knew that ecstasy well, and it was not this.

In the deepness of my heart I also knew the Lord Moteczoma had not possessed me as the slave Atahualpa would have done had he and I so dared in Moteczoma's own gardens. Even as my Lord did lay beside me and press hot lips upon my breasts, so did I wonder if Atahualpa had been freed and where he would go in his exile. My heart followed him upon his way, only returning to my God Quetzalcoatl when the long somber hours of night were gone.

18

MALINALLI

Upon first sight of Cempoalla, Aguilar turned to me with wonder in his eyes. "Never in my dreams did I expect to find a city such as this—and in so barbarous a country!" As we approached there were more words of wonderment and surprise, and even my Captain looked at me as if he saw me anew.

"It is like our tales of romance," Aguilar said to me, and when he saw his words bewildered me, he explained, "These are tales, Marina, about soldiers going on adventures to find exotic lands and cities fabulous and strange and with golden treasure, and women, called Amazons, beautiful and as fierce as warriors."

I smiled to myself that he was thus beguiled and that he also looked upon me with altered gaze, as if I were indeed an Amazon. "Tell me one of these tales, Aguilar," I asked, and so after we entered the city and were given food and sleeping chambers, Aguilar told me tales of conquest and dangerous adventure. Most unlikely did they seem to me, but not to him.

"Tell me, Aguilar. Do all your countrymen feel enthralled by these tales? Is my Captain also?"

"He, perhaps, most of all." All of them spoke among themselves about these tales, he told me earnestly. They had all heard such words or seen pictures painted upon paper in their country, so that every man was enchanted and yearned to adventure in strange and foreign lands. "We hoped this country would be full of wonders and great treasure, but it seemed so poor a place that until now we doubted there would be treasure enough for all."

"The Ueytlatoani Moteczoma has sent you golden jewels and other things of great value."

"Yes," Aguilar replied, "but we thought among ourselves that he must indeed have sent the best of what he had and therefore had little treasure left. The villages we have seen before this Cempoalla have been but poor, mean places and so we expected little more."

I had not known the soldiers were so dispirited, and I wondered if all believed this and if they were already half-persuaded to return to Spain. "No, Aguilar," I smiled, putting my hand upon his arm in a slight caress so that his flesh quivered beneath it. "These lands are only poor because Moteczoma has sent his tax gatherers many times to steal from us all our treasure. And not only treasure. The Azteca have taken with them our most beautiful women, whose bodies they mount like beasts in a field and then sell into slavery. They demand we give our men to the Flowery Wars so they may be sacrificed in Tenochtitlan. Oh, Aguilar," I said to him eagerly, "there is more treasure in that Azteca city than your storytellers could ever dream possible!"

"This you know, Marina, without doubt?"

"I swear to you on my life."

His eyes shining, Aguilar sought out Cortés to tell him my words and later, as I guessed he would, my Captain sent for me to converse in his private chamber. I was ready indeed for this command. All that day I had thought long and earnestly of Aguilar's stories. Though I had known nothing of these tales before, nor any like them, and found it amusing that men would cross oceans and brave dangers only because of some ancient storyteller's fancy, yet I better understood my Captain and his men. They said that they had come to this land to tell us of their Christian Gods, but these Gods did not seem so different from those we had already; they scorned sacrifice, as did Quetzalcoatl, but they sought selfish nourishment in other ways. It seemed strange to me that these men should leave a country where there was plenty, so Aguilar had told me, to come sailing across the earth to a country they knew nothing of and which perhaps had little.

Also I knew in my woman's heart that men made trouble when they had not other tasks to do, that they always sought to go elsewhere and anywhere in their male restlessness. Some of that restlessness I also had within me, but it was rare among our women and I was looked upon with censure and as if I were one of those women with whom the Gods made sport by giving her a male heart but no tepuli to go with it! Such is the way with people. Indeed, they insist if you are not one way then you must be entirely the other.

I saw at last into those Spanish hearts, and the heart of my Captain also. It was not that he wished for me to be but a poor slave, nor yet a Spanish Doña. No, indeed. He wished for me to be a marvel, one of the fabulous creatures he had sailed forth to find. What a disappointment it must have been to have found in the Tabascan lands nought but huts, small teocallis, mere ruins of what once had been vast pyramids, and with this also but scant food and treasure of little worth. Until Moteczoma had sent his gifts of gold, they must have thought their journey had been in vain. Well did Aguilar serve me that day, so opening my mind to these ideas both strange and instructive.

Cortés was indeed enchanted but our pleasant talk was too soon interrupted by other matters. Caciques gathered in my Captain's chamber, the chief cacique arriving upon his litter borne by slaves already sweating under their burden, for he was gross with fat. Immediately he raised his voice loudest in complaint that Azteca tax gatherers were even now in the city at their Lord's command. Flowers held disdainfully to their noses, puffed with arrogance and pride, the Azteca had chastised the caciques for having given us food and shelter, saying that the Ueytlatoani had forbidden this courtesy and would be most angered by the caciques' disobedience. They had demanded then twenty beauteous men and women as punishment for this offence.

I was dismayed in my heart to see that Moteczoma dared to so offend my Captain, whom I had hoped by now he would believe to be a God. My Captain comforted the caciques and pleased them by immediately taking the Azteca tax gatherers captive, collaring them to a pole even as I had been, gladdening my heart also. The caciques begged my Captain to permit them to sacrifice these captives, but this Cortés would not allow.

In the night Cortés did with stealth release two of the tax gatherers so that the caciques would not know who let them escape. He bid me instruct them to return to their Lord and tell him that we had come as friends, mindful of the greatness of the Azteca and their ruler, and that he would soon set free the other tax gatherers also. I told them that this mighty God who stood before them in human guise was merciful in all his ways, thus allowing them to take fair warning to the Ueytlatoani that he, Quetzalcoatl, was on his way to Tenochtitlan, where he expected a fitting welcome. The tax gatherers made obeisances and fear was in their eyes as they backed from him, bowing, as if his presence was scorching them.

Next day the Cempoallan caciques were enraged to find two of the captives had escaped their collars, but Cortés said nothing. Fearing that Moteczoma would exact revenge when he learned how his emissaries had been treated, the caciques implored my Captain to protect them. Cortés looked upon them with amusement, telling them—with my mouth—that his soldiers would from now on protect them so that they need never again pay tribute to Tenochtitlan.

Great was their rejoicing when they heard that they need no longer bleed dry at the dagger of Moteczoma, and in gratitude did they bring good food and much octli, and we feasted and drank so that many soldiers slept soundly upon the bare ground and greeted the dawn with their snoring.

I used the next day to devise a plan, then ventured forth to gather herbs and the other things I needed. A slave brought hot water to my chamber and I infused my herbs into that cup and then drank it down. I could feel the hot magic coursing down my arms and legs and nestling in my female parts to await my need for its power. Bathing and then steaming my body, I rubbed my skin with the oil of crushed flowers I had gathered. Thus when I received word that my Captain bid me come I went proudly, as if I were queen of lands beyond his dreaming.

I found him sitting on a chair in his chamber, head in his hands and eyes upon the papers he always studied, which were called maps; the one now before him had the name "New Spain" in one corner and the shape of the land drawn upon it. "Oh, Doña Marina," he said, gesturing for me to sit down but without raising his eyes, "I need to know from you how far it is from here to where the people live who are friendly with the Azteca."

I said nothing.

"Well, Doña . . . ?" he began impatiently, and then looked up. "Dear Christ," he breathed, his eyes drinking my beauty like the most potent octli, "you are as fair as the very angels themselves!"

I knew nothing of angels, but his words mattered not, nor what names he called me, for I knew he saw me with the eyes I had deliberately enraptured. As he sat, stunned, I slipped out of my garments and walked toward where he sat by fire and candlelight, watching as his eyes travelled my body and his tepuli rose and pushed urgently against his lower garment.

"Come to bed," he said in a voice made hoarse by desire.

"A moment first, Captain. I would like for you to share with me a drink to increase our pleasure."

"I have no need for any such tonic," he said, brushing away my words as if they were troublesome xexenes and moving to the bed. "I want you here, now."

I smiled at him and ran the tip of my tongue over parted lips. "Drink to please *me,* Captain."

Brusque and impatient, he called for the hot water I required and while we waited I caressed him and undulated my body serpentlike against him so when one of his soldiers brought the water to the chamber, he saw me naked and in my Captain's arms. I knew this news would reach Alonzo's ears and well was I pleased.

Crushing the peyotl in my hands, I infused it in the cup with a soothing herb so that his belly would not sicken. I drank from the cup myself and then held it out to my Captain. "Drink, and this night will be unlike any other."

He hesitated, as if I sought to poison him, and then he laughed. "I cannot see the end of my journey at a *woman's* fair hands!" and he drank.

I drew him to the bed and took from him his garments most caressingly. As the fire mounted in his loins so did the visions swarm into his eyes, so it was that night he did not join most passionately to the body of a woman, but to a Goddess from the barbarous land of his dreams. "You!" he whispered again and again, as if he could not believe what was astride him, and "Dear Christ!" he said and said again as he mounted to the heavens upon my flesh, sowing his seed in a fury time after time and until he could no more. I bathed him then, tenderly, and dried his body with my long hair while he shuddered and then slept.

I stayed thus in his bed beside him until morning and he, still half-asleep, to me saying, "I have need to send Moteczoma's treasure to my King to ensure his continued support of our venture. I do believe Alonzo deserves the honor of returning with it to Spain."

Thus did I become my Captain's mistress. Close I stayed to him in the night as well as in the day, and in all of these hours did I have his willing ear. Never again were we to have a night like that night had been, but as I knew many other enchantments I believed he would be well and truly my captive, given time.

Alonzo did not protest his return to Spain and did not bid me farewell. His anger did not reach out to my Captain, however, for his hands had been filled with gold more valuable to him than my body.

Aguilar was displeased with me also. "You think nothing of going from one man's bed to another's," he said to me next day as we rode forth from Cempoalla. "A woman like that has many names and none of them are courteous."

"What would you wish of me, Aguilar?" I said with scorn, "that I should lie down in no bed but your own?" Blushing, for we both knew I spoke the truth, he closed his lips and rode away. I rode on alone until the hated Alvarado reined in his horse near me. Gazing upon my body as if I were unclothed he said, smiling, "Our glorious Captain enjoys you now, but it will be my turn when he tires of you. And he *will* tire. That I promise you."

Unwillingly did I lose hold of my tongue and unleash words upon him in a fury. "I would sooner lie down with your horse, Alvarado!"

He threw back his head and laughed so merrily the soldiers near us turned to stare. "You are a hungry woman, indeed, to wish to bed a stallion. Perhaps you have never had the fortune of knowing a man who could do a stallion's work."

Later when I complained of Alvarado's words to my Captain, he said lightly, "Now *there* is a man with ready wit! I would bet all the gold of this land that he *is* hung like his horse."

I was so angered that I told Aguilar, though I knew he was still displeased with me, and he said, "You have not proven yourself to be aught else than what he believes you to be."

"I did not give myself to Alonzo! I was not born to be but a slave and passed from man to man." I flung my words at him and more loudly than usual, so that again soldiers turned to stare.

Aguilar softened his voice. "What you say is true of Alonzo, Marina, but is it also true of Cortés?"

"And what if it is not? Have I no right to choose but must take whatever is given me?"

Aguilar shook his head and left me, and did not again approach me in friendship for several days. To my surprise I missed his talk, his wondrous and amusing tales of his adventures and the strange ways of the Spanish in their own country. The journey northeast to Quiahuitztlan was wearisome without him, and when I sought to interest my Captain with tales both truthful and of my own invention, and to learn more about him, also, he spoke little and never of his heart or of me.

We slept in a small village that night, and by the late morning of the next day we had arrived at the great rocks and cliffs upon which Quiahuitztlan was perched like the nest of an eagle. As we approached this town, I was told to walk behind the soldiers while they prepared to face enemy warriors inside the city walls. We met with no one as we climbed the steep streets, and indeed saw no one at all until we had reached the sacred center of the town where there were several fine teocallis. Fifteen caciques met us there, dressed in bright finery and wearing their warrior masks of jaguars and serpents, holding toward us braziers in which copal smouldered. I hurried to stand by my Captain's side.

"What is it they say?"

"They bid you most welcome, my Captain. They make these obeisances to you in all honor and ask for your forgiveness that they came not out from their city to greet you, but they did not know whether you came to make war upon them and were thus afraid."

My Captain said all that was needful and before Aguilar could draw breath, I repeated his words to the caciques. My Captain then gave to the caciques the necklaces and other things of little value while I, as always, called them sacred gifts. I knew enough of the Spanish tongue that I rarely needed Aguilar's help, but I had not yet challenged his position as my Captain's interpreter, and so waited to see if he, thus humbled, would betray me to Cortés and tell him I spoke of him to all as a God. When I glanced sidelong at him he was looking at the ground. When he said nothing I knew for a certainty that my plans were safe.

19

Xochitl

No more could I go into the teocalli as priestess, or seek divine blessing for the people. I returned from Moteczoma's chamber to live again with his women and now as mere woman, although I was second only to his First Wife, Lady Green River Flowing, and of greater consequence than his five daughters.

It was a life of easeful luxury. On common days the food our Lord cared not to eat was given first to his nobles and the other two Lords of the Triple Alliance, and what they disdained would be sent to us. Though hot dishes had cooled, yet we ate only the finest of foods. When Moteczoma was neither fasting in ritual or withdrawn in misery, we would be bid on special evenings to sumptuous feasts. There would be great excitement on these days and much hurrying to and fro of the slaves who attended our whims and needs. For hours we would sit before our obsidian mirrors while slaves brushed our long hair to shining sleekness, then wound it elaborately upon our heads and wreathed into it pearls and other precious jewels that were brought us in chests from my Lord's treasurehouse. We also had special jewelry of our own, given to us when our Lord was pleased. Thus, on the day of the first banquet after my marriage, a slave brought to me in a jeweled casket a necklace all of gold and hung with the coiled shells of Ehecatl, and a most beautiful cape, also, oversewn with thousands of hummingbird feathers. In this way did my Lord show me honor and also make it known that I had been as a woman in his blankets. When these gifts had been presented and I had sent to him my thanks, the other women gathered round to admire them, most of them admiring and some envious, but all with knowledge of what this gift meant. The necklace was hung round my neck and it felt as if I were once more collared to the pole of slavery. The coldness of it oppressed my heart and the weight of it bore down upon me. Unlike Lady Green River Flowing and the concubines, dressing in jewels and costly garments did not please me for they were reminders of my lowly state and of him from whose lofty service I was now exiled. Oh, Quetzalcoatl, I cried to him in silence, this is not of my desire! But it was my tonalli to submit to whatever servitude the Gods of Fate decreed. In sorrow, I submitted.

After our hair was suitably arranged, then our bodies were stroked with fragrant oils so that our skin would glisten and taste of ripe mangoes, and we were offered the rare acagetl to sip so our breath would be sweet. This was done so that we would prove pleasing if selected by Moteczoma to share his blankets. Lastly were we dressed in our finest garments, woven with the fur of rabbits and of a softness and warmth I had never before known. If the evening was cold, our capes would be placed upon our shoulders before we walked in procession to the great dining chamber.

At these feasts where men and women ate together—and according to Azteca custom—I sat upon my Lord's left side and his First Wife upon his right. The concubines were by themselves at one table while at another were my Lord's mightiest warriors and counselors and fellow Lords. It was to my satisfaction that at these banquets the priests did not dine with us, for such merriment and pleasure were foreign to them and unbefitting their sacred solemnity.

Golden dishes were brought; ceramic ones from Cholulan sat with contents simmering above braziers so that the air was rich with the scents of roasted pheasant and tortoise in chilis, with tiny birds brown and crisp and but one mouthful each, and fowl in the most succulent and subtle of sauces. Great silver platters were heavy with oysters still shivering with life upon their opened shells and with the small salted bodies of fried waterflies, both having been brought by swift messengers from the oceans and swamps. Beautiful shells were heaped with the eggs of the waterflies, and these we ate with delicate translucent spoons carved from tortoiseshell.

As we ate, musicians played upon their flutes and teponaztlis and gongs, and the poets did recite. Warriors spoke eloquently of battle and the honor of the Flowery Death. Lady Green River Flowing herself did recite at my first banquet as Moteczoma's wife, and it was verse in praise of our Lord. Well was he pleased for did she, most artfully, wish him a "hundred and a hundred years of splendor" in his mighty empire. Concubines danced and warriors as well, while those too old to dance drank octli and made themselves warm in this way.

My Lord Moteczoma's dwarves romped in most humorous fashion, tumbling and leaping about and speaking amusing verse to give our Lord pleasure. While we ate of this and that, wolves and jaguars and bears were brought snarling in their cages to entertain us. From Moteczoma's menagerie monsters were brought to amaze us also, and several of these were the pitiable creatures I had seen with Chimalpopoca. The sight of them tore my heart, for they were not beasts, but men. Crippled in fantastic ways and of savage or hideous countenance, these beings were led stumbling and groping past us, some so twisted they needed to be brought in upon litters and set like objects of wood upon the floor. There was much astonishment at the most grotesque bodies and laughter at the ones deformed by artistry—as one would warp and break and bind a tree—into creatures of wildest fantasy. The faces of these monsters did quiver but slightly when the concubines did point to their naked bodies and make jest. Men with great buttocks were brought for our amusement, and men hung with tepulis the size of squashes and some with none at all. Loud would be the laughter and merry the jests when girls were brought who were linked by flesh into one body and females with breasts dangling to their knees, as well as one woman so white that she seemed dead and with eyes the palest blue. The guests would all gasp and laugh and point to the most ridiculous or hideous or strange, and all as if the beings who passed before their gaze were unable to hear or see.

Once such a sight might not have so sickened me, for I knew the Gods often made sport of us and so some men are born mad and some misshapen and others foolish. In this the Gods give pleasure to themselves and wonder to man. But all I saw in the eye of my mind was the body of Atahualpa in these bodies, caged as I had seen him caged, and wonder was replaced by sorrow that they should be created so and their sorrow our delight.

Moteczoma noticed my reserve. "Xochitlzin," he asked me, "why do you not laugh at this? These are indeed the finest monsters in all this land."

"I see no humor in their sad state nor find pleasure in their deformity, my Lord."

He looked upon me with astonishment and smiled. "You are as strange, perhaps, inside your bones as these creatures are *ouside* of theirs."

"Perhaps you speak truth, my Lord," I said, giving him a slight smile in return.

Lastly did slaves bring sweet pastry and cups of spiced and steaming cacao, and many guests then smoked their pipes and the aged were given yet more octli to warm their old bones while the younger danced again. Thus it was into the darkest hours of the night that the musicians did play and the guests danced, and this was so until our Lord rose to his feet thus to signal that the feasting was ended.

After that first banquet Moteczoma bid me follow

him to his private chamber, and as I left with him all eyes were upon me, priestess no more. In his chamber, then, he sat down upon his icpalli and bid me undress before him. In silence did he gaze at my body in the torchlight as if I were but another captive in his menagerie. "Unbind your hair," he commanded, and I reached up and uncoiled my hair, placing the pearl ornaments upon the floor. Then did my Lord smile upon me, but did not bid me lie down upon his sleeping mat. Bewildered at first, after a moment I felt a menacing in the air around me as if it hung in a vapor in the shadows of the chamber.

"Has your God, Quetzalcoatl, possessed you since the night I took you to wife?"

I looked with misery at the floor, for hollow had I been since my marriage night, and bereft of the sacred presence that had before run like golden blood inside my flesh. "No, my Lord, he has not."

Moteczoma was silent and watchful. When I raised my eyes to his face I saw he was well satisfied that this was so. "And has your shadow self returned to you?"

"I do not know, my Lord," I replied in truth, "I have not felt anything but emptiness and that my God is no longer within me."

He continued to stare upon me and to sit without stirring. I was made most uneasy by this and by the manner of his questioning and the menace I felt surrounding me. Suddenly my Lord struck his hands together. The door opened behind me and Moteczoma's favorite dwarf ran into the chamber and climbed like a child upon the Ueytlatoani's knee.

"Yes, my Lord?" he asked in a childish voice.

"Is the dish I requested now prepared?"

"Indeed it is so, my Lord.'"

"Bring it here."

The dwarf hurried from the chamber with a quick and curious glance upon me as he did. Soon did he return with a small golden bowl in his hands. My Lord told him to leave and he did, tumbling out as if this were but more entertainment for my Lord.

"Eat of this," Moteczoma commanded, holding the bowl out in one hand. I stepped near and took it from him. In it was something dark and shriveled and I hesitated to put it to my lips.

"I bid you eat."

The mushroom was dry and of noxious odor, and when I put it upon my tongue my mouth was filled with bitterness. Unease did mount within me to fearfulness, for I knew then what my Lord intended by this ritual. Bitterness spread from my mouth into my throat, and with it also spread a weakness and a sickening so that the golden bowl fell from my hands and rang loudly upon the stone.

As if this sound were a bidding, there emerged from the shadows of the room black-robed sorcerers hung with the sacred symbols of their craft and with the masks of fearsome beasts and Gods over their faces. They moved toward me in silence and when they were near I could see through holes the glittering of their eyes. With them came the scents of copal and fresh blood. A sorcerer with the mask of the dog-beast Xolotl, demonic shade to Quetzalcoatl's light, placed the palms of his hands over my eyes and I fell helpless into the arms of the sorcerers and into the very depths of their dark magic.

Carried forth into the night, it was as if I journeyed into the cold fires of Mictlan with the howling of men burning and being flayed by knives. My eyes did not regard those things that are above the earth but those that are below it; serpents with eyes of fire I saw, spitting venomous flame from their tongues. Beasts horrifying and hitherto unseen crowded around to devour me. Piece by piece my flesh was bitten from me until I was but bones and skull travelling alone through the night.

Hands were placed upon me then. I opened my eyes. Supported by the sorcerers, I saw unclearly that I stood at the foot of a great pyramid. In silence did the sorcerers support me up the many steps to the teocalli upon its peak. It looked to be quite dark, but as we drew nearer I could see a faint flickering within. At the entrance, the sorcerers withdrew their hands from me and I fell to my kneebones inside the entrance.

Before my eyes stood a statue of that beast, Xolotl, and behind him the monstrous figure of Coatlicue, Azteca Mother of Death, with her serpent heads and necklace of hearts and hands and skulls. Xolotl, with one eye dangling from its socket and mouth drooling, was no less frightful than the Goddess behind him. Fires in the braziers burned sluggishly, heaped as they were with many human hearts, and thick smoke rose so that the statues in this ghastly vapor seemed shrouded in the cloud and fire of a great and windless storm.

Suddenly, then, it seemed to me that stone was no longer stone, but quivering, living flesh. Xolotl's eyes turned to look upon me, and his mouth did gape wide. Inside that jaw, his face radiant, peered forth at me the twin, Quetzalcoatl, captive in the jaws of night yet robed with the splendor of the morning star. As he peered thus at me and with eyes as bright as jewels, I heard the murmurings of the sorcerers behind me. Smoke rose in heavier clouds as they chanted and the flames flickered higher, and the open jaws of Xolotl began to close.

I longed to cry out to my God not to return to the darkness but to shine forth in this, Xolotl's hour. But the chanting did increase and with it a low drumming, whether of my heart or something other, I did not know. The beast's jaws closed slowly and then was my God lost again to the darkness.

Xolotl, as if he were now but vapor also, grew dim and disappeared, leaving me at the huge clawed feet of Coatlicue, mother of Huitzilopochtli and also of Malinallxochitl and Coyolxauhqui, Goddess of the Moon. Spreading wide her legs, she crouched over and upon me so that I did enter her and become one with her. Slowly did I turn my face to the sorcerers, looking upon them from her monstrous eyes, and they did cease their chanting and were still, staring with white eyes at this Coatlicue I had become. Before their very gaze, then, did I turn from stone to flesh again. First upon me was the guise of a young girl with a sweet, flowerlike beauty and gentle manner; then, swiftly did I become abandoned woman, sensual, restless and cruel. For those sorcerers did I then turn priestess again, then Goddess, giver of fertility and all earthly abundance.

At last I could feel the chill of stone giving hardness to my bones and they did twist monsterlike as my fluid flesh shriveled into that of the most ancient crone, fearsome and destructive, enemy to all earth's blessings and devourer of men. Thus did I appear to the sorcerers as moon and woman, both, in all of her phases. The sorcerers fell to their knees and prayed for pity as the smoke from the braziers grew blacker yet, blinding my eyes. In the body of the Goddess, even as I was once Goddess of the Moon and sorceress Malinallxochitl, so did I feel myself grow small and living once again, mortal flesh from divine flesh, light from darkness. Through Coatlicue did I seek my way, and tight she held me in her black passage so that my flesh and bones did writhe through the very stone. At last did I emerge from her great body to lie as if dead upon the floor. In feverish haste the sorcerers gathered me up and wrapped me in a cape and carried me out into the night, back to the palace roof where my Lord Moteczoma awaited the results of their bewitchment.

"Has her shadow self returned to her?" I heard my Lord ask eagerly, "even as Quetzalcoatl to his twin?"

"It did not, Lord."

The moon was round and white above us. Suddenly one of my Lord's diviners cried out, "Look there, my Lord! Upon Coyoxauhqui's face!"

A dark star was passing slowly before the moon. It was the Morning Star of Quetzalcoatl, out of place at that time and most powerful augury. In great agitation, Moteczoma turned to his sorcerers and cried to them, anguished, "Is he not, then, to be stopped?"

And then Moteczoma knelt by my side and whispered sadly, "So you still serve him, even as you serve me?"

From a deathly weariness I whispered, "Even so, my Lord."

Slowly did our procession make its way down into the palace, and I was given to the women healers to bring strength back into my bones. And though life continued in all luxury after that night, there was a great change in my Lord Moteczoma, who in his thoughts grew strange and feverish. Often he needed me to stay by his side to comfort him, for he was now possessed by dreams and demons. In those hours I soothed him and urged that he, at last, welcome Quetzalcoatl's coming and with open arms and his heart rejoicing.

"It will be to welcome Death," he said once to me, turning his pale face sadly to the chamber wall.

20

MALINALLI

"I fear your men plot against you, my Captain."
"How do you know this?"
"I have heard words here and there. Some men are saying they have had enough of this adventure and wish to return to Cuba."
Cortés rose upon one elbow and looked at me with narrowed eyes. "Who is it that speaks so?"
"I have names of some of the men, but not yet that of the one who stirs this rebellion."
"Find out who chooses to betray us and bring me his name, Marina."
When it was dawn I made my silent way into the soldiers' encampment while my Captain met with the most trusted of his men, urging them to listen carefully and to bring him news of any who plotted against the success of their campaign. All swore most vigorously that they would do as he asked, that though they had themselves heard of no such treachery, they would gladly put to the sword any who did speak so.
"Only at my command, my friends," Cortés warned them with a smile.
We were at this time having successful dealings with the Totonacan people, and yet Cortés decided that we needed a fortress built beside the sea to protect us in the event of war and, perhaps, protect us from the traitors among us. Thus did we journey back from Quiahuitztlan with many Totonacan warriors to our first encampment beside the coast and there begin to build near the little village of Villa Rica de la Vera

Cruz. Cortés himself carried earth and stones upon his back, as did we all, and soon indeed did we have a mighty fortress with watchtowers and holes for his cannons.

During this time I watched and listened carefully, for I needed to find proof for my Captain of unrest and talk of treason. And I often went far from the shore to gather herbs and plants I needed for potions and enchantments, drying them carefully and wrapping them in cotton. If Aguilar or my Captain noticed what I was doing, I would say that I was collecting those herbs which gave strength to the weak and vigor to the ill.

"I trust there is no witchcraft in this, Marina?" my Captain once asked gravely.

"My Captain, I know nothing of sorcery," I smiled. "These are but women's simple remedies."

"Very well," he said, "but you should know that in Spain we put to death women who practice the unholy art of witchcraft."

"Then I will continue living, Captain," I replied lightly.

One day men came from Tenochtitlan. Four were caciques of high rank and two were male relatives of Moteczoma and were no more than boys. They brought gifts of gold and cotton cloth in gratitude, they said, for freeing Moteczoma's tax gatherers. Then they complained that we had encouraged rebellion against Moteczoma; he was greatly angered, they said, that some of his people now refused to pay tribute. Since Quetzalcoatl was of the lineage of Moteczoma, they asked, why did Quetzalcoatl stay in the houses of Totonacan traitors? I said what was needful for my Captain to know, and he replied that he had acted only as a servant for their great Lord and had kept guard over the other three tax gatherers so that they would not come to harm.

I interpreted thus: That our God protected these three Aztecas because he had come to this land in peace and not to make war, and that he would free them to the caciques' care. Then I turned to Cortés and said, "These men wish the return of the tax gatherers and when this is done they will leave and speak well of you in Tenochtitlan." Immediately, Cortés gave the order they be freed, and he sent soldiers to bring the captives forth.

"But tell these men, Marina," he added, "that I wish to complain about Cuitlalpitoc and how he left slyly in the night, and so we were forced to take shelter with the Totonacs." I interpreted this as he spoke, but not the rest of his speech, which was about how when we reached Tenochtitlan he would place himself most respectfully in Moteczoma's service and follow his wishes. I spoke other words of proud civility and the Azteca Lords bowed their heads in reverence to my Captain.

Necklaces of the green and blue stones were given to all, and they were pleased to have such sacred things. Then, to give the Aztecas more to tell their ruler, my Captain bade Alvarado and the other skillful horsemen to gallop dashingly along the shore, and daringly indeed did Alvarado make his animal rear and plunge so we could hear his horse snorting and making other sounds fearsome to the Azteca who still did not know if the beasts were flesh, or divine. With words of high honor to my Captain, and full of wonder at what they had seen that day, the caciques departed, bowing.

"It is fortunate for us that these heathen fear horses!" Cortés exclaimed after the caciques were gone.

"They have never known such things were on this earth, my Captain, and wonder if they are some kind of lordly beast."

Cortés laughed, "What savages these people truly are to see gods in every low and brutish thing. What an abomination they must be to the Lord our God and how desperately they need the salvation we bring."

His words stung. I could not tell if he saw me also in this way, as having but a brutish nature. Turning on his heel he walked away without knowing the pain he had given me. If he had known, perhaps still he would not have cared, I thought. I knew my power over him as his interpreter and the woman he sometimes desired in his bed, but he had never shown that he thought more of me than that. If only he would but once look at me with the eyes of Aguilar! But he did not. Often when he slept I would lie watching him, eager for words let slip from his dreams, eager for the sound of my name. But he kept his own counsel, however, awake and asleep, and said only what he chose.

At last I overheard the treasonous words I had been listening for. Swiftly did I hasten to tell my Captain that soldiers allied to his old enemy, Velasquez, were plotting to take one of the ships to Cuba. Cortés sent orders that these soldiers immediately present themselves to him. Proudly and with small respect they came, seven soldiers saying that they wanted no more of this expedition Cortés had forced upon them, but to return to their farms and homes in Cuba. They asked permission to depart with such stores of food as they would need for the journey.

Cortés looked at them as if he were surprised by what they said. "But we have a chance at great treasure, and if we leave we will never be able to return, for these Azteca will surely not let us land a second time."

The traitors replied, and with heat, that they were vastly outnumbered, that it was a mad scheme to undertake to subdue them all. Cortés, pretending their words did not distress him, continued to speak calmly. Though what they asked was desertion from their Kings's flag, he told them, he would still permit them to embark that day. They thanked him for this and eagerly made ready to sail.

When they had gone, Cortés turned to me. "Marina, go to Aguilar and Alvarado, and those others of my most trusted men. Tell them that I have permitted these seven men to desert our flag and our sacred endeavor and that they should come to me and plead for me not to permit this treason to occur. I, most unwillingly, will then revoke permission and command them to remain."

Aguilar and the other men came as my Captain had wished, all arguing most forcefully that our numbers not be diminished even by so few. Thus did Cortés revoke permission, and the seven were ordered from the ship and back under his command, where they were shamed by my Captain's men who called them cowards and other scornful names. I warned my Captain that he needed to watch these men most carefully, for if they would betray him once, so would they a second time. It would be easy for them, I said, to create unrest among his soldiers and so incite greater numbers to desert his cause. With this my Captain agreed.

The Spaniards were most courageous warriors, but easily swayed by thoughts of home. Soon there came to our ears more news of treachery, and Cortés ordered the same seven traitors arrested and brought before him, accusing them again of betrayal. Aguilar, for his part, told Cortés that he had heard they had planned that very night to embark for Cuba upon one of his ships. At Cortés' order, Aguilar wrote down their confessions, although they would only say that they wished to return to Cuba and to Velasquez' command, and that to speak thus freely was not treachery.

This was guilt enough, and Cortés ordered two of their number hung from a tree while the others of less consequence were lashed with a whip. The traitorous pilot, who had sailed one of my Captain's ships here, was taken to the central square and there his feet were cut from his ankles with a sword. After this was done, Cortés ordered all iron and other things of use and value to be removed from the ships and in the darkness he ordered Alvarado and a small group of men to set the ships on fire.

Well was I pleased to have those ships destroyed and my Captain firmly upon the land.

After prayers were said in the grey hours, we began

our march inland toward Tenochtitlan. There were some four hundred and more of my Captain's men and many Cempoallans did accompany us, as well as the women needed to grind maize and sleep with the soldiers who were their masters. Cortés rode his mare and sometimes I rode and sometimes I marched on foot beside Aguilar. First we came to the town of Jalapa, which was distant two days' march, and then to the fortress city of Socochima. In both cities my Captain insisted we set up crosses and tell the people of his Christian God, and in both cities I told the people what I always told them, that my Captain and his men were Lords and that this was the sacred sign of their passage. I told them Quetzalcoatl, this God now among them, wished only to be honored with fruit and flowers and that he most urgently demanded they cease their sacrifice of men. They bowed their heads in reverence, but whether or not they bowed them in obedience one could not have said. I was also much against such sacrifice, because of my father, yet I knew the Spaniards were moved to greater wrath when they saw evidence of that bloody ritual and were spurred more fervently onward.

Upon leaving Socochima, we began the long climb into the mountains. As it was the season of snow, that night ice dropped like stones from the sky and a rain fell that was no warmer. The wind cried down upon us from the mountainsides, moaning like the restless spirits of the dead. Men lay close to men if they could not lie with a woman, and my Captain kept me tight to his side and his hands warm upon my breasts. So did that bitter night pass. At morning light we marched on into wild lands where no one lived. Our supplies were low in the absence of those we depended upon to give us food to eat. The following night was the same and we shivered in a cold made colder yet by the emptiness of our bellies! As we climbed the mountain passes we found villages at last, but these had been abandoned and stripped of food. There was wood in the teocallis for the sacred fires and so my Captain and his soldiers in command warmed their bodies and those of their women.

We were relieved next day to find ourselves nearing a goodly-sized city, and my Captain commanded his men and the Cempoallans to march in good order and so as not to alarm the city's warriors. Glad were we to see a city so large and well-built, for there would be storehouses of grain, if nothing else, to ease our hunger. There were many teocallis and the grand dwellings of rich caciques, and the Spaniards gave to this city the name of Castilblanco because, they said, it reminded them of a city they knew in Spain.

If the city pleased Cortés and his men, even more were they pleased to find the people friendly, willingly leading us to warm quarters in which to pass the night and offering to us an abundance of good food. We all feasted until our bellies were as round as those of women bearing young. As we ate, the most important cacique of the city enthralled us with tales of Tenochtitlan, that great fortress reached only by three stone causeways with openings bridged by wooden planks that could be removed for the city's defence. Our men's eyes glittered when the cacique described Moteczoma's treasurehouse, how it was filled to its very roof with gold and jewels and other treasure past all imagining. At this my Captain and Alvarado, who sat nearby, looked upon each other with smiles and shining eyes.

My Captain bid me speak to the cacique in turn, and all about his Spanish King and his Christian God, and to beg them to desist from blood sacrifice, and all of these things that wearied and distressed me. I told them what was wiser for them to know. They bowed their heads and said nothing in their awe. While I told this cacique these things, so did the Cempoallans tell people of Castilblanco wondrous tales of these Lords come among them, so to win them more easily to our side. This was in part due to my cunning, for I had told the caciques from Cempoalla that it would be wise to put fear into the minds of all the people with tales of sorcery: our dogs were beasts that could kill any who annoyed them; our horses were even more powerful beasts who could run down any man no matter how swift; and the Lords could read men's thoughts as easily as if spoken aloud. These things the Cempoallans said, and other things also, about our magic weapons that spit death at anyone the Lords chose to kill. And with all of this the people were struck dumb with amazement.

In every city and village, I told the cacique, we were brought golden treasure. Why, I asked him, had we not received any from him? It amused me to see his face turn pale with dread, and he made haste to bid treasure be brought to us and laid at Quetzalcoatl's feet. There were golden necklaces and pendants and serpents fashioned artfully from gold, but it was gold of inferior quality and thus did not much impress my Captain. At last the cacique also presented us with four women for grinding maize and whatever else they were bid to do, and glad I was that they were ugly and all but one quite fat.

As we left that city, we marched through the sacred square where their teocallis were, and there we saw a great teponaztli with perhaps ten thousand skulls ranged upon it. Nearby was there also a mountain of thigh bones left from past sacrifice. This caused muttering and disapproval among the soldiers, but they marched in good order so as not to bring down upon us any disfavor.

It was my Captain's plan to gain the aid of all enemies of Moteczoma, and thus as we entered the land of the Tlaxcalteca, he hoped that we might pacify them before they could attack us. I knew not if they were awaiting Quetzalcoatl, or readying themselves for war, and as it would have been most unwise for me to go ahead and explain Cortés' presence, we made camp in a village where we were well treated.

Cortés sent forth from that village two Cempoallan caciques to Tlaxcala as messengers, and in their hands he put a letter he had written and a red hat such as they wore in Spain. I was content that my Captain wrote his letter as he wished, for it was not to be imagined that the Tlaxcalteca, anymore than the Cempoallan messengers, would see more than the meaningless scratches of chickens upon the paper. Of this Cortés was also well aware, but he explained that the paper might suggest to the Tlaxcalteca that our purpose was not to attack but to deliver an urgent message. Furthermore, he added, if they did attack, he would feel righteous in that he had attempted to do the proper thing in the eyes of his God.

"For truthfully, Marina, I do wish to bring to these savages not war, but word of our most Holy Lord and his Blessed Mother."

I lowered my eyes as if in respect, answering, "And good it is that you have come, my Captain, to save us from our savagery." At this he smiled upon me and was pleased, so he said, that the seeds of his words were planted in so fertile a soil as his faithful Marina.

Much to our disquiet, the messengers we had sent to Tlaxcala returned in fear and trembling to tell us that they had been seized as prisoners upon their arrival and had witnessed preparations for war. I told this to my Captain, who could see with his own eyes that these two warriors did not lie. They had easily escaped from the cage in which they had been placed as captives, and Cortés said of this, "I doubt the Tlaxcalteca are careless of prisoners. I would guess they saw to it that these men escaped so to bring to us news of their hostile intent."

Against the more than four hundred of our soldiers, and the scarce hundred or so Cempoallans and other allies that accompanied us, these messengers spoke of many thousands determined not only to kill us, but to eat our flesh and thus see what kind of Lords we had among us. The Tlaxcalteca believed, so said the messengers, that we were allies of Moteczoma and were coming in his name to destroy them. No words the caciques could say would convince the Tlaxcalteca how wrong they were. Cortés and his men were grave at this news, but valiantly indeed they behaved, offering up prayers to their God to help and protect them and give to their arms the strength they would need to defeat the heathen enemy. Then they unfurled their banner and marched on.

In time we came to a stone fortress, sturdily built. Cortés, well pleased, explained that such a fortress was excellently made for defense and that these Tlaxcalteca were likely to be great warriors, indeed. We rested awhile and gave water to our horses, and then Cortés climbed the fortress steps to speak to his men.

"Men," he cried, "let us follow our banner which bears the sign of the Holy Cross, and through it we shall conquer!" Thus he gave fresh vigor to his men. They gathered up their weapons and mounted their horses and all marched most cheerfully toward Tlaxcala. We had not gone a great distance before our scouts rode back. Tlaxcalteca spies were hidden nearby dressed in red and white and wearing black paint upon their faces and feather headdresses also. Cortés ordered the scouts to capture one of the warrior spies, and as protection for them he sent five horsemen. As these men approached the spies attacked and, battling furiously, wounded three of the horses. Riding back to report to Cortés, they told him, much to his displeasure, that they had been obliged, in the face of this spirited attack, to kill several of the Tlaxcalteca.

At the moment they said this, suddenly and without warning a sea of warriors rode down upon us from where they had been hiding in ambush in a ravine. I stayed behind with the other women upon a hill and from there could we see deadly combat. As our soldiers marched forth, so did the Tlaxcalteca run toward them with high and terrible screams, and more and more poured from that ravine until the ground was red and white with their vast numbers. Never did my Captain halt, however, nor did his men withdraw from the fray. Arrows flew in dark clouds from the Tlaxcalteca and they did great damage with their darts and yet worse with their macquauitls whose two sides were lined with obsidian flaked to the deadly sharpness of jaguar teeth. Our men battled most bravely, the smoke from their muskets filling the air and arrows from their crossbows whining like xexenes in flight and finding some of their targets with a fatal sting. Thus the battle continued until the fall of darkness and the Tlaxcalteca retreated, harried by our horsemen.

That night we made camp near a stream. Many men were wounded and the women cut open a dead Tlaxcaltecan, cutting the fat from inside his skin and melting it down to grease over the fire, and so with it and some cloth did we bind up the soldiers' wounds. There were dwellings abandoned nearby, but they had all been stripped of food and so we were hungry until, to our good fortune, their little dogs returned in the night to their masters' homes and our men killed them and roasted them over the fire. The Spaniards were not well pleased with roasted dog, for they said they raised them not for food but for sport in their country, but they ate them nonetheless, and even gnawed the bones of their tails! I am not sure what many of the common soldiers and our Mexica allies ate, for there was not dogmeat enough for all. I do know my Captain and myself, as well as many of the men closest to him, had meat enough to still the ache of hunger.

Soldiers that night slept ready for battle and the horses were kept bitted and saddled. But it was not until daylight, after we had arisen and marched on, that we met again to do battle. Vast numbers of Tlaxcalteca had ambushed us the day before, but now we saw twice that many and more, running toward us with fearsome cries and beating upon their drums and blowing the warning of doom upon their conch shells. Cortés sent three captives he had taken the day before to the Tlaxcalteca with words of peace, but the enemy paid no heed and came steadfastly on. Cortés then shouted, "Santiago, and at them!" and charged forth upon his horse, followed by his men.

From the plain came the sounds of war and the screams and cries of the warriors, and as I watched with the women we saw our soldiers press upon the enemy, driving them before them like beasts. But this was only the demonic cunning of the Tlaxcalteca, for as our men pursued them into land uneven with great rocks and ravines, so did the Tlaxcalteca in treachery rise from those ravines in numberless numbers. Even from a distance the noise of battle was deafening as hundreds upon hundreds of warriors swarmed from their hiding places and onto the rocky ground where they massed around the few hundred of our men who fought to gain more level ground ahead. Due to my Captain's wisdom, they kept together and even the horses were not let to charge from the ranks. Thus they battled on without faltering.

Later I learned that one mare had been killed and her head cut from her body, and that her flesh and even her iron shoes were taken for sacrifice, but her rider was, by our soldiers' fierce defense, saved from death. It was our great fortune to kill many sons of Tlaxcalteca caciques, putting an early end to the fighting as they retreated in good order to take counsel among themselves.

We withdrew to take shelter in and around some teocallis nearby, and that night the men slept like the dead in their great weariness. The women were posted to watch for the enemy to advance, but it was a night of most welcome quiet. I watched from the roof of a teocalli, while other women of less importance were sent further afield and yet not so far that they could not swiftly return if the enemy were sighted. Most able and courageous were our men, but I doubt they could have arisen from their hard beds had our enemy come upon us, so tired were they.

Daylight brought another battle. We managed as always to take captives, but we did not know the number of enemy dead or wounded because these had been taken from the battlefield by the Tlaxcalteca—so that, perhaps, we could not strengthen ourselves with their flesh and blood. Thus passed another night and then a day in which it was deemed necessary by Cortés that weapons be cleaned and repaired and his soldiers rest. It was to our fortune, indeed, that the Tlaxcalteca did not appear and force us into battle. After this day of rest, Cortés decided he could not allow the enemy to think our men weary and thus easy sport, and so he ordered two hundred of our fittest soldiers and all of our allies to march forth with seven horsemen and a few musketeers and crossbowmen. I accompanied my Captain this time, as did Aguilar.

We came upon towns and took captives, but Cortés ordered us to treat them with kindness and not to kill them or abuse them in anyway. Yet when it came to his ear that our allies were burning the towns behind us and carrying off dogs and fowl for food, he sighed, "Well, they must be satisfied with some spoils of war, or otherwise they might decide it more to their liking to return to the safety of home." And so he let them continue on in this way. However, he was stern with his own men and forbade them to do likewise.

Back in camp, my Captain ordered the captives to be set free. Food was brought for them at his command, and necklaces of stones were given to them also. He bid me say to them that we had come in peace and it was but peace we were seeking. Then he sent them forth to the Tlaxcalteca camp with this message, that we only sought passage through their lands to the lands of the Azteca, there to see Moteczoma. These messengers did as they were bid, but in turn they were sent back to us with a message from the warrior son of a great cacique, Xicotencatl. He bid them say to us—and this time I told my Captain the whole truth—that he would like to see us in his father's city; the peace we sought would be gained by their feasting upon our flesh and paying honor to their Gods with our bloody hearts.

Cortés was gravely angered by such an arrogant and warlike message, but to the messengers he spoke in all kindness, giving to them more necklaces, saying he would send them back to their master, Xicotencatl, as messengers of peace. Then he asked them questions and thus did we learn the Tlaxcalteca had even more warriors ready for combat than they had before and that five caciques from other places had brought with them ten thousand warriors each. Fifty thousand men were now armed against us. My Captain did not believe this, thinking it was only through Xicotencatl's cunning that these messengers told us what they did and so we would lose courage and retreat. Still he treated these Tlaxcalteca with generosity and let them return to their encampment unmolested.

Our men spent that night with the priests, confessing their sins so that their God would forgive them if they should die and not send them to burn forever in a place they called Hell that was underground, even as Mictlan, though one was hot and the other cold. My Captain also confessed and that night he did not mount me, nor did any of the other men take the bodies of their women because, we women had been told, if they did so they would go to Hell if they died on the battlefield next day. Even though we had been baptized, Aguilar explained, we were not joined to the men in marriage and in the sight of their God, and thus we would bring grievous sin upon the men and make them unclean if they put their tepulis inside us. My Captain still kept his hands warm upon my breasts, but nothing more than this.

The rising sun found all our men, even the wounded, readying themselves to do battle; but one man remained behind with the women and his wounds were so grievous that he later died. This battle turned out to be the most ferocious of all we had endured. Cortés kept his soldiers in their ranks most wonderfully, although there were those who did not stay so and thus could enemy warriors get close enough to do damage. Yet, as my Captain told me later, their wondrous swordplay was of greater skill than ever before that day. Many of the Tlaxcalteca were disemboweled or their heads cut from their bodies with but one mighty thrust.

Even with this uncommon skill, our soldiers and allies were a pitiful number against the multitudes ranged against us. Nonetheless, toward the close of that day the enemy began to withdraw from the battlefield, and it was curious they did so for light still remained in the sky. Our men did not follow them in their retreat. Cortés ordered them all, half dead upon their feet, to withdraw as well and though several of our best horsemen advanced to defend our tanks, they soon returned also to camp. After the brutality of that battle, it seemed a wonder that but one soldier had been killed and sixty wounded. All of the horses had been wounded likewise, but all were yet fit for riding, which seemed most amazing good fortune. Cortés with all of his men fell to their knees and offered thanks to their God, and I did likewise, for such reverence pleased my Captain. We buried our dead in a sacred cave beneath a pyramid and covered the entrance with dirt so that, my Captain said, the man would not be defiled by the Tlaxcalteca savages.

Then did I say to my Captain that it might well be of benefit if our enemies did not think us mere men of flesh and blood, and that after they saw our soldiers' skillful and courageous fighting it might well suit him if they believed the Spaniards gifted with Godlike power. Thus burying our dead, I told him, would serve two purposes. Before this day, my Captain would have seen no sense in this, but now he gravely considered my words and said, "You may speak sense, Marina. Such a credulous belief, were it sowed among them, might well give them reason enough to cease forcing these battles upon us."

Greatly was I pleased with the success of my cunning. Soon we would be in Tenochtitlan, if we were not killed first, and by then it would be of vital importance that Cortés present himself to Moteczoma, if not as a God, then as a man with Godlike power. No matter how many thousands might speak of him as a Lord, my Captain had to conduct himself as one or all was lost.

"Some indeed believe," I added cautiously, "that you might be the God that has long been foretold would return to these lands and in this very year."

Cortés looked at me in disbelief and shook his head. "Surely these barbarians do not expect God to walk upon this earth as but a lowly man!"

"But many *do* believe this," I replied, "and many might well wonder if you are that God. Indeed I have heard it spoken even among your allies, the Cempoallans, that they follow you because they believe you and your soldiers to be Lords returning from what you in your religion call Heaven."

His eyes narrowed with this new thought. I waited breathlessly to see if he would gain from it suspicion of me as truthful interpreter of his words. Furious would he be, I knew, if he ever discovered it was I who not only had pacified my people, but had encouraged my Captain with lies to persuade him to stay and seek Moteczoma's treasure in Tenochtitlan.

"This seems heathen foolishness, and perhaps sacrilege as well. However . . ." and he looked past me and over to where hills hid the Tlaxcalteca hordes, "I think it could be most fortunate if the enemy did not see our small army as mortal men. After all," he added, and looked at me with a wink of one eye, "there are as many ways to wage war as there are to wage the act of love. And well do *you* indeed know that, Marina!" He laughed and I laughed with him, full of joy that he would do as I wished and that he did not suspect my cunning.

It was fiercely cold that night, with a wind that blew

upon us from the snow. Our men covered themselves as best they could with rags and their weapons to keep from freezing. It was far into that night that I finally slept even as did my Captain in my arms, and I awoke to the morning with a most hopeful heart.

Three caciques we had captured the day before were sent with messages to the Tlaxcalteca encampment. I told them that the Lords were most impatient with the manner in which they were being treated in these lands and if they were not soon given due reverence, they would put all men, women and children to death. If they obeyed Quetzalcoatl in this, I said, he would be well-disposed toward them and would lend them his protection.

The horses stamped fretfully and with jingling harness, standing through all those hours, waiting impatiently as did we all. No messengers returned from the Tlaxcalteca, however, and as darkness fell Cortés ordered his men to remain ready for battle all through the night. The women and some soldiers were posted guard, and as I was one of these, the night hours passed slowly indeed and with every sound like musketfire. The moon rose. From the north and the west came men running, calling out as they ran that the Tlaxcalteca were advancing upon us in great numbers. Hurriedly we gathered together and did what we could to get the weapons and horses into our soldiers' hands. Also we let loose our dogs to frighten the approaching enemy.

"Be careful, my Captain," I said, but he laughed and put his hand upon my shoulder.

"If I were a careful man, Marina, I would still be in Spain." He leapt upon his mare, then directed his soldiers where they were to meet the Tlaxcalteca, all of them marching into the darkness, leaving behind the women to stamp out our fires and to await what was to be. Most of us waited in silence, listening to the progress of the battle we could not see. I wished with all of my heart that I could also fight, and I longed for a bow or a musket or even a small obsidian dagger in my hand. All I could have asked of this life was to be at my Captain's side, where I belonged. In my thoughts I saw myself slay those enemy warriors who came against him and so save his life with my own hands.

The Tlaxcalteca had surrounded us on four sides, three of the sides armed with arrows and spears and the fourth armed with the deadly macquauitls. This flank attacked so suddenly that our men scarce had time to dispatch a number of soldiers in defense.

The battle was over quite as suddenly as it had begun, and the Tlaxcalteca melted away into the night. Many of our men were most grievously wounded; all gave thanks to their God that but two Cempoallans had been killed and not one of our own men. After prayers the women were told to bury the dead and, while they did so, I bound up the wounded arm of Aguilar and the leg of my Captain with rags and the grease of a dead Tlaxcaltecan. We slept what remained of that night and at dawn we found most of our men had been wounded and some more than once.

There was muttering in the camp that day and solemn discussion. Many men came to Cortés protesting to him that they were weary of fighting, and if they found the Tlaxcalteca so difficult to subdue, then what of the vaster numbers Moteczoma must command? They were all suffering in one way or another, with wounds or fevers or the flux, and the chill of the nights sickened them more. Cortés, who had also awakened with a fever, listened courteously to all who came to him. After those who complained came men of more courage, Diaz and Alvarado and others, cheering him with words of valorous intent. I spoke when all else were finally silent, saying that it might suit our cause to send the captives we had taken in battle back to their army with words of peace and dire warning. With this my Captain did agree and thus were they sent forth to Xicotencatl's camp.

Two days passed without incident. We made good use of this time, all the while readying ourselves for battle. The women healed the soldiers with herbs and potions and I stayed close to my Captain to heal him with all of my skill. Aguilar I also healed, and gratitude was in his eyes when his fever cooled and his wounds ceased to bleed and ache.

"If I didn't know you for a Christian woman, Marina," he said to me with a weary smile, "I would think you mistress of witchcraft's black art, indeed!"

Upon the third day it was agreed among the men to march by night to the nearest town, not to kill but to seek food, taking our strongest men and musketeers and crossbowmen. Aguilar and I also rode that night. As usual, when peace or necessity allowed me a horse to ride, I was given the tamest and oldest of the beasts, and though I sat her well, still I had an uneasiness in my heart lest she should bolt out from under me in the darkness. We marched without harm, and after a short while we came to the town of Tzumpantzingo in the first light of day.

What terror we caused as we entered that city! Men and women fled, screaming that the Lords had come to kill them all, and children wandered lost in the streets and weeping. Cortés ordered us to halt in the square until it was full light. Priests came to us then, and ancient men and the oldest caciques, and in fear and reverence they bowed down and touched dirt upon their tongues. Cortés spoke to them gently, saying we had come in peace. Though these were great Lords, I told the Tzumpantzingo, while they walked the earth they needed to eat food even as mortal men, and so we required enough to feed us all. Relieved, the people eagerly agreed, and brought fowl to us and two women to grind maize and make tortillas. The caciques promised to send more food as soon as their people returned from hiding. Cortés thanked them and gave them the necklaces of stones, bidding them go to the Tlaxcalteca and sue for peace or else be swept from the face of the earth.

We returned to our camp, to more grumbling and disorder among the men. Many came to speak to Cortés, and I stayed close enough to hear their words and my Captain's soft replies. They longed to return to Villa Rica, they said, where the land was at peace. They wished to return to their homes and lands on Cuba and never again see another battle like the ones they had been fighting. To all of this my Captain listened, waiting patiently for them to finish. Then he told them gently that we would march forward, nonetheless, and any refusing to do so would be shot. Though still some of the men were angry and afraid, all yet agreed to continue on and not to falter in their holy purpose.

The following day, Xicotencatl sent forty slaves laden with baskets of fruit, cages of birds and also four old and ugly women. One of the men carried a message from his master. "My Lord," he said respectfully, "Xicotencatl, great cacique of Tlaxcala, bids you eat of this food. And he does say that if you are indeed Gods, then sacrifice these women and eat heartily of their flesh and blood. But if you are mortal men, then eat of this fruit and fowl."

Cortés, angered by these words, bid me most unwisely to say that they were not barbarous savages, but Christian men, and though they were not Gods, still did they come in peace and with the word of God. His words made grave my heart, for I had thought him well persuaded to pretend to be Gods and thus to subdue the many thousands ranged against us. I did not say what he bid me, for that would surely do nothing but condemn us all to death. Thus, said I, Xicotencatl knew well that human sacrifice was sacrilege to Quetzalcoatl, and why did the Tlaxcalteca persist in their irreverence? To this the slave said nothing.

For that day and the following night these Tlaxcalteca stayed in our camp as if it were their intention never to leave. Full of suspicion as to their purpose, I went to the Cempoallans and asked for someone to discover for me what it was they sought. It was nightfall when I took my accustomed walk through the soldiers' camp, and that of the Cempoallans also, to hear if anything of interest was being said. There did a Cempoallan sidle up to me, bidding me walk with him into the gathering shadows outside camp. The Tlaxcalteca were spies, he whispered, sent by Xicotencatl. It was their purpose to see if the strangers were Gods or men. Some had already left our camp with news and others had slipped in to take their places, seeking to learn yet more.

A spy had confided in the Cempoallan that the sorcerers and priests of Tlaxcala had sought for an answer in the sky and in their magic had divined that we were not Gods but men who ate fowl and fruit and the flesh of dogs. Sorcery had brought them knowledge that we could only be defeated in the night, and that was why they had attacked us at that hour. Xicotencatl even now awaited the news he sought and when he had fully decided we were not Gods, then would he again attack us with many thousands of warriors and not cease until every one of us was either slain or taken captive.

Giving the Cempoallan a necklace in gratitude for his day's work, I hastened to my Captain with this unsettling news. "Tell our allies to keep lookout for these spies," he said, "even as I will tell my men to be on the alert."

When this was done, Cortés requested Aguilar and me to choose two of the most honest-seeming of the Tlaxcalteca, which was a most difficult task indeed. But we did so, bringing them before Cortés who told me to ask them if they were spies, as we had been told. "Beware!" I warned them in a dire voice. "Our God knows that you are spies for your master, Xicotencatl, and if you do not confess and do penance for this grave sacrilege, surely will he torture you as you stand with bolts of fire and knives from the heavens!" The two quaked at my words, admitting that yes, they were spies, even as the God had divined. They were to return to their master, they confessed, with proofs that we were not Gods, and the Tlaxcalteca would attack us and slay us all. Cortés was white with fury. Crossing himself and muttering prayers, he sent for seventeen of the Tlaxcalteca spies to be taken captive. Then he ordered some to have their hands cut off and some to lose thumbs and fingers, and all of these he sent forth, clutching at the stumps of their hands to staunch the bleeding, back to their master's camp.

Afterward we heard that even at the very moment Xicotencatl was poised to march upon us, when he saw these spies come stumbling into camp he did not know what to do. He lost courage because of what he thought was our divine wisdom. Thus Xicotencatl, once our most steadfast enemy among all of the Tlaxcalteca caciques, sought to make peace, as did the other great caciques of that land. So ended in triumph our war with Tlaxcala. With all reverence were we then given food, our enemies bowing before us swearing to be our allies and most obedient servants.

The Ueytlatoani Moteczoma, filled with dread at our triumph over the thousands of warriors that had come against our small number, again sent to us treasure. Gold of most wondrous shape did he send, and jeweled ornaments, and also twenty loads of the finest cotton cloth, some of it sewn skillfully with bright feathers. His message was that this treasure was to do us honor and that he would give us yearly tribute of gold, silver, and chalchuite stones and what else the Lords did demand, but only if we advanced no further toward Tenochtitlan. The land before us was rough and wild, his message warned, and though it would have been honor indeed to meet with so mighty a host of Lords, still he did not wish to see such venerable Gods suffer the hardships of such a long journey.

I told all this to Cortés and he looked upon me and

asked, "So they do, even Moteczoma, believe me to be a God?"

"They do, my Captain," I replied, "and I most strongly doubt that we would be suffered to live if ever they learned the truth."

He sighed. "So be it. I pray that this will not offend God, our Father, and bring defeat upon us."

"Do not fear, my Captain. If your God truly wishes for his word to be spoken to the people of this land, then surely he will not be angered by the means by which you accomplish his desire."

"I am grateful to you, Doña Marina," he said, narrowing his eyes, "and yet it seems you might bear watching."

I smiled, though my heart was tight with dismay to hear his doubting words. "My Captain, you know I would willingly die at your command."

His face softened and he reached to put a gentle hand on my shoulder. "Forgive me, Marina, I spoke in haste. The strain of battle has disordered my wits. Well do I know you are the most loyal of women."

"Never do you need to seek *my* forgiveness," I said with a lightened heart. "It is already given and for whatever it is you do."

Thus we came to a fortunate understanding, and my Captain dealt with the messengers in a lordly manner, taking counsel with the Tlaxcalteca caciques with the arrogance of a God. Days passed in a long march and finally we reached the great city of their land where we were feasted and honored. Treasure was given us and also some beautiful daughters of caciques. Though the most beautiful cacica of all was given my Captain, he looked smilingly upon me and said, "I have Marina, and need no woman more." And I grew faint with pleasure and delight.

Alvarado was given this woman, instead, and the others were also bestowed after they had been baptized and made clean for us. The caciques said to me, "Malintzin, we do wish for our daughters to bear the sons of these mighty Lords, and so truly we might be brothers." Weeping with fear, for they were but maidens and thought they would die in coupling with Gods, the cacicas went to where they now belonged and submitted to the will of their new masters. Alvarado's woman was given the name of Doña Luisa, and a great cacica was she, indeed. With almost my own fierceness did she soon care for her master, but this made small difference in her master's desire, for he still pursued me and took other women to bed whenever he wished. Doña Luisa was willfully blind to this and thus he treated her well, and though he beat the bodies of other women, her he treated with respect.

We listened to the tales of the Tlaxcalteca in which they told us about their wars with the Azteca and about Tenochtitlan and the treasure to be found there. They told us that once the Tlaxcalteca had been giants, and for proof they showed us great bones they had found rotting to dust in the earth. Indeed these bones were huge and Cortés asked for one so he could send it to his King, so I asked for the greatest bone and told them it would be taken someday to the heavens from which our God and his Lords had come. They most eagerly chose the bone of largest size, presenting it to us with solemn pleasure.

Several days we spent in that city, resting and feasting, and only once was there a moment of disquiet. My Captain asked the caciques to destroy their idols and teocallis and in future worship only the Blessed Trinity. This I said in careful words and even still were the caciques distressed. "Malintzin," they protested, "you have only just now come before us and into our city. We know your God and his Lords are good, even as you are good, but they ask too soon that we give up worship of the Gods we have venerated through all time. Please beg of your God that he allow us to worship them still, or we will live in dread of their divine anger!"

"They know all the people of this land will rise up

against them," I said to my Captain, "and against you if you demand this of them." He pondered the wisdom of this, decreeing at last that the priests must only whitewash and make clean one teocalli for him, and so this was done. Narrow indeed was that passage, but well-content was I that we had passed so smoothly through it!

21

Xochitl

By my Lord Moteczoma's side I learned the ways of rulers and how it was they had power over their people. Lords of the Triple Alliance, the Lords of Tlacopan and Texcoco, did attend my Lord, and also did they summon to his chamber Cuauhtémoc, Lord of Tlatelolco, and Cuitláhuac of Ixtapalapan, one of these last warrior Lords most likely to rule if Lord Moteczoma died.

To my amazement, not only did these loyal Lords take common counsel, but there were also Lords from distant parts of Anáhuac, named "Enemies of the House," who often stayed at the palace of my Lord to take counsel with him, also. Thus did I hear them speak of Flowery Wars among themselves, arranging days for battle so captive warriors might be obtained for sacrifice to the Azteca Gods. Passionlessly were these battles arranged and as if they were to be no more grave than games of tlachtli—as if the losing side were to lose but one warrior, and not hundreds. My father's face was clear before me at these times. So had he, I supposed, been taken from us in a battle not fought between enemies, but arranged coldheartedly by rulers pretending to the people that the battles were honestly fought.

The priests in counsel with Moteczoma often complained that Tezcatlipoca and Huitzilopochtli were hungry for warrior hearts and that many must be captured for sacrifice. The Lords always agreed, rubbing their hands, though my Lord Moteczoma wavered and looked sidelong at me. I had always been scornful about the insistence of the priests that so many must die to feed the Gods, and this remorseless hunger of Tezcatlipoca and Huitzilopochtli seemed more the hunger of the priests who served them. As I increased in power at my Lord's side, so did I also understand more the nature of power, feeling even within myself how power could take root and grow. These Lords spoke calmly about the numbers to die, but never did I hear them speak of how honorable it was for the warriors to die thus. They agreed upon the number of warriors to be taken captive, and a day when the armies would meet, and then slaves were summoned to bring these weary Lords cacao. All having been completed to their satisfaction, they drank and smoked their little pipes and smiled.

One day when a battle had thus been arranged between the armies of Texcoco and Tenochtitlan, I took my anger with me into the palace gardens. With disordered mind I made my way along the paths through the fountains and trees and flowers, and saw nothing. For many months had I once been priestess, but now I wondered what was ordained by the Gods and what was merely the plotting of those men who ruled over us.

I had not felt Quetzalcoatl's presence for many days, and even when I beseeched him, he came not. Had I, albeit against my will, forsaken him by my marriage—or had he forsaken me? Once had he possessed me and given me dreams, but now my heart was swollen with pain and doubt. Once it seemed I knew something of this world and, if not content with it, still had accepted what it was. I knew life meant little and death, surrounding us like the very air we breathed, had meaning only for those who died in ways pleasing to the Gods—otherwise life and death were nothing but empty plains one traversed endlessly and without purpose. To love and honor our Gods was all we had the power to do to ensure that rain and warmth and harvests would keep us alive to do further worship. This had I known, this accepted.

But now my thoughts were in ferment. I had given my life to my God, Quetzalcoatl, and suffered much. Now in my extremity, when I cried most desperately to him, he turned away his face. I was taught at my mother's knee that he was a merciful, loving God, hating all sacrifice but the fruits and flowers and butterflies of this earth, that he cared for us as his children and sought to give us lives of peace and plenty. When all was taken from me in slavery and my body defiled, it had been he who had taken pity upon me and healed my body and the spirit it contained, and though he had used me with divine violence, so had he filled me with his peace.

Where had he gone? Was he marching toward Tenochtitlan to save us as his children or to destroy us? Either way, willingly would I have rushed forth to greet him. With all my heart would I have run to kneel at his feet, begging him not to forsake me, that though my body might be used as that of any woman, my maiden heart still belonged to him. I sighed, weary of the weight of my thoughts, and sat down upon a bench in the shadow of the trees.

"You are weary of warriors' talk, Lady Xochitlzin?" The voice came suddenly and most unwelcome to my ears, and I looked up to see Lord Cuauhtémoc before me. His brow furrowed at the look in my eyes.

"Yes, Lord, I am weary, but not from the talk of warriors."

"Then someone has been unkind? Some favor refused you?" And he spoke with the indulgent voice of a man to a spoiled child.

"No, my Lord," I said, and the anger in my heart crept out upon my tongue, "I do not sigh over trifles."

I could see he was taken aback by this small show of anger, and that he curbed his impulse to speak in kind. Also did I see curiosity on his face, for never had he seen me without my mask of cold reserve. That I would come into the garden with a heavy heart intrigued him in spite of his dislike for a woman whose beliefs were both influential and contrary to his own.

"Then for what matter of grave consequence are you so distressed?" Though he spoke mockingly, still could I tell he was curious to know.

"Perhaps from weariness, Lord, as you suggest." With this I hoped to put an end to an unwelcome conversation.

Raising an eyebrow at my discourtesy, he spoke again more coldly. "Perhaps my Lady, even in her great weariness, might explain to me why it is you still seek to persuade the Ueytlatoani that the army even now advancing upon us is not an army of men? The tale of Quetzalcoatl is an old and pretty fable, and one held dear by women such as yourself, but why should all of us face war because of ancient prophecy?"

"Do you believe the tale a false one, Lord Cuauhtémoc?" I asked him, matching ice with ice. "That Quetzalcoatl never lived upon this earth and thus never will return to it?"

"I do not know what I believe, Lady, not being either priest or sorcerer. But I *am* a warrior, and I do know more of men than ever a woman could."

"I am not so sure a woman does not have equal sight, if from unequal vantage point, my Lord. I also could say to you that I know men as *you* do not."

"You are bold in speech, Lady Xochitlzin."

"I have learned well that it serves women ill to remain speechless or to but echo their masters' words."

Cuauhtémoc leaned against a tree and, crossing his arms over his chest, stood regarding me as if I were a new oddity in the menagerie. "I cannot say that I agree with you, if your speech to your Lord and to me is any example."

Words came hotly to my lips and I rose to my feet that I might stand before him eye to eye. "And I tell *you*, Lord, that with every bit of my flesh and with all the conviction of my heart, it is a God who marches even now toward Tenochtitlan!"

"You have seen him and his retinue," Cuauhtémoc said mockingly, "even as you see me here before you?"

I held up my chin and gave him look for look. "Not in this way, my Lord. But I have seen much else, and all betoken his coming. Have you forgotten the fire in the sky and the stone that fell into the conduit, and did you not feel the earth move and see that the sculpture of my Lord Moteczoma cracked upon the cliff of Chapultepec where it was carved?"

"Yes, all of these things, even as you say. But I differ from you and believe they foretell disaster to us, a disaster that will surely befall us if we remain beguiled by your pretty fables."

"What you say is untrue. Lord Moteczoma knows, also, what you say is untrue."

"The Ueytlatoani has lost courage along with his clear vision, I fear. He sits listening to women's tales while he should be paying heed to the counsel of his fellow Lords. Sorcery has shown five hundred years of sorrow for our people if Anáhuac is destroyed. I believe you to be most gravely misled in your fancy, and that you mislead our Lord most grievously as well."

"You would be wise to guard your speech," I warned him angrily. "Moteczoma is Ueytlatoani still, remember."

Cuauhtémoc straightened in wrath at my words and spoke to me sharply and with eyes hard and black, "I forget *nothing,* Lady. Be on your guard as well."

He turned from me then and walked away, and I felt a chill foreboding. A man not given to religious piety, but with eyes fixed upon the Ueytlatoani's icpalli, might well make good the threat in his words. Well would it serve me, indeed, to be watchful.

Long did I wander in the palace gardens that day, and with thoughts like wild birds flying. Though I did not still see Quetzalcoatl marching in my dreams, yet could I allow no suspicion to enter my mind that it was not he who was on his way to save us from the endless bloodshed of the Azteca. And yet the question raised its serpent head again and again: Did I believe in Quetzalcoatl's coming because I was desperate to believe, or because it was true? Surely I had seen it in my swooning dreams, and surely I had not seen only the destruction of an empire but the purification of it as well. Through fire would we be cleansed and our God once more among us. Surely that was what my God had told me in my visions.

My God, I prayed there in the garden, do not forsake us.

That very night, Cuauhtémoc asked entry to my Lord's private chamber, and there spoke with him in the strongest words he dared. He glanced not once at me, but kept his eyes most respectfully upon the ground at the feet of Moteczoma. "Mighty Lord," he began, then fell silent, awaiting permission to continue.

"Yes, Lord Cuauhtémoc? Why do you disturb me thus and in the privacy of my chamber?"

"I seek to have words with you alone, my Lord."

"My Lady Xochitlzin is privy to all. You may speak before her even as you do before me."

Cuauhtémoc hesitated, but the finality in my Lord Moteczoma's voice did not escape him. "As you wish, my Lord. The army that does even now approach us . . ."

"The coming of our God, as foretold," Moteczoma broke into his speech, but in that slightly mocking manner that suggested he perhaps did not fully believe what he said.

"As you wish," Cuauhtémoc repeated. "You have heard of the battle with Tlaxcala in which the strangers' army did triumph and thus bring to their side our great enemy, the Tlaxcalteca?"

"Indeed so, Lord Cuauhtémoc, even as did you today."

"Messengers have just arrived who await audience

with you. They bring with them news of great interest, Lord."

"It is late and I am weary, can this news not wait until morning?"

I could feel Cuauhtémoc's attention briefly rest upon me and heavy it was with import. Then he turned it once more to Moteczoma, to whom he then spoke. "Several of our warriors did we send to Tlaxcala dressed as Tlaxcalteca warriors. After the battle had been fought, they were able to search the battlefield. In this way did they find the bodies of some of the God's slain warriors, and one of their beasts likewise slain. They cut from them their heads and hastened with them here, my Lord. Do you wish to see them?"

Moteczoma's voice quickened with interest. "Indeed would I so, Cuauhtémoc. Have them brought immediately."

Three messengers entered the chamber at Cuauhtémoc's bidding, holding in their hands woven baskets. Out of one did they lift a head, the hair upon it short and brown in color, the skin of the face and severed neck pale and heavily-bearded, even as the face and neck of our God Quetzalcoatl was foretold to be. A second bearded head was much the same only its eyes were open due to the suddenness with which death had come. The eyes were as blue as those of an albino. The third basket, much larger than the others, contained the great head of a monstrous beast. My Lord and I drew near to marvel upon it. Long was its nose and not dissimilar to that of a deer but not so delicate of bone. Long hair hung down between its ears and down along its powerful neck. One of the messengers pulled back the lips of its mouth and we could see teeth large in size and square in shape.

Moteczoma's chamber now reeked of bloody flesh on the verge of rotting, and so my Lord held a bouquet of flowers to his nose and bid the messengers take the heads away and clean them and then place them on the teponaztli rack with the other skulls. We were silent then a long moment, with both Lords contemplating what now to do.

"Think you," Lord Cuauhtémoc first took breath to say, "that those heads, however strange of shape or color, are yet those of Gods and their divine beasts?" He fell silent and was watchful.

My Lord Moteczoma glanced sidelong at me and then sighed and regarded Cuauhtémoc severely. "And dare you think them but the heads of mere men and mere beast?"

"I do, indeed, my Lord," Cuauhtémoc replied.

"Though they have a most unfamiliar aspect, yet they do also seem to be but flesh and blood." Moteczoma sat down upon his icpalli in deep thought. "Perhaps our God rides with mere men to allow them the glory of sacrificing themselves in his name. Do you not agree this might be so, Cuauhtémoc?"

I longed to speak, but it was not proper when men were in counsel together, for my thoughts were a woman's thoughts and unworthy of being considered alongside the thoughts of men.

"All is possible, my Lord," Cuauhtémoc said and in all deference, "but it also is true that prophecies might have been gravely misread. These may all be mere men, however fierce and strange, who have entered our lands easily because we fear a God may be among them."

My Lord Moteczoma rose from his icpalli and paced the chamber in that way he had when his mind was in a ferment and his thoughts led him one way and then another. "But . . . if it is indeed false that any of these men are Gods, and Quetzalcoatl is not among them, then this army seeks to destroy Tenochtitlan. And with the aid of our enemies."

"Yes, my Lord. I believe what you say to be truth." Cuauhtémoc shot me a look of triumph and contempt.

"I do not know what now to believe, Cuauhtémoc!" my Lord exclaimed in great agitation. "My sorcerers and sages have all foretold that in this year, One-Reed, would the God return to us. It would plainly be greatest sacrilege not to welcome him with all honor. And yet, if you and the other Lords are correct and my sorcerers wrong, then we lie like a woman before her master, submissive to the strangers' will."

"Exactly so, Lord," Cuauhtémoc said smoothly and without eagerness. "This is an empire founded not upon the humility and compliance of women and their meek Gods and Goddesses, but upon Tezcatlipoca who gave us power, with Huitzilopochtli, over all others in this land when we came from Aztlán. It was not with the power of Quetzalcoatl you became Ueytlatoani of all these lands and peoples, but with the warrior might of Tezcatlipoca and all the forces of night that do attend him."

Indecisive as he often was in those days, Moteczoma paced, his words first for one side and then for the other. Unwilling was he to offend either God, the one of his mighty empire or the one from whom he had descended as Azteca Lord. The shadows of Tezcatlipoca gathered in that chamber and also the morning light of Quetzalcoatl, and both shadow and light lay upon the heart of my Lord and flickered like torchlight in the dark chamber of his mind. Finally he bid Cuauhtémoc to send to Cholulan, by which city the strangers would pass on their way, a small golden teponaztli, which would warn them of war, and also his message for the Cholulteca to attack in ambush the army approaching them, for the strangers were in war most cunning and their weapons were of evil design. Cuauhtémoc made haste to fulfill a command so greatly to his liking and my Lord and I were left alone.

"I am weary and wish to sleep," he said, unwilling to look into my face and read what was surely written there.

"My Lord," I said softly, putting my hand upon his arm, "Did our God, Quetzalcoatl, leave this land with other Gods attending him?" I waited a moment but he did not speak. "No, my Lord. He took dwarves with him, even as you have dwarves by *your* side and accompanying *you.* Would not those dwarves bleed and die even as would your own, my Lord, if put to the dagger?" I waited in silence again, but he stood motionless and without speech, the color draining from his face as if he had sustained a mortal wound. "Thus would it not be more than likely that our God would also return with men of flesh and blood? Men not like us in aspect, and yet not divine. Could that not be so?"

Moteczoma shook me fretfully away from him. "I do not know what to believe," he snapped, "with all of you dragging me this way and then that with your words! One of you is lying or a fool! Which is it, Xochitlzin? Which one . . . ?" he repeated in a whisper and to himself.

"Come lie down with me, Lord, and rest." I spoke seductively and led him like the merest child to his sleeping mat, undressed him, taking from me my clothes also, and nestled his head upon my breasts. Like a child did he lie there, and though I was in a fever of impatience to change his mind before Cuauhtémoc's messengers reached Cholulan, still did I deem it wisest to let the night and my body subdue him to my will and the will of our God.

That night was a night of horror for me while my Lord, mightiest ruler on earth, slept like a babe in my arms. I dreamed of people dancing and singing and throwing flowers and of an army of most fierce aspect falling upon them, slaughtering them in their joy so that heads still wore smiles as they fell, and heads and arms and bellies lay thickly upon the ground, quivering and spurting blood and entrails. Into a sacred white chamber did I see a warrior come brandishing high his long, shining blade, and beyond him did I see a woman. She was Xocomoco. Long unseen, still I knew well that loved face, and it was screaming with fear and wide-eyed with terror. In my dream, this warrior crossed his chest with one hand while he tore from Xocomoco her white robes and threw her old woman's body to the floor and there mounted her in most profane sacrilege. When he had had his satisfaction upon her body, then did he slit her throat with his long dagger and thrust the blade into her belly. Making the gesture of a cross again upon his chest, he left her there, naked and in a pool of her own blood.

I awoke sobbing. "Can it be that you weep?" my Lord Moteczoma, awakening, said. "Never have I thought to see your tears."

"You must not let my God enter Cholulan without due honor, my Lord. All in the city will most surely die for such sacrilege."

My weeping as much as my urgency persuaded my Lord to stop the messengers from taking their words of war to Cholulan. But by dawn it was too late. Cuauhtémoc had moved instantly upon gaining Moteczoma's permission. My Lord sent a second group of messengers that day, commanding the Cholulteca *not* to ambush the God and his army, but to welcome them with reverence and honor. Thus did two messages reach that sacred city, and remembering the horror upon my beloved friend's face, I prayed with the whole of my heart that only the second would be obeyed and nothing done to incur my God's just wrath. In Tenochtitlan we waited in fear and trembling for news of the God's arrival, and for what would happen in Cholulan when they entered its holy walls.

22

MALINALLI

After seventeen days had passed, Cortés and some of his men were restless and longed to continue their journey. Emissaries that had come from Moteczoma with even more and valuable treasure at first tried to dissuade my Captain from an undertaking they warned him would be most arduous and fraught with danger. Some of our soldiers also said that it would be better to turn back now than continue on, possibly right into the murderous hands of the Azteca King and his many thousands of vassals. But Cortés insisted that they had come too far to turn back and that the only way led ahead of them; the road was blocked behind. There were those men this wisdom did not satisfy, but they still did as my Captain bid. After the emissaries saw no good would come of further words of discouragement, they said we would do best to take the road by way of the sacred city of Cholulan, where there was such treasure that they were sure the priests would honor us with gifts of great value. My Captain was pleased with these words. The Tlaxcalteca caciques warned us of the treachery of Moteczoma, saying that in Cholulan Moteczoma could deal with us as he wished. Most forcefully did they implore Cortés to take another road, one not chosen by the Ueytlatoani, but my Captain would not agree.

"Cholulan sounds a fair city indeed, and one with an abundance of everything most welcome."

"With an abundance of gold, as well," Alvarado added.

"Ill would it become us, Alvarado, to refuse gifts given with such willing hands." Both men joined in laughter, their words passing from man to man until all were most eager to undertake the journey, however arduous it might prove to be.

Moteczoma, in what appeared to us to be desperation, sent messengers to beseech us to accept their company on our way so that they could ensure us safe passage to Cholulan. They brought masks of fantastic design, one with the visage of Quetzalcoatl and covered with the green and blue bodies of plumed serpents all fashioned of small stones, and the other a mask of Tezcatlipoca, made with stones covering a man's skull with a man's teeth still in its jaw. Both masks wore feather headdresses and were beautiful and fearful to look upon.

"These are from the sacred city of Cholulan, my Lord," the emissaries explained, "and they are given to you with all honor."

Cortés accepted the masks in his hands and a dire foreboding filled me. I felt they possessed great magic; I could almost see the glittering of eyes in their empty sockets. I snatched them from his hands and he looked at me in amazement.

"I think it wise, my Captain, if I look carefully at these masks to make sure nothing harmful has been placed between the stones by Azteca sorcery."

Cortés laughed. "Do so then, Marina, but surely my God will protect me from heathen ritual and the toxins of ignorant savages."

I hastened away, the masks of an unearthly coldness in my hands. Studying them stone by stone, I found nothing to explain my dire foreboding. Giving them to Aguilar, I told him to keep them wrapped well and in a box until they could be sent with other treasure to his King. I was glad that my Captain forgot all about them and never asked to see them again. Well did I wish I also could forget them, but they remained a vision in my mind's eye for a long while.

One morning we set off at last for Cholulan. Glad were the soldiers to be marching, for most were men who tired quickly of comforts and the ease of soft living. My Captain felt stronger than he had in many days, he told me, and rode with a high heart. By nightfall we reached the sacred city of Cholulan and made camp on the banks of a river not far from where the bright pyramids and teocallis rose against the darkening sky. Men of Cholulan came forth to us that night, bringing us food and bidding us welcome to enter their city at dawn. We slept well and deeply that night, although many guards were posted in the event we were betrayed.

Pink and orange rose the sun on the morning we marched to the gates of the city. Priests and priestesses and the highest caciques all came in a procession toward us, bearing smoking braziers in their hands so that they walked in a cloud of copal. Dancers moved through the smoke as if they were but visions in a dream. Maidens tossed flowers which the horses and men crushed underfoot so that when the last of the soldiers had passed by, the road was stained red with torn petals.

All entered but for the Tlaxcalteca who, as mortal enemies of the Cholulteca, would not go close but camped outside the city walls. All amazed were the Spaniards to see so many great teocallis, and a pyramid the size of a mountain, though damaged by time. This was the pyramid dedicated to Quetzalcoatl, and its steps were wreathed in many thousands of flowers. Banners of glistening feathers, blue and green, floated in the breeze from the top where the teocalli itself had fallen into ruin. Hundreds of people thronged the streets, smiling and making obeisances. One priest bowed low before Cortés, saying, "My God, you are welcome in this sacred city of Cholulan! We bid you rest and partake of all we can provide to ease your hunger and your weariness. Your chambers await you in the palace." And he led the way to a great and beautiful building, severe on the outside but sumptuous within, as was the custom. My Captain and I were given the chamber of a high cacique. Its stone floor was hidden under mounds of red and yellow flowers, and when we stepped upon them their petals were soft underfoot and gave sweet fragrance. Tables had been placed about the room and upon them were wide golden dishes piled high with all the fruits in season, with many I had never seen before. A jeweled icpalli was in one corner and in another a mat covered with the softest of cotton blankets.

All of this pleased my heart and that of my Captain also, though even then he would not take his ease but went forth to see that his men were comfortably quartered and fed. While in weariness some soldiers slept, others explored the city and its great marketplace and I also wandered here and there to see and hear what I could. It was a simple matter for me to be invisible in any crowd, for I affected no curiosity of dress, but only that which any woman might wear, and my features were too regular to brand me an outsider. Thus it was I mingled with the people, my eyes full open and my ears missing nothing.

Most of the Cholulteca had by now returned to their labors, except for those who walked near Cortés, daring to raise their eyes but to his chest and no higher, overawed to see anything of a God at all. Well pleased was I to see this reverence, and I heard only words of praise and honor in the crowds. Leaving the marketplace, I took my way to where the ancient mountain of Quetzalcoatl's pyramid towered above all the rest. Priests and priestesses were busy burning copal beside the fallen teocalli, playing upon their teponaztlis and rattles and flutes, all in celebration of the coming of the God they served. Priests passed in and out through an opening at the pyramid's base, chanting their prayers and bleeding profusely from the thorns they had in reverence run through the lobes of their ears and the ends of their tongues. All walked sedately and with cloudy copal in their hands making sweet the air as they passed. My steps then led me to another teocalli and yet another until progress ceased in amazement at the sight of such vast numbers of them in that one city. It was as I stood there that I felt a watcher near me and I turned to see a priestess staring at me with eyes of wonder.

"Xochitl!" she cried, running to me with her arms spread wide in welcome. "Oh, you have returned with our God, great priestess that you are!" And with these words she clasped me in her arms and wept tears upon my neck.

I bore this embrace in mute shock. I had not thought of my sister in many months, but immediately I knew it was of my sister the woman spoke. Had she truly become a priestess, and she but a slave even as I had been? It seemed impossible, and yet as I suffered this strange priestess to weep in my arms, it truly appeared to have come to pass. I was amazed, and yet my wits did not depart from me at this sudden knowledge. I knew I could make use of anything she knew—as one can indeed make use of *any* knowledge—and so I stood upon the narrow wall between speaking the truth and learning news of my sister, or letting this woman persist in her delusion. My sister's face wavered in my mind's eye as if I looked into a dark mirror, and though I had loved Xochitl in my own way, still learning my sister's whereabouts could offer me less than what I might gain pretending to be her.

"Yes, I have returned," I said, wondering how to discover the priestess' name, "and in the company of our God."

The woman drew back from me, her face radiant behind her tears, but as she continued to look at me I could see uncertainty creep into her eyes. "You have changed, Xochitl," she said, "and yet I cannot tell how . . ."

I smiled kindly upon her. "My friend, even as you have changed. Time does not leave us unmarked by its passing, alas! Do tell me how you have fared in my absence." Thus I sought to turn away her hazardous scrutiny. Fortunately this was not difficult to do, since happiness made her easily distracted.

"Oh," she laughed, "I have been doing only what I have always done. You know as well as any that the life of a priestess does not alter from day to day, or even year to year! Do come with me to my chamber—I am so old now, I have been given that honor—and I will seek refreshment for us and we will tell each other everything that has come to pass these many months since you left us for Tenochtitlan."

She took my hand in friendly fashion, chattering eagerly of this and that, and led me to a building wherein lived the priestesses devoted to the few Goddesses still considered worth honoring. We entered into a garden but we did not stay there. "I want for us to be alone," she whispered, laughing and pulling me along behind her, "for I have grown selfish in this time we have been apart and I want you only to myself."

Half-listening to her witless prattling, I pondered the news that my sister had gone to Tenochtitlan. Most heartily did I wish my companion would let slip the reason for this departure. Surely it was not usual for a priestess in Cholulan to leave her duties and go elsewhere. However, the ways of priests and priestesses were foreign to me and all my speculations were, I knew, quite useless.

The priestess' chamber was small and white and empty. A brazier of embers smoked lazily and there was but a thin mat for her to sleep upon. The luxuries given these women were meagre indeed. We sat upon the floor and she looked with delight upon me and held both my hands in her own. "And how do you find Tenochtitlan?" she whispered.

I dreaded to make a reply, but knew I would have to drag forth words that would not betray me. "Oh, my friend," I sighed as if there were not words enough to paint the scenes of my memory, "wherever can I start?"

She was eager enough for both of us and from her chattering I sifted a word here and there to lead me more easily along. "But did you indeed see Moteczoma?" she whispered, her eyes wide with wonder. "We heard you made prophecy and then we heard no more. We thought perhaps you had been put to death, as had the others who prophesied the coming of Quetzalcoatl and the fall of Tenochtitlan. I have grieved for you so, Xochitl."

"Indeed have I also felt fear, dear friend. But, you see, the Ueytlatoani wished for me to prophesy again and thus decided not to put me to death." I wondered if this could be truth or if my sister had met her end in the fortress of our enemy.

"How did you live there? Were the people kind to you?" I saw the concern on her face and for one swift second I felt a stab of loneliness that no one had ever cared thus for *me*. How strange it seemed that my shy and sober sister should make so faithful a friend.

"They were, indeed," I smiled. "Life in Moteczoma's palace is in no way as austere as your own! But enough of me, my friend. I am eager to hear what has happened to you since we last were together, and what of Cholulan? The people give honor to our God, unlike the ignorant Tlaxcalteca whom he, in his mercy, spared."

"Oh, yes, we have been delighted and afraid. And yet . . ." her eager face grew grave. "Perhaps you knew that messengers were sent us from Tenochtitlan to tell us that the Ueytlatoani had gathered all of his sorcerers and priests together and that they told him our God was not a God and his Lords not Lords at all, but mortal men. Did you not hear word of this in Tenochtitlan before you left it?"

"There have been rumors. But some months I have been with my God upon his journey and have thus heard little."

The priestess' brow furrowed. "So you were not long at all in the Ueytlatoani's palace? Did you leave there soon after your prophecy, and how was it you were permitted to go?"

I found myself in dark and deepening waters indeed, and took my way as would a blind man and in all caution. "I was sent with some of Moteczoma's messengers, both to carry tribute and to see if he was indeed the God foretold."

"Which he is!" the priestess said, tightening her clasp upon my arm, eagerly, happily.

I smiled at her with assuring certainty. "Of course, my friend. How can you doubt me if I say he is so?"

She was a woman easily swept from side to side by her affections and she quivered with guilt that I might think she had doubted me. "Oh, Xochitl! Do not think I would ever disbelieve the smallest word you could utter. You, dearest of all women to me. Even dearer than that precious jewel of a child, if it does not pain you too much to hear me speak of her." She looked with grave compassion into my face. Here was a shadow indeed! What child could she possibly mean? A queer look crossed her face and I cast my eyes down so that she could not see in them the blank unknowing.

"It is hard for me to speak of her. I still feel pain, my friend. Forgive me."

"Forgive you?" Her voice was rich with pity. "You must forgive me for giving you pain. It was just . . . just that I think of her so often and I do so miss her even yet. Long have I wished to speak to you of her, but had given up hope I would ever again be so blessed."

I glanced hesitantly upward and her face was again radiant and full of trust. Never had I been looked upon nor spoken to as that woman did, and I was as bewildered as if she spoke to me in a foreign tongue and expected understanding. Her hands upon me were warm and fervent with an intimacy I had never known with a woman. I hastened to turn her talk to subjects less perilous. Smiling gently and sorrowfully I said again, "Tell me of things here in Cholulan. You say Moteczoma sent messengers?"

"Indeed he did so. First they came to tell us that his sages and sorcerers had divined that the God was but a man from a distant, hostile land, and bent upon conquest. We were told that armies would come from Tenochtitlan and that our warriors were to await a propitious hour to slay the strangers and take as many captive as were alive after the battle. Azteca warriors would wait hidden in the ravines outside the city, then come to our aid when our teponaztlis were sounded and the battle begun."

"When were you given this message?"

"A mere three days ago."

"What did then occur so that we were not attacked?" I asked, trying to keep my voice soft with unconcern.

"Messengers came upon the following day, as well. Most bewildering was this to our caciques, Xochitl, for the Ueytlatoani now bade us treat the strangers as our God and his Lords, and give them honor and offering in his name."

I breathed more easily. "Then truly all the people of Cholulan know the truth, that our God has come?"

The priestess looked away and in her uneasiness she slipped her hands from mine and clasped them tightly together in her lap. "Oh, Xochitl! Indeed I do not know. Some of our caciques have spoken one way and some the other. We have heard rumor that in Tenochtitlan the Ueytlatoani has grown foolish and is wrapped in the wiles of a woman so that he falters first one way and then another, and that the Lords of the Triple Alliance still doubt that Quetzalcoatl has come and thereby preach to Lord Moteczoma that he must make war upon the strangers before they reach the sacred Heart of the One World."

She looked at me in distress. "Please do not look upon us harshly, beloved friend. The news has been strange and of a significance our caciques and priests could scarce divine, but we are, indeed, overjoyed to have our God within our walls. Please do not be angry that we in Cholulan have ever doubted him."

I made her a small smile of forgiveness. "I know well my master is a God, and thus these petty doubts of men do not concern me. Continue, if you would, dear friend."

"The next day, when those second messengers hastened to our caciques, telling them the Ueytlatoani had changed his mind and we were to honor the God and his Lords when they reached our gates, glad were we to obey and honor has been most gladly done. But, Xochitl," her voice was rough with anxious concern, "I know you travel in the company of immortals, yet you are still a mortal woman, are you not?"

I nodded, smiling at her foolishness. "Indeed this is still so."

She took my hands again in her damp ones. "If the winds do blow this way and that, and if the Ueytlatoani does make war upon these holy Lords, whatever will happen to you?"

I squeezed her hands, although they were unpleasant to the touch. "I am a mere woman, but I am not afraid. My God will protect me."

"But if he can not?"

I gently withdrew my fingers from hers and rose to my feet, and the priestess stumbled gracelessly to her own. "Do not fear for me, my friend. Our God watches over all who believe in him and honor him. Now, if you will allow me, I must hasten to his side and see that he requires no further comfort. The journey, as you know, has been long and most wearisome and even a God must rest."

I suffered the woman to embrace me once again and promised that I would return and speak with her before we continued on our journey. She held me in her arms as if she dared not let me go. Finally I withdrew from her and she wiped the tears from her eyes. "I do not know why it is so, Xochitl, but I fear never to see you again. There is this darkness in my heart . . ."

"You are foolish, my friend," I replied cheerfully. "I have promised you I would come again, and so I will. But now I must bid you farewell."

I left her disquieting company, turning my hurried steps back to the palace with my mind full of what I had been told as well as what I would tell my Captain I had been told. I found him in his chamber, taking counsel with Alvarado and one or two others of his most trusted soldiers. They glanced at me indifferently as I entered, but were moved to curiosity when I interrupted their speech to ask Cortés to send them away so that I might speak with him in privacy.

"This is most unusual, Marina. I trust you have good reason for this intrusion."

Breathless from haste, I nodded, and he bid his men go. Quickly I calmed myself to speak the words I had to say with care lest they lead my Captain down a road he should not travel.

"My Captain, I was walking through the city today, listening to what was being said by the Cholulteca, and an elderly woman did sidle up to me in a most curious fashion. She said that I was beautiful and probably rich, and that her son was in need of a wife. She told me that it was unsafe in Cholulan and that I should fetch my possessions and return with her to her home and there marry her son."

Cortés was bewildered. "But why did she imagine you to be in danger?"

I took a deep breath. "Perhaps for no reason at all, my Captain. But when I asked her that question myself, she told me that Moteczoma had sent two messages to the caciques of Cholulan. The second, sent two days past, bid the Cholulteca to greet us peacefully and to honor us with tribute. But the first, coming the day before, was of a different nature. That message was that the priests and sorcerers of Tenochtitlan believe us to be the enemy and that Azteca warriors will be sent to help the Cholulteca battle us in their streets, taking captive all who are not slain."

At these words, Cortés grew grave. "And how had she come to have this intelligence?"

"She said to me that her son was a warrior and thus from him did she learn this news. All warriors of Cholulan had readied themselves for battle and when the second message came they were bewildered. It seems Moteczoma does not know in his mind if you are Gods or but men, and thus he wavers like a flame from one side to the other."

My Captain sat in thought, then said quietly, "There is no chance that the people of Cholulan will rise against us?"

"I do not know. I think not, but since things have changed from day to day, perhaps they may change still. It might be wise, my Captain, to keep some of our men on guard in the event of treachery."

"As always, you are of much help to me, Marina. This intelligence is sobering indeed."

My heart warmed with his praise. "I am glad to serve you in all ways, my Captain."

"I shall require from you service of another nature when this day is done," he said, putting one hand lightly upon my breast, "but meanwhile, we must keep on the alert for any sign of betrayal."

Thus it was that we listened secretly to what was said in the city and we warned our men as well as our allies to be prepared for ambush. Many were the signs, but they were contrary one to another. Large stones were found piled upon rooftops, betokening ambush, and yet the priests and caciques continued to do us honor and sing Quetzalcoatl's praises.

Cortés called for a council, and his trusted soldiers came to our chamber and spoke of what they had seen and heard. It seemed to us all as if the Cholulteca were convinced that Cortés was Quetzalcoatl, and yet there were murmurs that Moteczoma continued to lean from one side to the other and thus sow confusion in the land.

"What if," Cortés asked, "we were to find evidence, sound evidence, that an ambush is indeed in readiness. Then would we have ample reason to move against them first and without warning?"

Alvarado answered. "Admirably would it suit our purpose if we could strike at the heart of Moteczoma so he would not plan a similar treachery when we reach the Azteca fortress."

There was silence in the chamber. Glances of solemn significance passed from eye to eye.

"But we need proof, Alvarado, that we are being forced to act in our own defence."

"You shall have it, Captain," he said, and left.

When Alvarado returned soon before nightfall, he brought news that two priests had gone to the Tlaxcalteca with talk of bribery and when our allies gave them gold, confessed to them that, indeed, a plot of ambush had been laid against us."

"Where are these priests?" Cortés asked. "I would question them further, with help from Doña Marina."

"I have been told they grew remorseful, even as did Judas Iscariot, and that they slit their own throats and are dead."

I looked into Alvarado's eyes but they were as black as a moonless night.

"We must move at once," Cortés decided.

Calling to him his soldiers of command, he and they planned together where each would await the signal to strike and where in the city to lead their men. Alvarado was given the part of the city around the great pyramid of Quetzalcoatl, upon which Cortés would stand so that all could see him give the signal to attack. Orders were given to slay every Cholulteca, man, woman and child, until Cortés signalled the battle's end. All would then withdraw to their quarters, there to ready themselves to march next day to Tenochtitlan.

As soon as I could have speech with him alone, I

went to Alvarado. "There is a building not far from the great pyramid, and it is all of white and only priestesses and those training to be priestesses live within it. I beg of you to spare these guiltless women," I said, thinking only of the one priestess, the friend who was not my friend.

He looked upon me with a smile both shrewd and ruthless. "If I were to do so, Marina, then finally will you lie with me as I have long desired?"

"Never," I said, furious that he would again suggest this betrayal. "Never will I so dishonor my Captain! How can you still say such a thing to me when you know well my answer? Please," I said, and let my voice melt with pleading, "there is really just one old woman there who warned me of the disquiet in Cholulan, and she does not deserve to die. Be merciful for once, Alvarado. I beg it of you."

He seemed to pause in thought at this and then nodded gravely. "Very well, Marina, but are you still not sure this woman's life is worth an hour of pleasure?"

"Alvarado," I could barely speak to him, but I reined in my anger with a strong hand, "I have told you I will never lie with a man other than my Captain."

"Very well, Marina, although truly I do not believe Cortés would be so scrupulous. However," he went on, raising a hand to still my sharp denial, "I know you think ill of me and so it will be worth it to me to see your surprise when I ask nothing of you in repayment. Describe this woman you wish to save. Where again will I find her?"

I told him, and in detail. If she remained in her chamber, he could not help but find her.

At my suggestion, Cortés demanded that the caciques and priests announce to the people that there would be a celebration next morning in honor of Quetzalcoatl, and all must gather in ceremony, bringing with them fruits and flowers, in the streets around the great pyramid. Quietly and by stealth Cortés then had all the caciques taken captive in their dwellings and palaces and when all were gathered in our chamber, he bid me tell them that we knew of their treachery against us and that divine law decreed they be put to death. Though all protested their innocence, Cortés ordered his men to strangle the caciques with ropes, so as to give no alarm to any who might hear and then alert the people. After this was done, he went with some of his men and I to the great pyramid of Quetzalcoatl just as the sun rose pink in the sky.

When we reached the top, Cortés turned to me with a wink of his eye, saying, "A humorous place to begin a battle, is it not, Marina?" and then we heard the drumming of the teponaztlis and the birdlike music of the flutes, and all of the people of Cholulan came down the streets, dancing and singing, to the base of the pyramid where we stood. Cortés raised his musket and fired. The slaughter began.

From our place of vantage we watched our soldiers ride into the dancing crowd, trampling the bodies beneath their horses' hooves. Weaponless, armed but with flowers, the Cholulteca fell like a field of maize beneath our knives and muskets and swords. With screams of terror did they try to run, slipping upon the blood of the dead and dying, and our soldiers cut from them their heads and sliced open their bellies so that their feet became entangled in their own entrails as they scrambled to escape. Babes and children they took by their heels, smashing their heads against the walls so that the stone was slimy with blood and brains gushing from those fragile skulls. Our allies soon arrived, but little needed were they, only to put to death those who had fled from the city gates. Easily indeed were these cut down, and almost as if in sport.

The sun had reached the middle of its journey when my Captain gave the signal to cease. Slowly, the killing stopped. From the clamor of battle it soon grew quiet, except for the groans of the dying. "I think God has been with us today, Marina!" my Captain said in great good humor. "Now let us ask whatever priests or caciques who still draw breath to come to us for forgiveness for their foul treachery." Demanding horses, we rode back to our quarters, side by side, along streets so slick with blood that only with great difficulty did our horses not fall. Beneath their hooves unbroken skulls crunched with a cracking sound and daintily indeed did the horses step between the bodies of the dead, tossing their heads at the smells of battle.

In his mercy, Cortés ordered some of his men to go forth and dispatch with a sword all persons still dying and so put them out of their pain. Then we met in his chamber with Alvarado and the rest. After they had taken counsel and made their plans for the following day, then did I find a moment to speak privately with Alvarado.

"Did you find the priestess I asked you to save?"

"Indeed I did so, most particularly, Marina," he said with a cunning smile. "Your description of her was quite accurate. I doubt I could have found her without it."

"She is safe?"

"She could be no safer," he replied in a voice smooth with guile.

Though the woman had meant nothing to me, still my heart grew cold. "What do you mean?"

"First I used her body as I would have yours, if you had so permitted me. After all, you said yourself your body had more worth than hers. A man cannot always be over-particular about where he satisfies his hunger. Indeed, sometimes dry bread is as tasty as cake—although not in this case, unfortunately."

I could not speak. A most surprising sorrow mingled with my fury, and I could only stare at the man who smiled cruelly in return.

"I kept my promise to you, Marina," he then said with mock gravity. "She is, as I told you, safely beyond all danger."

"You son of a whore," I whispered.

"This for a man you begged—almost on your knees, Marina!—to take care of an elderly priestess. For shame, you ingrate. I merely did your bidding. I simply first made use of her, though I had to close my eyes to do it, and who could blame me? Remember, you had repulsed me quite unkindly, Marina. I slit her throat with merciful swiftness and so you should thank me."

"I will see you dead, Alvarado!"

He laughed, and if I could have killed him then I would not have hesitated. "You are an insufferably arrogant savage, *Malintzin.* Very well might it be you who die first. What do you say we place a wager?"

Shaken with a passion almost beyond my control, I turned on my heel and left him, though his soft chuckling followed me, like the laughter of a demon, from the chamber. All my days I would wish him dead, I knew, and await his undoing with keenest desire. I had hated him long before this day, but now I hated him with a deadly passion, and not only because he had played traitor to me. For I remembered that old priestess' embrace, and knew that she had lovingly embraced my sister so. For some reason I could not fathom, that made her death clutch at my heart with grieving and a most unexpected sense of loss.

23

Xochitl

I lingered sorrowing in the aviary, with fond thoughts of Atahualpa and where fate may have led his steps, when I did feel eyes upon me and turned to see Lord Cuauhtémoc regarding me balefully.

"Have you heard of events in Cholulan, Lady?"

I was silent, stricken with foreboding.

"I believe you will find my news interesting." He paused and when he spoke again his voice throbbed with anger. "The man you believe to be a God did order the people of Cholulan to arise at dawn to celebrate his coming. They did so and the streets were crowded with priests and warriors and women and children also. And they were dancing and singing and giving reverence to your God when he ordered his warriors to slay them. Hundreds died that morning, Lady, and as they were all of them unarmed, the slaying was but an easy matter."

So my dream had been true. And surely then must it be true that dear Xocomoco had been raped and slain. A shuddering coursed through my body and I swayed against the thin wooden bars of the birds' cage and would have fallen if Cuauhtémoc had not stepped quickly to my side and taken my arms. Though the man was my adversary, still did I lean weakly against him until I could stand alone.

"Lord Cuauhtémoc, is this certain?" I whispered, overcome with dread.

"Even as I have spoken."

"But why?" I asked this of my own self more than

I asked it of him. "What could have been the cause for such a massacre if they were, and at that very moment, giving honor to our God?"

"Indeed I wish you could tell me, Lady Xochitlzin," he said in a dry voice. "The Lords of the Triple Alliance and the Ueytlatoani, your husband, all of us await your words with great interest."

I leaned my face against the cage and gazed unseeing at the birds in their enviably heedless flight.

"Well, Lady? Even Tezcatlipoca does not demand the blood of ignoble massacre but the honorable death of warriors. What of your God's promise of a bloodless peace? Mictlan must be glutted with the numbers that pass this day through the caves of wind and fire and the knives that even now flay the flesh from their bones."

"Please," I whispered, raising my hand to bid him be silent. "Well do I know that you bear me ill will, but your mockery at such a time does you no service. I must think, Lord Cuauhtémoc! I must think what this could mean."

Lord Cuauhtémoc watched me then in silence as I struggled with my thoughts. How could it be that a God who forbade blood sacrifice would demand the dishonorable death of so many? And, if what Cuauhtémoc said was true, demand it while they were gathered in all innocence to praise him? If the Cholulteca had been plotting against him or had met his arrival with enmity, then could I understand dealing with them harshly. And yet, what of the priests and priestesses? Did not their sacred calling protect even them from his righteous anger?

I covered my face with trembling hands and tried to shut from sight the image of Xocomoco's death and from my ears the agonized screams of the dying. But the teocalli of Quetzalcoatl loomed with relentless portent in my mind and with it the holy city I knew so well—especially the sacred dwelling place of the priestesses. Spirits transfixed to the streets in terror would surely walk them forever, lamenting. Cholulan would be a city of wraiths wailing in all the nights to come.

"You have brought this to pass," Lord Cuauhtémoc said abruptly. "The Ueytlatoani otherwise would have bid our warriors to fight. Instead, and upon your urging, he has invited the enemy within our very walls, your shadow self by his side."

I raised my eyes to his face and therein saw both sorrow and wrath. "But it must be he who comes, if not . . ."

"Yes, if not!"

"But it *must* be Quetzalcoatl! All of the signs and portents . . . even Chimalpopoca has admitted this to be true. This is the time and the year foretold, and indeed in his face and with his garments and in all things does he seem the God of prophecy. You have heard and seen these things yourself, Lord."

He nodded grudgingly, but his voice made no room for my argument. "I saw and heard these signs, Lady, but still I did not feel they were summoned forth by a God. They were but the fruit of sorcery, sorcery most treacherous and vile."

I saw grave meaning in his eyes. "Surely you do not accuse me, Lord, of treachery! Even *I* needed to be told what I said in my swooning dreams."

"So you have led people to believe."

"Are you daring to accuse me of such low cunning?"

Lord Cuauhtémoc stared at me a long and silent time and then in a quiet voice said, "Yes, even of this do I accuse you. I accuse you of deepest and most evil artifice, and of using by magic your woman's wiles upon your Lord Moteczoma."

"I will stay to hear no more of this!" I began to hasten away, but was stopped by Cuauhtémoc who grasped my arm and turned me roughly around to face him.

"Know this, Xochitlzin. I will seek proof of your

falseheartedness and when I find it I will so inform Lord Moteczoma, so that he, himself, will see your foul wickedness and how you have used him to do your will. Then, Lady," he whispered, his eyes fierce upon mine, "you will die the death you deserve."

I could see my death in his eyes as I pulled away my arm. "You are wrong, Cuauhtémoc."

"I will be proven right."

With these words he strode away. Stunned, I walked to a bench and sat down. Where had my faith led me now? To truth or to delusion? Indeed I had induced my Lord Moteczoma to do my will, and with womanly wiles as well as prophecy and with what I had believed to be wise counsel. All signs and portents had signalled Quetzalcoatl's coming, but why did this most peaceful God come not in benevolent guise, but as avenging warrior? Or was Cuauhtémoc right, and the God not God at all?

Closing my eyes I did desperately beseech my God that he possess me once more—but once—and that by this blessing might I regain my faltering faith. As it had been since my wedding night, however, he came not to fill the vessel of my body and it was as hollow and echoing as an abandoned chamber. After a long moment I opened my eyes. At my feet lay the curved obsidian dagger a priestess always carries at her waist, as I had when I was priestess. I bent to pick it up and held it in my hand. There was fresh blood upon it and it stained my fingers. Was this a warning, I wondered, or an omen? I cleaned it with leaves and slipped it into the cloth tied about my waist, feeling the cold hard tip of it against my leg. Without quite thinking the thought, the words came to my mind; I might as well be armed.

Suddenly the music of flutes and rattles and teponaztlis rang forth, and I remembered that this was a day of significance and of solemn ritual. My absence would be seen as sacrilege and so I made haste to my Lord's side. Within the Heart of the Heart of the One

World a tall pole had been placed in a hole in the stones and as musicians played their instruments and priests chanted and burned copal, five men clad in the wings of eagles stepped to the base of the pole. One, the ko'hal, began to climb. I reached my Lord Moteczoma as the ko'hal ascended to the topmost top and turned to face the east. There he sought the divine blessings of the Gods and then, with the whistling sound of birds' wings flying, did he then turn to the four quarters of the world, offering to all Gods, the greater and the lesser, the vapor of octli he breathed into the air for their refreshment. Donning a headdress of red feathers, then he danced and flapped his wings, and most wondrous was it he did not fall. The four remaining men then played their parts. With ropes tied from the top of the pole to their waists, they climbed the pole also. There and all at once they leaped out into the air and, with arms outstretched, whirled around the pole in the guise of eagles, symbols of Azteca greatness. As they neared the ground in their circling flight one of the men broke loose from his rope, spinning out and plunging downward where his skull cracked open upon the stone.

The crowd gasped. Suddenly all was silence, for this was an omen of disaster. I dared not look at my Lord Moteczoma's face, but I saw that his hands gripped the sides of his icpalli and his knuckles were bloodless with the force of his grasp. Priests came in haste to gather up the body, and in an attempt to amend the evil, took it to the teocalli of Tezcatlipoca and there cut from it the heart, offering it to that God upon a burning brazier. But all knew this was of little value.

With uneasy minds we all proceeded then by custom to the tlachtli court. I walked beside my Lord's litter, upon which he rode most grimly. The game to be played upon this day was of grave importance. The two teams were to represent the Gods Tezcatlipoca and Quetzalcoatl, and our priest and sorcerers had determined that the team which was triumphant would foretell which of these Gods would triumph in Tenochtitlan.

Upon my Lord's right side sat his First Wife and I did sit upon his left. Surrounding us were other Lords and warriors and caciques who furtively glanced upon us. They were wearing the colors and signs of Tezcatlipoca as my Lord Moteczoma wore as headdress the green and blue quetzal feathers of the Plumed Serpent, Quetzalcoatl. In his nose was the golden symbol of that God and upon his chest as well. My hair had been dressed with flowers that morning, but other than the golden plug in my nose, I wore no other finery. Always did I dress with the austerity of the priestess I was no more.

The ball, hard and of rubber, was thrown upon the court, the players then knocked it back and forth between their opposing sides. With their heads and bodies did they send the ball flying, for they were not permitted the use of their hands. Fierce indeed was this game and all were most intent upon it. Loud were the cries and exclamations as first Tezcatlipoca's side was in the ascendant and then the side of Quetzalcoatl. It was a most punishing sport and the players often fell and injured themselves upon the stones, and the ball also knocked them into unconsciousness if they were not wary to avoid it as it flew swiftly through the air. As the game neared its end my Lord Moteczoma became more cheerful in the surrounding gloom, for the side representing the Plumed Serpent did most skillfully toss the ball through the stone ring in the courtyard wall and thus end the game in triumph. My Lord smiled and the people, some in earnest and some merely to please him, cried out in praise and thanksgiving as the First Player on the losing side had his head struck from his shoulders upon the central sacrificial stone.

"Perhaps we have been misled about the massacre in Cholulan," my Lord whispered to me. "Indeed, this could be so for our God knows what we do not know and would have had his excellent reasons, doubtless." Thus was he pleased and fearful all at once, and now gripped more by excitement than disquiet.

I looked to see the face of Cuauhtémoc. It was set and passionless. This was not also true of Chimalpopoca's face, however, when he sought audience that night with my Lord. The look he cast upon me then was black with malevolence. Yet he spoke meekly to my Lord and with solicitude did enquire into my Lord's health and say also that his sorcerers had told him the Ueytlatoani was unwell.

"Unwell?" my Lord said, furrowing his brow. "Indeed the opposite. Most vigorous have I felt this day."

"And yet, precious Lord, you know your sorcerers to be skilled in divining illness even before the one thus cursed by evil demons knows it himself. Would you not like for me to have brought to you a health-giving infusion now, before these demons have taken firm hold?" This he said in a meek and wheedling voice and with an anxious smile.

"Perhaps that would be best," my Lord replied, "for I will need all my strength to welcome my ancestor God to this city. Fetch it to me, Chimalpopoca."

The priest bowed himself out, soon returning with a gourd filled with a brew of earthy odor. "What is infused into this drink that it does smell as dank as a cave?" my Lord asked as he peered with a wrinkled nose into the cup.

"Oh, many and various herbs and roots, my Lord, and all of most potent qualities when taken correctly."

Moteczoma nodded and awaited instruction.

"Drink it just before you sleep, Lord," the priest told him, "and in no company but your own."

I glanced at Chimalpopoca suspiciously, for this was a most uncommon order and one I had never heard.

"Very well," my Lord said. "Even so shall it be done, priest."

Chimapopoca, rubbing his hands and bowing low, left us alone in the chamber.

"Well, Xochitlzin, let us go together and seek to content ourselves before you return to the women's chamber. Too many nights have I spent fasting and chaste in ritual and I wish tonight to be sated with pleasure." We passed through the door into his private chamber, and then he said, as if confiding a secret, "Today has been a day of adversaries, of one contemplating his opposite. We will thus end this day in symbolic delight."

Sitting upon his icpalli, my Lord bid me remove my garments and so stand naked before him. This he did frequently because my body pleased him and he would often stare upon me as he would upon a statue, from all angles and in varying brightnesses of light. Tonight, however, the diversion he desired was new, and he clapped his hands. The door opened behind me and a woman dwarf came into the room, bowing her way to my Lord's icpalli until she fell to her knees before him. My Lord bid her rise and undress. Stunted to an amazing smallness, she was as plain as I was beautiful.

"It pleases me to see such a pair as you are, one of most noble height and beauty and the other quite the opposite. Look upon my Lady Xochitlzin, dwarf, and admire everything that you are not."

The dwarf turned to me with eyes both curious and timid as she looked up and down my body.

"Stand close," my Lord then commanded, "and face each other."

We obeyed, though I made one futile protest, and the dwarf stepped toward me so that her face was but an eyelash length from my belly. I could feel her breath warm and moist upon my skin.

"This dwarf, Xochitlzin, was given to me today as a pleasant curiosity in honor of this day of opposites by a cacique from a distant city. As a baby she was left in the care of concubines who turned her from a woman with a woman's hungers to a woman with the hungers of a man." He paused, gazing with satisfaction upon us. "Do you want to know how this was accomplished?"

Uneasy and flushed with shame, I said, "Please, Lord . . . it is not necessary."

"But I want to tell you!" he protested, like a child accustomed to the devoted attention of others. "You see, she is supposed to be a most interesting example of what man can make of man. You know, Xochitlzin, of my interest in all such matters, for the Gods in such a way do take pleasure in making monsters of men. Though we mortal men are not so skillful, it is remarkable how like clay flesh can be, indeed."

I made no reply but prepared myself to endure, for my Lord's pleasure, what was to come.

"When but a babe, and a puny thing she was, too—as small as a dog newborn, the cacique did say—she was held in the arms of those women who fondled her most intimately, slipping their little fingers into her tipili and massaging it tenderly with arousing oils. When she was older, they played with her upon their sleeping mats and gave her sweet foods and little gifts when she pleased them. After awhile she needed no such gifts, for nothing gave her more delight than to lie with women and take her pleasure upon them. I was told that she indeed gives pleasure more skillfully than can a man, and the truth of this I am most curious to know."

I was horrified by his suggestion. Shame spread through me at the thought of lying, most unnaturally, with this poor wretch of a woman.

"After all, Xochitlzin, what I ask of you is not unlawful as it would be with a man. Adultery is most grievous sin, but what a woman does with another woman is of no importance. Now," he said eagerly, "recline upon this mat and let me see what this dwarf has been raised to do."

Most unwillingly did I sit at my Lord's feet and then the dwarf, nervously eager, sat by my side and pushed me gently backwards. Her small hands fluttered down upon me and softly did she begin to tease my nipples. First with her fingers and then with her tongue did she patiently draw my nipples forth, and I was hot with shame when I saw them stand erect upon my breasts with her delicate ministrations. Her little tongue then flicked between my breasts and down the length of my body, slowly and like the petals of a flower against my skin. Moving steadily downward to my feet, then did she suckle each toe and gradually, with little pushes, widen the space between my feet and begin to lick the skin of my ankles.

Thus did the dwarf insinuate her way upward until, at last, she licked with her puppy's tongue and stroked the insides of my knees and then softly, insistently, cleave passage to my thighs. It was then I began to quiver and I looked suddenly upward at my Lord to find him most intrigued and smiling with delight.

"So the cacique has told the truth?" he asked me, and I closed my eyes in humiliation.

Indeed had she been well trained, for even though I had been innocent of much subtlety in the area of fleshly passion, still did I know I had never been touched so skillfully and in so lewd a manner. Murmuring words I could not hear, the dwarf gently prised open my thighs and with the tip of her small tongue did she coax them to spread wider. With little fingers she caressed my tipili and took into her lips the pearl that lay quivering in its hidden place. I felt my belly tauten as she did her work, and my breathing was fast and ragged.

Though I could not forget myself even then, nor my shame, if she had stopped at that moment I would have been, most disgracefully, disappointed. My pearl she drew gently into her mouth again and as if to suckle upon it did she move it upon her tongue, and while she did this, and delicately, did she slide the whole of her small hand into me as a man would his tepuli, and therein did she flutter her fingers so it seemed a bird was burrowing its way inside. Suddenly, knowing well what the shuddering in my belly meant, she grasped me with surprising strength by my loins. Shaken then with a seizure I was, and the dwarf held me down while she kept her tongue busy upon me. Then did a second and a third spasm pass upwards from where she kept her mouth and almost did I cry out in the ecstasy that was almost as unbearable as pain.

I lay then as if in a swoon as the dwarf caressed me, and it was a long moment before I dared open my eyes. My Lord was looking down upon me with a contented smile. I looked away in shame, but he bid me watch as he directed the dwarf to busy her mouth upon *him*. Quicker work was this for her, as he was hot and ready and soon did he sow his seed into her mouth.

"Go now, dwarf, and receive your reward," he commanded, and wrapping herself in her garments, she bowed her way from the chamber. I heard later from my Lord that out of his need for secrecy, and wanting the dwarf never to describe what she had seen and done that night, he had had her strangled in the corridor outside his door.

"You have served me well, Xochitlzin," he said to me before I left. "I have been most pleased with you—as well as with the generosity of that cacique!"

In my disquiet, I did not go in obedience to the women's chamber, and instead braved the dangers of the night. Though restless spirits always choose to wander in the darkness, bewailing their fates and casting bewitchments upon the unwary, still did I dare to seek privacy in my Lord's garden. Cold it was, but scarcely did I notice. The chill in my heart was bitter. Well and truly was I lost. My faith was being stripped from me and I was as helpless as if I were in Mictlan with the flaying knives stripping the flesh from my bones. There had been a time, I remembered, when I had believed what my mother had told me, and even in hours of sorrow and distress that belief had nourished and sustained me. Now it seemed I was still nothing but a slave and subject to the whims of both Gods and men. My Lord Moteczoma sought to shame and oppress me even in spite of his need for my assurance that fate was wending its benevolent way toward the Heart of the One World, and there was nothing to be done but accept it with honor and grace. I had told him this many times, for it seemed to me I still saw clearly the shining path of my God pass over the land even as the moonlight. And yet, this beloved God no longer acknowledged me. I had beseeched his pity and he pitied me not. I had sought for proof he cherished me, and proof there came not. Not only was I alone in the palace, I was alone in the land as well, and could take counsel with no one.

Never had I known a moment's warm safety since I was a little child, I thought, and suddenly I felt a longing for my mother and for the chance to lay my head upon her lap and feel her fingers soft upon my hair. Still I knew even then that this was a world not of safety but of peril and that it made no difference if I railed against it or accepted it with the docility of a slave, for there was no change I could make in it, no way to alter it into the world my heart desired. Thus it was and thus it would be, world without beginning and without end.

Finally growing weary, and yet unable to face the inquisitive stares in the women's chamber, I found a bench by one of the fountains and sat down. The ceaseless splashing of the waters calmed the turbulence in my spirit. Folding my hands in my lap, I sat motionless as a figure carved from stone, moonlight washing color from my skin.

It must have been in that attitude that I fell asleep, for it seemed but the very next moment when I heard men shouting and opened my eyes to find the moon already low in the sky. On the roof of Lord Moteczoma's palace were men, moving about in the light of torches and making exclamations I could not comprehend at such a distance. It did appear that my Lord was observing the stars as he did every midnight and morning and when the sun set, so he would be prepared, as Ueytlatoani, for what they foretold of fortune or hardship. I knew his priests were there with him, and perhaps other Lords as well. According to ancient custom, they met together, observed and charted the stars in their courses, and then retired for the remainder of the night. However, it seemed that something had disturbed them for they moved this way and that and spoke loudly among themselves.

It was forbidden for me to accompany my Lord to the rooftop now that I was no longer priestess, but I wished for the courage to do so and thus gain knowledge of what so disquieted them. Much was hidden from others, as the priests and sorcerers did their work in utmost secrecy so that their charms and heavenly observations and prophecies would be pure from taint. Only when they had satisfied themselves of the truth did they make that truth known. And yet . . . did Chimalpopoca speak truth when he declared the ascendancy of Tezcatlipoca and his sovereignty over all other Gods, especially his counterforce, Quetzalcoatl? Perhaps he felt as strongly as did I, but our divinations had wavered this way and that even as they were interpreted. If he did not feel a like devotion, then it was possible he worked for his own mastery through the power of his God and sought to make of men vassals he could sway this way and that, according to his own will. Would he then still be servant to his God, I wondered, or would his God then be servant to him? And how could this be, when men and women were but unworthy instruments the Gods allowed to live through the fruitfulness of the earth watered with their blood? All we could do, so we had always been told, was to labor dutifully and give due reverence, give even our lives, if they were needed to slake the Gods' great thirst for blood they shed, in turn, for us. If Chimalpopoca was indeed suiting his divinations to his desire, why then did his God not strike him down? Or was the priest's desire but a reflection of his God's desire, and thus making manifest his will upon the earth?

My head ached with these thoughts. How could I, a mere woman, question the words of the greatest priest in Anáhuac? A prophetess of power I had been, but never possessor of the occult knowledge and dark secrets of the priesthood. Surely my doubts were sacrilege.

As if I had conjured him from the shadows with my thoughts, Chimalpopoca came hurrying across the garden toward the palace stairs. Upon seeing me sitting motionless, he stopped and drew a startled breath. Few there were indeed who would brave the dark, and they almost always were priests who had the power to pass protected through spiritual danger. I did not speak, for at first I feared that I would speak aloud my profane thoughts, and then I did not speak for I saw his fear of me was no less than mine of him.

"Leave here, spirit!" he whispered, passing his hand in a magical gesture through the air. I continued to observe him, without sound or movement, and he drew back his black garments with a hiss and, backing into the shadows, disappeared.

When I felt he was gone and I was unseen, I hastened to the women's chamber and lay down without awakening those who slept, softly breathing and murmuring in their dreams. At the first light, when we by custom pricked the lobes of our ears and the tips of our tongues with thorns in reverence to the rising of Tonatiuh from Mictlan, messengers came to the chamber to ask for me. A slave helped me dress and then I was led to my Lord Moteczoma's audience chamber where, much to my amazement, there stood only the priest, Chimalpopoca. With the blood still dripping from his ears and mouth and with his ornament of office upon his breast and the skull mask of Tezcatlipoca over his face, he stood before the empty icpalli as if he spoke for the one who usually sat upon it.

I approached and made my obeisances. "You did wish for me, Chimalpopoca?"

His eyes flickered in the mask's hollow sockets like dark flames and his lips pressed tight behind its gaping jaw. "What were you doing, Lady, last night in my Lord's garden?" His voice came low and rasping through his teeth.

"I do not know what you mean, Chimalpopoca. Surely you know I slept in the women's chamber even as my Lord, upon your suggestion, bid me do."

"I must warn you that to lie to me, you lie to Tezcatlipoca, Lord of the Smoking Mirror."

I looked at him in feigned innocence. "Surely it was not me you saw, but perhaps another woman who bears my likeness?"

At this sowing of the seed, he was silent. I could see a slight tremor in both hands clenched by his sides. "You swear this to me, Lady? Not only to me but the God who also stands before you?"

I nodded, a thin needle of ice piercing my belly. "Of course I so swear, if you wish it."

"And by your God, Quetzalcoatl, Lord of the Morning Star, as well?"

This indeed was a most solemn oath, and one I could not lightly take. "An oath to Tezcatlipoca should be sufficient, should it not, Chimalpopoca? I am sure he alone would be eager enough to punish me at your hands."

The priest's eyes glittered in the sockets and so did he seem to be the angry and vengeful God he served.

"Did you speak to this woman," I added, "whoever she was?"

The priest made no answer.

"I am sorry if my words do not satisfy you, Chimalpopoca, but now, if you have no more to say, I will take my leave."

"Go, Lady," he replied. "Take care not to put yourself in peril. Not only from darkness should the wise retreat."

Giving him a cold smile, I said, "Thank you for your kind advice. I will endeavor to follow it."

Hastening then to my Lord's chamber, I found him still asleep. I waited by his side until he awoke, but that was not until Tonatiuh had risen almost halfway into the vault of the sky. He turned to look at me and for a moment his eyes held no recognition, and his face was pale and drawn.

"Xochitlzin?" he whispered.

"Yes, my Lord," said I in a comforting tone, "shall I send for your cacao? You look ill, my Lord, and it will give you strength."

"I am weary unto death," he replied. "My bones are cold with sudden age."

"I will warm them for you," I said, chafing his hands and feet until blood brought new life into them. Then I bid a slave fetch my Lord's favorite drink and to add some chile to it to heat my Lord's flesh from inside.

"Ah, I do feel better, Xochitlzin," he said, sipping the hot cacao. "I do not know why I felt so old and almost as if Lord Mictlantecuhtli did tap his bone of death upon my body."

I smiled, "Perhaps you have but the ague, my Lord, and that is what chills you."

Moteczoma put down his golden cup with a trembling hand. "Never have I had such a dream as I had last night," he began in a hollow voice, "and never do I wish to dream so again."

"What did you dream, Lord? Do you remember?"

I chafed his feet, waiting for him to tell me what he would. For a time he sat gazing at nothing and then looked at me with a childlike confusion. "Do we dream scenes yet to come, do you believe, Lady, or are the scenes we dream but a disorder in the mind brought about by sleep? Which, indeed, could be more real—the thoughts of my mind or pictures painted upon it by hands other than my own? When do we see truly what is, and not what others invent for us to see?"

He paused and I replied, "My Lord, I have no answer for this. I, too, am bewildered by what is sometimes black and sometimes white, and sometimes myself and at other times someone other than myself. I am part of the whole, but what part?"

Moteczoma looked at me with a quickened interest. "Yes, I have felt the same as you! How odd that should be so. And yet, you have had extraordinary skills for a woman and most likely can think somewhat beyond what is common for your sex."

"Tell me your dream, Lord," I said quietly.

"It still seems so strangely real that I find it difficult to speak of it," he began slowly. "I dreamed that I lay here and when I opened my eyes I could see green plumes upon the floor, and when I sat up I saw that they grew from my own feet. Even as I looked, scales of feathers began to cover my limbs and so was I not a man with two legs and arms, but one long body melting into itself and clothing itself in feathers. I felt the lips of my mouth part and from between them uncurled a tongue, forked and darting, and then the torches in the wall flared and I looked upon myself in my dark mirror and saw I had turned into a serpent. A plumed serpent."

"Quetzalcoatl," I breathed.

"Yes, the God, himself. And then somehow I was upon the roof midway through the night, as always, and as I waited with my eyes upon the sky, I heard a low and moaning sound, and there in the darkness did a most monstrous being draw near. And, Lady!" his voice grew husky with fear, "It was Tezcatlipoca, himself!"

"Are you sure you were yet asleep and dreaming?"

"Surely I must have been, for I looked down at my body and it still was the body of a serpent and still covered with feathers that shimmered in the moon's light and in the light of the torch Tezcatlipoca carried in one hand." Moteczoma's eyes were wide with the memory. "And Tezcatlipoca did whisper to me that I was doomed, and that he would be Lord of all this land, with his hand upon the Ueytlatoani's shoulder. This he said without moving his jaw, for his head was but a skull without flesh and his mouth and eyes but holes of night and most awesome to look upon.

"He warned me not to go to Tenochtitlan, for Moteczoma, the Ueytlatoani, would forbid me to enter the city and would wreak great damage upon me and my warriors if we dared to do so. He waved his arm and commanded me to return to the eastern sea and thus depart from these shores forever. All this he said and with an aspect most terrible to behold. I fell at his feet and knew no more."

"Were you not upon your roof last night?"

He turned to me bewildered eyes. "Yes, I was. That is the strangeness of it. When I first awoke it was in the arms of my priests, and they told me I had come up somehow by myself and when they found me I was lying in a swoon. I looked about me and there was no one on the roof but myself and my priests, and where Tezcatlipoca had stood there was not even a feather or a stone to mark his passage. I told the priests this dream and they said to me that it was a dream of foretelling, and that Tezcatlipoca himself had come to warn me not to let the strangers into our gates. And yet . . ." he paused.

"Yes, my Lord? Have you doubt of them?"

He shook his head and sighed. "It all seemed so real that scarce could I believe myself to be dreaming! Of course I know I was, and yet . . ."

"Was Chimalpopoca there with you on the roof?"

"Oh, yes, of course," he answered, "as he always is."

"And did you drink the potion he gave you before you slept?"

"Yes," my Lord replied with a furrowed brow, "but I do not understand what this has to do with my dream, Xochitlzin."

I needed to speak now with utmost caution, for my

position in his court was a precarious one. "My Lord, your priest, Chimalpopoca, is most desirous that his God reign in triumph over your empire. Is this not so?"

My Lord Moteczoma nodded, then waited.

"Would it not be possible for him, in the service of his God, to persuade you that our Lord of the Morning Star is an unworthy rival, and to help you see this more clearly, to give to you a potion infused with the various herbs and mushrooms that make us see wondrous things?"

Before my Lord could protest, I hurried on. "Might he thus bring you to a state in which you see what he wishes for you to see in the darkness?"

Moteczoma held up one imperious hand. "Remember of whom you speak. Your words are perilous!"

I bowed my head. "As you say, my Lord. All I wish to suggest is that perhaps you have seen something both real and unreal, and that it was difficult for you last night to divine which was which."

It was yet another sign of the Ueytlatoani's weakness that he did not rise in anger at my presumption, as once he would have done, but merely bid me begone and to send to him a silent woman to bathe and massage his body. I returned to the women's chamber and rested, listening to their chattering with my eyes closed so they would not know I did not sleep. Thus it was I heard talk of what had happened in the night, and then talk of me.

"It is said the priest met Lady Xochitlzin's shadow self in my Lord's garden, and she did lament her fate for soon she would be slain. He said she wrung her hands most piteously, but he bid her begone, to meet her fate at our warriors' hands." One whisper followed another. "They do say the spirit of Quetzalcoatl drains our Lord's strength with powerful visions and that his Lady, Xochitlzin, is also drained. Her shadow self wanders these lands without her, and at night it returns to her to drink from her strength and vigor."

A third added, "Just look at her there sleeping! Surely there is truth in what you say."

I could feel many eyes upon me.

"I have heard also," came another whisper, "that she can do this, and indeed many other things, with black sorcery."

At that Moteczoma's First Wife, Green River Flowing, shushed the other women with words of stern reproof. It was quiet as they dressed for the midday meal, and most blessedly silent after they had gone. Much had happened that had to be considered, and much would yet happen that I needed to prepare myself to face. Tezcatlipoca moved in the darkness, and if I had indeed a shadow self, in darkness might that part of me do battle against whatever was ranged unseen against me. Well indeed did I wish I possessed the arts of sorcery, for I doubted not the priests made frequent use of all the sorcerers in Tenochtitlan to bend circumstances to suit their will.

Though my Lord Moteczoma still desired me by his side, after that last night he no longer used my body or the body of any other woman. It was said that the agony of his mind had rendered him impotent. However, I believed this was not so, for he was a man for whom lusts of the flesh were remote from the thoughts of his mind. I placed this new affliction at the door of Chimalpopoca, who nightly gave my Lord potions to drink. That the potions were a most powerful elixir I did not doubt. Under their influence did my Lord cry out in sleep or walk blindly through the darkness, preyed upon by visions so that by morning he was bewildered and afraid.

"I will die soon, Xochitlzin," he whispered to me when we had news that Quetzalcoatl's army had left Cholulan. "Whether he is God or man, I know I will die. If he is a God, then Tenochtitlan will be destroyed."

"And if he is but a man, as Lord Cuauhtémoc believes?"

A strange and crafty smile came to his lips. "Then he will be destroyed by my God Tezcatlipoca, who does protect this city."

"Who has told you this, Lord?"

Moteczoma's eyes glittered and a look almost of madness clouded his face. He began to pace, wringing his hands. "I do not know. Someone . . ." he began, then stopped and turned to glare at me. "Do you come in the night in your shadow self and tell me these things, that I will die? You do anger Tezcatlipoca by your words, Lady, and so I warn you!"

"I sleep in the women's chamber and walk not, Lord," I answered, "and as for my shadow self, it is said she is beside our God night and day and never leaves him."

Once more he paced, muttering to himself and casting looks at me of suspicion and entreaty. Most anxious was I for him, for now it seemed he wavered back and forth as on a precipice and I longed to pull him to safety. As I watched him, I thought of his words and the uncertainty he no longer had the strength to bear. A thought came into my mind and I immediately gave it words.

"My Lord," I asked with feigned diffidence, "you are unsure if this stranger is God or man. Even do I have doubts after what came to pass in Cholulan. Thus would it not be an idea to send forth emissaries laden with treasure and that one of these emissaries impersonate you before him? If he is tricked, then he cannot be our God, for a God would surely be able to tell the difference between his precious descendant and a common man."

Moteczoma was first doubtful and then excited at my words, and he bid to his presence the Lords of the Triple Alliance, Cacamatzin, Cuauhtémoc and Cuitláhuac. "I wish to send emissaries to the strangers who approach," he said, "and one will go feigning to be me. If the trick is discovered, then the stranger must be our God. But if the trick is not discovered, then he must be but a man and then may we march against him and destroy him and all of his warriors before they reach Tenochtitlan." He looked around him with some of his past assurance and the Lords glanced from one to the other in uncertainty.

Cuauhtémoc was the first to gain permission to speak. "I believe your plan to be sound, Lord," he said, and I smiled to myself that he, of all the Lords, should find my counsel wise. "Then will we know in truth what these strangers seek. We could send sorcerers also to place webs and walls of magic in their way to slow their progress. That will give us more time to prepare for war if, as I do believe, this is not a God who comes, but a man who seeks our destruction."

All agreed with these words, yet Cacamatzin asked how we could know our emissaries would not merely be slain, and making yet another question we must answer? It was argued that the strangers had not yet murdered messengers but had accepted the treasure brought them with good humor and words of peace.

"A peace he did not bring to Cholulan," said Cuauhtémoc grimly, and with this all did agree.

Then Cuitláhuac, a quiet and thoughtful man, did say, "It is truth that our messengers have returned alive and bearing the strangers' words and necklaces of quetzal stones. If he should slay them, then will we send more. And perhaps from this, and from our deepest sorcery, we will learn the truth."

This was wisdom and my Lord Moteczoma looked upon him approvingly. "You speak most prudently. Let us make no more delay, but send our emissaries forth this very hour."

Our finest warriors were sent upon this venture. One was dressed sumptuously with a pair of my Lord's gold sandals on his feet and a headdress of quetzal plumes upon his head. They journeyed forth with golden treasure: jeweled necklaces and pendants worked from precious stones and intricate metalwork, masks and feather capes and the fragile bodies of beasts all in purest gold. Also Chimalpopoca in his cunning sent with them flesh from a sacrifice made to Tezcatlipoca, and this was cooked in tomatoes and hot chiles so to disguise its taste. In this way did he hope to defeat Quetzalcoatl, if indeed the stranger were he. I knew that if my God could recognize my Lord's impostor, so would he divine the unholy meat, but Chimalpopoca believed that if he were unwary enough to taste, then would he disappear into Tezcatlipoca's darkness and leave that rival God triumphant.

We stood together upon the wall to watch our emissaries depart, my Lord's impostor seated upon a golden litter, surrounded by a retinue of our greatest warriors wearing the masks of eagles. The many men who pretended to be but slaves bearing the treasure were warriors, their weapons cleverly concealed. Thousands of Azteca warriors already waited in ambush, and if our emissaries returned with news that the stranger was not Quetzalcoatl, then would they attack and in utmost ferocity kill or take captive one and all. If, however, the emissaries declared that the stranger was our God, then were our warriors to hasten back to the city so my God would not know of our sacrilege.

It was a long day, and half of yet another day passed also without news. All would have been content to do nothing but listen and pace the palace walls, but it was the month to do honor to the Gods of the Mountains, and most improper would it have been to ignore them. Especially was this so since my Lord had been made unwell by the mountain spirits who did invade bodies with their cold and thus cause sickness. With even greater ceremony did we need to placate Tlaloc and his spirits and beseech them to depart from my Lord's body and return to their abodes of ice and snow.

When Tonatiuh arose on the second day of waiting, we went forth into the sacred square. There were five women and one man sacrificed and their blood poured upon the stone of Tlaloc until the priests stood in a pool that spilled out of the teocalli and dripped crimson down the whitewashed steps. Then there was dancing and singing. Figures made of blood mixed with amaranth paste were brought forth to represent the mountain spirits to be appeased. After due honor was given them, we of the Ueytlatoani's palace ate of them. With rejoicing, our musicians played and our priests and priestesses pounded upon their teponaztlis and blew upon their flutes, and as the shells were sounded from the tops of all the pyramids was there a sudden shuddering in the earth and the waters of the lake did rise and lash against its banks. People screamed in terror as the water came in waves over the streets, knocking children and the elderly to their knees. Someone shouted, "Look to our Lord Popocatepetl!" We turned toward the great mountain of sleeping fire but the fire was not quiet in the Lord's belly but spewing forth in sparks of flame, bright against a sky that had been blue and was now grey with smoke and the clouds of Tlaloc.

As suddenly as it had come, did the water then recede. The clouds billowed rainless to the watery edge of the world, and the fire in Popocatepetl ebbed back into his belly. At this moment did a warrior come running, accompanied by a breathless pochteca. The two men threw themselves at the Ueytlatoani's feet.

"Please, Lord," the warrior cried, and the pochteca held up a small cage and crouched, cowering, beneath it. Chimalpopoca took the cage in his hands and gasped.

"What is it, priest?" Moteczoma asked, peering closer at the little bird within. A most wondrous bird, indeed; it had upon its head a small mirror, but it was not the mirror that caused amazement. It was the vision clearly seen upon the mirror's surface. An army was marching toward us, armor and helmets shining Godlike in the sun. As if behind the bars there coiled a perilous serpent, Chimalpopoca thrust the cage back into the hands of the pochteca.

"Take this evil thing from the Ueytlatoani's sight!" he said harshly, and the two men scrambled backwards, terrified, and were gone.

All stood in silent wonder at what these portents meant. Truly did it seem that some God must have sent these marvels as a warning, but of what no one could agree. Even the priests were overawed, withdrawing to the teocalli of Tlaloc wherein they prayed for guidance. My Lord Moteczoma and I, surrounded by the other Lords and warriors, ascended to the rooftop to await the news our emissaries would bring. Thus we were there when our army came marching swiftly back along the causeway and into the city. The emissaries soon followed, approaching my Lord on their knees in fear and trembling.

"I bid you speak," Moteczoma told them in a voice tremulous with feeling. "What is he, God or man?"

Moteczoma's impostor did reply, "A God, my Lord! Scarcely had I spoken to them, or them to me, than he did know the truth. And not only that, but also did he know without tasting it that the food we gave to him was not animal but human flesh, and he threw it to the ground in anger. Not only that, my Lord . . ." he continued, licking his lips and casting a glance at me that was both amazed and reverent, "All of this was spoken through the shadow self of your Lady Xochitlzin—she is known as Malintzin—for the God did not deign to speak in words we could understand but in language mysterious and divine."

All eyes bore down upon me. I knew this by their heat alone, for my own eyes were fixed upon the breast of my Lord Moteczoma, who also did stare upon me with a gaze of wonder.

"So you do indeed bring him to Tenochtitlan," he whispered. "Now does it come to pass."

I did not speak, but with a breast full of painful longing, I nodded my head. He took a deep breath, then faced his fellow Lords. "We must send forth a party to welcome Quetzalcoatl to the Heart of the One

World, and make ready our city to receive him. And I," he added so softly that only the nearest of us could hear him, "I must prepare myself at last to surrender the One World to my God."

24

MALINALLI

I was glad when we set forth again on our journey. My Captain was a restless man when held captive by chamber walls and happiest when upon his horse and in the midst of dangerous adventure. At first this seemed foolhardy to me. Slowly, however, I found within myself a taste for such a life. I had been born with a restless spirit; danger was still a spice it took me time to crave. By my wits had I kept alive and I had no wish for dying, and yet days soon ceased to have interest for me if they were not, at least in part, given to the challenge of life pitted against life or cunning against cunning. Aguilar, when I told him this, laughed at me and said, "You should have been a man, Marina! And a Spaniard, at that!" His words pleased me greatly. That these men had been emboldened by old tales of romance still seemed reasonless to me, and to go to far lands for gold even more so, but as I marched along with them I discovered a fierce enjoyment of my strength and nimble wit. Not for gold did I journey forth, nor to bring tales of foreign Gods, but to be at my Captain's side and to be useful to him, and to see for myself the empire of the Azteca destroyed.

The way was rough into the heart of the mountains. Our Tlaxcalteca were fearful of the spirits dwelling there, especially as this was the month of their appeasement in sacrifice ritual. My Captain spoke words of encouragement through me, and they, thus heartened, followed him on. Into the dark forest we marched and then into the wasteland that rose steeply to the mountains of fire, Popocatepetl and Ixtacciuatl. Winds blew their shells of mourning across the snow and even the horses shivered in the cold. From the mountain Popocatepetl came groans and shudders. Several of the men asked Cortés permission to climb to the mountaintop to see why smoke issued forth.

"I hardly dare forbid you such adventure!" my Captain said, laughing, and we ate of our rations while several soldiers scrambled over the stones and dry brush to the top. By the time they had scrambled back down, we were ready to push onward. Full of tales they were, about the mountain simmering with fire even as a brazier smoulders with hot coals, and how beyond, in the valley below, there was a most wondrous city, like a vision in a dream. When we came to the last ridge before the descent to the valley floor, there spread before us the fabled and mighty Heart of the One World, Tenochtitlan.

"Mother of God!" my Captain breathed, as we all stopped, transfixed with awe.

Set like a cluster of gems in the midst of a vast and fertile plain lay the shimmering waters of a lake, and, like jewels set within a circle of lesser jewels, were the red and white shining towers and teocallis of Tenochtitlan. Columns of smoke rose from the great teocallis and long pennants of bright feathers floated from the palaces, curling and undulant like the bodies of skyborne serpents. All gleamed brightly in the cold white light, and though it was an awesome sight indeed, still did I feel those walls in the palm of my hand.

"A fine city, is it not, my Captain?"

He turned to me in great good humor. "A fine city, indeed, Doña Marina. Barbarous and beautiful, even as you once were."

"And am I not still?" I asked, masking my jealous disquiet with a teasing smile.

"Barbarous no more, Lady," he answered, to my relief, "but no less beautiful. Do you think, Alvarado," he added to the man who sat astride his horse nearby, "that that was a most gallant reply?"

"You lose none of your courtliness, Captain," Alvarado answered, "but then, with women, I have never seen you lack chivalry. Well do we know the many times that has stood you in good stead, especially with husbands returning home at inauspicious hours!"

Both men laughed. Thus did my Captain often seek to undo flattery with jest, and so I was always unsure what it was he meant and what was mockery.

"Why do you laugh, my Captain?" I asked, wanting the return of his attention.

"Well, Marina," he replied, winking at Alvarado, "surely you have seen that I walk with a limp?"

I inclined my head in answer.

"Well, that has nothing to do with a battlefield, but with a most sudden and necessary leap from the window belonging to a nameless, but very toothsome, young woman. I knew she had a husband, but I thought him more courteous than to return to his conjugal chamber before he was expected."

"Did he not know you lay with his wife? Did he not share her with you willingly?"

Cortés shook his head. "Perhaps you are still somewhat a barbarian, Marina. In Spain men do not willingly share their wives. And yet," he added laughingly to Alvarado, "many wives are shared unwittingly, nonetheless!"

"And many cuckolds thus unknowing created."

I was not willing to yield to my enemy my Captain's attention. "You say to me that you lay with a woman who was a wife. Then is it your custom to do so only if the husband does not know?"

At this both men laughed and Cortés said to me gravely, but with tears of amusement in his eyes, "It is adultery, Marina, and a grievous sin. But it was a sin I did confess . . ."

"Many times . . ." Alvarado murmured.

"Indeed," my Captain agreed, "many times. Sadly, I

have been cursed with a lustful nature that needs to be forgiven often by our most gracious Lord."

"If you stayed astride your *horse,* Cortés, you would have less need to kneel in the confessional."

Cortés laughed and slapped his knee at Alvarado's jest, and they rode cheerfully on together while I rode disconsolately behind.

"It scarcely seems real, does it not?" Aguilar said, riding abreast of me. His words at first confused me until it came to my mind that he was not speaking of my Captain's conduct but of the great city below us.

I nodded.

"Never did I think to see so awesome a sight, Marina." His voice was so full of wonder that I turned to him in some amazement. "This is such a marvel to you, then?"

"Indeed it is," he replied, his eyes fixed on the vista before us. "Never in all the tales I have read or the dreams I have dreamed have I met with such a sight. Truly this is worth all of the trouble we have endured."

"It is but a city of stone," I told him drily, "and not one of cloud. You are this amazed because you expected to see only a town of mud."

At this sudden rush of bitterness, he looked quickly at me and with a furrowed brow. "That is not so, Marina," he said quietly. "It is just that your cities are very beautiful and so unlike those we have in Spain. I never expected Tenochtitlan to be a town of mud, especially since Moteczoma is so mighty and rich a king."

"Yes," I said, "without Moteczoma we Mexica would surely still be wallowing about in the swamps and grunting like beasts. I tell you, Aguilar, that there was greatness in this land long before the greedy Azteca were spawned! But then," I added in a voice of obsidian, "I cannot expect so very *civilized* a man to believe the words of a barbarian."

"Marina!" he protested, but I dug my heels into my mare and galloped away. Angry, and pleased that I had hurt Aguilar as my Captain had hurt me, still I felt a vague uneasiness that I had done so. Aguilar never wounded me and was truly the most loyal of allies, and though I knew my power over him, still I had to acknowledge his usefulness. I would have to be kinder to him when next we spoke, I decided, and stir flame into the embers of his desire.

I returned to my Captain's side just as men were seen approaching us from the direction of Tenochtitlan. We met at the base of the mountains. A retinue of caciques and warriors marched in procession surrounding a slave-borne golden litter upon which sat a Lord in elegant dress.

"Could this be Moteczoma, Marina?" my Captain asked, and I shook my head that as yet I did not know who came to us in such splendor. The litter was set down gently and as his caciques and warriors parted, the Lord placed the golden soles of his sandals to the ground and then stood. One cacique, also sumptuously arrayed, stepped forth from the others and announced, "The Ueytlatoani of the One World, Lord Moteczoma!" The one so announced graciously inclined his head, as my Captain did also. Richly was he garbed in golden jewels and feathers, and the headdress he wore fanned outward like tongues of green flame. Altogether he was a most imposing sight and for a moment I forgot my vengefulness in awe.

"What did he say, Marina?" Cortés asked impatiently, and I realized that I had been standing in deaf thought.

"He says this is Moteczoma," I said bluntly, wondering why he came so far from his city to greet us.

"Tell Moteczoma I am honored to meet with such a great prince and seek but brotherly peace and affection."

I said what was needful and then the Ueytlatoani replied, "I am also honored, and give due reverence to such a mighty visitor to our land. Please accept these poor trifles we have brought with us in friendship," and he clapped his hands and slaves came forth with jewels and cloth and set them in piles before my Captain.

"My God," I said to them, "is pleased that you show him this mark of your devotion. If you had not done so, he would surely have destroyed you and your city as he did, for like reason, in Cholulan." My Captain asked what I had said, and I told him I had given them thanks and warned them that we had come peacefully and to bid for peace.

"Very well," he said. "Now tell them I wish to proceed to Tenochtitlan."

As I turned to the Ueytlatoani with these words, I saw a quivering in his hands and a spasm, slight but arresting, jerking at the corner of his mouth. My attention sharpened at this and gave me to notice that the slaves were all men of good size and muscular, not in the sinewy way slaves are muscular but in the rugged way of warriors. Likewise they did not have the servile expression of slaves but glanced about with eyes both keen and watchful.

"Careful, Captain," I said in a gentle voice. "There is something wrong. I do not know yet what it is, but I sense things are not as they appear."

Cortés smiled at me as if I had just said some pleasantry, but I could see grim understanding in his eyes. "Very well, Marina, we will tread with care. I have noticed Moteczoma is not wearing the medal of St. Francis I told his caciques he should wear upon the day of our meeting."

This omission meant little, I thought, but still there was something missing, something wrong, and I felt the hair rise on my head like the fur on the back of a jaguar when he is stalking his prey in the jungle. Just so did I smell danger in the air.

"You have had a long journey this day and thus do we bring you food to eat, Lord," a cacique said, bowing, and a bowl of stew was set before Cortés and a gourd was filled and held out to him. Before he could take it into his hands, however, I took it in mine and held it to my nose. It smelled good and rich with meat and ripe tomatoes. I tasted it and chewed a piece of the tender meat. As I did this I glanced up and the cacique who had presented the gourd was regarding me with uneasy speculation. What could be the reason for that, I wondered, unless something of significance had been added to the stew.

"My Captain," I murmured with a face of unconcern, "I believe this to be a hoax. I do not think this man before us is Moteczoma. I have heard it said that he will not speak in public except through interpreters. Furthermore, these slaves appear to be more noble warrior than slave, and this stew . . ." I paused, gauging his reaction and what he would show the Azteca, "you must not eat it, for if you were indeed Quetzalcoatl, you would fiercely shun such a gift of sacrilege."

"Am I now cursed to continue playing this absurd God of yours?"

Controlling my impatience at having to tread again this well-trodden ground, I said pleasantly, "Truly, my Captain, their believing you a God is the only reason we have not been slain where we now stand."

He sighed. "Very well, so be it. What do we do now with these impostors?"

Alvarado, who had overheard, said carelessly, "We greatly outnumber them. Mayhap we should just kill them and be done with it."

"We would then bring upon us thousands more after them," Cortés said. "Let us sue for peace."

I touched my Captain upon his arm, something I rarely did, and he looked at me questioningly.

"My Captain, I believe they are not certain if you are Quetzalcoatl. Thus they seek to determine your nature by the use of trickery. You must cast down this gourd of food when I hand it to you, and with great disgust should you berate the Azteca for their treachery." I handed him the gourd and then I said, "The meat in it is not meat, but human flesh they seek to feed you." In most unfeigned disgust did Cortés hurl the gourd to the ground.

"You unholy savages!" he began, and in his loathing

did he let loose other words of horror and contempt. Most impressive did he look, with his helmet and armor new-polished and shining, and though the Azteca could not understand his words, his righteous horror was most apparent. When he ceased speaking, I cried at them, "You have profaned your God, Quetzalcoatl! How dare you give him the meat of sacrifice when he has forbidden it! Now must you bow and touch your tongues to the dirt and there make all obeisances to him or he will surely strike you dead!"

Terrified, they did so, even the man who had pretended to be Moteczoma. Then they begged for his forgiveness.

"Speak graciously to them, Marina," my Captain said when I told him they sought his pardon. "I feel we stand very close to the gates of Tenochtitlan."

I told the frightened Azteca—and with what relish did I tell it!—that out of my God's vast benevolence they were forgiven, and that they might return to their true Ueytlatoani whom my God wished soon to see.

"Tell several of these savages that I order them to carry a message of peace to their master. Then, when they have gone, allow the others to leave also." I did as he bid me. Several of the Azteca departed with my Captain's message, bowing as they backed away, and as soon as they had hastened off over the first hill, I sent the others after them.

Cortés breathed a sigh of relief. "I am glad that this has been so easily smoothed over. While you were berating them, Marina, a scout came to speak quietly in my ear that thousands of Azteca warriors are massed beyond that low hill, painted and dressed for battle."

"But you seemed quiet unconcerned, my Captain," I exclaimed, "and as if you did not know of such immediate peril."

"Marina," he smiled, "I simply found it wisest to treat our visitors mercifully and let them go in peace. Little comes of driving men beyond their endurance." At this we all laughed, and heartily, for it was only due to my Captain's iron will that his men had come so far and through such discomfort and danger. After a short moment he raised his sword above his head and cried, "To Tenochtitlan, and by God's blessing, to her treasure!" and his men all shouted and slapped each other on the back, speaking eagerly of returning rich to their homeland as we proceeded thus merrily along. We had not journeyed far before we met another group of emissaries bearing more treasures.

"Malintzin," they asked respectfully, "please tell the God the Ueytlatoani wishes for him to accept these gifts, and also does the Ueytlatoani wish for him to know that he understands he and his fellow Lords have travelled far from distant lands and endured much hardship to see him, and that he has given him already much gold and silver and chalchuites along the way as tribute.

"But now the Ueytlatoani sends us to ask our God most humbly not to continue his journey further. If he and his Lords return to the sea, the Ueytlatoani will give to him many loads of gold and silver, precious stones and feathered capes, and these things will be sent to where his great houses will take him home again, across the water."

"Your Ueytlatoani is very inconstant," I replied for my Captain. "First he says one thing and then another. We choose, despite the Ueytlatoani's generosity, to continue to Tenochtitlan."

"But the road is not good and our God will grow weary," they protested with a kind of desperate weakness.

"Tell them," Cortés said, "that we are determined to speak with Moteczoma and if our presence is not of benefit to his people, then we will return from whence we have come."

The messengers bowed and departed. We journeyed on, with some less valiant of our men muttering about becoming entrapped and then murdered inside the great city ahead of us. Cortés that night bade his priest say soothing prayers about their Spanish God protecting them from all harm. We slept well and were well-fed that night in a town called Ayotzingo, which was built half upon land and half on water in a most marvelous fashion.

The next morning, four caciques arrived to beg counsel with my Captain. "I do not mind more treasure," he told me in weary good humor as he dressed, "but I am heartily sick of all these uninvited visitors. And yet, I suppose, they do us a service by flattening the road ahead of us!"

These emissaries were well and elegantly dressed, and they made deep obeisances to Cortés, begging him to await the arrival of the Lord of Texcoco, Cacamatzin, who was nephew to the Ueytlatoani, Moteczoma. Soon, that Lord arrived and in sumptuous grandeur, in a litter of silver bedecked with plumes of quetzal feathers that shimmered in the sun as it was carried along. Golden serpents had been fashioned along its sides and their eyes glittered with precious stones. Great caciques, wearing the honorable masks of eagles and jaguars, bore the litter on their shoulders as if they were mere slaves. When they were near, they lowered the litter to the ground and two helped the Lord Cacamatzin alight while a third swept the ground with feathers before his feet. With deep obeisances, Lord Cacamatzin asked permission to speak.

"You may, Lord," I said, well pleased by this auspicious display of reverence.

"Malintzin," said he, "I have come with these my caciques to place ourselves at our God's service and at the service of his Lords, as well. We wish to give you all you need for your comfort and to lead you to Tenochtitlan where the Ueytlatoani, Moteczoma, awaits to do you honor. He asks forgiveness that he has not come himself, but he has been unwell." All this I told my Captain, and we were both well pleased by the words. If such a great Lord as Cacamatzin showed such reverence, then surely Moteczoma himself would not show less.

Cortés embraced them in the Spanish manner, much to their surprise that a God would deign to show such affection. Then he gave to them necklaces of blue and green stones and also stones of various other colors they called margaritas.

"If it pleases our God, Malintzin, shall we now begin our journey?" Lord Cacamatzin asked, and thus we proceeded, with fanfare and in splendor, toward Tenochtitlan. People gathered as we passed, singing and dancing and throwing flowers at our feet. Their eyes were wide at the sight of our horses, and Alvarado made his stallion prance sideways and toss its head. In this way we marched to the great stone causeway and proceeded then upon it through the towns that were built on land and over the water.

"This is like an enchantment," Aguilar said softly at my side, "like a fabulous tale of ancient times. Never did I think to see anything so splendid and strange."

Though I hated Moteczoma and the Azteca, yet was I pleased to hear these words. Such artful skill could not be the work of mere savages. Such lofty and impressive teocallis could not have been built by barbarians, nor the lush gardens of flowers and vegetables that floated like bright and tiny islands on the surface of the lake. Though I was not Azteca, neither was I from Spain, and it pleased me that since my Captain thought of me as Mexica, he could now see about my shoulders not the coarse mantle of mere jungle, but the elegant mantle of Tenochtitlan's artful beauty.

Aguilar chattered on about the wondrous sights and how he was reminded by them of the tales of adventure he had read, and I listened to his eager voice with one ear and kept the other open for what I could overhear from the crowds. Finally we reached the town of Ixtapalapan. Caciques in all their finery came in a procession to greet us, including in their number the Lord Cuitláhuac and the Lord of Culuacan, both powerful rulers in Anáhuac. After their obeisances and words of welcome, they showed us to their palaces and begged us to rest. My Captain was anxious to reach Tenochtitlan, but he complied with most amiable words. Our chamber was large and very beautiful, built of carved stone and sweetly scented woods. Ceramic dishes of red and white design held small mountains of fruit for our refreshment.

Then were we bidden to a feast and I accompanied my Captain as always, though the other women dined in a separate chamber. A long table was covered from end to end with gold and silver dishes and strewn with fruit and flowers. Ceramic bowls rested upon small braziers so that their contents simmered and made fragrant the air. My Captain was given the seat of highest honor and I sat by his one side while the Lord Cuitláhuac sat upon the other. Down the table, in order of rank, sat other caciques and warriors and the highest officers of my Captain's men. The Azteca were dainty in their ways and took small morsels of food from each dish, but the Spanish ate with avid hunger and with moist noises from their mouths and a great smacking of their lips. I could see the caciques were bewildered by these foreign ways, but courtesy, as well as veneration, kept them silent.

Young girls were brought in to dance and sing and play upon their instruments, and they wore cotton so white and fine that their slim bodies could dimly be seen through their cueitls. They were maidens with their hair loose and flowing and all of them were beautiful. One, who could not have been more than eleven years of age, came dancing near my Captain and one shoulder of her huipilli slipped down her arm so the top of one young round breast could be seen. I heard my Captain's breathing quicken and was dismayed. Always I feared banishment from his bed, and yet I knew he was a man of lusts and that it was not his nature to be sated with one woman alone. I had long worked to become for him more important than a passing hunger. If he wanted a woman it would be to my benefit, I knew, to procure her for him, thus to trade an hour of pleasure for an increase in his gratitude to me. Procuring this young girl proved a simple matter indeed. Lord Cuitláhuac addressed me.

"Would it offend our God, Malintzin, if I were to give to him my daughter for this night? She is a maiden yet, but has come into her courses and thus might bear noble fruit from such an exalted coupling," he said anxiously.

"While on this earth our God does indeed eat and drink and couple with mortal woman," I explained cautiously, "so to more perfectly understand the common plight. I will ask if he will deign to lie with your daughter, as you wish."

I turned to Cortés, who was watching the girl with eyes that laid her body bare, and I told him what Lord Cuitláhuac had said. If I had not been so pierced with jealousy, I might have been amused by my Captain's struggle to slake his thirst as he wished while acting in righteousness before the grim eyes of his God. It would have taken but a word from me to remind him of his pious duty, but I knew I would gain more by helping to quiet the promptings of virtue. One way to secure my place with him, I knew, was to provide him with excuses to do as he wished.

"My Captain," I said, with my eyes lowered modestly. "I am afraid that you are in a most difficult situation. The Lord Cuitláhuac wishes most eagerly for you to lie with his daughter so that perhaps she might become with child." I paused, then added softly, "If this did prove to be so, it could only help our cause."

"How could it, Marina?" he asked, longing for a reason to do as he so clearly desired.

"The Azteca Lords will be far less likely to attack you if their daughters carry your sons."

"You speak wisely as usual, Marina." Relieved, he gave me a grateful smile and then turned his gaze once more to the Lord's young daughter.

"Marina," he asked quietly, without taking his eyes from her, "is she not, perhaps, over-young?"

I remembered myself at eleven, preyed upon by my mother's second husband, and how his hot impatient ways had given me much pain. "She is a maiden, Captain, but in this land she is not over-young. And yet," I added, for her soft eyes touched my heart, "she will need a gentle hand."

"I will be most gentle with her," my Captain said, rising to his feet. "Now tell her father that I accept his gift and will gladly take her with me now."

I obeyed him, watching as he held out his hand to the maiden who, with fearful eyes fixed upon the ground, went to him. "Tell her she is not to be afraid," he asked. "Tell her that I will use her tenderly."

The child cast at me a grateful glance before she was led away, and I departed the chamber also, for without Cortés present it was improper for me to remain. Thus I wandered into the garden enclosed by the palace walls and tried not to envision what was happening in my Captain's chamber. Aguilar saw me leave and followed my steps into the garden, coming upon me so quietly that I was startled from my dark pondering to see him standing so near.

"Did I frighten you, Marina?"

I tried to smile as if there was nothing in my mind but idle thoughts. "Yes, Aguilar, for you walk like a spectre on noiseless feet."

"Shall I leave? Do I disturb your solitude?"

Surprised was I to realize that his presence did not disturb me. Indeed, I was grateful for it and smiled at him truly as I said, "No, I am glad to see you. I am not sure why."

"Perhaps I know."

"Perhaps."

He slipped his hand under my arm. "Let us walk, Marina, and enjoy the night and this beautiful garden."

Again I was grateful to him that he did not speak about the matter further but led me along the garden paths, through the trees and past the ponds and fountains, speaking of this and that but not of anything that mattered. After a long while I said, "Perhaps I should make sure my Captain does not have need of me, Aguilar."

There was a long moment and then he replied, "Do you wish for me to remain here waiting, if—" he paused, choosing his words with care, "he does not bid you stay?"

I could not look at him and see the pity I knew would be in his eyes. "Yes, Aguilar, if you would."

"Then go. I will wait."

I hurried to my Captain's chamber but one of his men stood outside its door. "Does Captain Cortés have need of me?" I asked, feeling shame rise to redden my cheeks.

"Not tonight," the soldier replied. "He bid me say to you that you must be weary after our long journey, and that it would be well for you to sleep in another chamber where you may rest more easily."

Then he was going to keep the girl with him all night, leaving me to find a bed as best I could. I returned to the garden with my heart in a fever of jealousy and shame. There Aguilar waited, as he said he would, and I went to him with magic in my eyes, looking long upon him so he caught from me some part of my fever and began to tremble. I reached for his hand and slid it over my breast.

"No, Marina," he whispered, "it would be wrong."

"Why? You owe nothing to Cortés—nor do I! He takes his pleasure elsewhere, why do we not also? Is it that you no longer want me, Aguilar?" I swayed against him, pressing my body to his, moving my hips against his tepuli so that it stiffened with desire.

"You do want me, I know you do," I whispered. He groaned, giving ground for a moment before he put his hands on my arms and pushed me gently away.

"I do, Marina, God help me. I want you more than any woman I have ever known."

"Then why will you not lie with me?" I whispered, drawing near him once more. "Because your God would not approve? Then do as your Captain does and seek out a priest in the morning for forgiveness."

Aguilar gazed upon me sadly. "You do not understand, Marina. I cannot."

I lashed out against him in anger, then, for twice had I been not wanted. Never had I questioned that if I bent my finger toward Aguilar he would come running. Why did he not seize this chance to have what he admitted he had always desired? "What do I not understand?" I cried hotly. "That you are not man enough, Aguilar? That I am like one of those useless women in your fables for whom you yearn from a distance but truly want not?"

"I am sorry if I have given you pain, Marina," he said softly. "I would never wish to hurt you."

"Give me pain? You?" I cried at him in a fury. "How could you ever hurt me? You mean nothing to me, less than nothing. I only wanted to lie with you because . . ." suddenly I could not go on, could not tell the truth.

"I know why," he said wearily, then turned and walked away, leaving me alone in the darkness. When it grew cold I went back inside the palace, uncertain where to sleep. On the floor near the doorway to my Captain's chamber was a woolen cape such as the soldiers had brought with them from Spain. As I wrapped it warmly around me I noticed where it had been clumsily mended, and remembered Aguilar once sewing with difficulty by the fire. Even though my heart still burned with anger at him, I knew he had left it there, certain I would not seek another chamber and that I would be cold. I curled up like a dog in a dark and quiet corner and awoke when light first crept along the hall. Hiding myself, I saw when the girl left my Captain's chamber, and after a few moments more Cortés himself appeared. Feigning that I had but wandered in from a stroll in the garden, I looked all surprise to see him.

"You are up early, Marina," he said. "I trust you slept well?"

"Indeed yes, my Captain."

"Good, Marina, good," he said brusquely. "Now let us ready ourselves for our entry into Tenochtitlan."

"Whatever you wish, my Captain, I will do."

"I know, and I will never forget that is so." He looked at me and our eyes met in understanding.

It was but a short journey that day and we went in grand procession as if we were Gods indeed, accompanied by a number of great caciques, and we were stared upon from rooftops and walls and from the canoes which covered the lake and its canals. Cortés and his men surely did appear Godlike in their bright-polished armor and shining helmets; unmistakably Lord over all, my Captain rode ahead on his high-stepping mare, looking neither left nor right. Finally we reached a crossroads where another causeway lay upon the lake to our left. Elegant stone teocallis were crowded with warriors wearing their masks and carrying shields of feathers, and there also were the caciques of Tenochtitlan in their finest headdresses and golden jewels. In the middle of the causeway stood the mightiest caciques of all the Azteca, and they made obeisances and touched dirt upon their tongues, announcing they had been sent by their Ueytlatoani, Moteczoma, to welcome us to the Heart of the One World. Speeches were made back and forth, so courteous and flowery on one side and so pious on the other that I needed not only to translate the words but somehow make them carry sense as well. Often did it seem the Azteca and the Spaniards not only spoke two separate tongues but saw two different worlds. This was all to my advantage, of course, for I could thus more easily bend meaning to my will.

Led by these mighty Lords we proceeded on along the causeway where, swift approaching, came a splendid litter of gold. My heart quivered within me, for this could be none other than Moteczoma, at last. Moteczoma, my enemy. When the litter drew near I saw it was shaded by a canopy of blue-green feathers fringed with pearls and chalchuites. Two caciques supported the Ueytlatoani to his gold-shod feet and two others supported him from behind. Other Lords swept the ground before him, laying down gold-embroidered cloths so that he walked upon gold in his golden sandals. People fell to their faces as he passed them by.

"This is indeed Moteczoma, my Captain," I said, and Cortés leaped from his horse, and strode up to the Ueytlatoani. I followed swiftly, leaving our horses in the care of Aguilar. Cortés wished Moteczoma good health, and in turn the Ueytlatoani bade him welcome. My Captain reached to take Moteczoma's hand but as this was never done, the Ueytlatoani was startled and drew back.

"My Lord," I said in reverent tones, not raising my eyes from the royal chest, "this is the manner in which our God Quetzalcoatl shows to you due honor. Surely you do not find such an embrace unacceptable?"

Moteczoma, in obvious discomfort, offered his hand. Cortés grasped it heartily in his right while bringing forth with his left a necklace of margaritas that had been infused with a musky scent. This my Captain placed around the neck of the Ueytlatoani and made as if to embrace him in the custom of the Spanish, but two caciques drew Moteczoma slightly away, and I murmured, "My Captain, it is better not to touch Moteczoma. That is not the custom here."

Cortés shrugged. "Very well, I have no desire to offend. Tell him this, that I am overjoyed to at last meet with such a mighty prince and that I consider it a great honor that he should meet me thus in person. Also thank him for the many fine gifts he has bestowed upon us so generously."

I suppressed a sigh of frustration. Still my Captain spoke as a mere mortal would and not with the arrogance of a God. I said to Moteczoma what was more to our profit, and he listened to my words with increased veneration. While he listened, I studied the caciques to gauge their thoughts, and some wore faces blank with awe and some of concealed suspicion. Well did I know we must move cautiously, for all had not yet surrendered to our will.

Believing the Ueytlatoani to have no interest in a mere woman, I dared to raise my eyes to his face, a blasphemous act for all but his most intimate relations. To my surprise I found him staring at me with a most perplexing expression upon his face. Amazement was there and something akin to resentment and, startling to discover, something of awe. I looked down quickly, disconcerted. Surely Moteczoma could not be so disquieted by the fact that a woman could have wit enough to speak another tongue or that I bore a great resemblance to a priestess he had once heard prophesy. It had to be that he was amazed by my closeness to a God, and that the tongue I knew was therefore divine. That would be explanation enough, I thought.

In solemn ceremony did we then walk together to the entrance into Tenochtitlan. I stole many glances at Moteczoma as we went, believing myself no longer noticed. He was a man small in stature but with a most prideful bearing. His face was narrow and grave, and upon his chin he wore a thin black beard, fastidiously clipped and combed. Coiled the length of his arms were golden serpents with eyes of precious stones, and his maxtlatl and cape were covered entirely in green and crimson hummingbird feathers. A headdress of gold and jewels and with plumes of quetzal feathers seemed overheavy for such a slender neck and frail-seeming skull. Cortés was not a much larger man, and it gave me amusement that these two almighty Lords, while they were in power so masterful, should yet in size appear less formidable than many they governed. Alvarado, with his broad chest and head of golden hair, was the more obvious Lord and master, and yet there was something mysterious, a familiarity with command, perhaps, that made one turn to those two smaller men and know them for the sovereigns they were. The manner in which they walked and gestured with their hands, the way in which they held their heads, all of this they did with lordly bearing. The common people fell to the ground on their faces as we passed, thus they did not see us—but the caciques busily glanced this way and that and, quite often, I found their gazes resting upon me. There is some mystery here, I thought. Surely I cannot seem to be a person of more than minor interest.

Our procession wound along wide streets and over the bridged canals, past the great houses of the rich and the floating chinampas, bright with flowers, lying upon the lake waters as the earth floats upon the breast of the sea. When we came within sight of the sacred part of the city, the Heart of the Heart of the One World, there were grand teocallis indeed, their narrow steps lined with black-robed priests holding braziers of sweet copal to scent the air. Encircling this sacred plaza was the serpent wall, just outside of which were palaces and other large and sumptuous buildings. Immediately we were taken to a splendid palace that had belonged to the Ueytlatoani Axayácatl, Moteczoma's father. Its halls and great chambers were canopied with embroidered cloths and the walls were garlanded with fresh flowers. Everywhere were there bowls and wide platters of fruit and bouquets of blossoms in honor of Quetzalcoatl. Well was my Captain pleased to see such signs of welcome, and I hastened to remind him that they did him this honor because they believed him to be a God.

"I ask that you do not think me presumptuous, my Captain, but I must warn you to be most careful lest they suspect you are but a man."

Cortés saw the reason in this but was nonetheless displeased by the necessity. "Marina, I would far rather see this honor given to the one who brings word of the Holy Trinity to these pagans, and not to yet another of their vile and imaginary deities!"

"I know, my Captain," I said soothingly, "but that is not yet to be. Perhaps later, after they have taken your words to heart."

He nodded, heaving an exasperated sigh. "Unfortunately you speak truth. I will be careful."

Soon were we invited to Moteczoma's audience chamber in his palace nearby. Caciques led us in ceremony beside the palace of Ahuitzotl, ravaged by floods some years before, and past what the caciques described as a menagerie of exotic beasts. Moteczoma's palace was no grander than that of Axayácatl, but grand nonetheless. Up stairs and through a large garden we were led, at last reaching the door of the chamber wherein the ruler of the Azteca awaited us. With bows and words of reverence my Captain and I were entreated to enter, while the others among us were asked most politely to remain outside.

Moteczoma stood before his golden icpalli, and though I kept my eyes respectfully to the floor, still I saw one figure standing close beside him and some others at a distance. My Captain gasped and crossed himself. "In the name of the Blessed Virgin, what is this witchery, Marina?"

Startled, I looked up. It was my sister who stood beside the hated Moteczoma, staring back at me as if one of us was real and the other but a reflection. She stepped slowly toward me, whispering, "Malinalli? Can it be you?"

"Indeed, Xochitl," I answered, as my thoughts darted this way and that behind my eyes. "Of course it is I."

"Answer me now, Marina!" Cortés demanded, looking from one to the other of us in grave disquiet.

"This is no witchery," I said, straining for calm. "This is but my own sister, my twin, from whom I was separated many ages ago."

"You swear to me that you had no idea she was here?"

"Of course I did not know, my Captain. I am as startled as you are."

He looked doubtfully at me a moment. "Well, it seems the greatest impossibility. And you are as like as two candles."

"I agree, and yet this is an accident of fate that may serve our interests well." I turned back to my sister, who stood staring at me still. Beyond her Moteczoma regarded us both in silence.

"Are you willing to embrace me, after we have been apart for so long?" Smiling uncertainly, Xochitl opened her arms and I stepped uncomfortably into their embrace. "I never thought to see you again," she whispered.

"Nor I you," I replied. "And what are you to Moteczoma that you stand beside him?"

"I am his Second Wife," she answered.

Thus it was I learned my sister had left Cholulan to become the Ueytlatoani's whore. I drew away from her embrace, masking my contempt that she should thus ally herself with the man who had murdered our father. I longed to shout these words into her face, but ill would that have served us. No, I would bide my time and make what use I could of her and then, when she could no longer be of service, I would tell her of my scorn.

25

Xochitl

It seemed to me that day the wonder of all wonders that my sister had brought our God to Tenochtitlan. This was more astonishing to me, indeed, than if my shadow self had been upon that journey, though I was careful not to let Moteczoma or his Lords and priests know the truth, that she was but my sister. Time might come when that disclosure would need to be made, but not yet. Overjoyed as I was to see her, flesh of my flesh and companion of my God, I knew she did not feel equal delight. I felt her body stiffen in my arms and when I looked into her eyes they were cold. Most sorrowful was I that she believed me an adversary, even as were our masters in part adversaries. I longed to hold private counsel with her and so plumb the depths of her heart, but that chance did not come for several days.

During that time I was much with my Lord Moteczoma, and privy to the talk that ebbed and flowed around him in arguments about the divinity of the Lords now among us. Prophecy had been fulfilled, but Lords Cuauhtémoc and Cacamatzin argued courteously and yet most forcefully that they who had thus fulfilled it were not sacred beings but mere men. When alone with my Lord, I would repeat to him that godly beings on earth necessarily take on aspects of mortal man, but that this did not lessen their divinity. Though I spoke with solemn assurance, at the same time I heard stories that made my faith, as after the massacre in Cholulan, weaken. I no longer had any direct connection with my God Quetzalcoatl and though I saw him but few times, he looked upon me not with almighty knowing, but with curiosity and suspicion most bewildering to me.

At last I found a way to see my sister alone. One day I did go to my Lord's chamber and say, as had I planned, "Well would it advise us, my Lord, if I were to hold private converse with my shadow self and thus discover if the God requires any little thing we may provide for his comfort." He agreed, and thus did I have servants sent to the palace of Axayácatl with a message for my sister to come to my Lord Moteczoma's palace alone. She was led to where I awaited her.

"You wished to see me, sister?" she asked in a voice so cool that I did not seek to embrace her.

"Malinalli," I began hesitantly, "my Lord wishes to discover if there is, perhaps, anything your God requires for his comfort that he has not already been given."

My sister crossed her arms over her breast, regarding me without expression. "My Lord requires due reverence with gold, sister, and that may you tell your master." I heard the scorn with which she spoke that last word and I hastened to relieve what I perceived to be her mistrust of me.

"Malinalli . . ." I began, but she interrupted me.

"I am now Doña Marina, Xochitl, even though these people call me Malintzin. I have no fondness for the years in which I was known by that other name, and I must ask you to cease speaking it to me."

"Very well, sister," I said, bewildered by her angry bitterness, for I did not know what I had done to deserve it unleashed upon me. "I know you have always spoken of my Lord Moteczoma as if you hated him." I paused, but she gazed darkly upon me in silence. "I did also, sister, as well you must remember."

"Indeed? And so great was your loathing that you became his wife?"

Words rose hotly to my lips and with some difficulty did I bite them back. "Sister, listen to me. As a priestess I came here from Cholulan, and I was priestess *only*. When it was decided I should become my Lord's Second Wife my own wishes in the matter were not considered."

"I would have died before submitting to the man who killed our father!"

So that was it. Never had she allowed that old anger to depart. Though I had early accepted the unhappy truth that our father was a warrior who had met a warrior's death, my sister had continued to lay blame for his death upon my Lord. Was this, then, the true reason for her taking part in this journey to Tenochtitlan? Not as Quetzalcoatl's mortal aide, but to exact revenge? Prophecy had been fulfilled either way, but I could not believe that she would make the journey simply to avenge a childhood wrong.

"Doña Marina," I said reproachfully, "you have come here as the devoted servant of our God, have you not? You have not come here merely out of old anger?" I felt something cold clutch my heart. "Indeed there are many in this palace who believe him not to be our God at all, but a mortal impostor. What say you to this?"

At first her face hardened, eyes glittering like ice, and into my mind came the thought that her face was indeed an exquisite mask, tooled by anger and ambition, her features capable of assuming expression as effortlessly as a shallow river rippling over stones. Before my eyes, then, her mouth softened tenderly and the narrow eyes widened like those of a child.

"I must leave now, Xochitl. My God has need of me." And with that she left the room without a backward glance.

26

MALINALLI

Bored with my sister's credulity as I was pleased with her guileless tale of court intrigue, I hastened back to Axayácatl's palace in search of Cortés. He was checking on his men, making sure they had what was needed and that they knew not to go outside or behave in any way that might jeopardize our campaign. Cannon had been placed on the palace roof in the event of an Azteca uprising against us. He counseled patience, but I knew the men were starting to grumble at the manner in which gold was being doled out to them and in quantities—so they said among themselves—that ill-rewarded the risks and privations they endured to earn it. This I had listened to, in my stealthy manner, and reported to my Captain. In this way, as in all others, I sought to be indispensable to him.

"Captain," I called when at last I found him, "I need to have word with you in private."

Raising an eyebrow at this, for usually I waited for the night to take counsel with him when we were alone, he followed me to our chamber.

"What is it, Marina?" he asked. "More signs of unrest?"

"No, my Captain, a matter of gravest urgency. My twin sent for me to come to her chamber in Moteczoma's palace. There she told me that many have held counsel with the Ueytlatoani, insisting to him that you are not a God, but a mere man. My sister wanted to know the truth, for indeed few can easily believe Gods are among them when they have the habits of men, and some with all the vices."

Cortés smiled briefly at this and then grew serious. "Indeed this does not surprise me, Marina. I have been chafing at this ruse and well do you know how I have longed to cast it off. Perhaps that time has come."

I held up a cautionary hand. "I agree with you, but in so doing we will avoid one peril only to invite another. There are many who would not kill a God but will have no hesitation about spilling the blood of an enemy."

"You understand these heathen minds better than I, Marina," he said casually, "so what do you think it wise for us to do?"

I looked at him a moment and with what magic I could draw up into my eyes. "Captain, I think it best to take Moteczoma prisoner."

"What?" my Captain said, amazed. "In his own palace? His own city?"

"With guile, my Captain, so that he will not know he is being taken captive. That way he will not rouse his men and we will be able to escort him easily to our palace with none the wiser. No one will dare raise a hand against us if Moteczoma could be struck down as well."

"And how do you propose we do this?" he asked drily. "Drugged and at dark of night?"

I smiled. "I have an idea. Let us go to him today as if we wish to speak to him again of our holy religion. Let us send word that we come as usual so he will not be alarmed by an unexpected visit. Then let me speak to him. I will say that we have heard treacherous words in the city and that we do not wish him to come to harm through his graciousness to us. I will say we seek to protect him from his enemies."

Cortés thought deeply upon this before he made reply. "Yes, this might be of advantage to us, especially since Villa Rica has been attacked by the Tlaxcalteca, proving an unrest that might also turn against him.

Tlaxcaltecan spies have brought us word the Azteca are not to be trusted and our men, as you know, are restless with disquiet that perhaps we are as much captive as guest in this palace. What you say sounds reasonable."

I took this for his consent. "Oh, and one thing more," I added lightly. "We must make certain that my sister is not present when we take her husband captive."

He shrugged. "If you persuade him so subtly, why would she protest? Would he listen to a woman anyway?"

"I have heard it said that Moteczoma is greatly influenced by my sister. We know not what she will counsel if she is there to hear what we say. And there is another reason, my Captain . . ."

He raised one eyebrow in enquiry.

"My sister is not to be trusted, for her jealousy of me may cause her to be contrary as she has been many times in the past."

He shrugged again, as if the issue of my sister was beneath his notice, and I hastened to make ready for our visit to Moteczoma's palace. Cortés sent word that we would wait upon the Ueytlatoani later in the afternoon, and Moteczoma sent back word that he would be pleased, as always, to hold converse with us. I ordered a slave girl to quickly sew for me the same white huipilli and cueitl that my sister wore and, when this was done, I had the girl seek out Xochitl and in utmost secrecy give her the message that I longed to speak with her in Axayácatl's palace and then escort her to me. Never shrewd enough to question her affections, she came even as she was bid to my chamber.

"I did not expect to see you so soon, sister," she said quietly, "since you have such contempt for me."

"Ah," I answered with a sweet smile of pleading, "I am indeed sorry for my words; please forgive me. However angry I am at Moteczoma, still I should never have let that anger flow so cruelly upon you."

I could see she was still torn between doubt and blind loyalty, and I placed my hand gently upon her arm. "Please, Xochitl, forget words said in haste and bitterly regretted."

She smiled then with a warmth that reached her eyes and I clapped my hands and said heartily, "We will drink a cup of octli to seal our friendship!" and in a moment the slave girl brought us two golden cups and a golden vessel of octli as I had planned.

"Octli, sister! This takes the form of debauch, not sober vow!" but she said these stern words in a cheerful voice.

"Should we renew our sisterhood with water?" I jested, motioning for the slave to leave and then filling both our cups full of the potent drink. "To you, sister, and to our reunion." I lifted my cup and drank.

"And to you," she replied, sipping from the cup in the delicate way I well remembered. "We should also drink, do you not agree, to the return of our God, Quetzalcoatl." And she sipped again, adding, "How odd this makes one feel. Could I be drunk already?"

Suddenly looking into my eyes, she saw with a sister's uncanny insight the cunning with which I watched her drink the octli. Startled, she glanced into what remained in her cup.

"You have poisoned this, Malinalli," she said in a leaden voice.

"Xochitl," I replied, "you have always been a fool." She dropped the cup to the floor and began to walk, waveringly, to the door. Before she reached it, I went to block her way.

"Let me go, Malinalli . . ." she tried to push me aside but by then her strength had ebbed and so it was but a simple matter to resist.

"You will go soon enough, sister," I said pleasantly, "just as soon as Captain Cortés and I have your master safely here and under our protection."

For a moment she looked at me stupidly, then staggered to the wall and leaned against it as if she had sustained a mortal blow. "Cortés?" she whispered.

I smiled. "*My* master, with whom I have come to destroy Moteczoma."

So pale that even her lips had no color, she sat upon a chest that was beside her and I helped her so she would not fall. "He is not . . ." she faltered, unable to speak the words.

"No, my sister, he is not." For a moment I could feel her pain within my own breast, but I hardened my will against such weakness. It was time, at last, for truth.

"I have seen him wounded in battle and weary unto death, Xochitl," I said as she stared dully into my face. "I sleep nightly in his arms and we do not always *sleep,* sister. Proof of that do I have here," and I laid a hand on my belly. "You are the first to know of this, even before my Captain, Cortés."

"No, please no," she whispered, her eyes no longer seeing, her head too heavy for her neck. As I bent to lay her out upon the chest, she closed her eyes and in a voice softer than a sigh she said, "What have I . . . done."

Unwilling to suffer her reproaches when she awoke, I had two slaves carry her under cover of darkness to the garden outside Moteczoma's palace. "Guard her until she wakes," I ordered them, wrapping my sister's body in a warm blanket before they took her away.

Having overcome the greatest obstacles, my plan became effortless. My Captain and I, Aguilar and several of our men went to Moteczoma's palace and were readily admitted to his presence. After the customary words of honor and reverence, I spoke for Cortés.

"Well do I know what a great and mighty prince you are, and that you have declared yourself our friend. Thus am I shocked and saddened to hear the news that your men have risen against us and at your command. What say you to this?"

"But never have I commanded my warriors to attack

you," Moteczoma stammered, rising from his icpalli. "Whoever told you this has told a grievous lie!"

Cortés assumed an angry pose and spoke words the coldness of which Moteczoma could not fail to understand, even as I conveyed their meaning. "I have heard that you meet in secret with your captains and Lords and make plans to slay us all."

"No!" Moteczoma cried. "No, you cannot have heard truth. Never would I . . ."

"If I learned that you did so, I would have no choice but to destroy this city and everyone within its walls."

Upon hearing this, Moteczoma, who had been glancing at me uneasily, suddenly spoke directly to me. "Malintzin?" he said querulously, and I gave him a bleak smile.

"I am even as you thought, my Lord. I am the shadow self of your wife, Xochitlzin, though I am known as Malintzin. I come with these great Lords as prophesied." His face paled at these words, and he looked from one to the other of us and as if he eagerly wished we would all turn into vapor and disappear.

"What do you wish for me to do?" he asked at last in piteous tones. "Never have I raised a hand against you, nor uttered a falsehearted word, since you came to Tenochtitlan."

"He wishes to know what you want him to do," I said with clear meaning to my Captain, whose eyes grew shrewd with cunning.

"Tell him that for his own good he must come to live with us in the palace of Axayácatl. There he will be treated with all courtesy and protected from those who speak against him."

This I told Moteczoma, and he begged that we take his daughters as hostages, instead.

"That would hardly suit our purpose," Cortés muttered under his breath when I told him what Moteczoma wished.

"Shall I persuade him to come without protest, Captain?"

"Very well, Marina. We can hardly drag him from his palace by force."

I turned back to Moteczoma, who was trembling with fear and indecision, and said to him in soothing tones, "We are most upset for your safety, Lord. And more than this, indeed! You have taken the counsel of my other self, Xochitlzin, but now it is time you listened to *me*. The time foretold is at hand, and only I can tell you what actions these times require of you." I drew magic into my eyes and looked deeply into his. "You will come and live with us in luxury until we know that it is safe for you to return here. I will stand beside you and protect you and help you to keep Tenochtitlan from destruction."

He looked upon me with doubt and hope. "Do you swear this, Malintzin? Do you swear you speak truth before our God Quetzalcoatl, even as you do before his dark twin, Tezcatlipoca?"

"Most happily and reverently do I swear upon them all, Lord," I said smiling. "Now come with us and my Lord will protect you, and I will stand by your side and with deepest sorcery keep you safe from enchantments even now being wickedly worked against you."

He gazed upon each of us in turn, and like a hunted thing. Finally he nodded his head and clapped his hands for a slave. "Have my litter brought," he commanded in a weak voice. "I go to the palace of Axayácatl."

Thus was the mightiest ruler of the land taken captive without force. Cortés had guards and watchmen placed around him, seeing to it that though Moteczoma was never allowed to leave the palace, still was he let to feel little restraint. He did not seek to escape, however, and lived as sumptuously with us as ever he had lived before.

I took it as my duty to provide all the pleasure he wished for, inventing for him potions that gave to him great potency. As I had with my Captain, I provided beautiful women upon whom he could slake his thirst.

I prepared for him teonanacatl mushrooms so that he would have dreams and visions. So vivid were they that sometimes he could not tell if he were awake or dreaming. Thus it was I went to him some nights and lay with him, and as he slept powerless in my arms I wove for him enchantments which bound him to delusion at night and bewilderment by day. In his mind's eye, therefore, the black and the white of life clouded with confusion and were gray.

When my Captain wished to share his bed with one of the many women who had been given to our men for their enjoyment, I went forth to the chamber of Moteczoma and beguiled him with dreams. And this I did in all secrecy, for well did I know that Cortés would have called it witchery and forbidden it. Sometimes they were not dreams of power and mastery I gave him, though; sometimes they were visions dire and bleak, and the Azteca's mighty ruler would shiver and cry out in my arms as I gazed upon his rapt and terror-ridden face with cold pleasure.

27

Xochitl

I awoke to a world forever changed. By the time I reached my Lord's chamber with the dire news, it was too late. By then, my sister, in the company of Captain Cortés and his men, had taken Moteczoma captive. In his captivity in the palace of Axayácatl, he soon became beguiled, although he did learn also that the strange warriors were not Lords and their Captain no God. He was caught in the web of prophecy and there was no one, not Lord or priest or wife, who could persuade him that our fate could still lay in our hands and not in the greedy ones of the conquistadores. Lords of the Triple Alliance took counsel with him there, pleading with him to return to his rightful place, but he would not do so.

"He believes," Lord Cuauhtémoc told me with contempt, "that your shadow self, Malintzin, guides him as she did guide Cortés. As a whore, with a whore's womanly wiles, she persuades him this is as it was foretold and he obeys her every treacherous word."

I flinched at his harsh words, but accepted his anger as my due for having misread prophecy and for having trusted that my sister would not so betray us. Indeed in great part it was my fault that our enemy now lodged within our walls. With good heart and pure conscience had I prepared my Lord for our God's coming. Thus unwitting had I also prepared our doom. In those hollow days I scanned the heavens and the nine underworlds with the eye of my faith, and Quetzalcoatl was not in one or the other. Perhaps it had all been but a flower tale told by the overhopeful to the overly innocent. Perhaps, I thought, this is all it ever was. My heart yearned for Cihuacoatl, for Xilónen, for all of our lost Goddesses. And it ached for my mother, lost as well in the dark passage of the years.

Once having accepted Cortés for the mortal he was, I wondered how the ways of his men could ever have been accepted as the ways of divine beings. Their customs were barbarous. They stank foully from the filth they would not wash from their bodies and they drank to contemptible excess. They used our women as they would dumb beasts, and if there were not women enough for them indeed would they then stand in a line for whatever woman was available and take her there and in sight of all. Many a woman returned weeping and with her tipili torn and bleeding, and when some found that they carried the offspring of so odious a union, they would thrust pointed sticks inside themselves so to rid their bodies of such vile issue. Some later bore the babes and then strangled them, or gladly gave them up for sacrifice. There were those women who kept their young, for they were by nature too tender to do aught else, but these were children everyone else did despise.

At first noble cacicas were sent to the Captain's men, but when they returned so defiled, then slaves were sent and later, loose women, for these were seen as beasts and to be used as beasts. It made no matter to the Spaniards, who did not seem to mind who or what the woman was so long as she had that place for them to stick their tepulis. I believe we could have sent them a corpse and they would not have noticed or, noticing, would not have cared.

The Spaniards spoke long and forcefully about their Gods and placed the statue of a woman and a cross of sticks with a man hanging upon it in a hastily-cleaned teocalli, but other than that I saw little difference in their ways and those of other crude and brutish men. Cortés and several other warriors possessed more restraint, yet even they were most repellent in their ways. It seemed my sister was devoted to Cortés, and had learned his tongue, rode by his side and bore his child within her, and yet he dismissed her from his sleeping mat when a slave did charm his eye. This was not unlike the men of my own land, of course, but our men did not often prate of their Godliness; one moment ravishing a woman and the next kneeling piously for priestly forgiveness. Indeed, in our land we did not see the act between man and woman a matter of divine curiosity needing either censure or blessing, unless it was adultery, which required the punishment of death by stoning. Man's seed needed planting in the body of a woman, we believed, as the rain needed to make fertile the earth. That there should be pleasure in it at times merely ensured the sowing.

Days passed while we waited. My Lord Moteczoma, it was said, grew increasingly strange. His eyes, once so keen and clear, were glazed with a fever and he rambled often in his speech. Yet he did have wit enough to make impossible his replacement as Ueytlatoani. Only if his mind became quite overthrown was it then possible to choose a successor. There was talk of Moteczoma's surrender and thus the surrender of his rule, and while I heard that some spoke one way and some the other, the Lords of the Triple Alliance were loath to commit such a heinous act without greater reason.

Slaves sent to Axayácatl's palace were well paid for what they could discover to tell our Lords, and they spoke not only of the Spaniards' filthy ways but also of other things. They told us that our enemies were restless in their confinement and greedy for more gold. They saw them searching the walls for doors to a secret treasurehouse and also saw them daily grow more vexed with failure. Then the conquistadores found what it was they sought.

It was their custom to set up small altars and kneel before them, speaking aloud to their Gods. In one chamber several had gathered together to set up yet another of these homely teocallis and in so doing did they discover the markings of a walled-over door. With swiftness born of greed, they tore down the stones and thus did discover one of the small hidden treasures of Axayácatl. We were told that they gaped with wonder upon the riches therein, touching the golden bars and jeweled ornaments as if they touched the body of a God. Most reverent were the warriors as all heard of the discovery and came to worship not at their altar of wood but at that altar of gold. Then, it was said, they sought to hide their discovery by walling up the door once again, not knowing our slaves already knew and had already told.

Lord Cuauhtémoc told me all of this, for I saw but few persons in those days. I kept to a small private chamber, attended by one faithful slave. Lord Cuauhtémoc, come to mock and berate me, was surprised to see such austerity.

"Do you do penance for your errors, Lady?" he asked, looking about my small white chamber.

"No, my Lord. I have done penance enough in grief. I now seek but a life alone and without power."

"I cannot agree you have been punished enough for what you have done, but well indeed do you seek to rid yourself of the power you most grievously abused."

"My Lord," I said to him quietly, "I do not ask for forgiveness nor do I ask for blessing. I ask but for solitude, and I ask that from you, as well."

Cuauhtémoc raised his chin and stared upon me with a wrathful eye. "You are arrogant as always! Well would I like to chastise you with my own hands to bring you properly to your knees."

I could not but smile at this and then shake my head. "Lord, I have no doubt you could do with me whatever you wished, so I must believe you have other plans for me. I did not wish to sound arrogant when I said that I ask no one's forgiveness or blessing. I have no hope of either, Lord Cuauhtémoc, neither on earth nor above it nor below. We have been forsaken by Quetzalcoatl and now I await nothing but the flames and knives of Mictlan. For now I know," I said, turning away from him so that he would not see the wretchedness in my eyes, "there is nothing to hope for, nothing to believe."

"You have been thwarted in your wishes, Lady, that is all," Cuauhtémoc replied coldly. "Do you wish for pity?"

"I wish for nothing, as I have already said, Cuauhtémoc." I looked into his face and was startled to see a shadow almost of compassion upon it. In silence did we stand thus, gazing at each other, until Cuauhtémoc cleared his throat uneasily. "Chimalpopoca would be most interested in the sacrilege you speak. Take care he does not learn of your words."

"That is up to you, my Lord," I said, turning one palm upward. "For my part, I will never deny what I have said to you."

"Do you wish to die?"

"I have lost everything and everyone in this life. How can I fear death?"

"You speak also of that slave, Atahualpa, that you had such base affection for?"

That name, so suddenly spoken, pierced my heart. "Yes, even as I lost my God did I lose my love as well."

"It was but a foolish passion," Cuauhtémoc said sternly. "An adulterous passion."

I looked at Cuauhtémoc a long moment and until he grew uneasy. "*You* might know of both, my Lord, but I do not. The only foolish passion I have ever cherished was for a God who was not a God. The only adultery was with my Lord Moteczoma, who kept me from both the divine ecstasies of a priestess and the humble happiness of a woman."

"This is pointless talk," Cuauhtémoc said irritably, walking to the door, "mere female chattering."

When he reached the door, some impious spirit unloosed my tongue and he turned back at my words.

"And yet, my Lord, you spoke my love's name first. Can it be that you bear an envious heart?"

I was darkly amused to see blood rise to the very crown of his head. "I warn you, Lady, I will not help you take one step away from the mortal peril you surely face!"

"You do not need to convince me of that, my Lord," I said softly, "but perhaps you would do well to so convince yourself." Cuauhtémoc, speechless with vexation, hastened from my chamber.

I was fortunate in the loyalty and intelligence of my slave woman, for in my solitude she brought me news of events in Tenochtitlan and thus it was I heard, among other useful things, that my Lord Moteczoma held court in Axayácatl's palace. Because my sister was always there to tell Cortés what was being said, private conversations were impossible and all things were made known to our enemy. At first it seemed astonishing that Lord Moteczoma should submit to captivity so docilely. Well did I recall the days when one was forced to appear in his presence as humble petitioner, never daring to raise one's eyes above his chest. Now he was approached even as one could approach Cortés, and though the Azteca would never dare such liberties, the Spaniards behaved most irreverently and with bold words and bolder glances. I believe they were courteous when they desired gifts of women or gold, and otherwise they treated my Lord with a patronage for which they once would have been slain.

In the beginning, our Lords could not be of one mind about which road to take and they sought their way as if travelling on a moonless night. Then it was, at Cortés' behest, my Lord sent for the caciques involved in the uprising at the village the Spaniards had named Villa Rica. They were brought from that place in chains. The day following their arrival, I could see from my rooftop logs of wood placed upright in the sacred Heart of the Heart of the One World and well within sight of the palace of Moteczoma. There were the five caciques held captive, bound to the logs with thongs and with wood piled high around them. When all was ready, then was a torch applied to the dry wood and it smoked into flame which, as the warrior caciques stood silent, crept upward. From their knees to their waists the flames rose, and as their naked bodies had been smeared with fat, their flesh crackled like roasting meat before it blackened and burst. Hard would it have been to hear anything above the sound of the flames, but I have no doubt these men, trained from boyhood to endure pain without complaint, made not the slightest sound as they were burned alive. The smell of roasting flesh drifted out lazily over the serpent wall and over the palaces, and I retired to my chamber to escape it. Even yet the clinging sweetness of it stayed in my nostrils for hours. Indeed had I seen human flesh on fire before, and had myself opened the bodies of the sacrificed, but there was nothing sacred about this day's burning, and nothing given reverence. My people also punished the wicked, but it seemed to me that this punishment was without reward, for those noble caciques were not accorded the Flowery Death of warriors but the death of mere beasts. Not even of beasts, indeed, for even beasts were not roasted alive.

Our Lords were aggrieved and among the warriors was there great disquiet. Late into the night the highest in the land held counsel, some arguing that the slightest wish of the Ueytlatoani had to be obeyed, and some saying Moteczoma was no longer in command of himself but was the toy of Cortés. Strangely, I heard few words against my "shadow self." They despised her for what they saw as betrayal of her people, but it was a woman's betrayal and thus of little account. None of them seemed to have the least suspicion of her cunning and power for never would they have guessed such things could belong to a woman's nature. A warrior they would have treated both more harshly and with more respect, but a woman like my sister was as a xexene, not so much perilous as annoying. Some men showed their contempt by calling Moteczoma "Malintzin," as if he were but my sister's creature and no longer quite a man. I often wondered if he were more at peril by the division within our own people or by the Spaniards within our walls.

My slave woman came hurrying one day with the news that trouble had arisen again in Villa Rica. However, this time it was trouble between Spaniard and Spaniard, and our Lords were heartened by this sign of disorder in our enemy's camp. Also did she say that my Lord Moteczoma seemed at times to be half-witted, and at others quite sensible, and that he spent more and more of his time in the arms of many women and dreaming upon his sleeping mat. It was whispered, she said shyly, that his hungers were whipped to a frenzy in which he could take woman after woman, or but one poor woman for many hours, and at the end of it still find no release.

"His tepuli will not slacken," she whispered as if there were others in my chamber, "and it drives him into a fever which none but your shadow self, Malintzin, can satisfy. Indeed, I know of one slave in this palace and she was sent for cacao. When she returned with it she saw the Ueytlatoani beseeching Malintzin to give him rest, and this slave saw her put something in the cacao from a ring upon her finger and then give it to our Lord to drink. She did not see what happened next, for she was ordered from the chamber, but it is said this potion Malintzin gives him cools his fever and so he can sleep. It is said that Malintzin knows such sorcery that even the Ueytlatoani is in her thrall."

"Do the Lords believe this also?"

She shook her head. "They say she is but of little value and that it is her master, Cortés, who knows of this craft."

I could not help but recall the day I sipped octli with my sister and how I awoke into mindfulness some hours later in the palace garden. I was certain that she, given the opportunity, would have made herself mistress of the sorcerer's black art.

From this same slave did I also learn that all hours were not grave ones in Axayácatl's palace. Often Moteczoma and the enemy played totoloque, which was a game played with stones among the commoner people, but in the palace with little balls and bars of gold. I suspected that the game did not entice the Spaniards so much as the markers with which it was played. Cortés and my Lord played also, their score most often kept by the Spaniard the Azteca called "Tonatiuh" because of the golden color of his hair. It was said that for every ball and bar my Lord lost, Tonatiuh did say two, and for every two Cortés lost, he would say one. Thus it was a game not so much of skill as of cunning, but Moteczoma did not protest.

A day of high ceremony came and the Ueytlatoani, roused from languor, asked Cortés if he might go to the Heart of the Heart of the One World to give due reverence to the Gods. When it came to our ears that he pleaded for this permission, all our Lords and priests were much aggrieved. Many did believe—though, I myself, now did doubt—that the Ueytlatoani's supplications were necessary for the ripening of the harvest and the health of the people. Already he had not worshipped at a teocalli for many days, which never had a Ueytlatoani failed to do. Cortés told him he might go, but that he could not conduct any human sacrifice, and with this Moteczoma did agree, saying he would sacrifice but beasts.

"Will you return to us here, Lord?" Malinalli was reported as asking him, "and without protest?"

"Indeed, yes," my Lord answered, "for it has been shown to me that my God wishes me to be here with you." We were told that when he said this my "shadow self" smiled upon him as if he were a child.

Surrounded by our enemy, Lord Moteczoma went forth upon his litter to the teocalli of Tezcatlipoca and there did he ascend with the support of his priests, the chief of whom was Chimalpopoca. I could not find out what was said in the teocalli, but I am certain the priests seized that rare chance to have speech with him and to exert their persuasions. Soon, however, did he descend back into the company of Cortés and return to captivity without protest.

Much to our Lords' dismay, Cortés had brought to him in greatest secrecy materials with which to make two of their great canoes, and these they readily built and fitted with the perilous cannon. Moteczoma was taken out upon the lake in one of these and taught to shift the great white cloths that caught the wind and moved the canoe over the face of the water, and all of this was done as if to humor an invalid.

One day quite suddenly I was summoned to appear in the Ueytaltoani's audience chamber. In anxious haste did I make myself ready to obey what was by now a most unusual command. As I hurried along the corridors, I wondered if I were to finally be punished for my part in the turmoil. Expecting soon or late to be held to account, I had kept my mind always prepared for death.

I was given permission to enter. Before me I found the two mighty Lords, Cacamatzin and Cuauhtémoc, dressed in all of their warrior finery. From within the gaping jaws of their jaguar masks, their faces were ruthless, their eyes regarding me with cold disdain. "Lady Xochitlzin," Lord Cacamatzin said in greeting.

"My Lord," I replied, inclining my head.

Cuauhtémoc spoke. "You must wonder, Lady, why we have sent for you thus."

"Indeed I do wonder, my Lord, although I have long expected such a summons."

Lord Cacamatzin said, "There was nothing to be gained by speaking to you before we had use for you."

I folded my hands in front of me and waited in courteous silence.

"You have heard what is happening in the palace of

Axayácatl?" Cuauhtémoc said in the harsh voice he used with me. "And of the plight of the Ueytlatoani, your Lord and husband?"

"I have heard little in my solitude, Lord."

"And yet I suppose you have your ways of not remaining entirely ignorant. Perhaps your shadow self, Malintzin, visits you in this 'solitude'?"

"I hear but the talk of slaves. My shadow self is as separate from me as if we were but sisters."

Cuauhtémoc fixed upon my face a piercing stare. "Some say that indeed she *is* your sister, and that all this is but a sorcerous plot between you to destroy Tenochtitlan."

"Those who speak thus are fools, my Lord, and all who would believe such gossip fools as well."

Cuauhtémoc stiffened and Cacamatzin then spoke. "You would do well to guard your tongue, Lady. There was a time when you could speak as you wished, but that time is past." He paused and I looked stolidly into his face, for I had little to gain, indeed, and sought to keep what small dignity I still possessed. "You realize we could have you put to death," he warned, "and none would be the wiser."

"I am aware of that, Lord. I only wonder why my death has not been ordered before now." I looked calmly from one to the other. "I do not question that you believe me responsible for much of what has taken place in Tenochtitlan, because I had faith our God Quetzalcoatl was returning to us. Many men have been put to death for less than that, no matter how innocent the motive. Thus it comes as no shock to me to hear that my death hovers near."

"It hovers," Cuauhtémoc said harshly, "nearer than you can imagine."

I looked at him for a long moment and without a trace of passion I said, "Lord Cuauhtémoc, you and I have spoken before this. Well do you know my death is of no importance to me. As I have said to you, I have no one and nothing to make my life more than an unpleasant duty. I would welcome the jaws of Mictlan, but that is of no concern to you, as I know well. You wish to speak of something other than my immediate death," I paused then, "or so it seems to me."

"You are right, Lady," Lord Cacamatzin replied.

I nodded but said nothing. I had little to give to remedy Tenochtitlan's wrongs, but that little they would have to labor for.

"The Ueytlatoani once had respect for you and listened to your words, however unfortunate that was for all of us. Now he seems to listen thus to the words of Malintzin, your shadow self. Have you heard this is so?"

I nodded but again said nothing.

"We believe that if the Ueytlatoani could be alone with you again, he might listen to your words once more." Cacamatzin paused, watching me narrowly, and then continued. "Thus have we planned intrigue, that you shall go to the Ueytlatoani's chamber while the Spaniard Cortés and his accomplice, Malintzin, are away. There you will persuade the Ueytlatoani to escape with you and return to his rightful place in this palace."

"How am I to have these words with him, surrounded as he is by the Spaniards who, I am certain, guard him well?"

Cuauhtémoc snapped, "You will but do as we say. You do not need to know more than the part you will play."

"I do not need to tell you, my Lord," I said coolly, "that when one is seeking an accomplice in one's strategy, one does not leave that accomplice unprepared to face suddenly discovery. If I do not know the whole of your plan, I might give much away, unknowing."

Lord Cacamatzin glanced at Cuauhtémoc and then turned his cold gaze back upon me. "You are shrewd, Lady Xochitlzin. Perhaps, indeed, too shrewd."

I smiled, meeting the thrust of his gaze with one as unyielding. "Perhaps so, my Lord. And yet, in these last days of my life, I find an obstinacy in me that quite takes me by surprise. I find that I now refuse to surrender myself in blind service, but require that my eyes be open and my way made light before me."

"And if this is denied you?" Lord Cuauhtémoc asked, angered by my polite insolence.

"Then you may have me slain, if you wish," I shrugged. "It matters little."

Cuauhtémoc made as if to speak, but Cacamatzin silenced him with a small wave of his hand. "You will do as we request, Lady Xochitlzin?" he asked, somewhat more civilly than he had spoken to me before.

I nodded, "Yes, my Lord. I have also been most disquieted by the plight of my Lord Moteczoma, and will do what I can to be of service in freeing him."

"Very well," Cacamatzin replied, and though I had gained but a tiny victory, I felt a faint stirring of pride that though I did not love myself, nor care about what became of me, still I had not willingly bowed my neck for another's foot to rest upon.

"This is what we plan . . ."

Thus it was that Cortés and Malintzin, together with some of the Spaniards, were to be invited to meet in counsel with the Lords Cacamatzin and Cuauhtémoc, and they would keep the enemy thus engaged while I slipped into Axayácatl's palace pretending to be what the Lords still believed was my shadow self. The chamber wherein my Lord did sleep was mapped for me so I could find it quickly even in the dark, though the hour of dusk was chosen to make it both a reasonable hour of meeting and a good time for the passage of those who needed to remain unseen. Thus would I more easily gain access to Moteczoma's chamber and thus together escape the palace more easily if he came with me, as we planned.

"Remember, the Spaniard Cortés does work sorcery, and we do not know what webs and walls he has woven in Axayácatl's halls."

"I will be careful."

"It matters not at all what becomes of *you,*" Lord Cuauhtémoc said, "but the Ueytlatoani must not be harmed."

Almost amused, I replied lightly, "Do you wish so badly then to put me to death yourself, my Lord? Then it would indeed be most unfortunate if I were not to return alive." I turned to Lord Cacamatzin. "I will endeavor to use all the persuasion at my command to bring Lord Moteczoma back here to his palace, even as you desire." As I left, I swept a mocking glance over Cuauhtémoc and had the small satisfaction of seeing his hands curl tightly into fists.

28

Malinalli

There was intrigue in the palace. I could feel it damp upon my skin like groping hands. And not in the palace only, but in Tenochtitlan as well. Cacamatzin, Lord of Texcoco, was said by our well-paid spy to be plotting treachery against us, for he coveted the icpalli of the Ueytlatoani for himself. It was therefore with a wary curiosity that my Captain accepted Lord Cuauhtémoc's request for a meeting.

Almost at dusk on the appointed day we ventured forth, my Captain and I and a guard of twenty of his finest soldiers, to meet the Azteca halfway, at Moteczoma's famed menagerie. The menagerie was wondrous indeed, and while we awaited the arrival of Cuauhtémoc, we wandered through that great building, amazed. Beasts of all kinds filled numberless cages and there were humans, also, though it sometimes took a long moment to discover something which was but man or woman and not monster. Cortés and his men all looked with contempt at the stone Gods set into the walls, sheathed as they were with dried blood, and viewed with equal disgust the human beasts beneath them.

"The very moment I begin to see these Azteca as men like us, then am I reminded most forcefully of their savagery." Cortés exclaimed.

"This is most nauseating, Captain," Alvarado remarked. "Creatures like this should be strangled at birth before they are caged thus like animals. Look at this brute!"

We all looked in the direction of his pointing finger and saw a very monster of a man, indeed. He was wearing a rag that scarcely covered his loins and, crouching, he looked out at us from a face grotesque with thick red scars. The muscles in his face had been recently slit so that half of it hung slack, his left eye almost on a level with his nose and the corner of his mouth drooped and drooling. So had his large body also been slashed and scarred and where his tepuli should have bulged against the thin rag of his maxtlatl, there was a suggestive flatness.

"Oh, my dear God," Cortés breathed, "was this once a *man*?"

"I will find out what happened to him if you wish, my Captain," I said, and he nodded. I turned to the creature in the cage to find him staring at me in what could only have been delirium. "Why are you here?" I asked him, and though there came to his eyes a faint glimmer, he said nothing. "What is your name?" I asked him in both Mayan and Nahuatl, but he was silent.

"I believe that he is dumb," I said to Cortés, "for though he seems to have heard me, doubtless he is too deranged for lucid speech."

"Let us go outside," my Captain said, shaking his head with disgust. "This place is an abomination."

We left the menagerie then and entered the garden where we saw the Lords Cacamatzin and Cuauhtémoc, in company with a few priests and caciques, coming toward us through the dying light. They bid us greeting and then low stools were set out for the Lords and for Cortés. I, as always, stood beside him.

"Why do you persist in keeping our Ueytlatoani captive?" Cuauhtémoc began. "That is a most grievous insult to our people, who welcomed you as guests within our gates."

With this words flew back and forth, my Captain most courteous and firm in his refusal to admit Moteczoma was anything other than a willing visitor.

To this Cuauhtémoc took offense, heartily denying the possibility that Moteczoma would choose to be a prisoner within his own city.

"If this is all you wish to discuss," Cortés bid me say, "then we will return to our quarters."

At this the two Lords stiffened slightly and then Cuauhtémoc spoke. "There is another thing as well, Malintzin," he said as if Cortés bore my name, "and that is that Cacamatzin, Lord of Texcoco, is returning to his land tomorrow and thus wishes to bid you farewell."

Surprised by this courteous leave-taking, Cortés offered his farewell with equal civility, and then, with empty words on one side and the other, we returned to Axayácatl's palace.

"There is something in this I do not like Marina," Cortés remarked thoughtfully, "something that perplexes me."

"What is that, my Captain?"

He shook his head. "I cannot put my finger upon it, but damme if that does not seem a most unlikely meeting, somehow. Mayhap you can discover something if there is, indeed, anything of truth to my suspicion."

"I will try," I promised. I thought I would need one of the Azteca spies willing to act the traitor for our gold, but this did not prove to be necessary. When we returned to the palace Cortés sought another woman for his bed, so I went to Moteczoma's chamber wherein I found him most bewildered.

"Xochitlzin?" he asked in a quavering voice, "is it you?"

"Of course not, Lord," I answered sharply, and he cast down his eyes in confusion and began to pace and wring his hands.

"Why would you think me to be Xochitlzin when you know I am her shadow self, Malintzin?" I asked him but in a more soothing voice so that I would not alarm him into incoherence.

"But you were here, Xochitlzin, were you not?" he asked, looking sideways at me. "You said you were!"

"Of course, my Lord, of course," I murmured comfortingly and went to lead him to his bed. "You thought you saw her here in the darkness, but it was only a dream."

He snatched his hand from mine like a fretful child. "You do not believe me!" he cried. "You think I no longer know what I see, but I *did* see her. I did!" Then he fell silent and a look of cunning crept into his eyes. "You told me that you know everything, Malintzin, but how can it be you are truly wise if you still do not know that she came to me this evening and spoke to me?"

I was startled, and yet doubtful, and knew I needed to shrewdly make my way to any truth there might be in Moteczoma's delusion. "You know I am Xochitlzin's shadow self, for that is what I told you. But I must test you, my Lord, to see if you trust me."

Moteczoma smiled craftily. "If you know that she came here, then tell me what it was she said."

I raised my chin. "I do not need to answer questions as if it were *I* who needs to be tested, Lord." At this show of strength, Moteczoma withdrew, but still he would say nothing further about my sister's most unlikely visit.

"I wish to go to sleep," Moteczoma said with some of his old arrogance, "and I want you to go away."

"Very well, Lord," I answered sweetly, "but first let me have a cup of cacao brought to you to soothe your sleep."

"I wish for no dreams, Malintzin!" he said, again in the voice of a fretful child. "I have too many dreams in this, my father's palace. Perhaps it is the cacao which brings them."

"No dreams," I promised, "just sleep." Without further words, I summoned a slave and she prepared cacao for my Lord and brought it in all haste. "Here it is," I said, making use of the darkness to drop a powder into his gold cup. "Drink it all, my Lord, and then I will leave you to your rest."

He did as I bid him and then, overcome with drowsiness, he lay back upon his blankets and closed his eyes. Soon he began to toss from side to side, muttering and groaning.

"My Lord Moteczoma," I whispered, "open your eyes and look at me." He continued to toss as in a fever, and so I gripped both his hands in mine and moved my face closer yet to his. "Open your eyes, my Lord!" I commanded, and with a shudder his eyes opened and stared into mine.

"Xochitlzin came to you today," I said softly. He shivered and nodded his head. "What did she say to you?"

"I . . ." he began, then swallowed hard and again attempted speech. "I . . ."

"What did she say?"

"She said . . . she said I was to come with her, that my life was in peril," he said dully, forming words as if his tongue were swollen. "My life . . ." he repeated, and then some sense of what he was saying must have entered his mind for he then said in a thick voice, pleading, "Am I going to die? Am I to die like she said?"

"No," I comforted him, patting his hands and smiling. "If you do everything I say then you will not die. I promise you, my Lord." He nodded slightly and his eyes closed, and though he still tossed, beset by dreams, he said no more. I slept beside him, having nowhere else to go. Not until first light did I leave him, knowing it would be a good while before he would awaken from his drugged slumber.

"I believe," I told my Captain that morning, "that my sister might indeed have come to Moteczoma's chamber while we were with those Azteca Lords."

Cortés narrowed his eyes in thought. "Then perhaps that meeting was arranged merely for the purpose of getting you and me out of the palace."

"Perhaps so, my Captain," I replied. "Remember that you felt there was something strange about the meeting."

"Indeed. But why would your sister be sent, and how could it be that our guards did not stop her, knowing you were with me?"

"It is possible, my Captain, that my sister pretended to be me and the guards simply thought I had returned early. Remember also that my sister once had influence over her husband, Moteczoma, and perhaps she thought to influence him again. She might easily have gotten him from the palace in her company, if the guards believed her to be me and acting upon your orders."

"That sounds indeed possible," Cortés said, stroking his beard, "and if it is, then we have proof that the Azteca are plotting against us. We would be wise to see that this does not happen again. Ask Alvarado, de Lorenzo and Aguilar to come to me and we will decide our next plan of action."

I did his bidding and then hastened back to his chamber. "Marina, go to Moteczoma and say to him that you fear for his life. Say to him that we have proof the Lords of the Triple Alliance are plotting heinously against him. Say to him that upon no account must he venture one step outside the palace, for they will surely take him captive and put him to death. Say," he continued, pacing as he carefully selected his words, "that we need for him, for his own safety, to send his warriors to Texcoco to seize Cacamatzin who plots against him and to deliver the traitor into our keeping. Do this and then return to me with Moteczoma's reply."

Moteczoma listened to me with a most wretched countenance. After I finished he paced back and forth, wringing his hands in distress and speaking first one way and then the other. Finally he agreed to send caciques to Texcoco to take Lord Cacamatzin captive.

This was done. Lord Cacamatzin arrived grandly by canoe and golden litter and in his arrogance he seemed not to be captive at all, addressing Moteczoma with scorn and with scorn refusing to speak one word to Cortés. After this great Lord was imprisoned in chains the other Lords refused to pay their respects or take counsel with Moteczoma, blaming him as well as Cortés for Cacamatzin's plight. It became easier to convince Moteczoma that they all plotted against his life; it needed but moments for Cortés and I to convince him to take as many of the Lords captive as we could. Thus, in the space of eight days, several were in chains except the most powerful Lords, Cuitláhuac and Cuauhtémoc. In obedience to my soft suggestion, Moteczoma then called to him all the lesser caciques of the Triple Alliance and said to them that they must render allegiance to Cortés, for he, Moteczoma, Quetzalcoatl's earthly descendant, knew the God commanded them to do so. Prophecy, thus, would be properly fulfilled. In sorrow did he speak, for even in his muddled state he knew he was giving up his empire with these words and actions. The caciques left his presence, their faces drawn with grieving. Cortés was pleased by all we had accomplished with so little dissent and I was pleased also with the successful part I, myself, had played.

Despite our triumph, great trouble came down upon us. Moteczoma sent forth tax gatherers to levy tribute—at my Captain's polite request—but they all returned with empty hands. Cortés bid me tell Moteczoma that his soldiers were distressed by the insufficiency of gold being given them in payment for their services and that they might make loud and violent their grievance. Moteczoma, while he knew now that the Spaniards were but men, still was he as fearful of them on the one side as he was fearful of his fellow Azteca on the other. Caught between the conquerors and the conquered, he sought to pacify them both; he ordered his father's treasurehouse opened and all the gold in it given to Cortés. In this way he wished the Spaniards to be content and, as he confided to me, to return to the land from whence they had come and thus content the Azteca as well.

"For, Malintzin," he said fretfully, "it was better before you brought the Spaniards here. Everything was as it had always been. If you and Cortés and all his men were to be satisfied with treasure, then perhaps you would go away and everything would return to the way it was."

I agreed with him. Always I agreed so that he would believe me a loyal friend, dedicated first to his welfare. In this way I learned his secrets and could lay them before my Captain. When I repeated his words to Cortés that night, he smiled. "His wish is quite unsurprising, but unfortunately one I cannot yet grant. The kindly gift of his father's gold is not the end of his benevolence, I am certain. There is no reason to doubt that this tidy sum he has given us has at least its equal in his own palace."

Cortés and all his men were pleased to hold Axayácatl's treasure in their hands; especially were the common soldiers almost frenzied by their sudden wealth. They threw golden necklaces into the air and danced about so that some of the more delicate pieces were crushed underfoot. Some of the golden objects were preserved whole, but many others, together with the hills of golden dust, were melted into bars and stacked upon each other like bricks. Cortés ordered that a mark be made with an iron stamp on the bars and lesser goods, but decreed that the finer works should not be marked and their beauty and value spoiled.

I watched as one fifth of this treasure was set aside for their King and then the rest divided, though Cortés, his priest and highest officers kept to themselves the greater share. There was grumbling among some of the men that to divide the treasure so was unjust, for they had all suffered equally the hardships of the Conquest, but I knew that they would have had nothing at all were it not for the skill and cunning of their Captain since most of them would surely have long since abandoned the venture. The priest, de la Merced, hoarded his new wealth in his chamber, locking it into his chest with his holy books and necklaces of counting beads, and even in his priestly gaze there was the fever one saw unsubdued in the eyes of the less Godly. Their first flush of joyful greed abated soon enough, however, as more men grew vexed by the injustice with which they believed the gold was meted out. Cortés, alerted to the growing dissatisfaction, gave larger shares to the men closest to him and to those who had brought their own weapons and horses, and secretly gave greater amounts to those noisiest with discontent. He still satisfied very few, but while the rest grumbled, they held their tongues in his company.

Gold produced a kind of fever in the Spaniards. Games of chance they played all hours of the day and night, gold passing from hand to hand. Some gained much by this while others were once again as poor as they had been when they set forth from Cuba. Not only gold was sent flying from palm to palm by these games of chance, but women as well. The most beautiful women were sold from one unlucky gambler to another more fortunate, and those men bereft of both gold *and* women were sullen indeed and given to murderous talk and violent ways. Frequently I heard and witnessed fights among the men, and even as frequently one would hear women scream in the more distant chambers. It was common that certain men, impoverished and ridiculed, sought to release their anger upon the female slaves who, cowering and powerless, were easy sport. There were those quietly disposed of who died from some over-eager rape or who bled to death from continuous rape by many men who did not have enough gold to procure a slave for private use. Many women awoke to find raw chancres on their private parts and the flux of fever, and so had this been true with me also, but it was of short duration and troubled me little.

Cortés tried to keep the wilder excesses of his men in hand, but he did not wish to clamp too heavy a fist on their revelry for they did not often stir from the palace and were restless and fiery by nature.

"They have been under rigorous restraint for too long," he explained to me, "and will be more docile to handle if they are allowed to do as they wish."

What he did not say—nor did he need to—was that he feared open rebellion if he tried to keep them completely at his heel. Dissatisfied first by their share of gold, then frenzied in the spending of what they possessed, these men were ripe for violence.

"They might as well have their sport with women," he added, "than provoke the Azteca into open war."

No one dared touch me, of course, especially after I told my Captain I was bearing his child. Clapping me on the shoulder, he cried, "Well done, Marina! Another bastard for Spain!" and then called for octli to be given his men in celebration. I knew that his public announcement of my condition further forestalled the chance of attack. His soldiers might have had little restraint where the use of women was concerned, but never would they touch a pregnant woman unless the provocation was sharp and no other woman available. I believed this to be a rule of their religion as it was a practice displeasing to their God. Thus was I made safe in the midst of riotous debauch.

During this time my Captain met often with Moteczoma, and with his Christian priests he sought to turn the Ueytlatoani from pagan ways. They entreated and pleaded with him to command an end to all human sacrifice. They also threatened that Cortés would destroy the teocallis if one was not made ready for his God. Finally, after much argument, this was done. The great teocalli belonging to the God Tlaloc was cleaned and whitewashed and a cross and their Holy Mother were placed upon an altar therein. Then Cortés ordered the Azteca priests not to touch the altar, but to bring fresh flowers to adorn it and to keep wax candles always burning in reverence.

Then, suddenly, all talk of gold and Gods ended. Spaniards from Cuba who were enemies of Cortés landed in Villa Rica and declared war. All other concerns vanished. Cortés took with him most of his men and marched from Tenochtitlan to the eastern sea, leaving Alvarado in command. All of the men who remained were enjoined most fiercely to keep their horses and weapons in readiness and to be prepared at all times for attack. I was given the task of watching continuously over Moteczoma, so he would not escape or be used to unsettle the treacherous Azteca.

While I pacified the querulous Moteczoma, my mind flew in its disquiet to my Captain's side in Villa Rica. It seemed so strange to be apart from him, as if half of myself were gone. Meanwhile, free from Cortés' shrewd rule and under the lax hand of Alvarado, life in the palace grew ever more wanton. Since the mightiest soldiers had gone with Cortés, the wounded or less capable had been left behind to wallow in the excesses usually denied them by their more powerful compatriots. Thus were the women's lives unchanged by the absence of two-thirds of our army. The remaining third made good use of its sudden fortune, and though under orders to remain booted and ready for battle, the satisfaction of their appetites was in no way thwarted. Alvarado himself, as drunk with power as he often was with octli, encouraged licentiousness and turned a deaf ear to all but the most furious brawling amongst the men. If the Azteca had known how perilously weak we were at this time, perhaps even their fear of Moteczoma's disapproval would have been overthrown. Fortunately, they seemed not to know of our weakness and went about their way.

Rumors were rife, of course. We heard news of Cortés from time to time and most victorious was he said to be, and then in the next breath we were given news of his defeat. Our Tlaxcalteca allies brought us weekly word and I subsisted upon that as upon maize. Rumors were there also in Tenochtitlan. In disguise I often ventured forth and so heard the whispered complaints of many who wished us ill. These I held to myself for I did not care to take them to Alvarado, preferring to stay hidden from his sight. There were times when he needed me to speak for him but Aguilar always accompanied me, at my request, and so Alvarado was never given the chance to take liberties with me in my Captain's absence. When he sent for me to attend him by myself, which he did from time to time, I merely pleaded my indisposition or the indisposition of the Ueytlatoani. He could do little but look darkly upon me and with unspoken threat. Even in my condition I knew I was not safe from him, for he had sworn himself against me and was vile enough to make good his oath. I took Aguilar into my confidence for I knew he would defend me if need arose.

"Marina, surely he would not attempt to . . . surely you are safe from him now," he stammered, trying to keep his eyes above my rounding belly. "Not even *he* would so defile a woman who is . . . the way you are."

I smiled inside myself at his innocence. He was not a man given to debauchery and did not understand men of lesser virtue. Alvarado, I knew without doubt, would not be so tender of conscience.

"You will stay beside me when I need you, will you not, Aguilar?" I asked him sweetly, and he looked at me with that veiled yearning that at once pacified and annoyed me. I did not need his worship, but his faithful service.

"You know full well I will, Marina," he solemnly promised, and I smiled upon him, hoping to appear the guileless maiden he knew me not to be.

Unrest grew in the city and in spite of all Alvarado's excesses he was not unaware. I warned him not to take our safety for granted but to remain alert for the display of hostile intentions. A loose and heedless man, still he was a soldier of courage and cunning and thus he did not treat my warnings with contempt even though he did not behave to me with respect. As I spoke to him, his eyes travelled up and down my body and even when I would not look at him, still I could hear lechery in his voice. Aguilar heard it too, and he witnessed my modest conduct with approval. It was with some bitter amusement that I realized Alvarado probably saw me with clearer eyes than Aguilar, who was blinded by devotion.

To my dismay, Aguilar then sickened. Though feverish, he accompanied me in the presence of Alvarado until he grew so ill that he could not rise from his bed. Thus was I forced to go alone to Alvarado when he summoned me.

"Where is your faithful hound, Marina?" he mocked the first time I went to him alone. "Or is he more to you than that?"

I looked at him in cold silence and he laughed. "Oh, Marina! I have seen the great cow eyes he makes at you. Never fear that I will tell Cortés the truth about your chaste union, though I feel certain he would be interested. But then, perhaps he would not."

I waited in stony silence, concealing my hate under a mask of contempt.

"And yet, somehow, I imagine that our Captain would have no trouble believing you are not the noble woman you have told him you are, but only a woman of the streets. You simply ply your trade a little differently, yes?"

With a cry of rage, I rushed with fist upraised to strike him, but he grasped my arm hard by the wrist, twisting it so that my arm bent behind my back as if broken.

"You are a hot little bitch, indeed!" Pulling me tight against his chest, his arms were like iron manacles and I could scarcely breathe. "It is too late, Marina. What is one more man to you?"

"I will kill you!" I whispered. "I will tell my Captain and he will . . ."

"He will what?" Alvarado interrupted me, still laughing. "Believe your word against mine? Even if he were to do so, you are but a woman and I am his most loyal and well-loved brother in arms."

Even as I fought, I knew he had won. I was of more use than Alvarado would ever know, but Cortés was not a jealous man and even if he were told that Alvarado had raped me, still he would think little of it. For a moment my fury turned from Alvarado to Cortés, and I found myself hating my Captain with the same vengeance I felt for the man who held me captive. Startled, I felt more afraid at that moment of what I was feeling than of the coming violation. And so I cast aside all thought and refused to feel anything but devotion for my Captain and blackest hate for Alvarado. All I could do was hate, for I was no match for him.

While he held me with one hand, he took hold of my huipilli with the other and tore it from me. "You would be wise to enjoy this, Marina," he taunted. "Even Cortés knows I am the superior cocksman."

I willed myself not to speak or think or feel. All I had in my power was to give him nothing, as if he lay with a corpse. Pressing me to the floor, he grasped my breasts with both hands and twisted them, smiling, and though this grew most painful, I would not cry out. In this battle, I decided, I would be a warrior, enduring whatever passed without surrender.

"You have treated me badly, Marina," he said with mock sorrow, "and now you must be punished."

As I lay there, I fixed my eyes upon him and filled them with visions of his death, and when he bent his face close to my lips, I bared my teeth and bit him savagely in the face. With a cry of pain and surprise he drew back, letting go my breasts, and then swiftly masked his face with a smile of utter menace.

"Is this what you want? Battle? Very well, battle it will be." While he held both my hands in an iron grip, he pulled my cueitl from around my waist and so I was naked beneath him. Then he pulled out his tepuli and while his grip on me did not relax, he stroked his tepuli with one hand until it grew to a great size.

"I am afraid this may wound you, Marina, even though I have no doubt the many men you have had have made in you ample passage!" Pushing my knees apart, he pushed it relentlessly inside and with searing pain. "I see you are determined to prove to me that you feel nothing," he said in a pleasant voice and as the wound on his face dripped blood upon my breasts. "You will need to be stoic, indeed, before I have finished with you."

Never in my days of slavery had I endured the like of what was to follow, and all the while Alvarado gazed upon me with a smile and took his pleasure. I closed my eyes so that he would not see my suffering, but he struck me hard, threatening that if I did not keep my eyes open he would take his knife and cut them out. Though I did not think he would ever dare do such a thing, nonetheless I sought no further torture.

"That's better, my sweet bitch," he said softly, pleasantly, "I want to see in your eyes that my skill remains undiminished."

With that he pulled himself from me and wrenched me over upon my breast, tying my wrists together with a leather thong. "Get on your knees," he said in a low voice, and when I could not obey him he took from his belt a short knife and held it against my throat. "I have coupled with a dead woman before now, Marina, and you would be just another." I sensed that he was perhaps by now so maddened by lust that he might, indeed, make good his threat so I pulled my knees to my chest and he put his arms around me and lifted my buttocks as he wished. Soon I was moistened enough with my blood for his passage and when he once more threw me onto my back, he bade me look upon his rigid, dripping tepuli. "Are you enjoying this, Marina?" he asked softly. "Have you ever known a man so able to pleasure you?" and he lowered his face near to mine and whispered, "If you bite me again, I will do things to you that will make what has passed seem all delight." Slowly he lowered his lips to mine.

I struggled not to gag with revulsion as he forced his tongue into my mouth and ran it softly over mine. Gently, then, did he slip into my tipili one finger, stroking and teasing the pearl he drew forth with the tips of his fingers. From my mouth he moved his lips down my body, pausing at my breasts before moving yet lower, until he drew the pearl into his mouth. "Do you like this almost as well as the other?" he raised his head to ask. "I wonder . . . are you pleased? If not," he added, "I can give you more . . . vigorous . . . lovemaking." I knew what it was he wanted. Through all of my hatred and fury and pain I could see he was giving me a moment to choose further agony or the degradation of pleasure. It was with crushing shame that I turned coward.

"Well?" he asked, "which is it to be?" And he set his teeth upon those hidden lips and so, slowly, bit down.

"This," I whispered.

He smiled. "I think you are wise. However," he added, his voice darkening with menace, "there will be no pretense at pleasure, as you undoubtedly pretend to Cortés. I want none of your wiles. Is that understood?"

In utter humiliation I nodded assent, and he untied my hands. Thus did I learn that even in the blackest hate and through the red mists of anguish, still it was possible to be betrayed by one's own flesh. Hollowed of thought, I finally grasped Alvarado to me, meeting his thrusts with hunger, shaken as I had never been before, and never since, with the throes of shameless, mindless passion. When Alvarado finally pulled himself from me I was sobbing at the dark edge of unconsciousness.

"Was I right, Marina? Am I indeed unrivalled, even by your adored Cortés?" I made no answer. Alvarado placed a hand gently between my parted thighs. "Am I?"

"Yes," I whispered through swollen lips. "Yes."

Not once but many times after this did he take me thus, and in time my surrendering was no longer in doubt by either of us. Pain and pleasure twined like serpents and soon I did not want to have one without the other. In his cruelty Alvarado heated my blood, and with his skillful passion did he finally let it cool. My hatred of him grew no less vigorously than did my lust, but even that intensified the pleasure. I wished him dead in all the moments I was not joined to him in wanton abandon.

Aguilar, still weak with fever, learned of my shame and fixed upon me looks of sorrowing reproach. I would never before have thought his opinion had weight with me. His love for me had never mattered, nor had I ever felt the slightest desire to return it, but when I saw the lessening of his regard I found to my disquiet that I was most unwilling to lose it.

"I will pray for you, Marina," he said through lips still parched from fever, "and that our Lord God may have mercy upon your soul."

I avoided Aguilar after that, even when he was stronger and could again accompany me. I no longer requested this of him, for his presence was now an annoyance. In any case, I no longer needed protection from Alvarado, nor a witness to the use we made of our solitude. Days passed. Murmurings of unrest were common in the palace, but little word came from Villa Rica. I longed for my Captain's return, even though the pleasure I took with Alvarado must then cease.

The thought came to me one night that perhaps my Captain's return to Tenochtitlan would be hastened if he heard there was perilous unrest among the Azteca. I told Alvarado that an uprising was most likely and that it would occur quite soon, hoping he would immediately send a messenger to Cortés. Instead, inflamed by arrogance and rage, Alvarado waited until the Azteca were gathered in sacred ritual in the teocallis and crowded in the sacred square, and then he ordered their massacre. From his horse he watched the slaughter, and I was at his side. When the battle was over and hundreds lay dead, we returned to his chamber to copulate like beasts upon the floor. "Death adds a fillip to desire, does it not, Marina?" and I hated him more at that moment than at any other in the past. For what he said was true.

29

Xochitl

Until the end of life, never could I forget the horror of that day of butchery in Tenochtitlan. As I stood upon the palace roof watching the rites in honor of Tezcatlipoca, the warriors of Cortés streamed forth into the sacred square, slaying all before them. Unarmed were the people as they danced and sang and gave homage and they fell before the weapons of the enemy like grass in a great wind. Unlike grass, they did not rise again, but lay in pools of blood so vast there was not a stone left white by the end of that day.

Gripped by the ghastly scene below, I could not turn away my eyes or move or speak. Even in the most evil of dreams there would not come such a sight. Screaming, the people could only try to run, but there were so many of them they could not escape the weapons of lightning and the thundering hooves of the horses. Swords flashed in the sunlight, slashing off heads and limbs so that pieces of bodies flew right and left as the assault advanced. Blind with fear, people tripped over the fallen, tripped over heads and trunks that gushed blood like ghastly fountains into the air. Some were disemboweled with a single stroke and as they ran their entrails fell from their bellies and tripped them in the coils of their own flesh. Women's breasts were sliced from them, if the warriors had momentary leisure for such amusement, and children were grasped by the feet and slammed against the pyramids and so their skulls shattered like gourds and their brains splattered those sacred walls.

The horses stood upon their hind legs and plunged downward, crushing any who stood in their way, and as they did this their riders fired death from their weapons and soon there hung a cloud over the spectacle as if all were but phantoms in a dream. So had it been in Cholulan, I was certain. There also had the enemy made war upon the defenseless. Even as these women now found themselves dying, so also had my only friend, Xocomoco. It was a sight so terrible I almost went forth to share their death rather than face living with such a memory.

The slaughter went on for hours and then, as suddenly as it had begun, on a signal the enemy withdrew. It was quieter then; one could hear the groans of the dying. I gathered together what cloth and healing potions I could in my haste and ran to the square. Gutted and headless, with shattered bones thrust into the light of day, bodies were everywhere. Heads lay bodiless, faces frozen with terror. Coils of entrails sprawled like serpents and the stones underfoot were slippery with the blood still streaming from the dying and the dead.

I found a little girl, half her face slashed from her head, and though I held her in my arms and tried desperately to staunch the wound, there was nothing I could do. She clung to me, sightless, believing me to be her mother, and I held her tenderly against my breast while she died.

I stumbled on, then, to the great teocalli of Tezcatlipoca through a wilderness of mangled flesh, helping some of the wretches to stand, bandaging what wounds I could with my cloth and then with the cloth I tore from bodies no longer in need of it. Soon I had used all of my healing potion and could do little but comfort those who cried to me for help. There was nothing more I could do. Nothing. The helplessness within me turned to rage, at myself as well as at the enemy, for in the face of this suffering still was I whole and well, and powerless.

Finally I reached the sacred stone of Tixoc. Bodies

had been flung upon it in unholy offering. I climbed the narrow steps of the teocalli in obedience to some blind urgency and found Chimalpopoca inside—although I would not have been able to recognize him had he not been wearing the stone pendant of his calling. A Spaniard had taken special care to mutilate the priest, and though I bore the man no fondness, still it sickened me to see him thus. A brazier of burning coals had been poured over his upturned face, and at first it seemed strange that he could have lain motionless under such torture. Then I saw, where his robe had been pulled away, that his legs had first been severed at the knees and his arms at the elbows, and so he had been helpless as a babe when the burning coals fell upon his eyes. I looked to the idol of Tezcatlipoca, a most indifferent witness. Justly was he to seem so, for as God of War, bloodshed and slaughter were for him a pleasing reverence. At that moment I was glad no God could touch me, neither to give me pain nor pleasure, for well did I now know they lived, if they lived at all, far beyond all interest in human suffering.

From the teocalli I made my way to the entrance of the serpent wall and out of the sacred square. Again led by impulse, I went on past Moteczoma's palace to that of Axayácatl. In the garden beside the canal there came to my ears a moaning. Quietly did I then draw into the shadows, darker than the darkening sky, and crept to where the sound had its source. An enemy warrior lay there in the bushes, felled by a stone but coming back into mindfulness. He stared up at me and in one undamaged eye there was pleading mixed with pain. I knelt by his side and stared back into his eyes. This was some woman's son, I thought, my heart softening within me. Once he had been but a child, like those whose blood now dried upon the stone walls. My heart grew hard once more. I saw his one good eye brighten as I reached to my side, then widen as I drew forth the sacrificial dagger I kept always with me. With the skill of long practice I drove it deep into his heart.

"Now die," I whispered, watching his body shudder as the hands of death took hold.

From behind me there came a familiar voice. "You surprise me, Lady. You moved to kill more swiftly than I." Stepping from the shadows came Lord Cuauhtémoc. "It is unsafe for you to be here. I will accompany you back to your chamber."

I went with him in silence, and in silence he left me at my chamber door. Covered in blood, with the bloody dagger in my hand, I leaned against the wall and, for the first time since I lost Atahualpa, I wept.

Much to my surprise, I was summoned next day to the presence of Lord Cuauhtémoc. One of the few Lords not yet imprisoned by Cortés, he awaited me in the audience chamber, alone. I made him a proper greeting and, gruffly, he did likewise.

"Messengers have come with news that Cortés has defeated his enemy in the east and that they have now joined him in war against us. Already messengers have been sent from Axayácatl's palace with news of the great slaughter of our people," he said, studying me with a brooding intensity. Taken aback, I wondered why he should now call *me* for counsel. He wasted few words before reaching the heart of the matter. "Not only are we besieged by these foreigners from without, but also from within are we assailed."

"Do you speak of traitors, Lord?"

He was silent a moment, as if he were measuring me against an unseen rival. "I was interested to see you in the palace garden yesterday. Many women could not have done as you did."

"I had never killed like that before, Lord Cuauhtémoc, and I never will again," I said quietly.

"You killed him in mercy, Lady?"

"I killed him in anger," I replied evenly, "but of that I am not proud."

Cuauhtémoc nodded. When he spoke his voice gave nothing away. "You must do our people a service, Lady," he said, pacing from me several steps and then returning to fix upon me again his dark assessing eyes. "You went once to see the Ueytlatoani in the palace of his father and you failed to persuade him to return with you here. I want you to go there again, and this time you will not fail to do as you are bid."

"If I did not succeed the first time, Lord, how do you know I will the second?"

"A ruler either defends his empire against the enemy or he must be taken from his icpalli," Cuauhtémoc answered. "He must either do this willingly, when his people are in peril, or he must be . . . removed . . . without his consent."

In silence I pondered his words, their meaning suddenly flooding over me. "Surely you do not dare to ask me to slay my Lord if he refuses to return?" Cuauhtémoc but looked at me, and I cried, "How dare you suggest such sacrilege! Never would I consent to such a treacherous act."

I turned to leave but Cuauhtémoc moved swiftly to my side and grasped me by the arm, pulling me around so that I once more faced him. Roughly then did he speak to me and in a low and furious voice. "*You* are responsible for much of this, Lady. Do not speak of what I dare or dare not to do when you are guilty of a far greater treason than the removal of a ruler who deserts and betrays his people! If you had not led his neck into the rope we would have long since slain the enemy to whom you surrendered our Lord." Though his voice grew no louder, it increased in fury and his hand clamped tighter upon my arm.

"You saw one result of your treason yesterday, and well will you pay for it and with what act *I* will decide."

My gaze faltered under his and I whispered, "I cannot do what you bid me, Lord. I cannot."

"You will," he said, taking his hand from my arm. "You will once more dress as your shadow self and you will go to Lord Moteczoma's chamber and there use all of your wiles to persuade him to return with you. If you are not successful in this, then you will make use of your dagger."

My body began to tremble and my teeth chattered as with cold. What Cuauhtémoc suggested was a most heinous offence. Set upon his icpalli by the will of the Gods—or so I had once believed—none would dare remove the Ueytlatoani unless the Gods took possession of him first with divine madness. Then he was simply replaced. Never in memory had a Ueytlatoani been slain by his own people.

"Cannot you or another Lord rule Tenochtitlan in his absence?" I pleaded. "He can do nothing against you while Cortés keeps him captive."

"In the company of Cortés he still has power over us. He encourages the greed of the foreigner. They will not rest until they take from us every grain of gold we possess and slay or enslave us all."

This I knew to be true. All we had seen or heard confirmed it. "I will go to my Lord Moteczoma," I said, "and I will do all I can to persuade him to return with me. But I am certain I could never raise my hand against him."

Lord Cuauhtémoc pierced me with a darkling look. "You will do as I say, Lady Xochitzlin. Or you will die."

"It is likely that I will die in any case, Lord."

"Even so, you will obey."

Wordless, I turned to go and, unhindered, left the chamber. I would don disguise and I would go to Moteczoma, I decided, and with all of my wiles would I seek to enchant or terrify him into submission. For how could I add my husband's murder to my many transgressions? Thus it was I awaited an opportunity, but my sister rarely left the Ueytlatoani's side. Cortés returned to his fortress in Tenochtitlan and terrible battles were waged, and in all of this time I could not fulfill my task. I grew hopeful as our warriors won one battle after another and so I began to hope that the Spaniards and their allies would all be slain or flee the city. Such salvation seemed possible one day when, announced by cannon fire, Cortés appeared upon the roof of Axayácatl's palace accompanied by the Ueytlatoani and my sister, and attempted to persuade us to cease our fight against them. Warriors quieted in the street below, but when Moteczoma in a trembling voice commanded them to lay down their weapons in peace, then were there angry shouts from the crowd and the embers of rebellion flamed hot once more. I saw Lord Cuauhtémoc adding his voice to the angry din, for by then I had crept close to the palace in hope of gaining entrance and thus I could see all as it happened.

"Lord Cuitláhuac is now Ueytlatoani!" Cuauhtémoc cried out, and all took up the cry and chanted it in mockery of Moteczoma.

Roused to action, some men took up stones and threw them upwards. One of these struck my Lord upon his chest and the next upon his forehead, and he fell to his knees. In the resulting confusion, I managed to slip into the palace two mornings later with my face hidden in my shawl and I made my way past the guards who took me for but a harmless slave. I arrived undetected at Lord Moteczoma's chamber wherein he lay unconscious and alone.

Kneeling by his side, I slipped my sacred dagger from where it was hidden in case of need, keeping it close to my thigh so that if the Ueytlatoani awoke, he would not see it. Although it would have become most profane to beg the attention of my Lord Quetzalcoatl, I did seek that of Coatlicue, mother of Huitzilopochtli and his slain sister, Malinallxochitl.

"If you have ears to hear," I prayed, "let them hear, and bring to my lips words of sorcery." Surely if she did still exist, she above all others would understand the necessity of what I might be forced to do.

As if she indeed had heard my whispered supplication and materialized as a shadow from the shadows of that unlit chamber, a figure moved toward me. Overawed in that moment, soon I could discern with grave misgiving the features of my sister, Malinalli, who knelt upon my Lord Moteczoma's other side and smiled.

"And so at last we think as one, my sister."

If she had struck me, I could not have been more repulsed, so torn from purpose. I needed only to look at her eyes glittering with malice, her body rigid with ancient hate, to know that what I had set forth perhaps to do was wrong. It was as if I had shouted vile obscenities against my Lord of Dawn, so shamed was I. Silently I rose and turned away. I did not hear the rustle of my sister's garments as she pursued me. Like Tezcatlipoca, shadow-still and swift, she struck me upon the back of my head and I fell senseless to the ground. When I awoke it was to find my Lord Moteczoma dead, a bloody dagger in my hand. Voices stirred me into flight, the dagger rattling onto the stone behind me as if to alert those who would soon be seeking my capture.

30

MALINALLI

Our victory was short-lived, yet there was good come of it. Moteczoma became ever more helpless in our hands and Alvarado sent word for my Captain to return because the Azteca had arisen against our depleted ranks. I could sense that Alvarado was not eager for the return of Cortés, and it delighted me to see his discomfort. Even in the throes of coupling I smiled within myself to know he had misgivings about the justice Cortés might visit upon him for his rashness. I let drop a word here and there, amusing myself with his disquiet. It was not punishment enough, of course, but I took pleasure in the thought that more would follow. I would see to that myself.

At last my Captain returned and, with his valiant, weary men and some loyal Tlaxcalteca, he peacefully reentered the gates. He took small notice of me, but I reveled in the sight of him. He patted my belly and said, "My son prospers, eh, Marina?"

"He does, Captain," I replied, refusing to ever admit the possibility of bearing a mere girl who would naturally mean nothing in her warrior-father's eyes.

There was little time to speak of private matters. The situation in Tenochtitlan had utterly changed since my Captain was last here. Many problems had arisen in his absence and he dealt with each in turn, but the first concerned Alvarado and the massacre.

"I have been told the Azteca sought and were granted your permission to have a festival," Cortés said to him, having gained that piece of intelligence from me.

"That is true," Alvarado replied, growing uneasy as would a rat edged into a corner, "but I also heard from a priest that after they finished their lewd rituals, they were plotting to turn upon us in attack."

Neither Alvarado nor I volunteered from what source that information had come.

"This was not well done of you," Cortés said angrily. "It was not the time to act so rashly and without my consent."

"But you were gone from here and I was in charge," Alvarado said sullenly. "I did what I thought best."

Cortés made a scornful noise and bid him be gone, and I was pleased to watch him leave the chamber with his tail between his legs in disgrace. Word now came that several of our soldiers had been transporting cacicas from Tacuba when warriors attacked them and only narrowly did they escape, leaving the women behind. As they told their story, it had been only by the grace of God they were not taken as sacrifice and eaten. My Captain decided to send four hundred men under the leadership of de Ordás to learn the reason for such a warlike act, while Alvarado was left to brood in his chamber for punishment. Scarcely had de Ordás and his men gained the road when they were fallen upon by the Azteca, who attacked them suddenly from the rooftops. So fierce and unexpected was the attack that eight of our men were killed in the first assault and nearly all were wounded. In retreat, de Ordás battled bravely against the swarming numbers of the enemy but still could not reach the palace. From all sides the Azteca waged war, until they began attacking the palace as well, and the air was dark and hissing with arrows and stones. In great numbers they overwhelmed us until we trained our cannon upon them and with those and with musketfire drove them back so that de Ordás could forge a passage into the palace for himself and his men.

Still the battle did not end. It raged all that day and even into the darkness of night. Worse, Azteca warriors managed to enter the palace and set fire to some of the lower chambers, and our women were sent scurrying to throw dirt upon the fires so we would not be smoked from our quarters like bees from a hollow log. In the late hours of the night we mended both the wounded as well as our fortifications for the morrow. Well did we so, for the next day the fighting raged more fiercely yet. Soldiers, wounded not in one place but in many, were carried inside the palace walls all that day and the women staunched blood and bound wounds until they were as weary and bloody as those under their care. The Spaniards were most amazed at the ferocity of the Azteca warriors, saying in wonder that they never had seen such warfare, although fought with lowly weapons. Those soldiers seasoned by the wars of many lands said they had never seen warriors more courageous. Finally our men retreated into the palace amid the clamor of the Azteca who called them cowards and other insulting names.

The very air stank with fear that night. The Spaniards were valiant warriors indeed, but the numbers and relentlessness of the enemy caused great uneasiness. "Weakness from within is more perilous than any from without," Cortés exclaimed, exhorting his men not to fall prey to despair. I told my Captain to warn his men that the Azteca were telling how they would first feed their Gods and then themselves with our bodies, and that the beasts in Moteczoma's menagerie had been left fasting for two days so that they would be ravenous for our flesh. After considering, Cortés did say all this to his men and from their fear and disgust rose fresh resolve. Nothing aroused them so much as an insult to their dignity—the challenge was for them quite inescapable.

Moteczoma was all this time in great fear and trembling. At all hours did the Azteca cry to us to give up the Ueytlatoani. Tortured with indecision, he said to me that he did not know whether they called for him to return to his icpalli, or to meet his death. I gave him soothing infusions to quiet him and so he spent many hours dazed and unaware of what was going on outside his solitary chamber. Most urgent was it to keep him captive, for the Azteca would rally around him should he escape. Though I heard some speak against him, the Azteca fist had not yet been lowered full upon us in the palace for fear of injuring their captive ruler.

"It would be easiest if we put him to death," Alvarado, too valuable for further banishment, said hotly to Cortés in counsel.

"As usual, you do not foresee the outcome of reckless action," Cortés said with grave disapproval. "That is something you must learn, Alvarado."

Alvarado was silent under the rebuke. Once he would have been swift to reply, but now that his standing was in peril, he only grew sullen and visited his anger on others less powerful than himself. Men he would fight at a fancied slight, but women were often more convenient. I heard them sometimes cry out in the night as he tormented them, and always felt relief that I was no longer the object of his passion.

My Captain told me such stories about the battles waged in Villa Rica and his glorious part in them I was certain there had never been a warrior to equal him. Now, when it grew clear that the Azteca were determined to slay us all, he had his men build small wooden fortresses from which soldiers could shoot their muskets and yet remain protected as they ventured into the ranks of the enemy. On the following day most of our men and the Tlaxcalteca left the palace with their crossbowmen and horsemen and the wooden fortresses going on before. Under orders to help defend the palace, women and the wounded stayed behind. When we heard the drums and cries and other sounds of combat, we women took up rocks and the soldiers their weapons, and sought to prevent those who, from time to time, attempted to scale our walls. We fulfilled our task, though many women were seized by the enemy and unceremoniously slaughtered, whether they were Azteca or not, for having served the conquering army. Few Azteca women had remained with us, many having escaped the palace at the onset of war, yet there had remained some who had been taken in battle as slaves or given to Cortés as gifts, and of all these perhaps a hundred were slain. Rocks were but paltry weapons against the deadly arms of trained Azteca warriors.

As Cortés told me later, our soldiers in the field fought bravely but on difficult terrain, laced as it was with canals spanned by removable wooden bridges. The horses often slid and fell on the stone streets and the wooden fortresses were either destroyed or cast aside as too unwieldy to carry across that hazardous ground. In the face of thousands of fierce Azteca, my Captain fought to gain possession of the great teocalli of Tezcatlipoca in the center of the sacred square. Hundreds of warriors lined the steps as Cortés led the charge, and as its steps were narrow and slippery with the blood of the recently sacrificed, it was a perilous ascent. From all directions came arrows and lances, and most skilled were the Azteca with their knife-edged macquauitls. Still, Cortés pressed on with cries of victory to encourage his men.

At last they gained foothold on the top of the pyramid and then entered the teocalli itself. With righteous zeal they pulled down the idols of Tezcatlipoca and Huitzilopochtli and pushed them to the edge of the pyramid and then over, and watched them crack upon the stones below. For a moment the fighting ceased as the Azteca awaited a sign of divine wrath, but of course the Gods were still. Setting the teocalli on fire with the wood kept piled inside, our men then descended, slaying the enemy as they went. Yet no matter how many they slew, there were hundreds to take each corpse's place and so, wearied, they struggled back to the palace and safety.

Never had there been such unrest among my Captain's men who muttered against him most ungratefully. The soldiers of Narvaez, who had accompanied Cortés from the battle of Villa Rica, were the noisiest of all, cursing not only Cortés for leading them into danger but cursing the whole country as well.

Fearing rebellion among his men no less than he feared the enemy ranged by the thousands against us, Cortés took counsel among his officers and decided to sue for peace. "Marina," he said in unwilling defeat, "go to Moteczoma and persuade him we need for him to speak to his people from the rooftop. Tell him to say that if they will let us leave peacefully, we will go from Tenochtitlan and never return."

"Very well, my Captain," I replied with a heavy heart. Had I helped him all this way and for nothing? Yet to remain stubbornly in Tenochtitlan would be to tempt death, for it would be only days before our food supply was gone and we had but a small spring of fresh water that had sprung up most miraculously, so Aguilar said, when the men had dug a well.

"I will not speak," Moteczoma replied sullenly, "for these foreigners are not the Lords I thought them. I now know they are not even great men. They are but mortal and like mortals they will soon die." He sighed. "I think perhaps I will die, also, for I was wrong to let them into the city. I should have waged war against them when they first landed upon our shore and killed them all before they could bring such trouble upon us."

"It is difficult to confound prophecy, Lord," I suggested softly. "You have acted reverently, and so it will be remembered."

"It will be remembered that I was a fool," he said darkly, and he spoke in a voice of firm conviction that I had not heard for many days. "And that you were a traitor and a whore," he added bitterly.

I saved in my heart these discourteous words, adding them to the store I had already gathered. Soon he would regret them. "If the Azteca invade this palace,"

I warned him, "you will surely die, my Lord, along with the rest of us."

"Should I care? What more, Malintzin, do you and Cortés want from me? I neither wish to live nor to listen to him, for to such a pass has my fate brought me and all because of you."

Weary unto death he might be, I thought, but still too arrogant with life to truly desire his own doom. Bald pleading would only set his back more rigidly against submission to my will, and so I took a more persuasive manner. "My Lord, you know my loyalty to you and that it is my sorcery which has kept you safe from all of your enemies, both within and without this palace. Is this not so?"

He would not meet my eyes. "I do not know what to believe of you, Malintzin. If these men are not Lords, and Cortés no God, then why should I believe you are my Second Wife's shadow self? She was blindly deluded, even as was I. Why should you not be blind likewise?"

I smiled. "Surely you have seen my power in your visions. Have you not heard me speak into your dreams?"

"That could mean nothing. Your words could mean nothing."

I pretended to be offended. "Very well, my Lord, you must have your way in this as in all else. I will leave you to your fate and trust it will be merciful," and I made as if to leave.

"Malintzin!" he called after me. I was pleased by the note of panic in his voice. "Do not leave me right at this moment."

I regarded him coldly, letting my voice be indifferent. "I do not wish to share your fate, Lord. Farewell."

"No, no!" he begged, hastening to me and taking me by the arm. "I will do anything you say, Malintzin. I have no one else to trust but you."

I kept cool eyes upon him until I knew he was truly mine to command, and then I let a small forgiving smile touch my lips. "Very well then, I will stay beside you and protect you with my sorcery. But first you must speak to your people and sue for peace, that we might all safely leave Tenochtitlan."

"Even I?" he asked in piteous tones I did not pity. "The Ueytlatoani cannot leave the Heart of the One World without his warriors. What would I be then?"

"Stay, if you wish, and perhaps your Lords might again submit to your rule. With my help, perhaps they will still do so."

"But you will stay with me and work your sorcery upon them, will you not, Malintzin? *You* will not leave?" he asked pleadingly.

Again I smiled. It had been such an easy triumph that I could have wished for a more challenging enemy. "I will be with you until the end, Lord." This would be one promise, I knew, that I would keep most faithfully. The years of hatred would finally be laid to rest. I would soon be free of them, at last.

31

AGUILAR

What is it about this country that is at once so beautiful and iniquitous? What is it that scents the bright air with noxious vapor and with the hands of divine inspiration builds splendid monuments to evil? Since landing upon this shore I have been bewitched and repelled, certain of only one thing; that God never blessed the Mexica nor saved them from their wrongdoing. Only with our coming did they have chance of salvation, and they wanted it not. Too black with wickedness they were, too deeply mired in sin. In all fairness, I cannot so harshly judge them alone, for I, in my enchantment with the woman they now call La Malinche, was also infected with corruption and my soul a long time lost thereby. Sometimes I fear that my immortal soul will never rise within sight of the Divine Throne, but will wander in this wilderness that is Land of the Mexica!

The Scriptures enjoin, "Each person is tempted when he is lured and enticed by his own desire. Then desire when it has conceived gives birth to sin; and sin when it is fullgrown brings forth death." Would that death had come before my transgression. Would that death had wrapped me in my shroud before I ever met Marina, the beautiful and perfidious. Marina! I swear I loved her the moment I saw her and though I struggled against temptation she bewitched me into most grievous sin, a disgrace to the priestly calling I sought to embrace. But that fall from grace was not the beginning of the story, though it foreshadowed what would be its end.

When first I put to sea a full lifetime ago, or so it seems to me now, it was in prospect of doing my duty to my King and to my God. I determined to take Holy Orders upon my return to Spain, but first, being but a youth, it seemed to me of utmost urgency to accompany our army to heathen lands and help convert the impious to Christian ways. Fabulous were the tales of adventure I read with the avidity of a starving man falling upon meat, and though I knew the color of the cloth I would wear someday forbade partaking of the coarser pleasures of such an enterprise, still I could taste seemlier ones and, in fulfilling my duty to God, ready myself for the priesthood as well.

Before we embarked the talk was pious, thickly larded with prayers and devout intentions, while once upon the sea words were closer to the bone and not so godly-minded as they were gilt. Gold was what my companions yearned for, and heroic adventure. All were determined, even as I, in my less-carnal way, to bring the pages of romance to life. We had all read about the fabled land of Californio where dwelt the most beautiful women; Amazons they were and black as night, fierce and valiant and, of rather more interest, exceedingly comely. El Dorado and Californio, land of gold, land of women sweet as honey; we were in truth in search of these. Women were denied me by my choice, and gold was of no great interest, but peril in the name of God and King could not leave me unmoved. Foolish we are in our youth, and in our middling years worse than foolish.

But my words outpace the tale. Looking back in time it seems my youth flew past and that only the last few years have crawled by. So it is that when I peer over my shoulder I see a very young man, dutiful, chaste and by romance beguiled, sailing with the swiftness of a storm cloud across the sea to Hispaniola, and thence to the coast of Yucatan. I see him hold fast the rail as the winds rise and the clouds darken, and watch him grow pale as the waves mount higher and higher. With a groan and a cry, as of a beast in pain, I behold the ship broken asunder upon the rocks and the young man leap from the deck into the dark water, grasp desperately some wooden flotsam and so make his way to shore. There he is joined by the few others who survive the ordeal, and there they are set upon by savages and if it is romantic to suffer and perish thus, then they are glamorous indeed! Several are shot dead with arrows, and some are sacrificed and stewed for supper, but that young man I know so well does not tarry around to greet the reaper or the cook, but makes his way into the jungle. If it is romantic to be lost in a distant wilderness, bitten by mosquitoes, starved and parched with thirst, then this youth is the very embodiment of poetic legend!

No, I did not find it marvelous to be shipwrecked, nor was it heroic to slog my way onward to a doubtful safety. As a future man of the cloth it would seem I should have travelled with pious prayers upon my lips and a constant sense of holy martyrdom in my heart, but the sad truth was that, if indeed there were prayers of a most desperate nature on my lips, so also were there curses and words of despair. Tribulation does not of itself bring forth nobility of spirit.

Late the third day I found myself surrounded by heathen and was poked and prodded ahead of them like a stray donkey into their village. There my invisible but quite substantial lead rope was handed over to their cacique, and I entered thus unceremoniously into slavery. This cacique—a position akin to that of our Spanish hidalgo—was known by the name of Teoamoxtli, without benefit of baptism, and was the proud ruler of a few miles of trackless waste inhabited by perhaps as many as four thousand unchurched souls. As if I were some sort of exotic beast, he had me undressed and then stared at me from all angles. His several wives did likewise, sparing their blushes and tittering with amusement at this naked phenomenon. I kept my eyes raised inches above their heads and kept my distracted thoughts in sufficient order so that *my* blushes would be spared. It was a curious and unsettling experience.

Then began my trial. It commenced with various subtle and brazen temptations in the form of nubile young women, both placed before me and ordered by night to creep to the section of dirt floor where I slept, and despite the comeliness of a very few, I had no desire to succumb. I must admit to a certain consciousness of virtue; that when the parade of temptresses slowed and then ceased, I was aware of the very pleasant sensation of having had my virtue rewarded. Though I must have seemed odd to them, possibly even freakish, Teoamoxtli put me in charge of his harem of wives and concubines, apparently satisfied that I held no carnal yearnings—at least for members of the weaker sex. The hard labor to which heretofore I had been put was restored to the slaves, while my new duties, decreasing in arduousness, increased in complexity. In time I became something of an arbiter among them, settling disputes and suggesting courses of action, enabled to do so by the readiness with which I embraced their mother tongue. It was through knowledge of that language that my perception grew keener. I discovered that while they were indeed idolators, still they were human and with human curiosities, sorrows and passions. They danced with joy in the maize and caressed and fondled their children and grieved when death came among them. They squabbled over trivial matters and pondered solemn issues and if their religion was barbaric, yet they did solemnly enact its savage rites with the veneration of Christians.

Yet Christians they were not, and so from time to time I spoke to them of my Lord God and Holy Mother Mary, and Christ, his martyred Son, and they nodded and listened gravely and then, I suspect, ended up believing the Holy Trinity contained but three more members of their overwhelming pantheon and that the

Virgin Mary was but another goddess of maize. They had gods and goddesses for every conceivable living and lifeless thing: dirt, plants, sky, rain, fire, all had their little demigods. When the people spoke of their religion, though well might it be blasphemy to call it that, my head swam with their deities' names and functions and appearances. Surely the names were all most bizarre and their stone idols fearsome and terrible to look upon. Remembering our loving Jesus Christ, I pitied these misguided people most sincerely, for I could never imagine praying for solace to gods of such hideous aspect!

Unlike the Azteca, these people of the Maya were in the main content with the sacrifice to their gods of feathers and precious stones and the occasional beast. Perhaps influenced by their more bloodthirsty neighbors far to the north, they did also on rare occasions sacrifice men. It was this ritual that most revolted my nature, of course. With music and dancing the people would watch breathlessly as priests slashed open the chest of some unfortunate to yank forth his still-beating heart, and while I could scarcely keep myself from puking at the sight, these people were largely indifferent to it. While they did show themselves capable of human feeling, still this callous insensitivity proved them savage at heart.

Seven years passed in this strange company and in many outward ways I became one of them. I spoke only their language until it seemed almost my own mother tongue, and I learned and adopted their manners. In my heart I kept my Spanish self and in my soul I was still fully Christian, but in order to survive with any comfort I sought to appear as if I had adapted to life in Yucatan. I kept myself chaste, according to my solemn vow, and the words of our Christian prayers were firmly upon my lips, and I went from day to day in an existence in which I kept each foot planted in one of two quite dissimilar worlds.

One day there came word from the coast that foreigners had landed upon our shores and, miracle of miracles, they had heard of a man like them living in the jungle. Offers of various goods were proposed to the cacique who was my master, and with some slight show of regret he accepted the little bells and trumpery beads he accounted equal to my worth. In the custody of twenty warriors I was escorted to the eastern coast only to discover that the ships had sailed on without me. My chagrin can only be understood by someone who learns he has been released from long servitude only to find himself awakening from a dream and in slavery still.

However, God was merciful to me in this as in all other things and I learned ships had been sighted farther south, so to the south I journeyed, greeting the sight of them with a most heartfelt thanksgiving! Sighting my frenzied gesticulations of greeting on shore they sent forth several boats, and in the first was the captain of the exploit, Hernán Cortés. I greeted him in the Indian manner, by touching dirt to my lips, and Cortés embraced me with tears in his eyes and covered my near-nakedness with his own cloak. Castilian came brokenly to my lips and it was most embarrassing to find myself speaking my native tongue like a stranger. My ways, for seven years ingrained, made me something of a curiosity until they wore off in the company of my fellow countrymen. Oh, with what a glad heart did I put to sea with them, and the creaking of the masts and the popping of the sails came as music to my ears.

Captain Cortés called me to his cabin and asked if I would stay with his company as interpreter, since I had learned the Indian tongue, and with a grateful heart for my salvation I told him it would be an honor to serve him. And honor it was, until we came to Cintla and I fell in love with the woman who would become Cortés' mistress and harlot of the charming ruffian, Alvarado, as well as the one temptress I could not spurn.

Never will I forget her, kneeling on the sand at Cortés' feet, raising her bewitching face to look upon him as if he were the mightiest of her heathen gods. Her glossy black hair, which fell to her feet when unbound, was coiled about her small, exquisite face and set with flowers. When she raised her eyes they were so beautiful, so sparkling with life and bright with adoration, that a saint would have struggled against temptation. My struggle was brief; I loved her instantly, with a passion devoid of reason and as urgent as any fleshly hunger. I wanted her in a way I had never wanted a woman in my life, carnal lust being but a small drop in the elixir of that new enchantment. I wanted her to look upon *me* with those eyes and with that same intoxicating adoration. I wanted to unwind that soft hair and put my arms around that voluptuous, perfect body. I wanted her for myself solely, my possession, my secret. In that abrupt and unsettling moment I learned why the servants of God must be celibate. I wanted to worship her. As a living shrine I yearned to place my love and hope and fondest desires at her feet. From one who had vowed to love and worship only God, at that moment my spirit divided as a river divides so it flows in two directions instead of one, and with half of myself I adored the Lord my God, and with my other half I worshipped at the pagan shrine of Marina. It would have done no good to struggle; the battle was waged and lost the moment I saw her face. Daily I prayed for deliverance from impurity of heart and daily sought her company.

Marina, or Malinalli as she was first known to me, was given as bed partner to a soldier twice her age and I escaped his groans of pleasure upon her body by going to sleep upon deck. As it was spring this was no hardship to one who had known the rigors of slavery, and indeed I was glad for the small penance of crisp night winds. Seeking further penance for the good of my soul, I slept without blankets and wrapped a coarse rope tightly around my waist lest I forget the menace of even worse transgression.

The adoration in Marina's face altered with time and became mixed in even part with yearning and guile. Even as she ceased to believe Cortés was a god—and one must say I fulfilled my duty in this by bringing her back one step from the absolute heathendom in which she was ensnared—she remained adamant about keeping the native populace ignorant of his mortality. With her charm she persuaded me to keep silent in conspiracy, and salving my conscience with the excuse that if this subterfuge were not undertaken then we would die to the man and so be unable to continue our mission of salvation, I silently agreed.

Speaking not one word of Nahuatl for some time and relying as we all did upon Marina, I was almost at the very gates of Tenochtitlan before I began to realize how false she had been in interpreting events, how she had built us a road of lies through a wilderness of delusion. It was too late by then to warn Cortés or attempt to dissuade Marina. We were in the city of sin itself.

Infected by the moral corruption that seemed to seep from the very walls of the palace, our men grew ever more rapacious and lustful. Wicked as they had been before, they were a hundred times more wicked by the time Cortés needed to leave the city to crush a rebellion in Villa Rica de la Vera Cruz. Wallowing in every conceivable form of debauchery, drunken soldiers fornicated not only in private but full in public as well, and with the very lowest Azteca wantons. Gambling rose to fever pitch when the curse of gold was laid upon us by Moteczoma's opening his father's hidden coffers. Lust for gold vied with lust for flesh and so the palace chambers rang night and day with voices better lowered in shame.

Sick at heart at these signs of our moral weakness, my body sickened as well and I lay helpless with the flux as Marina acted the harlot with Alvarado in

Cortés' absence. So filled with horror and disgust by this was I that I could scarcely look her in the eye, and as for her body—to me it was the body of Eve herself, fouled still by Adam's fall. Unable to stop my ears, I overheard whisperings about what went on in Alvarado's chamber, and sicker yet was I, though on the mend, to find the shameful stories a vile aphrodisiac. Even as I beseeched and preached to her in vain—and she with a look of chaste innocence on her face—yet I acted the voyeur, spying upon that chamber in my thoughts and standing within its walls in my dreams. I cannot describe my self-disgust nor the many penances I undertook to scourge the wickedness from my soul, but Marina, with that bewitching body and enticing face, kept flitting into my mind like a phantom.

Upon the return of Cortés, Alvarado was insufficiently punished for the utter laxity of his command and the cruel massacre of the Azteca innocents. At least, to my relief, Marina no longer shared his bed. Less often than formerly did she share the bed of Cortés, for he was at heart indifferent to women and never to be satisfied with but one, either. Moteczoma by this time had become quite dependent on Marina, as he had once been, so I was told, upon her twin sister who was one of his wives.

"You never told me you had a sister," I told her once this knowledge had reached my ears.

"I had not thought of her for years," she said lightly. "We were never of one mind in any matter."

"That is unfortunate," I said, desiring any and all information about her life, about which I knew almost nothing. "I should think twins, and especially sisters, would often be in agreement."

Marina's reply was cold. "We could not be any more different from each other, nor more complete strangers."

I did not pursue the matter in the face of her obvious

hostility to the subject, and began to speak casually of other things.

Cortés returned from Villa Rica to a city in open rebellion. The heinous massacre, result of Alvarado's plotting, had stirred native restiveness into a most unsurprising revolt and we posted many guards on the watch at all hours. Marina's duty was to guard Moteczoma so that he would not have the chance to escape; he chafed at his captivity at last and it was feared a second attempt to rescue him would not find him again unwilling to decamp. A most wretched sovereign he was, quite unable to pursue a single course or keep to one opinion. As for myself, I was quite interested in the man and with my fragile grasp of Nahuatl I often attempted to converse with him on matters of religion and Azteca life. Despite his pagan benightedness he was not a vulgar man and his manners approached those of a Christian gentleman. Given to a rather surprising degree of introspection, on the days when he was not plagued by capricious fits of madness, he was a most stimulating conversationalist indeed! Little headway could I make in matters of our Most Holy Faith, however. He listened politely and then changed the subject to one of more interest to him. Thus did I find myself describing in broken tongue my native Spain and my boyhood, and he in turn told me of his maturing years and the battles he had fought and victories enjoyed, and so could we almost have been old campaigners discussing a common, if dissimilar, history. Of course he was a well-educated man, or at least educated in what passed for culture in his country, and if much of his knowledge was erroneous, still it was thoughtful and his reasoning often quite elegant. Clearly, the man he had become was but the hollow carapace of the man he used to be. What befell him, whether to the man or to the shell of the man, was sad indeed.

To still unrest among the Azteca, Moteczoma was enjoined by Cortés and Marina to speak to the people from a balcony of the palace in which we held him, at least at first, a most willing captive. After listening attentively to his words, and to our unhappy amazement, stones were thrown from below wounding several men, among them Moteczoma himself.

Carried to his chamber and laid down upon his bed, Moteczoma seemed too stunned by the treachery of his own people to desire a return to health. As soon as Marina bandaged his wounds he removed them, quite as if he wished to hasten the arrival of death.

It wasn't from the effects of the stoning, however, that the great ruler Moteczoma died. One morning soon after, he was found white and still upon his sleeping mat, a deep wound made as if by a dagger in his breast. Marina, smeared with the Azteca king's blood, had discovered the murder and announced his death.

"I am sorry, Marina," I said, knowing of her devotion to the unfortunate man.

She looked at me strangely, almost as if I had babbled to her in a strange tongue, and when I looked at her more closely I could see her eyes were sparkling with what I might have mistaken for joy had I not known of the tragedy.

"He has been sacrificed," she said in a curious voice. "That is quite proper, is it not, Aguilar?"

"A most unholy sacrifice, Marina," I replied in mild rebuke for her return to impious Indian thought.

"It was indeed," she answered gravely. But before she turned to leave the room I thought I saw her smile.

Moteczoma's body was clothed in royal finery and given to our Azteca servants to return to his own people for burial. We heard their lamentations and the doleful thunder of their drums as the funeral procession passed through the streets of Tenochtitlan and beyond, so we were told, to the burial grounds of Chapultepec.

It became apparent that we needed to make our escape before revolt brought the full might of the Azteca down upon us. Conferences were held and there was much debate whether it was wiser to hold fast or depart by day or under cover of darkness in which we might be able to reach the end of the causeway before our flight was discovered. In daylight, so it was argued, we might have surer knowledge of strategy as well as firmer footing on unfamiliar ground, but finally the decision was reached to depart and, since the Azteca rarely fought after sunset, to leave at night to allow our movements the element of surprise. This argument was strengthened by the astrologer-soldier among us, Botello by name, who urged us on this course, saying our evacuation by dark would prove most propitious on a certain night, although he knew he himself would perish. Our Captain's was the final decision to leave on the night of good omen.

Most of the men had cleverly turned their gold into ornaments or objects easily transportable: necklaces, chains and the like. There were those, however—and most of these were Narvaez' men lured from Villa Rica by tales of plundered gold—who had gazed with unconcealed cupidity upon the heaps and piles of shining treasure. Cortés, after assigning the Royal Fifth to the care of his soldiers who possessed the strongest horses, said to his men, "Take what you will of it. Better you should have it than these Azteca hounds." Raising his hand to arrest for a moment the pending onslaught, he added, "Be careful not to overload yourselves. He travels safest in a dark night who travels light."

These men of Narvaez, starved for riches, fell upon the golden mounds and thrust about their persons bars and wrought pieces, filling small chests and pouches and any other containers they possessed. Staggering under sudden wealth they looked the very picture of drunken bliss and the more seasoned of us regarded them with contempt and no little concern that they should be that night not so much soldiers as beasts of burden.

At the blackest hour of night we were all armed and ready for the march. Father Olmedo said Mass and we all fell to our knees to beseech the Almighty for safe passage through the perils lying before us. Kneeling beside me, Marina clasped her hands properly at her waist, but kept her eyes upon Cortés as if it were to him that she addressed her supplication. When she noticed me watching her, she smiled and leaned close to whisper, "I see no bars of gold stuck into your boots, nor troves of Azteca necklaces hung about your neck. Have you therefore no greed to repent of, Aguilar?"

It was a rare moment for jesting and I was astonished to see she showed no sign of fear for what lay so soon ahead of us. "Gold is not the treasure I seek," I replied somberly, to which she smiled again and shook her head. "You are not like other men, my friend. If it is not gold—and I know it is not women—what is it then you seek?"

I looked into her eyes and with grave import said, "Salvation, Marina. That is the gold you should seek as well."

At this she raised her chin so that her long dark eyes were hooded. I grew uncomfortable in her gaze but would not avert my eyes from hers. "The only salvation I seek," she at last replied, "is that which I can provide with my two hands."

After this exchange I was afraid she would not march by my side, as was her wont when opposed, but happily, as we threw open the gates of the palace, she was there next to me, wrapped in a mantle and with her hands quite empty. I saw she also did not seek to enrich herself with Azteca gold, and I commented upon this in a humorous vein. It was her turn to grow somber at a jest. "Every grain of that gold is cursed, Aguilar. I feel it."

I must admit that I shivered at the prophetic sound of her words and tried to make light of them. "However, now you have nothing to show for your stay in Tenochtitlan, unless that mantle you wear is your spoil of war."

She turned to me with a smile, but it was not the

merry smile I thought to see, but one almost cruel. "Oh no, Aguilar, you are wrong. I have indeed what I came to this city for, and that is worth far more to me than any treasure."

I smiled uncertainly at her words, but understood them not. It would not be for some time that I at last would know what heinous "treasure" it was she meant.

That night was to be known in years to come as the Night of Sorrows, the events of which I still shudder to recall. A light rain had been falling all that day from a cloudy sky and the streets we marched along were strewn with corpses from the last days of fighting. At every step one expected Azteca warriors, painted and befeathered, to come leaping from the dark doorways, but all life save ours seemed stilled in unsuspecting slumber. As we passed from the gates of that accursed city, there came to our ears the sound of a great rushing, as if winds had risen from the far corners of the sky and were fast approaching. Cortés cried out for the wooden bridge he had ordered made and it was thrown over the breach in the causeway just as the Azteca were upon us. In canoes upon the lake and on foot from the city there came warriors by the thousands, and the only sound above that fearful rushing was the eery drone of the conch shells from atop the pyramids and the thunder of the great drum in the temple of the war god.

On all sides were we attacked and the arrows flew into our midst like hail. Soldiers fell dead and wounded upon the road and over into the lake, and those that were but wounded were taken up into the enemy's canoes to be saved for later, more hideous death. When the first ranks came to the second breach in the causeway, desperate word was sent back to the last ranks to send the wooden bridge forward, and though many men were killed in this valiant attempt, the bridge had become too firmly embedded in the causeway to be removed. Alvarado, to the amazement and disbelief of all, vaulted the abyss, but the rest of us were stranded, Spaniard and Tlaxcaltecan alike, in a length of road in the middle of the waters of a vast lake, surrounded by thousands upon thousands of our foe.

Vulnerable as we were, it became every man for himself, and many of the weaker were trampled beneath those who sought to save their own skins. Burdened by armor and gold, the greediest of our number dove into the lake only to drown upon its cold bed. Others of us, including Marina and myself, divested ourselves of boots and mantles and as quietly as possible entered the water and sought to swim to shore. Unaccustomed as I was to such exercise, I was far from safety by the time I feared I could swim no more and I slowed, grasping at the edge of the causeway, panting. Noting that I was no longer near her in the greying morning light, Marina turned about and swam back to me. Over my fierce objections she took hold of me and pulled me along behind her like a log of wood. Since it would have made matters worse to struggle with her and so call attention to ourselves in the melee, I submitted to the dubious relief of being saved from drowning by a woman.

At last I lay gasping on shore with Marina half-reclined beside me. Suddenly she leaped to her feet and ran to the water's edge and pulled a sword from the scabbard of a fallen comrade. I heard a rustling and turned my head in time to see an Azteca in his white garment like a spectre in the dusky light running towards us, his obsidian-edged bludgeon raised. I pulled myself to my knees and, unarmed as I was, prepared to meet my death. As I knelt there awaiting my fate, Marina dashed forth and engaged the Azteca in battle, swinging the sword with a strong and steady arm. The Azteca, taken aback by this most unconventional opponent, faltered at the fatal moment and Marina swung the blade across his throat. Dripping with the blood of her enemy, and breathless, she turned to me with eyes shining in triumph. "There is some pleasure in killing, is there not?" and picked up the dead man's weapon and handed it to me. "It is your turn, Aguilar," she said, and then laughed.

We battled together, side by side, farther and farther from the shore of the lake, until at last, as the sun was fully risen, we rested with some other of our men in the shadows of the jungle. For four days we fought, Marina no less fiercely than the rest. Struggling to put land between us and Tenochtitlan, we pushed ahead in ever-dwindling numbers until we came to a pyramid with its fortress-like temple at the summit, and there did we finally lay down our weapons and sleep. We later learned that over eight hundred of our number had been killed, and some unknown number of women, as well as over a thousand Tlaxcalteca. It was a defeat of staggering proportions.

Marina, when the light of battle had faded from her eyes, was all on the lookout for Cortés, and until she discerned his figure through the bloodied and ragged crowd, she knew no rest. Running to him, pushing aside those in her way, she fell upon his neck in her joy, weeping as would any other woman. I must in all truth admit he seemed pleased by her survival, though he soon put her from him and began shouting orders. Returning to me, Marina was almost beside herself with relief and delight. "Is it not wonderful, Aguilar! My Captain has only three wounds, and they are all slight! How glad I am!"

Since she had sustained a wound to the side and a painful blow to the shoulder, and I had suffered deep cuts on my arm and across my back, this news did not fill me with equal joy. Never had she shown the slightest concern for my wounds, nor had she indeed for her own, and I was both envious and disgusted that she should show such care for Cortés who was, after all, in great part to blame for the whole debacle. I was relieved the Captain of our weakened forces still lived, but it was with two minds that I welcomed his return. I prayed God to forgive me for that, as I pleaded his merciful forgiveness for all else. I had fallen into a cursed abyss, indeed, to wish death to someone, and he a fellow Christian who had never done me an injury.

Beyond the hill where we were encamped we could see the hills of Tlaxcaltecan country and it was with an uneasy delight that we saw them, unsure as we were of our welcome. Scouts were sent ahead to espy the lay of that unsteady land and to sniff the air for the scent of treachery. Fortunate we were to find welcome, and we marched to the capital where we were received with both cries of joy and lamentations for the dead. The chief cacique of that impregnable city wept aloud to learn that his daughter, given to one of our men, had been killed on the tragic night of escape, but soon he dried his eyes and bid us stay and heal our wounds, and called slaves to lead us to shelter and wait upon our needs.

It was insanity to rouse our allies and march again upon that Azteca Sodom, but that was what Cortés was resolute to do. Vainly did I, in company with several of his staunchest soldiers and advisors, seek to remonstrate with him. Vainly did we beseech him to turn his back upon this black adventure and sail for home. He would entertain no such thought.

"I can and I will conquer the Azteca," he said boldly, "but all of you unwilling to accompany me may continue without harassment to Villa Rica and from there embark to Spain and safety."

Perhaps it was the subtle emphasis laid upon that last word, so offensive to manly valor, that turned the tide. For me, I cared nothing if Cortés thought me cowardly, for to return to that abyss of sin and horror would involve more than physical peril. I implored Marina, thickened with child, to leave for the coast with me, but she refused.

"I will go wherever my Captain goes," she said in a voice stony with resolve, "and do whatever he bids me do."

All of my silent and spoken prayers went unanswered. She would go with Cortés even to Hell itself, I had no doubt. I readied my few possessions for my lonely walk to Villa Rica and went to bid her farewell.

"You are not *truly* going, Aguilar?" she asked, and most sincerely did she seem disturbed. "I thought you would stay with me! I have few friends but you, and none so faithful."

"I cannot, Marina. Even if you think me a coward, I must not. You know too well my reasons so I will not tire you with their repetition, but I know in my heart that if I were to march again with Cortés I would lose my soul. It would be to march into the wilderness where, in my own weakness, I would fall into temptation. I beg you, Marina, come with me! For one last time I ask you. I will care for you and keep you and your infant from all harm." I hesitated, then added with a full measure of embarrassment, "You know you would be as safe with me as the child you will soon hold in your arms."

She did not move, but there came into her eyes a look that even now defies description. It was neither seductive nor was it pleading, but it pulled upon me as if she had sunk talons of gossamer into my heart. She moved toward me so I could catch the fragrance of her body and the musk of her hair, and she fixed those eyes upon me and I could not turn away.

"I would have you with me, Aguilar. I would have you by my side forever. Do you not know that?" Then she said in a voice soft and yearning, "Do you not know that, my love?"

I was struck mute with surprise. Never had I, but for one moment only, ever thought I meant anything to her, and she was confessing she did love me, after all. As if they had been but vapor, at that unexpected word "love," all my plans and protests disappeared. As God is my witness, it was as if she had with her two delicate hands pushed upon the walls of my being and, like the walls of Jericho, caused them to fall in ruins around me. I could see in her eyes she knew this. It was pointless to attempt to hide my inability to deny her anything, now that I knew, or thought I knew, with desire and despair, that she loved me. All my pent emotion rose from the depths to which it had been with prudent reason submerged, sweeping over me like sudden fever.

"Dearest Aguilar," she whispered, laying a hand on my arm, "indeed I do love you, and my Captain as well. Can a mere woman command where her heart travels? No," she smiled tenderly and I longed to take her right there into my arms. "I must go where my heart leads me, and if it leads to you as well as to my Captain, then to both of you will I go."

Still I stood mute, and her smile warmed. She took my arm into her own as confidingly as a child. "Let us walk a little way, love, for I grow weary of this talk of battle and gold."

Like a beast she had tamed, I walked at her side along the broad streets of that Tlaxcaltecan stronghold and out its gates into the sparse forest beyond. The day was white with heat and the hot air simmered with mirage so that upon all sides in the near distance lay pools of sparkling water. The intermittent shade of the wood was darkly cool in contrast to the light, and as our steps led us into that darkness I prayed for a like cooling of my blood.

Soon we were beyond sight of the city and Marina stopped in a pool of shade. "I am so pleased that you will stay with us here, Aguilar," she said.

"If you love me," I said weakly in reply and in a last desperate effort, "you could come with me to Spain. Cortés does not really love you . . . he loves no one, Marina, but himself."

For a moment she stiffened and the pupils of her eyes swelled with anger. Then, as if it were but an ebbing tide, she grew soft once more and her face adoring, even as she had been on the first day I saw her, gazing upon the man she thought a god. "Aguilar, my love," she whispered, "surely you will stay," and she reached up her hands and pulled the covering from her breasts while I stood frozen with shock and hunger. Heavy and tipped with upthrust, swollen nipples, she held them uplifted with her fingers. Then she slowly, caressingly, moved her hands downward to unwind the skirt at her waist, and she was naked. Her belly round with child, she was as fertile and opulent as a pagan idol. With a groan I reached for her and, smiling, she moved willingly into my arms.

So the chastity that I had preserved for twenty-eight years I gave not to God, but to Marina. I drank the milk of her breasts and thrust myself to the very womb where Cortés' bastard lay, and even in that moment of ecstatic union, I wished for the earth to crack wide and swallow me into death and eternal darkness. After the act was over, I rose to my feet and with shaking hands clothed myself. Casually, Marina did likewise. Unwilling to look at her until I had mastered myself, I kept my eyes on the ground and thus it was I saw an object shining at my feet. Bending without thought to pick it up, I found it was a curved obsidian dagger carved with barbarous designs.

"That is mine," Marina said, reaching to take it from my hand. "My sister gave it to me," she added, though I had asked nothing. She slipped it into her clothing and, speaking lightly of this and that, spoke of that strange object no more. In the babble of my own inner confusion there was a small clear wonder. Why did she keep upon her person no Indian thing but that small dagger, and why had she seemed so eager to keep it hidden? Through my numb anguish, still I wondered.

Bemused by her, captivated by romance and suffering, I too marched forth on the second, and successful, Conquest of the Aztec Empire. Soon I found out that the reason Marina had been so badly in need of me was that Cortés suspected she had been the foul murderess of Moteczoma and was for the first time gravely angry with her. She denied committing such an act, placing the sin upon her sister's head, but never to my knowledge did she ever show her black dagger to Cortés. Embroiled in his deeper concerns, he let the matter die its death and only I was left to wonder.

"Did you, Marina?" I asked her once, shortly after she had given birth to her son, christened Don Martin. "Tell me you did not slay Moteczoma and I will believe you."

She gazed at me with the weary, radiant face of new motherhood. "Oh, my friend, let the dead lie buried! What difference could it be if I, or someone other—my sister, perhaps—put an end to that traitor? Look upon my comely son and ask me not again," and though she spoke in dulcet tones, they masked that iron blade I did not wish unsheathed.

"As you wish, Marina," I said, and was rewarded with her glorious smile.

32

ATAHUALPA

My poor mother gave birth to a slave and from her poverty did she, but a slave herself, give what she could: her love and a noble name. Atahualpa she named me, a name fit not for a slave but for that slave's master. Very much was I like my mother and if I were as well like my father I had no way of knowing, for I had been planted in my mother's womb by a stranger. This made him a curiosity to me, but no more. Huddled like featherless birds in our rude nest, my mother gave to me all she could, from her warm arms and breasts to her songs and comic stories that grew no less amusing with frequent telling. She was sky and earth to me, my mother. She bore me into a life of slavery and gave me the strength to endure it. Even as she was driven to her tasks like a beast, she took me with her. When I grew sturdy enough to work beside her I did my best to please her, scrubbing stone floors or gathering maize, anything a slave was born to do. Weary work it was indeed, but never so dreary that my mother could not lighten the burden with a glance or a hand placed briefly upon my shoulder.

Such a poor man's paradise could not last. With grief did she tell me one day that our master had sold me to a trader and I would be given up to his command when Tonatiuh arose in the morning. Ah, what a night of sleepless sorrow that was as we wept and prayed! Though I was a large youth of eight years, yet I passed that night in my mother's arms, clasped against her breasts like a newborn child. I sobbed unmanfully and spoke foolishly of hiding in the jungle nearby or running far away with her to a place where we never would be parted, and my mother loved me enough to let me babble on while she kept still. At last, exhausted, I was silent, too.

"You are my warrior, Atahualpa," she whispered, "and though I may never set eyes upon you again, I know that you will grow into a good man, a man of bravery, strong of heart. I do not need to see you to know this will be. So do not leave me in sorrow, my son, for I will not grieve for you," she said in a voice hardened by the tears she would not shed. "I will think of you with a proud heart, and I will thank the Gods every day that you once were mine." Those last words were faltering, and I knew she was trying to smooth our parting with courage and sweet memory. I drew myself from her arms and looked at her quivering mouth and the way she clenched her jaw against its betrayal.

"I swear by the Gods that I shall become a man even as you are a woman, my mother. I will remember you in every hour. I will pray the Gods protect you from all harm."

That night I became a man. When Tonatiuh rose from the underworld I set forth with my few possessions—a second set of clothes, a stone that my mother found when I was very young and we had gone wandering one rare, free hour—and entered my new life. I turned once to look behind me as we marched, loosely collared to the slave pole, and saw my mother, small and slender, standing with the straight back and proud face of a mother watching her warrior-son set off for the Flowery Wars. Her features have grown indistinct with time, but the look of her is not what brings her memory back to me. No, it is the scent of a flower or the wind at a certain season, the sound of a woman singing or her sweet laughter, a glance into a rude shelter wherein sit a mother and a child before a small fire. The memory puts arms around my body and brings comfort to my heart.

I set forth to become the man she believed me to be and though I was never the son she deserved, still I preserved within me some small goodness and a trace of courage. They were never enough, as well the Gods do know, but enough to let me feel that had my mother suddenly come upon me she would not have been ashamed. This, more than all else, made me strong enough to bear the life the Gods have given me. I have never complained, for my life has also given me much joy.

In those long solitary days of my captivity in the menagerie, pain did not become my only companion, nor did it truly become a scourge, but it was a reminder of my humble state from which I could not rise to protect Xochitzlin, my love. Many were the hours I spent remembering the day I first saw her in the camp of Icpitl, as I stood upon watery legs and with a mouth suddenly dust. Her beauty was not of this earth. Her eyes, her hair, her body, all were perfection. Her head was high with pride, but fear clouded those sorcerous eyes and I longed to place my arms around her and give her safe shelter.

I had grown by this time into a man both taller and sturdier than many of my kind, and thus I had become the guardian of my master's doleful herd, my task to watch upon them by night and capture those who sought escape. I found reasons at first to stay near my master's shelter and so I knew with pain in my heart that he used her cruelly. On the night she escaped I had moved to greater distance to avoid hearing her stifled cries. She crept from Icpitl's hut without a witness, and it was only when I saw a dark form hurrying past the great fire at the center of our encampment that I gave chase, unaware who it was I pursued. She was young, but strong and filled with purpose. Nearly did I lose her in the darkness. After she fell and I pulled her to her feet I saw who I had hunted down; her beauty was even more unearthly in the moon's light. She stared upon me with the eyes of a wild creature. I was rough in speech for she touched my heart, and when she offered her body for her freedom it was not temptation I felt but shame that I should have the power to force a woman to yield where her heart was not. Further shame did I feel in taking her back, pale and trembling, to her master, and with every step I searched among my thoughts for one with which to save her punishment. It was true what I had told her, that the life of an escaped slave was nothing to flee toward, and yet I was filled with self-loathing to return her to camp.

Glad was I indeed that Icpitl believed I had borne her away to satisfy my lust, but that I was no longer man enough for the act. Xochitlzin was led away and I kept from her lest I find myself forever bound to her in a feeling no slave had the right to lay claim to. It was better so, for Icpitl was a most suspicious man. A few days later I saw her harnessed to the slave pole and led away to a fate I could only hope would be kind. Never did I think to see her again.

My Gods, hear my words of gratitude at your mercy! For I did see that phantom of my dreams again, and this no longer a slave, but the great priestess she was before becoming the Second Wife of the Ueytlatoani, Moteczoma! I could not believe the words I heard when I gained courage to ask fellow slaves about her. Though I was comforted that her tonalli seemed less burdensome than I had feared, still it appeared to lie heavily upon those small, unyielding shoulders. At last we met, and she spoke to me, my Gods, and in that honeyed voice, and her words were liquid even as they were sweet, flowing into me like octli and turning my bones and flesh to warm and quaking sand. I spoke to her in turn and then, wonder of all wonders, we soon spoke of our affection, and then, marvel of marvels, did we speak of love. Love from those lips lay like a mantle of feathers around me.

My heart beat as it never had before and like a great drum within my chest.

What was it after that for me to suffer? To the Gods above and below, I swear it was nothing. To have but seen her again, for just that moment alone would I have been flayed. To hear her voice again, and speaking those words, what did I give that I would not have gladly doubled! To know she would be safe after we were discovered was all my fear and desire. Though the priests unmanned me in their daggers and disfigured me, yet through the pain of that was my heart still comforted with our love. I overheard slaves working in the menagerie speak of palace affairs, and though I was overjoyed to know that she was safe, also was I anguished with envy that Moteczoma should see her, hold her, caress that body I had but touched in awed devotion. I was caught between two river banks and the sweet grass and sharp rocks on either side both soothed and wounded me.

Time passed on dragging feet. Days and nights were filled with the cries and grunts of captive beasts and the rustle of serpents in the great pottery jars wherein they bred their young. Corn tlaxcallis were given us, and sometimes a fragment of raw meat, and the slaves who tended the menagerie were not unkind. They pitied the humans among us, for they saw we were not without human feeling, and they did not seem to look upon us with either disdain or ridicule. For that I was most grateful. Though I did not know how ghastly a mask the priests had left me for a face, still I was certain I had earned the right to abide in the menagerie as a monster.

Indeed, I was not aware how hideous I looked until that day when came a group of men, stopping before my cage and uttering words in a strange tongue. I had heard of Tenochtitlan's lordly visitors, and so, curiosity overleaping my usual lethargy, I looked up to see who stood outside the wooden bars.

Xochitlzin! As I crouched, dumb with surprise, she

spoke to the bearded strangers in their tongue and then turned laughing to look upon me, wrinkling her nose in disgust while the others wore expressions of revulsion and contempt. Thus it was I could see at one and the same moment my beautiful love and my own grotesqueness. A faint shadow crossed her face and even now I cannot explain more than that I knew it was a shadow alien to the woman I loved. It was dark with cunning, as sideways she looked at the stranger who walked with a limp, and in that glance I knew, likeness to the contrary, that it was not Xochitlzin who stood there but that shadow self I had heard about in whispers. Xochitlzin could not have changed, however subtle my proof, into a woman in whom cunning and debasement had taken root. Nearly did it seem I was lost in nightmare, for she was my love and she was not. Swiftly, then, they were gone.

I had unending hours to brood upon that meeting with one who looked so like the woman I loved and yet again so unlike her as to chill my heart. Never would Xochitlzin have become a woman whose chaste good mouth was tight with bitterness and twisted with scorn. No, in all the ways Xochitlzin was radiant with goodness, this shadow self was dark and dire, as cold as the side of a stone upon which the sun shines not. As dearly as I may have desired to see my love yet again, still I was glad it was this shadow self who had seen how monstrous I had become.

Day followed night; in the ill-lit darkness of the menagerie one was much like the other, except that food was brought to the cages only in daylight hours. Many times I lived the years of my life again, remembering small things that once were lovely or strange or dear to me. I spoke words to the Gods and in their silence I was not uncomforted, for they had ever thus been silent and silently all-knowing. In the world there was much to please one, and so it was with a grateful heart that I uttered the words of the old prayers and the songs of the earth's blessing that my mother had taught me long before. Often did I pretend to be not in a cage, but in the pleasant shelter of my childhood. I was near no fellow being who had the wit to speak, so I sometimes lay upon the wooden floor and listened to the grunts and cries of the beasts, pretending they told tales of magic and adventure one to the other. This became easier to imagine as time went on and their rough sounds seemed less strange. We became in a way companions, for they were no less lonely than I, I was sure, and no less needful.

So it was I grew resigned to my fate and to my death, and then one day there came to my ears the sound of Azteca voices. As they drew near I moved to the back of the cage, turning my face to the wall. They came to my door and, to my surprise, opened it. Fear gripped me that yet another punishment was at hand, but there was only a slight scuffling sound and then the door of the cage closed shut and there was silence. Attuned by now to every noise and breath around me, I knew I was no longer alone. I sensed, if I did not hear, a soft breathing, and my nostrils quivered at the scent of clean flesh. Carefully, not knowing what it was I had to brave meeting, I turned. It was only at a sudden startled gasp that I dared raise my eyes to see before me, at last, her face, her beautiful, gentle face, white with horror.

"Xochitlzin!" I pleaded, hiding my face in my hands, "please do not be afraid of me!"

After a long moment she breathed "Atahualpa?" and without another word did she take my hands in both of hers and pull them from my face. In shame did I lower my eyes. Once my body had been that of a man and even handsome, so that women had looked upon it with approval, but it was the body of a man no longer. I knew her eyes moved from my face downward, and she saw how certainly the priests ensured I would never know her, or any other woman, as a man. Without another word she slipped her arms around me and gradually, trembling, I ceased resisting the revulsion I knew she must surely feel at my touch, and I embraced her in return. In silence stood we thus for many moments.

"Xochitlzin," finally I whispered, flushed with shame, "you need not try to hide from me your . . . your disgust at what I am now. Indeed it would be strange and . . . most unwomanly if you did not feel so."

She drew away from me, but not outside my arms' encirclement, and almost smiled. "My dear love," she said in a voice both strong and yet unsteady with feeling, "the only disgust I have is for those who lied to me that you were let go safe and free." She leaned her head against my shoulder then and whispered, "Your body may bear the scars of their deceit, but you are still Atahualpa." She paused for a moment, then looked up at me with a slight blush upon her cheeks. "Well do I have reason to believe you love me, and well do I know I love you. With this union we do not need . . . the union of flesh is not . . ."

"Xochitlzin," I hastened to say, "make no promises and no pledges to one who does not need them."

"We have found each other again, Atahualpa," she replied, her eyes gravely upon mine. "Let us make all we may of this time the Gods, if they exist or care, allow to us."

How could I not have obeyed my heart's desire? Currents of tenderness and passion were not dammed as I would have thought, but flowed one to the other and back again, and even as she later whispered, mere flesh was not enough to hinder such a flood! Later, after we had filled the emptiness of our hearts to overflowing, she told me that it was believed she had slain the Ueytlatoani Moteczoma with the sacred dagger of her calling and that captivity in the menagerie, rather than death, was to be her punishment. I awaited in silence the truth of what she had said.

"Lord Moteczoma is dead," she began shortly, and I shrugged with indifference at the news. "I was in his chamber when he died, sent in secrecy and cunning by Lord Cuauhtémoc." She was whispering, not as if she sought to keep her words from any listening ear, but as if shame lay too heavily for speech. "I refused to satisfy my Lord that I would commit murder, as he charged me to do if Moteczoma would not come forth with me from his captivity, but also I did not say I would not.

"My sister, Malinalli, found me beside my Lord. She believed I had come to slay him, even as she wished to do. I saw how she hungered for his blood, like a beast, Atahualpa! And I knew that I stood in a place of great danger."

"At your sister's hands?" I asked in horror.

Xochitlzin gazed back into that grievous memory and then raised her eyes to me. In them was the look of someone who has narrowly escaped death by her own hand. "No, it was that suddenly I felt the same beast crouched within *me* and I knew that if I raised my hand against my husband the beast would be fed. My sister has fed the beast within until that is all she is. And her mind is dark with such a hunger."

She was quiet for a moment, then continued on with a small sigh. "I fled in disgust but my sister was swifter than I, and when next I saw light, she was gone and Moteczoma lay dead, killed with my sacred dagger. Hearing cries of lamentation and shouts for vengeance, I ran unhindered from the palace. Shortly did my Lord Cuauhtémoc come to my chamber, and though he had wished this course upon me, still did he say other Lords were demanding my death, principal among them Lord Cuitláhuac, and that it was the will of the new Ueytlatoani that I die.

" 'But I do not forget that I did ask this of you,' he said to me, 'and thus I have persuaded the Ueytlatoani Cuitláhuac to punish you in another way.' And thus, Atahualpa," she finished, smiling upon me, "here I am, punished by nothing but joy," and with that Xochitlzin kissed my ruined face.

I did not ask her why she bore the burden of her sister's evil, guessing that she would say it was her tonalli to do so. Tightening my arms around her, I replied, "Though it is terrible for me to feel, and worse of me to say, no matter what has brought you here, I am most heartily grateful."

I had grown used to captivity and needed nothing but Xochitl in my small caged world, but she was soon as restless as is a creature when newly captive. Pacing the narrow confines of our prison did not tire her—indeed it increased her agitation. Soon did she begin to plot our escape.

"Slaves would surely see us, Xochitlzin! Surely they would not, upon sight of me, think us but visitors here."

She shook her head, pacing like a jaguar in angry grace. I was saddened to see her disquiet, dismayed to be so helpless. At last one morning when we awoke she set to work, scratching at the base of one of the thick wooden bars with a sharp fragment of bone. At the end of the day her patient labor had earned but little progress. Nonetheless, she labored on day by day, and to be of company and in sympathy with her brave, if futile, scheme, I worked upon the post next to hers and by the end of the day we had at least the pleasure of physical weariness which brought sleep more swiftly over our eyes.

One morning we awoke and Xochitzlin sat up, rigid with listening.

"What is it, my love?"

"I do not know," she began, "something . . ." and then she paused and I too heard a most peculiar rumbling in the far distance as if a storm were approaching us. I offered this as explanation, but she shook her head. "It is war."

Truly this did seem to be so. The rumbling grew and the earth itself did shudder. The air, even in the menagerie, was heavy with smoke. Sounds of battle droned on overhead and all about us, there in the Heart of the

One World, while we stayed captive below as if in the center of the wild and random winds of Ehecatl. Ill indeed did we sleep that night, if we slept at all. Screams and the sound of stone dragging upon stone haunted the darkness. Tonatiuh rose, unseen by us as always, and the sounds did not lessen but grew. In this uncertainty did we pass the hours, laboring at our escape with the blind persistence of insects.

How many days we spent in this way I could not say. Day swam into night and night into day, our hours like echoes of each other. It was as if we had been fated to live each previous moment over and over, the only sign that this was not true being the deepening furrows in the wooden bars. At this Xochitlzin was pleased—her pleasure mixed with impatience—but I was strangely indifferent, for I knew that once free I would be but an object of disgust and a burden to her: A beautiful woman in the company of a monstrosity. Unwilling to let her go, still did I love her far too well to shackle myself to her with her compassion. Thus I noted our progress with secret dismay.

One morning we arose and began our task, one ear as always listening for the slaves bringing food. As the hours went by they did not come. More disquieted than hungry, we pondered together the meaning of this omission. At last even the oldest and most sluggish of the men joined in outcry at this neglect and the menagerie walls reverberated with the thunder of the beasts' protest.

Suddenly Xochitlzin sat back upon her heels, head high and eyes peering into a distance greater than the far wall of our prison, and she whispered, "The enemy has taken Tenochtitlan."

We had been too busy with our work and our thoughts to note that beyond the loud laments of the beasts, all was silence. As the animals quietened one by one into listless despair, we waited with ears keen for any sound beyond the menagerie walls. There was nothing but silence. Slaves did not appear the next day, nor the next, and the gourd of water we had left contained but a few mouthfuls more for the both of us.

The beasts began to die. First with doleful cries and then with a low moan as each grew too feeble for further effort, one by one they met their fate, and it was most grievous to overhear. Worse yet were the piteous sounds of those who were human, giants and dwarves and those disfigured even as was I. A word would come to us, a pleading more terrible in that we were helpless to give help or comfort and could but sit listening, hour by hour, to the prayers and cries and groans of the desperate and the dying. Once I said to my love, "Xochitlzin, what will we do when we are free? There is nothing I can do, and no way to live. It would be better, far better, for me to die now while there is yet water and . . ."

She took me fiercely by the shoulders and her eyes were like black fire. "Silence, Atahualpa! If you love me you will never speak like this again. You must promise me that. Promise me *now.*" And she shook me with an ardor that would have been humorous, but the moment was too somber for that, and too dear.

One night I awoke to find her at work on the wooden bar. I asked her to return to my arms but she did not turn nor did she speak or yield. Next morning I found her curled against the bars, asleep, and when I carried her to our worn blanket I found her body hot with fever. I prayed for her and uttered all the charms of memory, but in the night she had been possessed by the demons that bring illness, and as they wasted her frail body mine grew numb in a cave of despair. The Gods were deaf to my pleading and demons remained in her.

Into a well of grieving did I fall. Resting my face lightly upon her breasts, I gave myself up to death. Time passed and then, in the direction of the cage door, there was a small sound. Near a whisper of sound did it seem, but I heeded it not. Illness of flesh and spirit had seized us both in merciless arms, bearing us downward into evil dreaming. Greater despair was mine when Xochitlzin was no better in the morning. Dull and numbed as I was, yet did my body still ache with inaction and so I rose to pace a few steps forward and back and then, overcome, I leaned against the door of our cage.

The door moved outward, the chain that had bound it dangling loose. Somehow in the night this act of mercy had been done—by God, demon or fellow man I did not know or care. In awkward haste I knelt at Xochitl's side and bid her awake. "We are free, my love," I whispered. She moaned and her eyes opened briefly, then shut again. I lifted her body in my arms and stumbled on my ill-mended legs out of the cage, out of the menagerie, into the light. Her body was as slight as a hand's grasp of flowers, but still did I stumble and stagger with its weight, resting often upon the way. Few people indeed were there in the streets, and those were thin and sickly.

"Brother," I said, approaching one who sat with eyes closed upon a stone. He looked up, but as I had carefully placed myself between him and the sun he could not see me clearly enough to be frightened. "My wife and I have been ill for many weeks. Can you tell me what has befallen our city?"

"Can it be you do not know what all else do?" the man replied in a voice with dull despair. "We are under siege. There is nothing left to eat and nothing to drink but the salt water of the lake. That illness the enemy does call the pox rages even in the palace of the Ueytlatoani, Cuitláhuac."

For a moment I was stone. Was there, indeed, nowhere we could go in our new freedom? Were we but captives still? Xochitl stirred in my arms and whispered words too low for me to hear. I walked on, onto the very causeway leading to the sacred hill of Chapultepec. As Tonatiuh sank into the darkness of Mictlan, I entered the woods of the Ueytlatoani and sought shelter beneath the low branches of a tree.

Leaving Xochitl sleeping there, I went in search of the famed spring whose water rises pure from the earth. Although it was sluggish and muddy, it filled my cupped hand with water sweet enough to drink. Returning to Xochitl, I carried her there and gave her water in my palm. Fresh strength did she gain from this and so she could open her eyes.

"Never did I think to see you again," she whispered through dry lips.

"And now I do believe you will get well." I smiled upon her and caressed her cheek. "The Gods have heard my prayers."

"Not the Gods," she said quietly. "Only *you* have saved me."

We slept and rested and ate what we could find to eat—roots and bitter leaves—until the gates of Tenochtitlan were breached and the few of us who had survived starvation and disease became slaves and captives once more. Cortés ruled over us and with his priests and soldiers forced our feet along the roads of obedience to the ways of our conquerors and the rules of their remote and nameless God. Through cunning and labor I remained with Xochitl, even after she had been branded on the forehead with the hot iron of slavery, even after she was allowed to give up her duties in the world to take up those in the women's house of the foreign God. I saw her but rarely, in her black robes so strange to Mexica eyes, and times there were, more rare, when we could speak. But she was safe, and as long as she was so my heart was safe, as well.

The years passed, and the days of horror in which our people, Azteca and the rest, were tortured and slain and forced into the perilous depths of caves wherein the earth was veined with gold, and we died by the thousands and thousands until all left in the land were but slaves to the will of Spain. The foreign priests urged our women to breed like captive swine, telling them that if they did not give to each year a new birth the nameless God of Spain would speed their descent into a pit of fire, where they would burn forever. Born into poverty, into slavery, into a grievous time where their lives counted for little and the Gods remembered them not, nothing remained for these children but flower tales of the past which grew fainter and fainter year by year until the music of the teponaztli and the flute and the conch shell were but echoes from another world. Unrest was swiftly and brutally quelled. Voices of protest were strangled. Under a shroud of blood the people were still. Upon the broken stones of Tenochtitlan and the bodies of the Azteca Cortés did build his city, a great temple arising on the very place where the great teocalli of Tezcatlipoca had stood. A new house of women was built over the place where once was the stone of Tixoc, and this was the house where Xochitlzin, after much urging, went to live in safety, if not in comfort. Many years have fled from our lives and with time change has come, but never freedom. Yet knowing Xochitlzin was well and that she loved me has been, for me, enough. I have never asked the Gods greater blessing than this.

33

MALINALLI

How brave my Captain was! How gallant! Mother, I could forgive even you—and I do so because I am a Christian—for in casting me off into slavery you made this life possible. More so than any of Aguilar's tales has my life been romance. And the tale was not fully told at the end of our victorious conquest, for greater adventure and higher honor were yet to come. Ah, but honors must wait upon the heels of glorious action, Mother. The tale must first be told.

Many days did we spend readying our men and our allies for the siege of Tenochtitlan. My son, Don Martín, was born with a most pleasing resemblance to his father. At my Captain's behest I suckled Martín, though I was much excited in the midst of war and so my milk slowed and then ceased to flow. A peasant woman was found with milk in plenty, and thus was I freed to listen to the talk of the men and learn who it was that plotted against us. By day and night I listened well and any treachery or unrest was swiftly quelled and protest silenced. Indeed was I the right arm of my master and heedful as ever to see he was well and truly served by all in his command.

So began the siege. Watching upon a rise near the causeway, I saw our new ships set sail upon the waters of the lake darkened in the dying light of the Year of Our Lord, 1521. At first the battles were fiercely waged and our men suffered many wounds and a few died, although many fewer did we lose than did our enemy. Most cunning was Cortés and wise as a God, indeed. Skillful and shrewd of judgement, he sent his men and our loyal Mexica allies surging upon the weakest places in that fortress and so successful was he in this that soon the Azteca were living like beasts in their captive city, unable to leave their gates in search of food, and soon without sweet water. The pox then swept into their midst and thousands must have died, we thought, judging by the smell and the great number of black shadows circling silent overhead. Even on the hill where I stood a spectator I could smell the corpses rotting in those once-proud streets. We waited then with patience upon the hills and causeways until the city lay white and still as a well-gnawed bone and the walls were easily breached in that month once known as the time when flowers bloom and die.

I will not speak of the foulness we encountered upon riding through the gates; wasted bodies like skeletons lay strewn everywhere, over 200,000 of them, putrid and black with flies. We were all forced to keep fragrant cloths over our noses to lessen the stench. Once more we made camp in Axayácatl's palace, but not through the arrogant patronage of the dead Moteczoma or his overproud caciques either. Though great treasure we had expected to find, it was with both surprise and disappointment that Cortés discovered but small recompense for his army's dangerous adventure. Of course this meant little to me, since I had gained what I had set forth to find, but the Spaniards were angered by what they saw as Azteca duplicity and sent survivors in Anáhuac to labor in the mines and rivers to fill the coffers of Spain. Every stone was leveled or buried, and Cortés ordered a fine Spanish city built upon the ruins. Indeed, in four short years it engulfed Tenochtitlan entirely, and it was called Mexico City, the largest in New Spain. A grand cathedral of great size rose from the very place where the teocalli of Huitzilopochtli and Tezcatlipoca once stood, the broken bodies of the idols its foundation. A nunnery for women was built where the stone of Tixoc lay, and the giant idol of Coatlicue was buried nearby.

Cuauhtémoc, his haughty bearing unmarked by defeat, was discovered in his hiding place by Pedro de Jaramillo and brought back in chains to the city, where he surrendered. To honor Jaramillo, as well as to secure his valuable loyalty, my Captain gave me to him in marriage. Though I fought him in this, Cortés insisted, saying it was only fitting for the mother of his son to be married to so fine a man. "I would marry you myself, Marina," he told me in all sincerity, "but you know I am already married." I submitted to Jaramillo in my Captain's name and with no further protest, proud to do whatever Cortés required of me.

At long last my Captain was made Governor of New Spain by his King and many of his restless demons were thus laid to rest within him, but not all, for it came ever more forcibly to his mind that to secure his empire he needed to conquer the lands to the south, the first being that called Honduras. My son, by then a sturdy boy of four years, was left to stay with a woman newly come from Spain as I accompanied my Captain upon his quest. This adventure was even more exciting than the last. Aguilar was with us as always, but changed somehow, and grave with some strange sorrow about which he would not speak.

"Tell me why you no longer smile, Aguilar," I asked him once after a jest in which all but he had joined in laughter.

"You would not understand, Marina," he said quietly, and though from time to time his sorrow troubled me, I knew not what to do to heal him and so did nothing.

In the green shade I once chanced upon the new Ueytlatoani, Cuauhtémoc, brought with us to ensure his fellows' loyalty, sitting with his fellow caciques and plotting base treachery. As always, I hastened to my Captain and bore witness against the traitors in our midst. Cortés was pleased with me and at that moment ordered that they all be hanged from the very trees under which they had laid their evil plans. Cuauhtémoc, arrogant to the last, handed Cortés his obsidian dagger, saying, "I have done my duty in defence of my city. Take this dagger and kill me." Instead, Cortés ordered Alvarado to torture this last of the Azteca Ueytlatoanis, and with his thirst for such entertainment, Alvarado took his time before his thirst was slaked and Cuauhtémoc, too, was led to a tree and hanged. I watched their bodies dangle from the trees until it grew too dark to see.

All of the house of Moteczoma were now no more. None had died in a Flowery War which in their minds would have given them the right to spend eternity in the warriors' underworld. I smiled to myself as I thought of this. Never would my father have to brush against the shoulders of his enemy. They were forever to wander the empty, bleak shade of Mictlan like the most common of men. What a triumph it was for me, and how I hugged myself to myself in my joy. My Captain and I were victors over all.

After two years passed we returned to Mexico City. My husband, Jaramillo, died upon the way and we had buried him with proper blessings and so I was free again to sleep with Cortés. Glad was I to see the face of my son and I held him up to his father so he could behold how like himself the child was. He took him for a moment in his arms and dandled him upon his knee, then returned him to the servant who tended him.

In the midst of our triumph there were murmurings of unrest and plots of envious treachery. Our days and nights were not spent resting in the luxury due us, but in discovering who was against us and who we could still trust. Cortés believed my every word, for I was always zealous not to let one suspect word or glance go undetected. At times my knowledge of sorcery came well to hand and though my Captain would not have approved, still he was pleased to be rid of his enemies so easily.

Then there came a day my Captain said to me, "Marina, I am off for Spain to seek the blessing and the rewards my Sovereign has decided to bestow upon me."

I could at first but stare at him, and he took my hand in his and pressed it. "I will return soon, I promise you, and then will you be given your just reward as well, my faithful Marina."

I fell weeping to the floor. I lay my head upon his foot, pleading with him to take me with him to Spain, for never had he left me, never but for that one time of unrest in Villa Rica, and never since. I clung to him and wet the leather of his boots with my tears. Desperately I spoke words of love and loyalty and how I would gladly die for him, but that he should not leave me alone, without him, in this land we had conquered together.

"I must go, Marina," he said, "but I promise you I will return."

And I was forced to be content with that. I do not remember how I lived out those many days without him, since all hours were without interest, all food was dust, all company but that of Aguilar unbearable. I yearned for Cortés in the days and nights and there was not one hour in which I did not think of him with a full heart and beg his nameless God to return him to me.

With my mind so full of thoughts of Cortés, I paid little heed to Aguilar. It was not until he told me he had been called for questioning in Mexico City that I learned at long last what troubled him and that, in his youth, he had planned to become a priest.

"I am so glad you never did, Aguilar," I told him, "for you have been a dear and loyal friend to me."

Gazing upon me with a most bewildering expression, he replied, "Indeed. But not a friend to God . . . or to myself."

At his own insistence, Aguilar was to meet with the Spanish priest, Zumárraga, who was the hand reaching to Mexico from the body of the Spanish Inquisition. In Zumárraga's grip many who could not prove their utter faith to the Catholic God were tortured and killed.

"But why, Aguilar? Why do you do this now, when Cortés is gone and I am alone?"

"Because, Marina, I must."

When he returned after a month of fasting and penance imposed by Zumárraga, he was pale and weak. Alarmed, I made healing potions he would not drink.

"But you will die!" I cried to him.

"That is my hope," he said wearily, turning his face to the wall. From that moment on I never left his side and never ceased urging him to drink, to eat, to fight for strength.

"My fight is over, Marina. It was lost a long time ago."

I was stricken by his words. Had he not wanted adventure even as I had? Did he not love me enough to be pleased with my pleasure? Where, along the many roads we had travelled, had he taken another route and watched, without speaking, as I rode on by? It was almost as if I had brought this to pass and his death would be by *my* hand.

"Do you hate me then, Aguilar?" I asked him.

"No, Marina," he said without looking at me, "It is your misfortune that you gained what it was you desired. I have forgiven you long ago. Now I must forgive myself."

A month of days went by. One evening, just as I placed a cool cloth upon his forehead, Aguilar opened his eyes and, for the first time in many days, smiled. "I will miss you, Marina," he whispered, then closed his eyes.

"And I, you," I replied. By the next morning he was dead and his voice stilled forever in my ear. For days

I would think I saw him at my side, but when I turned, startled, he would be gone.

One day, not long after, Cortés returned, and with his lady. Now he was the Marquess of Oaxaca, in possession of vast lands and thousands of slaves marked with his noble brand. In the town renamed Cuernavaca, near Mexico City, he built a house worthy of his noble position, and then did he establish as well a great sugar plantation beyond the town a little way. In that place I took up my life again, in the Hacienda de San José de Vista Hermosa. What noble living we enjoyed, saluted and served by all! Even if I were not my Captain's wife by law, it made no matter. The station of noblewoman was mine most securely, and I was treated with great deference. Men and women newly come from Spain bent their heads to me, for well was it known in what high honor my Captain held me. What dances we had, what fiestas! What gowns I wore, and with what jewels did my Captain insist upon adorning me! Feasts there were nightly, and always with the finest wines from Spain and skilled musicians to play as we dined at our ease, and the laughter was gentle and the talk most elegant and refined. Never was there another moment of treachery or discord or dishonor. My Captain sat at the head of the table like King Carlos himself, and like a King did he ride forth upon his lands and survey the size and beauty of his kingdom. Content and happy was I, and well was this so, for after all of our trials we deserved to live lives of pleasure until the end.

Every night my Captain came to my sumptuous chamber, leaving his wife alone and weeping in her own, and every morning did he leave me with fond regrets and promises for the festive evening to come. My son did adore me also, and our servants placed my boot upon their necks, but there was only one being to whom I gave all my heart, and that was ever and always my Captain. My life had begun upon the shore of the eastern sea many years before, but not because of *you,* Oh Mother. First taking breath when first he spoke to me, the woman I became was created by him from she who knelt on the sand at his Godly feet.

34

Xochitl

At last I look on my days unwound behind me and my footprints upon them leading to where I stand, nearing the end of my journey. Well does it cause me to wonder, to see the distance I have travelled and in such varied company. And yet, what true difference was there, I now ask myself, between Spaniard and Azteca? Truly there was little to choose between them.

Ah, I am old and my mind wanders. I must relive those days though, so I may push them from me and so put my life in order. Thus it is that I see the menagerie once more and endure our flight only days before the Spaniards set it afire and burned to death whatever miserable creature yet breathed its foul stench. The days in Chapultepec were the last—and the only—days of freedom for Atahualpa and me. Soon we were found and gathered up like stray beasts. It seemed unnecessary to our new masters that Atahualpa be branded, for he was so clearly marked a slave by his deformities. I submitted to the branding without uttering a sound, my one small triumph, remaining a woman of the Mexica by my stoic silence. There had been murmuring among the men, perhaps because some did not want me branded and therefore made less desirable to lie with, but cooler heads prevailed and mine given the mark of slavery. From that moment on I possessed but one damaged face among many.

A long time passed and it was my fate to witness much sorrow: my people, including the once-hated Azteca in our common plight, were hunted down and taken as slaves, or put to flight and into exile. Those who escaped those destinies often died from the pox or from the disease the Spaniards gave to our women. Syphilis, it was called, and it ravaged the bodies and minds of our women as well as the bastards they bore. Malinalli, my sister, surely the shrewdest of survivors, did not escape this last; Cortés left it her as a final gift by which to remember him.

Thus enslaved, Atahualpa and I could no longer be together. After much persuasion I sought sanctuary in the house of women, the convent built upon the stone of Tixoc and then, by degrees, became a postulant of the Catholic faith and then an avowed nun. We stayed as close as we could during these times, with Atahualpa bringing me news from beyond the convent walls. Finally permitted his freedom—for his master, who could not bear to look upon his face, found no other master who would pay to look upon it either—he became at last a pochteca and by his wit soon bought and sold goods enough to keep flesh and spirit together. Often over the years I was able to see him without suspicion, not only because of his disfigurement, but because his charity ensured his welcome and the rare goods he gave to us were most gratefully accepted by the lean sisterhood of which I was a member.

It was on a sunny day he came with his dark news. I had arisen early to prayers, scourging my flesh for a foreign God and humbling myself upon the stone floor of my cubicle, then beginning the ceaseless task of weaving altar cloths and vestments for the priests who every day, it seemed, arrived in what was now called Mexico City, far from their Spanish homeland. As I sat in the sun that day, thinking of little, there came a nun with the message that Atahualpa was at the convent gates with cotton goods he wished me to accept. She whispered this, bending close, although I was the only one in the garden that morning. I smiled my thanks, gathered up my work and went to where Atahualpa waited for me. My heart lifted at the sight of him, as it did always. He smiled and without a touch did we take hold of each other and embrace. Pretending an interest in his bundle of cotton, I listened to his words with the tranquil smile that marked the nun no less than the brand on my forehead had marked me a slave. Well did my training aid me in this seeming indifference, for what I heard was of a nature most disquieting.

It was about my sister who, even after her marriage to another Spaniard, still had followed at the heels of Cortés into the far reaches of lands to the south. Her husband had died—conveniently, it was whispered—and Malinalli returned with Cortés and took up residence with him in the hacienda he had built upon the shores of Lake Tequesquitengo. His wife returning to him from Cuba did not dislodge my sister, nor indeed did his second marriage, as a widower, to a noblewoman from Spain. But it was whispered that she had gone mad. To find out if this was so, Atahualpa had gone to the hacienda with the excuse that he had goods to trade. Invited to join the servants at their midday meal, he quickly learned that the rumors he had heard were true. A pitiable shell of a woman she was now, he told me, neglected and treated as an unwanted dog. Even her bastard son had abandoned her. Did I wish for him to bring her to me, he asked, his eyes anxious upon mine to see if his words brought me sorrow.

"I will seek permission to go myself, Atahualpa," I said in answer, "and I thank you."

"At least let me accompany you," he replied, knowing argument was futile, "for it is unsafe for you to travel alone. These days, even your nun's garment may not protect you."

"I will ask if that may be permitted also," I said quietly, but he caught the glow upon my cheeks at the thought of being once more with him, and he chuckled softly.

"Tell them that I will come to these gates no more if permission is denied you . . . Sister."

"You are most unseemly," I said, turning away to hide my smile.

Mother Mary Gabriel deliberated for a trying two days before she consented. "But you will be responsible for your sister in all ways. She is not to further impoverish us with her presence."

"The pochteca, Atahualpa, promises that he will help provide what food and clothing she will need, Mother."

"And you are not to let this intrude upon your prayers or lessen your community labors."

Most humbly did I bow in submission and in my broken Spanish say to her words of gratitude.

"You do not need to thank me," she said, holding up one white, chiseled hand. "I trust you will do nothing to make me regret my decision."

With my head bowed, I left her chamber even as I had once left that of Moteczoma, the ruler, the husband it once was said I had slain. At the unbidden vision of his still, pale body and the bloody dagger, all joy at the thought of being with my beloved for the moment fled. There would be no place in heaven, I feared, no matter the promises made or the prayers uttered, for so treacherous a murderer.

Even with such a mind, and despite sad thoughts of my sister, still I must admit that the three days it took to reach her were happy ones indeed. It was the gentlest season of the year, with the first blossoms sweet upon their branches and the road sunny before us all the way to Cuernavaca and into the limitless beyond. Earnestly did I wish we could go on together along that road to the sea. A happy dream it was, of course, and nothing more.

The hacienda of the conqueror was easy to find, as there was nothing else built on so grand a scale. Humbly we went to the servants' gate to seek entry. However, it was not as difficult as I had imagined to reach my sister. A slave led me to her without a question. Passing through an archway we entered a garden around which the grey walls of the hacienda rose high as those of a fortress. An aqueduct built upon stone archways ran across the garden, flanked by trees in early bloom and large broken idols brought from the ruined teocallis nearby. It was a scene both beautiful and malevolent; peaceful and yet with an undercurrent of misery.

My sister sat in the shade, shielding her eyes from the sun as I drew near. I knelt beside her chair so that we could look well upon each other and she lowered her hand from her face. She was thin, her face lined and gaunt as much from temperament, I thought, as years of weathering, and her mouth was pinched. Her eyes were still her own, however, shrewd but beautiful.

"So you have turned crow, sister," she said. "Sister, indeed!" and laughed unpleasantly. I was silent and soon she, too, was still.

"I have come to take care of you, Malinalli," I said, and she flinched away from me at the sound of her birth name.

"Go away," she said harshly. "I do not want you here."

If I had ever thought my life lacking in happiness, it soon became clear that my sister's had been one of even greater emptiness and sorrow. Cast off by Cortés years before, while he now embraced a rich and noble wife, this faithful accomplice lived upon memories and delusion. My poor sister, once the right arm of the conqueror of all the Mexica, lived the life of a forgotten pet.

Readying himself for a second voyage to Spain, so my guide informed me, Cortés would be relieved to know she would be well cared for.

"Naturally he wishes to be free of her," I said, the gentleness with which I spoke belying the bitterness I felt, "and soon will he be thus relieved. First, however, I wish to speak with him."

Thus did I at last greet the conqueror face to face, and greatly was I surprised to remember that he was but a puny man as he limped toward me standing at his chamber door.

"Ah," he said, "Marina's sister! You caused us some worry in years gone by, but time passes and old feuds must be laid to rest." I was further surprised by the weary disappointment so deeply chiseled upon his face, though he did smile at his own jest. "My servant tells me you wish to be with your sister once more, and very proper that seems to me . . . Xochitl, is it not?"

I gave him look for look. "Xochitlzin, Sir." And this I said in ragged pride, for my name in the world now was a Catholic one.

He nodded, then seated himself and motioned for me to do likewise. "Very sad, your poor sister." He gazed thoughtfully down at his clasped hands and as if he spoke to himself, said, "She was the bravest woman I ever knew, with a wit as sharp as a dagger. It was after the death of her old comrade-in-arms that her mind began to be disordered."

His words roused my curiosity. Indeed, I thought, she must have loved the man to have become so addled with grief. "His name was Aguilar, Jeronimo de Aguilar, and a finer man and soldier never drew breath."

Then, as if awaking from a dream, he rubbed his eyes with the back of one hand and his voice grew brisk again, concerned with the issue at hand. "I have done all I could for her, but I leave for Spain in a matter of weeks and your poor sister is in no fit condition for such a journey."

"Which she would not enjoy, whatever her condition."

Cortés laced his fingers beneath his chin and stared at me, the pair of us with eyes locked in most civil combat. In this moment I could well observe a glimmer of the cunning warrior he must have been and my skin prickled at the thought that I was but a mere step from the direst of my country's foes. Suddenly he spoke, and with a most peculiar change of subject.

"You have aged more gracefully than your sister, Xochitlzin. Is it your choice of the religious life, think you? Your gallant sister being out in all weathers, scorched and soaked and freezing like any man, it is a hard life for a woman and is engraved upon her face."

"Even as is greed, Sir, or venery."

His eyes widened and, much to my surprise, he threw back his head and laughed until tears were in his eyes. "Oh, you make me yearn for the woman your sister was. Another vixen like you, with a tongue like an adder!"

I rose to my feet, inclining my head to him with all the appearance of unstirred calm still at my command. "All I request of you, Sir, is that you supply servants and a litter for my sister to ride in back to my convent. She will be well cared for there." I placed a slight stress upon the last word.

For a moment he looked beyond me and I felt certain he looked into the past where he was still the proud conquistadore and she the beautiful maiden, and then he rested his narrow gaze upon me once more. "I will take you at your word, Sister. And may she fare well."

I looked at him a moment longer, for well did I know I would never see his face again. As if it were the face of my beloved, I drew his likeness upon my memory.

"Go with God, Sir," I said, and he replied with a most ironical piety, "May he grant you and your sister His peace." Slaves were given us for the journey and they carried my sister strapped to the litter, raving and weeping by turns, issuing threats against us one moment and in the next making pitiful pleas to be returned to Cortés' side. It was grievous to hear and painful to witness. I was glad Cortés did not appear at our departure to see this further degradation of the woman to whom he owed his very life. The walls of his hacienda melted in the distance, the walls she had helped build with her cunning and misplaced devotion.

On we went to the city she helped bring to ruin, passing over streets which had once been causeways leading to the very center of the city where the Heart of the One World rose to the sky. The great pyramids and palaces were dust, as were my ancient adversaries. On the night the Spaniards choose to call Noche Triste—though sadder for the Azteca by far—Cacamatzin had drowned in the bloody, golden water alongside so many of the enemy. Later, Ueytlatoani Cuitláhuac died a common death of the time, of the Spanish pox. It was Cuauhtémoc, my foe and my savior, who outlasted the other Lords of the Triple Alliance, meeting his fate at the end of a rope in a faraway land.

In time my sister ceased her raving, but by then everyone knew who and what she was. Already there were whispers, naming her "La Malinche, the Traitress of Mexico," and worse. I do not believe my sister ever fully understood what she had done in saving our people from the Azteca only to give them into the tighter fist of Spain. She never seemed to question that what she had done was good. At first, some of the Mexica honored her courage, but in time whatever questionable good she had done was forgotten as stories concerning her grew.

At the same time, strangely, there arose a legend concerning me. The Second Wife of the Ueytlatoani Moteczoma, it was said, drowned her only daughter. In the dark hours of the night, it was said, she wandered lamenting through the city, searching for the child lost to her forever. "La Llorona," they called me, "Weeping with Small Cause." In time the legend changed—that it was not I who lamented my sin, but my sister, La Malinche, who wandered the streets of the city wailing her remorse at betraying her country. All of this talk always amused me, for I knew what time and wagging tongues could make of me and my sister, who never for a moment allowed regret or remorse to dog her heels. Well did I know the ways of men, and more than this; I have witnessed in my long life the way history is remembered, as if but one sex had lived through time, while the other was composed of wraiths and shadows. It would not surprise me if, from those days of battle and treachery and broken faith, only the names of Moteczoma and Cortés survive and those of my sister and I perish as if we had never been born, as if my sister had not thrown wide the gates of Tenochtitlan and I had not dreamed of the Conquest and the end of the One World.

If memory of me grew preposterous, my sister's became vile. At last she was known by all as "The whore of Mexico" who had, some insisted, murdered in cold blood the noble Moteczoma. People hearing of her presence in the convent soon brought crowds of the curious, eager to catch a glimpse of her. Sitting in the garden, busy with some simple task, suddenly she would hear foul names and lewd remarks hurled like stones over the wall and a nun would come in search of me to lead Malinalli, dazed and bewildered, into the chamber next to mine where she slept.

This was not to be borne for long, of course. Mother Mary Gabriel, not unkindly, bid us journey to the monastery of the Franciscans in Texcoco, where she had gained permission for us to live within their walls. I was to help in the kitchen, where my sister could also be given tasks simple enough for her to do. So, like thieves, did we journey to Texcoco in the night.

"Please tell the pochteca, Atahualpa, where I have gone, if you would be so good, Mother," I said in a cool, indifferent voice, but the elderly nun put her head on one side and looked upon me with suspicion.

"Judging from the cross he bears, I suppose there is no need to ask if you harbor any . . . improper fondness for the man, Sister."

"No, Mother," I replied through lips suddenly trembling. "It is but that he supplies me with the cotton goods I need for my work."

"But you will be in the kitchen now, Sister, do not forget. You no longer have need of his wares." She studied me closely, watchful for any symptom of that human connection so discouraged among the religious. If I betrayed the slightest attachment, she would make certain Atahualpa never discovered where I had gone.

"You are right, Mother; I had forgotten that."

There was a very old woman, deeply religious and devoted to us, who had often accompanied us as chaperon upon our rare journeys about the city. I sought her out before we left and asked her to tell the pochteca, when he next appeared, where I had been sent. She agreed most cheerfully, but my heart was not at rest. Surely he would be ill at ease to hear of my sudden departure, and he might betray emotion to find me gone. I was cold with disquiet.

Ah, all of this now seems so very long ago—or does it seem but weeks in the past? Beneath my white hair there are such youthful, such passionate memories. Indeed, it seems to me most remarkable of all that a human can endure, day by day, when all hope for happiness is gone.

But my story is not done. In Texcoco, Malinalli was lost to everything in life but Cortés. He took her arm in the garden and stood talking by her side when she made tortillas in the kitchen. Once I awoke in the darkness and knew she was not in her bed, and I threw her robe over my shoulders, praying to be unseen, and hastened into the garden. She was dancing in the moonlight, her face uptilted and radiant, her arms outstretched. She was laughing. I could not bear to put an end to even so deluded a joy, and so I huddled myself into a shadow and waited. After awhile she stumbled and then stopped, her arms lowering slowly to her sides. She stared, bewildered, into the darkness. I went to her then and took her arm.

"Come to bed, Malinalli."

She was dazed. "But he was here with me, sister. We were dancing. Then he went away." She looked at me, her eyes black with sorrow. "Where did he go? He knows I go with him always, always . . ."

"Yes, I know," I soothed her, "but now you must come to bed and rest."

She went with me like a docile child and I watched her face in the dim early light of dawn until she at last closed her eyes and her breathing became slow and even.

I do not know what strange sense she had for Cortés, but in some way she knew when he returned from Spain. She was often to be found by the monastery gates, patiently waiting for him to come for her. Fortunately she did not have the same sense about her old enemy Alvarado, villain of her many tales. She never showed sign of knowing that he had been crushed to death beneath his horse in the mountains far to the south. Fearful that she would gloat in unseemly fashion over his corpse, I did not tell her of his passing and, as far as I knew, she never thought of him at all. Nor did she think of her son. But with Cortés . . . Ah, that was different.

It was a cold day in the time of Tlaloc, which now the Spanish call winter, and rain had fallen without sound or spirit all morning. I overheard the brothers' conversation as I served them their midday meal. They spoke of Cortés.

"He is said to have died in poverty, though this is somewhat difficult to credit. His lands and his great haciendas must be worth much, indeed."

"It is said that his son by one or another of his lewd alliances will inherit everything."

"Much better would it have been if he had given his worldly goods to his Mother Church and so in part seek dispensation for a life of dissolution."

My enemy, Mexico's enemy, was no more. To my surprise, I felt nothing. Nothing for his death, nothing for his memory or cruel triumphs, nothing for what he had made of my sister's sad life. All I felt was the need to protect Malinalli from this knowledge, though indeed she had already made the man a phantom. I went in search of her, but she was not at her tasks in the kitchen, nor walking in the garden, nor sitting in our chamber. She was in the last place I thought to find her, in the chapel, on her knees. She was praying, not to the Catholic God she had never taken to her heart, but to her old and once-beloved deity, Quetzalcoatl. I knelt beside her and watched her from the corners of my eyes. Hands clasped tight, face solemn, she was speaking in our native tongue, not the Spanish she had so fiercely adopted as her own.

"God of my heart, I will give you flowers and I will give you fruit, and then will you come to me as you did promise me? Will you come back, shining from the sea, my Lord, in your gold clothes and your crown of gold and feathers?" her whispering voice grew higher, and plaintive as a child's. "You promised you would come to me and, oh, I am so alone, Mother!" She lowered her face into her hands and wept.

Sometimes I was of the belief that, with his death, Cortés' hold upon her mind had been released. She was no less deluded, yet from that time on she was a little girl again, living in Coatzocoalcos beside the sea and the river she had loved. The neat monastery garden was the jungle of her memory, and as she patted out tortillas she talked sometimes to me and sometimes to the father she still remembered. Never, after that day of prayer in the chapel, did I hear her mention our mother. I was amazed that even in her madness she could still seem to hold that grudge of unforgiveness in her heart. I tried to tell her that what had happened was no more our mother's fault than it had been our father's for dying and thus making way for the second father who so cruelly abused us. But she would have none of this. Her face turned to stone, and stone was her heart as well for the mother she would not, perhaps could not, forgive.

At least she was content and fairly at peace, and time passed with the daily rhythms of a woman's life. I cooked and cleaned and served with Malinalli's help, like any woman with her daily duties. My black garments gave me leave to do this in a monastery, though they did not absolve me entirely of being female. I kept my distance and my tongue and never raised my eyes in the presence of priest or brother, insofar as was possible making myself not flesh but shadow. My sister stayed away from them entirely and of her own accord, going to the garden only when it was time for the brothers' devotions in the chapel. Soon, though she was not of their faith nor rid of her madness, she knew to the exact moment when the brothers had filed solemnly into the chapel, or had filed as solemnly out. She would raise her head, an expression of intent listening upon her face, smile and say, "They are all gone now. They cannot see me," and then she would hasten out into the garden where she would stay, in sun or rain, until she knew devotions had ended.

In the twenty years that passed in this quiet way, never did Atahualpa come to the monastery gates. Thus I did not know if he yet lived or had died somewhere, perhaps alone. The thought of his death clutched my heart with pain, for I had long prayed whatever Gods might exist that I be given the grace of holding him in my arms at his last breath, and now it seemed that this could never come to pass. For my part, I was too old to search for him except in my dreams. Waking, I was held captive still, by age, by memory, even by the garments I wore. Perhaps in death, I thought, we will at last be together again.

I do not know how or why my sister left the monastery one day and wandered into the streets of Texcoco, whether she imagined herself going further into the jungle or following a phantom none but she could see. I had missed her for some time, but as it was Matins, I thought her most likely in the garden. However, when I went to fetch her back to her kitchen tasks she was not there. Nor was she in our chamber, nor—and I was certain of this—could she be among the alien holy men in the chapel. Distraught, I did what I never before had done. I left the monastery grounds in search of her. I had not known when word of my sister's presence reached Texcoco, but given as people are to idle chatter, all knew that Cortés' mistress was a madwoman who lived in the monastery of the Franciscans. They had not attempted to molest her before as people had done in Mexico City, but this day, apparently, she had been followed by curious witnesses whose numbers had grown as they hunted her down. It did not take me long to find her; I followed the sound of jeering voices.

Huddled on the ground, her face white with fear, my sister was surrounded by a crowd of the hostile, the amused, and the merely inquisitive. I had heard the taunts cast upon her before, but I am not sure *she* had ever truly heard them. One young man, who could not even have been born until long after the Conquest, grabbed her by the arm and yanked her to her feet and another reached over and tore away her huipilli, exposing her sagging breasts. Cruelly did they jeer at her, calling her Cortés' old crone and throwaway, and another man pulled her to him and, to the delight of the onlookers, made as if to couple with her, kissing her wrinkled face and stroking her white hair. Sobbing, she pulled away, covering her breasts with her hands.

I pushed my way through the crowd to her side. Perhaps it was my nun's habit that stopped their voices; perhaps it was the fury with which I tore off my veil and wrapped it around her nakedness. In my haste and by accident I pulled off my wimple as well, and the crowd gasped and drew back from me to see the brand of slavery, that relic of Spanish cruelty, upon my brow. Maybe it was to excuse their own cruelty—suddenly perhaps they felt no better than our conquerors—that a man muttered, "She murdered our Ueytlatoani, Moteczoma!"

I looked him in the eye, then turned deliberately to look at all of the faces surrounding me, perversely amused, and curiously emboldened by the danger we were in. "No," I replied, "*I* killed him."

It would have been likely for those people to turn

upon me then, but they did not. One reached down and handed me my wimple and another made passage for us through the crowd. In a silence broken only by the sound of footfalls we walked back to the monastery, the people following us to the very gates.

I put Malinalli to bed and as I smoothed the blanket over her I was startled to see that she was looking at me with clear eyes. Then she spoke, and with a lucidity I had not heard for years. "It was not you, you know," she said.

I was at first bewildered by her words. And then I understood.

"I killed him. I told them it was you, but I took your dagger and I . . ."

I bent down and kissed her on the mouth. "There is no need to say more, Malinalli. I knew. It is over now, and it is time to forget."

She nodded, like an obedient little girl, and then she smiled. "I did a good thing, though, to make up for it. It was in the menagerie where they had put you in a cage."

"*You* were the one who unlocked the chain!"

Suddenly she reached both her arms out to me and drew me down beside her on the narrow bed, holding me as she had not done before in all of our long lives together, not since we were little girls. I felt a kiss on my hair like the flutter of a hummingbird wing, and she whispered, "I love you, Mother, I do."

She slept then and so, after a long while deep in thought, did I. The relief in my heart that the truth had at last been spoken blended with the contentment of knowing that my sister had at last embraced our mother with forgiveness. It was nearly morning before I rose from her bed and went to lie sleepless in mine, my head too full of startling new thoughts to permit further rest. Maybe this was why we endure, I realized, because in our hearts we know evil does not always conquer goodness. We know times of change will come as we know the sun will rise and the Gods will walk this earth once more. And Goddesses too, I thought, suddenly filled with longing for those phantom shadows of my childhood. I was surprised, when I turned my face to look gratefully at my once-deluded and now redeemed sister, that my pillow was wet with my tears.

That morning I found the monastery walls echoing with debate. In the troubles of the day before, I had not heard the news. According to the wishes of his family, and to my astonishment, Cortés' bones were not to be re-buried in the convent he founded in Mexico City, but here, in the chapel of the Franciscan brothers. On one side would be reinterred the body of his mother and on the other the bones of a daughter who had died many years before. Much disquieted, I sought audience with the prior and begged him to keep talk of Cortés' burial quiet for, as I told him, such news might seriously upset my sister who finally seemed to have found some small measure of peace.

"I will do what I can, Sister," he said, and though I did not raise my eyes to his face, I could hear the gentle compassion in his voice.

The day of the burial, I kept Malinalli occupied in the garden. There was a procession to the chapel from the street, and the bells were tolled. Although my sister seemed restless, she made no enquiry as to the reason for the unusual activity. I heard Mass sung and devotions chanted. Then it was afternoon and all was silent once more. My sister and I went to the kitchen to prepare the brothers' supper, for they had fasted that long day. I kept one eye always on Malinalli, but she never gave any sign that she understood what had come to pass that day in the very place where she lived. After I served the brothers their supper, I returned to the kitchen to find her gone.

There is something that comes to one, a dread certainty, a dark and hollow foreboding, that foretells tragedy. As I searched in the garden, in our chamber, in the dining hall, I knew all the while where at last I would find her. At first glance she seemed to be sleeping. Of course I knew she was not. Curled upon the stone laid fresh that morning, my sister lay like an innocent child at rest. I knelt beside her and pulled her into my arms.

My priestess' dagger, taken from my hand on the day Moteczoma was slain, had been plunged to its hilt into my sister's breast. Quietly she was dying, her life seeping from her as her blood spilled over the gravestone of Cortés. Soon she shuddered slightly and then lay still. I held her body against me until it was cold, and then I lowered her again onto the stone. But it was not with sorrow that I gazed upon her face so like my own, for she was with her Lord, come at last from the eastern reaches of the sea and the heavens beyond the sea and the underworld that could not hold him captive. Reaching forth his hand to her, he set my sister free.

AFTERWORD BY THE AUTHOR

We all become phantoms of history, at least those of us who haven't the greed or the genius or the tenacity to be memorialized and our names remembered. The contributions of most of us are doomed to be forgotten, even though the times in which we have lived linger on in history books. Sadly, women are far more likely than men to disappear without a trace, commemorated perhaps by an inscription on a family tomb. Leaving behind not even that, the remarkable Doña Marina is known to us only as "the traitress of Mexico."

It is my belief that Cortés never would have succeeded in the overthrow of the Aztec Empire were it not for the help of the woman who translated for him so eloquently, so cunningly and—as events turned out—so tragically, that the bloody foot of the Aztecs was replaced by the brutal boot of Spain. If the litmus test of civilization is the way the most vulnerable members are treated by the most powerful, then neither empire could win that distinction.

In fifteenth and sixteenth century Spain there flourished a literary genre which greatly influenced daring young men of the time who sought fame and riches and exotic adventure in faraway lands across the still-mysterious seas. Idols of gold and palaces of emerald were to be found at the end of a sea voyage, as well as monsters and beautiful, nubile maidens. These fabulous tales were woven of fantasy and ignorance, but they lost none of their enchantment for all of that. One of these mythologists was Garci Ordóñez de Montalvo, who blithely asserted the following:

> Know ye that at the right hand of the Indies there is an Island called Californio, very close to that part of the Terrestrial Paradise, which was inhabited by black women without a single man among them, and they lived in the manner of Amazons. They were robust of body with strong, passionate hearts and great virtue. The island itself is one of the wildest in the world on account of its bold and craggy rocks.

This sort of literary enticement was fuel to the fire. Added to the conflagration was missionary zeal on the part of the Catholic Church and the desire of the Spanish Crown to discover, map and plunder lands of the "New World." That these lands already supported civilizations of great antiquity and culture did not matter to those bent upon their conquest.

Hernán Cortés arrived on the eastern shores of Mexico in the spring of 1519, with six hundred men, sixteen horses and an untold number of dogs, cannon, muskets and swords. Against him were nations comprising thousands of native people who, although at odds with each other—and especially at odds with the oppressive Aztec Empire—could have been expected to repulse this warlike invasion. And yet Cortés and his army were triumphant, able to overthrow Moteczoma and his empire in slightly more than two years. He succeeded with the aid of Mexican allies who thought at first that Cortés was the god, Quetzalcoatl, whose coming had been foretold for that year. Although they later discovered the mortal nature of the strangers in their midst, many of them joined forces with the conquistadores in order to overthrow the Aztecs' cruel regime. In so doing, they also destroyed the cultural fabric into which the lives of the Mexica were interwoven. What the Aztecs had succeeded in usurping and debasing, the conquistadores crushed absolutely. Gods and goddesses fell from the Mexican heavens like dying stars, and though rechristened by the Church, generations of the dispossessed must have found their nights dark, although faint aureoles of light from their ancient divinities have lingered for many years about the figures of Mary and Jesus, her Son.

Bernal Diaz del Castillo, one of the conquistadores, wrote a lengthy and detailed memoir of his experiences, *The Discovery and Conquest of Mexico.* Although he wrote "... without the help of Doña Marina, we could not have understood the language of New Spain and Mexico," he devoted but three pages in his book to her. Cortés, who gained fame, a noble title and land from the enterprise, penned five letters to King Carlos I of Spain, in which he referred to Marina briefly and dismissively.

Born Malinalli, later christened Doña Marina by Cortés, she was by then his mistress as well as his interpreter to the Mexica, who first called her Malintzin, and later La Malinche. There is little known about her early years and in later ones she makes so few appearances in print that she slips into the mists of history as if she were, in truth, but one of those phantom Amazons the Spaniards pursued in daylight and dreaming.

In the tragic aftermath of the Conquest, most of the literary treasures of the Aztec and Mayan cultures were put to the torch, destroying much that would have explained those exotic societies. In the case of the real Malinalli, we know so little about her that there is no choice but to fictionalize her in order to hear her speak. It is unfortunate that someone with her brilliance and daring was not more fully memorialized by those eyewitnesses to the Conquest, and thus remembered by more than a casual epithet in our own time.

GLOSSARY

Acuecueyotl	Goddess of the Waves
Anáhuac	the Aztec empire
ayachachtli	gourd rattle
Aztlán	legendary place of origin of the Aztec people
cacica	noblewoman
cacique	nobleman
calmecac	temple school
chalchuite	green, jadeite stone highly prized by Aztecs
chinampas	floating gardens
Cihuacoatl	Earth Goddess, Snake Woman, Goddess of Childbirth and Death in Sacrifice
cinatlamacazqui	priestess
Coatlicue	Serpent Skirt, Goddess of Fertility, mother of Malinallxochitl, Huitzilopochtli and Coyolxauqui
copal	transparent resin used as incense in religious ritual
Coyolxauhqui	Goddess of the Moon, sister of Malinallxochitl and Huitzilopochtli, daughter of Coatlicue
cueitl	long wrapped skirt
cumal	stone oven upon which tortillas were baked over a fire
Ehecatl	God of Wind

Huehueteotl	The Old God, Giver of Fire
huehuetl	vertical drum used in religious ritual
huipilli	blouse, often embroidered
Huitzilopochtli	God of War, God of the Sun
icpalli	throne
Ipalnemohuani	Giver of Life
Ixtacciuatl	White Goddess
ko'hal	chief of the aerial dance sacred to the Azteca
macquauitl	a blunt sword lined on both sides with sharpened obsidian flakes
Malinallxochitl	Goddess of Witchcraft and Sorcery, Tamer of Wild Beasts, sister of Huitzilopochtli and daughter of Coatlicue
maxtlatl	loincloth
Mictlan	Land of the Dead
Mictlancihuatl	Goddess Consort of the Lord of Death, Mictlantecuhtli
metatle	curved stone used in the grinding of maize for tortillas
Nahuatl	language spoken by the Aztecs
octli	fermented beverage made from the maguey cactus
Ometeotl	God of All, One Who Created All, both Goddess and God as Lord and Lady of Duality
omichicahuatstli	musical instrument made of human bone
peyotl	hallucinatory drug made from the mescal cactus
pochteca	itinerant trader
quetzal	Central American bird with long, flowing tail feathers
Quetzalcoatal	Lord of Dawn, Lord of the Morning Star, Feathered Serpent
Snake Woman	second in power to the Ueytlatoani, a position held by a male in the Aztec empire

temazcalli	sweat house used for purification
Tenochtitlan	capital of the Aztec empire, site of Mexico City
teocalli	temple
teonanacatl	hallucinatory mushroom known as "flesh of the God"
Tepeyollotl	Jaguar God
teponaztli	horizontal drum used in religious ritual
tepuli	male sexual organ
tetzontli	mortar
Tezcatlipoca	God of War, Lord of the Smoking Mirror
tipili	female sexual organ
tlachtli	a violent game played with a ball and symbolizing light over darkness
Tlaloc	God of Rain
Tixoc	sacrificial "war" stone, carved with battle scenes
Tlatoan	lesser ruler in the Aztec empire
tlaxcalli	tortilla, corncake
Toci	Great Mother, Goddess of the Harvests
Tollan	legendary birthplace of the Toltecs, home of the mortal ruler Quetzalcoatl, before he became a god
tonalli	destiny
Tonantzin	Our Holy Mother, Earth Goddess
Tonatiuh	The sun, He Who Goes Forth Shining
tzompantli	a raised stone rack upon which skulls from the sacrificed were hung in rows on sticks
Ueytlatoani	Great Speaker, sovereign ruler of the Aztec empire
xexenes	mosquitoes
Xilónen	Goddess of the Tender Maize

Xipe Totec	God of the Sowing of the Seeds, The Flayed God
Xiuhtecuhtli	God of Fire
Xolotl	God of the Underworld, Dark Twin of Quetzalcoatl

SIGNET ONYX (0451)

SWEEPING ROMANCE by Catherine Coulter

[ ] **EARTH SONG.** Spirited Philippa de Beauchamp fled her ancestral manor rather than wed the old and odious lord that her domineering father had picked for her. But she found peril of a different kind when she fell into the hands of a rogue lord, handsome, cynical Dienwald de Fortenberry. . . . (402065—$4.99)

[ ] **FIRE SONG.** Marriage had made Graelam the master of Kassia's body but now a rising fire-hot need demanded more than submission. He must claim her complete surrender with the dark ecstasy of love. . . . (402383—$4.99)

[ ] **SECRET SONG.** Stunning Daria de Fortesque was the prize in a struggle between two ruthless earls, one wanting her for barter, the other for pleasure. But there was another man who wanted Daria, too, for an entirely different reason. . . . (402340—$4.99)

[ ] **CHANDRA.** Lovely golden-haired Chandra, raised to handle weapons as well as any man, was prepared to defend herself against anything . . . until the sweet touch of Jerval de Veron sent the scarlet fires of love raging through her blood. . . . (158814—$4.99)

[ ] **DEVIL'S EMBRACE.** The seething city of Genoa seemed a world away from the great 18th-century estate where Cassandra was raised. But here she met Anthony, and became addicted to a feverish ecstasy that would guide their hearts forever. . . . (141989—$4.99)

[ ] **DEVIL'S DAUGHTER.** Arabella had never imagined that Kamal, the savage sultan who dared make her a harem slave, would look so like a blond Nordic god. She had never dreamed that his savage love could make her passion's slave. . . . (158636—$4.99)

Prices slightly higher in Canada

Buy them at your local bookstore or use this convenient coupon for ordering.

PENGUIN USA
P.O. Box 999 – Dept. #17109
Bergenfield, New Jersey 07621

Please send me the books I have checked above.
I am enclosing $__________ (please add $2.00 to cover postage and handling). Send check or money order (no cash or C.O.D.'s) or charge by Mastercard or VISA (with a $15.00 minimum). Prices and numbers are subject to change without notice.

Card #__________ Exp. Date __________
Signature__________
Name__________
Address__________
City __________ State __________ Zip Code __________

For faster service when ordering by credit card call **1-800-253-6476**

Allow a minimum of 4-6 weeks for delivery. This offer is subject to change without notice.

SIGNET ONYX (045

ROMANCES TO TAKE YOUR BREATH AWAY

☐ **AUTUMN RAIN by Anita Mills.** When Elinor Ashton's debt-ridden father forc her into a loveless marriage with the elderly but enormously wealthy Lo Kingsley, she becomes the most unhappy bride in London society . . . and t property of a man whose jealousy leads him to concoct an unspeakab scheme. "Powerful . . . a story to touch all of your emotions."—Janelle Tayl (403282—$4.9

☐ **BEYOND THE SUNRISE by Mary Balogh.** She is the daughter of a Fren count; he is the illegitimate son of an English lord. Both cast in a storm violence as England and France fight a ruthless war, they come together in passion that flares in the shadow of danger and a love that conquers t forces of hate. (403428—$4.9

☐ **A VICTORIAN CHRISTMAS by Edith Layton, Patricia Rice, Mary Jo Putne Betina Krahn, Patricia Gaffney.** Capturing the very essence of Victori times and the spirit of Christmas, these five holiday love stories are writt by some of the most beloved and acclaimed historical romance authors. (174429—$4.9

☐ **BEYOND EDEN by Catherine Coulter.** A beautiful woman hides behind a ne name to protect herself from a past of betrayal and treachery, and a prese filled with sinister shadows. "Spicy romance and mystery . . . heady, intriguing —*Publishers Weekly* (403398—$5.9

Prices slightly higher in Canada

Buy them at your local bookstore or use this convenient coupon for ordering.

PENGUIN USA
P.O. Box 999 – Dept. #17109
Bergenfield, New Jersey 07621

Please send me the books I have checked above.
I am enclosing $__________ (please add $2.00 to cover postage and handlin Send check or money order (no cash or C.O.D.'s) or charge by Mastercard VISA (with a $15.00 minimum). Prices and numbers are subject to change witho notice.

Card #____________ Exp. Date ________
Signature____________
Name____________
Address____________
City ________ State ________ Zip Code ________

For faster service when ordering by credit card call **1-800-253-6476**

Allow a minimum of 4-6 weeks for delivery. This offer is subject to change without notic

ONYX

TIMELESS ROMANCE
BY BERTRICE SMALL

A LOVE FOR ALL TIME Conn O'Malley is an Irish rogue no woman can resist. Known as the handsomest man at court, he has been seducing and abandoning wenches and royal ladies alike, until he meets heiress Aidan St. Michael. By command of Britain's powerful Queen Elizabeth, Conn and Aidan marry. But a cruel scheme makes Conn a prisoner of the queen and Aidan a harem slave to sultan in a distant land. (159004—$5.99)

ENCHANTRESS MINE This is the magical tale of ravishingly beautiful Mairin of Aelfleah, called Enchantress by the three men who loved her: Basil, prince of Byzantium, who taught her passion's tender secrets; Josselin de Combourg, gallant knight of William the Conqueror; and Eric Longswood, the Viking whose tragic love for Mairin would never be fufilled. (158326—$4.99)

BLAZE WYNDHAM "A rich, robust historical saga full of sumptuous period detail and tempestuous romance. Bertrice Small's best book yet—a colorful, captivating tale certain to enchant."—Jennifer Wilde, author of *An Angel in Scarlet*
(401603—$4.99)

*Prices slightly higher in Canada

Buy them at your local bookstore or use this convenient coupon for ordering.

PENGUIN USA
P.O. Box 999 — Dept. #17109
Bergenfield, New Jersey 07621

Please send me the books I have checked above.
I am enclosing $_______________ (please add $2.00 to cover postage and handling). Send check or money order (no cash or C.O.D.'s) or charge by Mastercard or VISA (with a $15.00 minimum). Prices and numbers are subject to change without notice.

Card #_______________ Exp. Date _______________
Signature_______________
Name_______________
Address_______________
City _______________ State _______________ Zip Code _______________

For faster service when ordering by credit card call **1-800-253-6476**

Allow a minimum of 4-6 weeks for delivery. This offer is subject to change without notice.

$1.00 REBATE when you buy next month's blockbuster action thriller!

SPANDAU PHOENIX

GREG ILES

"A scorching read." —John Grisham

The secret is out. The most riveting novel about WWII's most deadly plot—that will shake the world today.

- When you buy Greg Iles' SPANDAU PHOENIX, you can get $1.00 back with this rebate certificate.
- Just mail in rebate certificate, original sales receipt of SPANDAU PHOENIX with price circled, and a copy of the UPC number.

Send to:
SPANDAU PHOENIX REBATE
P.O. Box 1182-A
Grand Rapids, MN 55745-1182

NAME____________________

ADDRESS____________________

CITY____________ STATE______ ZIP______

SIGNET

Offer expires 6/30/94 • Mail received until 7/15/94
This certificate must accompany your request. No duplicates accepted. Void where prohibited, taxed or restricted Allow 4-6 weeks for receipt of rebate.
Offer good only in U.S., Canada and its territories.

PENGUIN USA

Printed in the USA